A FACE LIKE GLASS

AMULET BOOKS
NEW YORK

FRANCES HARDINGE

A FACE LIKE GLASS

Cataloging-in-Publication Data has been applied for and may be obtained from the Library of Congress.

ISBN: 978-1-4197-2484-8

Text copyright © 2012 Frances Hardinge
Title page illustrations copyright © 2017 Vincent Chong
Book design by Alyssa Nassner

First published by Macmillan Children's Books, a division of Macmillan Publishers International Limited, in the U.K.

Printed and bound in U.S.A.
10 9 8 7 6 5 4 3 2 1

Amulet Books are available at special discounts when purchased in quantity for premiums and promotions as well as fund-raising or educational use. Special editions can also be created to specification. For details, contact specialsales@abramsbooks.com or the address below.

To my one-year-old nephew Isaac, in whose
eyes I see the world reflected, and find it to be
wondrous and full of surprises

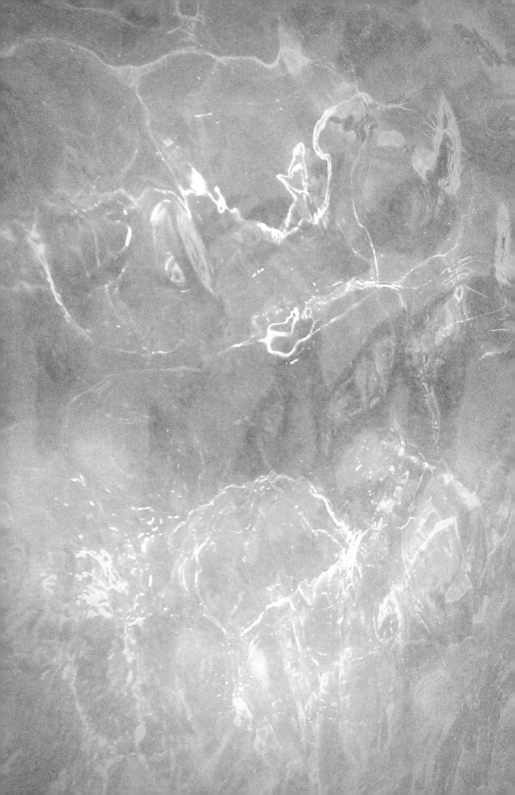

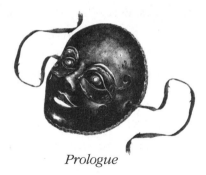

Prologue

THE CHILD IN THE CURDS

ONE DARK SEASON, GRANDIBLE BECAME CERTAIN that there was something living in his domain within the cheese tunnels. To judge by the scuffles, it was larger than a rat and smaller than a horse. On nights when hard rain beat the mountainside high above, and filled Caverna's vast labyrinth of tunnels with the music of ticks and trickles and drips, the intruding creature sang to itself, perhaps thinking that nobody could hear.

Grandible immediately suspected foul play. His private tunnels were protected from the rest of the underground city by dozens of locks and bars. It should have been impossible for anything to get in. However, his cheesemaker rivals were diabolical and ingenious. No doubt one of them had managed to smuggle in some malignant animal to destroy him or, worse still, his cheeses. Or perhaps this was some ploy of the notorious and mysterious Kleptomancer, who always seemed determined to steal whatever would cause the most chaos, regardless of any personal gain.

Grandible painted the cold ceiling pipes with Merring's Peril, thinking that the unseen creature must be licking the condensation off the metal to stay alive. Every day he patrolled his tunnels expecting to find some animal curled comatose beneath the pipes with froth in its whiskers. Every day he was disappointed. He laid traps with sugared wire and scorpion barbs, but the creature was too cunning for them.

Grandible knew that the beast would not last long in the tunnels, for nothing did, but the animal's presence gnawed at his thoughts just as its teeth gnawed at his precious cheeses. He was not accustomed to the presence of another living thing, nor did he welcome it. Most of those who lived in the sunless city of Caverna had given up on the outside world, but Grandible had even given up on the rest of Caverna. Over his fifty years of life he had grown ever more reclusive, and now he barely ventured out of his private tunnels or saw a human face. The cheeses were Grandible's only friends and family, their scents and textures taking the place of conversation. They were his children, waiting moon-faced on their shelves for him to bathe them, turn them, and tend to them.

Nonetheless, there came a day when Grandible found something that made him sigh deeply, and clear away all his traps and poisons.

A broad wheel of Withercream had been left to ripen, the pockmarked skin of the cheese painted with wax to protect it. This soft wax had been broken, letting the air into the secret heart of the cheese and spoiling it. Yet it was not the ruined cheese that weighed Grandible's spirits to the ground. The mark set in the wax was a print from the foot of a human child.

A human child it was, therefore, that was trying to subsist entirely on the extraordinary cheeses produced by Grandible's refined and peculiar arts. Even nobility risked only the most delicate slivers of such dangerous richness. Without as much as a morsel of bread or a splash of water to protect its tender stomach from the onslaught of such luxury, the unknown child might as well have been crunching on rubies and washing them down with molten gold. Grandible took to leaving out bowls of water and half-loaves of bread, but they were never touched. Clearly his traps had taught the child to be suspicious.

Weeks passed. There were periods during which Grandible could find no trace of the child, and would conclude with a ruffled brow that it must have perished. But then a few days later he would find a little heap of nibbled rinds in another under-alley, and realize that the child had just roamed to a new hiding place. Eventually the impossible fact dawned upon him: The child was not dying. The child was not sickening. The child was thriving on the perilous splendors of the cheese kingdom.

At night Grandible would sometimes wake from superstitious dreams in which a whey-colored imp with tiny feet pranced ahead of him, leaving tiny weightless footprints in the Stiltons and sage-creams. Another month of this and Grandible would have declared himself bewitched. However, before he could do so the child proved itself quite mortal by falling into a vat of curdling Neverfell milk.

Grandible had heard nothing untoward, for the creamy junket was already set enough to muffle the sound of the splash. Even when he was stooping over the vast vat, admiring the fine, slight gloss on the setting curds, and the way they split cleanly like crème caramel when he pushed his finger in to the knuckle, he noticed nothing. Only when he was leaning over with his long curd-knife, ready to start slicing the soft curds, did Grandible suddenly see a long, ragged rupture in their surface, filling with cloudy, greenish whey. It was roughly in the shape of a small, spread-eagled human figure, and a row of thick, fat bubbles was squirming to the surface and bursting with a sag.

He blinked at this strange phenomenon for several seconds before realizing what it had to mean. He cast aside his knife, snatched up a great wooden paddle, and pushed it deep into the pale ooze, then scooped and slopped the curds and whey this way and that until he felt a weight on the end. Bracing his knees against the vat, he heaved back on the handle like a fisherman hauling in a baby whale. The weight strained every joint in his body, but at last a figure appeared above the surface, shapeless and clotted with curds, and clinging to the paddle with all the limbs at its disposal.

It tumbled out, sneezing, spluttering, and coughing a fine milky spray, while he collapsed beside it with a huff, breathless with the unexpected exertion. Six or seven years old, to judge by the height, but skinny as a whip.

"How did you get in here?" he growled, once he had recovered his breath.

It did not answer, but sat quivering like a guilty blancmange and staring from under pale soupy eyelashes.

He was an alarming enough sight for any child, he supposed. Grandible had long since abandoned any attempt to make himself fair and presentable in a way of which the Court would approve. In fact, he had rebelled. He had deliberately forgotten most of the two hundred Faces he had been taught in infancy with everybody else. In his stubborn solitude he wore the same expression day in and day out like a slovenly overall, and never bothered to change it. Face No. 41, The Badger in Hibernation, a look of gruff interest that suited most situations well enough. He had worn that one expression so long that it had carved its lines into his features. His hair was grizzled and ragged. The hands that gripped the paddle were darkened and toughened by wax and oils, as if he were growing his own rind.

Yes, there was reason enough for a child to look at him with fear, and perhaps it really was afraid. But this was probably nothing but an act. It had decided that terror was more likely to win him around. It would have chosen a suitable Face from its supply, like a card from a deck. In Caverna lies were an art, and everybody was an artist, even young children.

I wonder which Face it will be, Grandible thought, reaching for a bucket of water. *No. 29—Uncomprehending Fawn Before Hound? No. 64—Violet Trembling in Sudden Shower?*

"Let's see you, then," he muttered, and before the curled figure could react he had thrown the water across its face to wash away the worst of the curds. Long, braided hair showed through the ooze. A girl, then? She made a panicky attempt to bite him, showing a full set of milk teeth with no gaps. Younger than he had thought at first, then. Five years old at the most, but tall for her age.

While she sneezed, spluttered, and coughed, he grabbed her small chin and with a heavy rind-brush began clearing the rest of the clogging Neverfell curds from her features. Then he snatched up a trap-lantern and held it close to the small face.

However, it was Grandible, not the child, who gave a noise of fear when at last he saw the countenance of his captive. He released her chin abruptly, and recoiled until his back halted with a clunk against the vat from which he had saved her. The hand holding up his trap-lantern shook violently, causing the little glowing flytrap within the lamp to snap its fine teeth fretfully. There was silence, but for the tallowy drip of curds from the child's long, clogged braids, and her muted snuffles.

He had forgotten how to look surprised. He was out of practice in changing his expression. But he could still feel that emotion, he discovered. Surprise, incredulity, a sort of horrified fascination . . . and then the heavy onslaught of pity.

"Thunder above," he muttered under his breath. For a moment more he could only stare at the face his brush had revealed, then he cleared his throat and tried to speak gently, or at least softly. "What is your name?"

The child sucked her fingers warily and said nothing.

"Where is your family? Father? Mother?"

His words had as much effect as coins dropped in mud. She stared and stared and shivered and stared.

"Where did you come from?"

Only when he had asked her a hundred such questions did she offer a whispered, hesitant response that was almost a sob.

"I . . . I don't know."

And that was the only answer he could get from her. *How did you get in? Who sent you? Who do you belong to?*

I don't know.

He believed her.

She was alone, this child. This odd and terrible child. She was as alone as he was. More so than he, in fact, despite all his attempts to hide away. More so than a child that age could possibly realize.

Suddenly it came to Grandible that he would adopt her. The decision seemed to make itself without asking him. For long years he had refused to take an apprentice, knowing that any underling would only seek to betray and replace him. This child, however, was a different matter.

Tomorrow, he would organize a ceremony of apprenticeship with his strange, young captive. He would invent a parentage for her. He would explain that she had been scarred during a cheese-baking and had to keep her face bandaged. He would guide her pen to enter her name as "Neverfell Grandible" on the documents.

But today, before anything else, he would send out for a small, velvet mask.

DEFACED

ON A CERTAIN MURKY HOUR ABOUT SEVEN YEARS
after that fateful day, a skinny figure could be seen capering
sideways beside Grandible as he growled and slouched his way
through the tunnels with a great white loop of braided rope-
cheese over one shoulder, and a ring of keys bristling in his fist.

She was no longer the little cheese-clotted scrap of life that
blinked white lashes at Cheesemaster Grandible and so terrified
him. Nor was she like her master, grim-jowled, solemn, and
taciturn, dogged and careful in word and action. No, despite her
best efforts she was a skinny, long-boned tangle of fidget and
frisk, with feet that would not stay still, and elbows made to
knock things off shelves. Her hair was twisted into a mass of
short, twiggy red pigtails to keep it out of her face, the cheese,
and everything else.

Seven years had passed. Seven years in the cheese tunnels,
struggling after Grandible's round-shouldered rolling gait with
pails of milk or pots of hot wax. Seven years turning cheeses onto
their bellies, cheddaring, clambering up the wide wooden shelves
like a monkey, sniffing scoops of cheese paste for ripeness.
Seven years learning to follow her nose through the darkened

tunnels, for Cheesemaster Grandible was stingy with the trap-lanterns. Seven years of sleeping in a hammock strung between the shelves, her only lullaby the fluting of the Whitwhistle cheese as its emerald rind heaved and settled. Seven years of helping Grandible defend his territory from the murderous attempts of other cheesemakers. Seven years of tinkering and taking things apart to fill the unyielding hours, inventing curd-shredders and triple-whisks, and learning the pleasure of seeing cog obey cog.

Seven years in which Grandible never permitted her to step out of his private tunnels, even for a moment, and never let her meet anybody without wearing a mask.

And what of those five years that had been hers before she was apprenticed? She could recall almost nothing of them. She had tried a thousand times, but for the greater part that section of her memory was as featureless and numb as scar tissue. Sometimes, just sometimes, she convinced herself that she could remember stray images or impressions, but she could not describe them properly or make sense of them.

Darkness. A luminous coil of purple smoke rising around her and upward. A bitterness on her tongue. These were her only memories of her lost past, if memories they truly were.

Nobody's mind ever remains a blank page, however carefully they are locked away from the world. In the case of Neverfell, she had made her mind into a scrapbook, busy filling it with the fragments, stories, rumors, and reports she could scavenge from talking to the delivery boys who came to pick up cheeses or drop off milk and supplies, and failing that, the wild scribblings of her own imagination.

By the time she had reached the giddy age of twelve-probably, she knew everything about Caverna that could be learned through nothing more than sharp ears, a good memory, tireless questioning, and an overactive imagination. She knew of the glittering Court, teetering always on the tightrope of the Grand Steward's whims. She knew of the great ceaseless camel trains that crossed the desert to bring wagonloads of provisions to Caverna, and carry away tiny portions of luxuries created by Caverna's master Craftsmen, each worth more than his weight in diamonds. The overground had its own makers of delicacies, but only in Caverna were there masters of the Craft, capable of making wines that rewrote the subtle book of memory, cheeses that brought visions, spices that sharpened the senses, perfumes that ensnared the mind, and balms that slowed aging to a crawl.

Hearsay, however, was no substitute for a real live visitor.

"When is she coming? Can I make the tea? Did you see I swept the floors and fed grubs to all the lanterns? I can serve the tea, can't I? Shall I fetch the dates?" Questions were too big and wild for Neverfell's mind to rein, and they always escaped her, usually in packs of six. Questions annoyed Master Grandible, and she could feel them annoying him, but somehow she could never help it. Even his grim, warning silences just filled her with a desperate urge to fill them. "Can I—"

"No!"

Neverfell flinched back. She lived in a quiet, pragmatic terror of those rare times when her persistence or puppy-clumsiness pushed Master Grandible into true anger. Though she had developed something of an instinct for his moods, nothing ever showed in his face, which remained grimly static and weatherworn like a door knocker. When his temper snapped, it did so in an instant and did not right itself for days.

"Not for this visitor. I want you hidden away in the lofts until she is gone."

The news hit Neverfell like a physical blow. In the drab and pungent calendar of her life, a visitor was more than a holiday—it was a blessed intrusion of light, life, air, color, and *news*. For days before such a visit her excitement would be almost painful, her mind a hornet's nest of anticipation. For days afterward her lungs filled more easily, and her mind had new memories and thoughts to turn over and play with, like a child with freshly unwrapped gifts.

To find herself denied contact with any guest at the last moment was agony, but to be denied a chance to meet this particular visitor was beyond bearing.

"I . . . I swept all the floors . . ." It came out as a pathetic, broken little mewl. Neverfell had spent the last two days taking special care to fulfill all her duties, and find yet more to complete so that Master Grandible would have no reason to lock her out of sight before the visitor arrived.

She felt her throat tighten, and had to blink back the blur of tears. Master Grandible stared at her and nothing changed in his face. No light moved in his eyes. Perhaps he was going to strike her. Or for all she knew perhaps he was just thinking of Cheddar.

"Go and put your mask on, then," he growled, and scowled away down the corridor. "And no gabbling when she arrives."

Neverfell did not waste an instant wondering at his change of heart, but scampered away to extricate her black mask from the heap of tools, ragged catalogues, and disemboweled clocks under her hammock. The pile of the velvet was now rough and flattened by years of greasy handling.

It was a full-face mask with silver brows and a silver mouth closed in a polite smile. It had painted eyes, each with a little hole in the center for her to peer through. She pushed her pigtails back, and tied the mask in place with its frayed black ribbon.

Once, many years before, she had dared to ask why she had

to wear a mask when visitors came. Grandible's response had been blunt and searing.

For the same reason that a sore wears a scab.

In that moment she had realized that she must be hideous. She had never asked again. From then on she had lived in dread of her own blurry reflection in the copper pots, flinched from the pale and wobbly visage that greeted her indistinctly in the whey pails. She was a horror. She must be. She was too horrible to be allowed out of Grandible's tunnels.

However, deep in Neverfell's tangle of a mind there was a curious little knot of stubbornness. In truth, she had never resigned herself to the idea of a life spent cloistered away among Stiltons. Thus, when she had discovered the identity of the woman who had so confidently invited herself to tea, a small bubble of hope had formed in Neverfell's mind.

Neverfell flung off her leather apron, and hurried on the jacket with all the buttons or near enough. She had barely had time to make herself presentable when she heard the door's string of bells ring to announce the arrival of Madame Vesperta Appeline, the celebrated Facesmith.

Facesmiths could be found only in Caverna. The outer world had no need of them. It was only in the labyrinthine underground city of Caverna that babies did not smile.

In the overground world, babies who stared up at their mothers' faces gradually started to work out that the two bright stars they could see above them were eyes like their own, and that the broad curve was a mouth like theirs. Without even thinking about it, they would curve their mouths the same way, mirroring their mothers' smiles in miniature. When they were frightened or unhappy, they would know at once how to screw up their faces and bawl. Caverna babies never did this, and nobody knew why. They looked solemnly at the face above them, and saw eyes, nose, mouth, but they did not copy its expressions. There was nothing wrong with their features, but somehow one of the tiny silver links in the chain of their souls was missing. They had to be forced to learn expressions one at a time, slowly and painfully; otherwise, they remained blank as eggs.

These carefully taught expressions were the Faces. Those at the cheapest crèches learned only a handful of Faces, all suitable for their station, for what need had they of more? Richer families sent their children to better nurseries where they would learn two or three hundred Faces. Most Cavernans spent their lives making do with the Faces they had learned in infancy, but the affluent sometimes hired Facesmiths, specialist Face designers, to teach them new expressions. Among the fashionable elite, a new, beautiful, or interesting Face could cause more of a stir than a string of black pearls or a daring hat.

This was Neverfell's first opportunity to meet a Facesmith, and her heart was punching against her ribs with excitement as she sprinted back to her master.

"Can I be the one to unlock the door?" she asked, aware that she might be pushing her luck.

Cheesemaster Grandible was always careful to hide his front-door keys away from Neverfell's curious grasp, and dug them out only when a visitor was imminent. On this occasion he tossed her the great ring without a word, and she ran back to the door, her fingers thrilled by the cold weight of the keys.

"Only let her in if she's alone—and take a sniff before you open that door!" barked Grandible from down the corridor. Cheesemaster Grandible always responded to any outside intrusion as a potential invasion, even when the visitors were nothing but delivery boys.

Her fingers clumsy with excitement, Neverfell pulled out the waxed cloth that plugged each of the locks to keep out poison gas and glisserblinds, the tiny sightless snakes that sometimes slithered through rocky fissures, using their uncanny sense of smell to search for something to bite. She unlocked the seven locks, pulled back thirty-four of the thirty-five bolts, then obediently halted and stood on tiptoe to look through the goggle-glass spyhole set in the door.

In the little passageway beyond was the figure of a solitary woman. Her waist was so slender it looked as though it might snap. She was dressed in a dark green gown with a silver-beaded stomacher and a lace-adorned standing collar. Her mahogany-colored hair was all but lost amid a forest of feathers, most iridescent green and black, which made her look taller than she was. Neverfell's first thought was that the lady must have come straight from some wonderful party.

A black silk kerchief was wrapped around Madame Appeline's throat, so that her pale face was thrown into relief. Neverfell decided instantly that it was the most beautiful face she had ever seen. It was heart-shaped and perfectly smooth. As the lady waited, various expressions twinkled in and out of existence, a strange and charming change from Grandible's perpetual glower. Her eyes were long, slanted, and green, her brows utterly black. Only a little cleft in the chin prevented her face from being perfectly regular.

Remembering Grandible's instructions, Neverfell opened a small hidden hatch and took a quick careful sniff of the air. Her sharp cheesemaker's nose picked up only hair powder, haste, and a hint of violets. The lady was wearing perfume, but not

Perfume—a pleasing scent but not one that could be used to enslave minds.

Neverfell dragged back the last bolt, heaved on the great iron ring, and pulled the door open. Upon seeing her, the woman hesitated, and then softened slightly into a look of politely amused surprise, tinged with kindness.

"Can I speak to Cheesemaster Moormoth Grandible? I believe he is expecting me?"

Neverfell had never been looked at quite so gently before, and her mouth dried up instantly.

"Yes . . . I . . . He . . . he's in the reception room." This was her golden moment to steal a few words with the Facesmith, and apparently she had forgotten how to form sentences. She felt her face grow hot under the mask as she glanced furtively about her. "I . . . I wanted to ask you something—"

"Neverfell!" came the gruff bark from the reception room.

Neverfell abruptly remembered her master's instructions. *No gabbling.* That probably meant he did not want her talking at all.

She hesitated, then bent a neat little bow, and stepped back, miming an invitation to enter. No friendly chatter today. This was a guest to treat well and attentively, but not one to make too comfortable or welcome. So Neverfell waited for Madame Appeline to enter, fastened the door behind her, and then showed her toward the reception room, a dapper little mannequin with white eyes and a silver smile.

The light in the passage was dim, a sure sign of a shortage of people. Just as people counted upon the little carnivorous flytrap plants in the trap-lanterns to draw in stale, breathed air and turn it into fresh, breathable air, so the traps needed people to provide a supply of stale air for them to breathe. If there were not enough people around, they ran out of stale air, turned off their glow, and went to sleep. The little flytraps themselves had the blind, dappled, pallid look of toadstools, and seemed to be yawning their blind mouths out of boredom rather than the hope of luring in fat cave moths with their murky, yellowish light.

Fortunately Madame Appeline followed neatly behind Neverfell, without showing any temptation to wander off or touch anything. Grandible distrusted visitors, so by now all his booby traps would have been set. Doors would be locked and their handles smeared with a paralyzing veneer of Poric Hare-Stilton just in case. Besides such precautions, there were also the ordinary hazards of a cheesemaker's domain. Open the wrong door and you might find yourself faced with shelves of Spitting Jesses, rattling on their dove-feather beds and sending up a fine spray of acid through the pores in their rinds, or some great mossy round of Croakspeckle, the very fumes of which could melt a man's brain like so much butter.

The cozy antechamber that Grandible used as a reception room was the only place into which visitors were ever permitted. Here at least the reek of cheese was slightly fainter than in the rest of Grandible's domain. As Neverfell showed her in, the Facesmith drew herself up and changed manner completely. Suddenly she was grandiose and glittering, and seemed to have gained a few inches in height.

"Cheesemaster! I had heard rumors that you were still alive. How delightful to be able to confirm them!" The Facesmith swept delicately into the room, the longest feathers of her headdress kissing the roof of the antechamber. Peeling off her yellow gloves, she settled herself on the appointed guest chair, a carefully judged eight sword-lengths from Grandible's great wooden seat. "After such a dramatic and complete disappearance, half my friends were convinced you had despaired of life and done something ghastly to yourself."

Grandible examined the cuff of his long, gray greeting-visitors coat. His expression did not change, but perhaps for a second it deepened a little.

"Tea" was all he said. The cuffs did not respond, but presumably they knew the instruction was meant for Neverfell.

It was agony leaving the conversation at such a moment, just as it seemed Neverfell might finally learn something of Grandible's reasons for withdrawing from Court. The only aristocracy of Caverna were the Craft, the makers of True Delicacies that crossed the invisible line between the mind-blowing and the miraculous. As a maker of True Cheeses, Grandible was a member of the Craft class, but he had never told Neverfell why he chose not to take up his rightful place at Court.

In their rocky little kitchen, Neverfell hauled on a wall lever to summon hot water. Somewhere far above in the furnace caverns a little bell would be ringing. After a minute or two the water pipes started to hum, whine, and judder. Neverfell tugged on her protective gloves and turned the gray and scaly tap, releasing a torrent of steaming water into the teapot.

Neverfell made tea, scalding herself in her haste, and by the time she re-emerged guest and host were mid-conversation. When Neverfell placed a cup of peppermint tea and a plate of dates on the table beside Madame Appeline, the latter paused mid-flow to flash Neverfell a small, sweet thank-you smile.

". . . an extremely good customer," the Facesmith went on, "but also a close friend, which is why I promised to try to help him. You can understand his worry, surely? This is such an important diplomatic occasion, and the poor young man does not want to disgrace himself in front of the Grand Steward and the rest of the Court. Can you blame my friend for wanting to make sure that he has all the right Faces prepared?"

"Yes." Grandible's blunt nails tapped at the arm of his chair, near the catch for the hidden compartment. "I can. Fools like that keep the Face market running, even though everybody knows that two hundred Faces are enough for anybody. Damn it, *ten* would do."

"Or . . . two?" Madame Appeline narrowed her long, slanting eyes. Her smile was knowing, but there was a hint of warmth and sympathy beneath the mockery. "Cheesemaster, I know that it is almost a matter of principle with you, but you should actually be careful wearing the same Face day in and day out. It marks the countenance. Someday you may want to use one of your other Faces and suddenly realize that your face muscles can no longer remember them."

Grandible stared at her, his face dour as a gibbet. "I find this one very suitable for most situations and people I encounter." He sighed. "I fail to see why you want to talk to me, Facesmith. If this whelp wants a hundred new expressions so he can react differently to every shade of green he sees, then go ahead and sell them to him."

"If it were a matter of shades of green, then, yes, that would be an easy matter. Mock all you like, but In Contemplation of Verdigris and An Apprehension of Apple Boughs are very popular right now. No, the problem is the banquet. If he wants to prove he is a true judge of all that is fine, he must be able to react the right way to every dish. Are you getting a glimmer of my motives now, dear Cheesemaster?"

"More of a glint."

"I already have him primed with the right Faces for all four Wines, the songbird jelly, the soup, the pie, the cordial, the ices, and each of the sugared fruits. But your Stackfalter Sturton will be making its *debut*. How can I devise the right Face for something that I have never experienced?"

"That particular cheese was commissioned by the Grand Steward. It is his property."

"But there are always broken cheeses?" persisted Madame Appeline. "Failed cheeses? Scraps? Spills? Crumbs? My friend would only need the tiniest crumb. Would you not be willing to spare even that? He would be most grateful."

"No." The answer was very soft and final, like a candle dying. Madame Appeline was quiet for a long time, and when she spoke again she sounded very serious. Her smile was melancholy.

"Dear Cheesemaster, has it never occurred to you that some day—however improbable it may seem to you—you might wish to return to Court? That you might *need* to come back to Court? Hiding out here may feel safe, but it is not. It offers your enemies a thousand chances to move against you, whisper in the right ears. It makes you vulnerable, and if you lose your standing some dark hour you will not be safe even here. And you have posterity"— she directed a fleeting glance at Neverfell—"to consider."

"I'm sure you mean something by that." Grandible's hands were fidgeting on the arms of his chair, and Neverfell suddenly realized that he was nervous, more nervous than she had ever seen him.

"I mean that sooner or later you and your protégée are going to need allies, and for years you have been doing your best to push away everybody who tries to make friendly overtures. What if you have to deal with the Court again? How will you manage with no friends and two Faces?"

"I survived last time," muttered Grandible.

"And perhaps you could again," Madame Appeline continued quite calmly, "or you could let me help you. I know a lot of people and could make introductions. I could even make a new look for you, to make the whole thing easier." She put her heart-shaped head on one side, and scrutinized Grandible through her long, green eyes. "Yes, I think a touch of Twinkle or Wry Charm would suit you very well. Or perhaps World Weary, with a Hint of Sadness and a Core of Basic Integrity. Perhaps even Amused Shrewdness, with a Well of Deeper Wisdom? Cheesemaster, I know that you have a prejudice against my trade, but the truth is I can be a good friend, and I am really quite a useful person to know."

"Biscuits," said Grandible with venom.

In the kitchen, Neverfell's haste tripped her on a rug edge, sprawled her over a chair, and forced her to spend maddening extra minutes picking up the spilled biscuits from the floor and flicking the specks off them. She arrived back in the antechamber just in time to see that the conversation was over. With a sting of desperation she observed the Facesmith gliding back toward the great door with its thirty-five bolts, her expression a mild glow of wry amusement, regret, sympathy, and resolution.

Breathless, Neverfell ran to catch up with her, then dropped her deepest bow. She felt the Facesmith's smile tickle over her as gently and iridescently as the headdress feathers had touched the ceiling. Neverfell's heart lurched at the thought of breaking her orders from Master Grandible, but there would never be another chance to speak with a Facesmith, and this chance was slipping away.

"My lady!" she whispered urgently. "Wait! Please! I . . . you said you could make Faces that would make Master Grandible look good, and I just wanted to know . . ." She took a deep breath, and asked the question that had been buzzing around in her mind for months. "Could . . . could you make a Face for somebody who has none worth the name? I mean . . . someone so ugly they must be hid?"

For a few seconds the Facesmith regarded Neverfell's mask, her expression perfectly motionless. Then it softened into a gleaming sweetness, like a droplet welling at the tip of a thawing icicle. She reached out a hand toward the mask, apparently intending to remove it, but Neverfell flinched back. She was not yet ready for this beautiful woman to see whatever lay beneath.

"You really won't let me see?" whispered Madame Appeline. "Very well, then—I have no intention of upsetting you." She glanced up the corridor, then leaned forward to whisper.

"I have had many people come to me who were called ugly, and every single time I have been able to design them a Face that makes them pleasant to the eye. It is never hopeless. Whatever you may have been told, nobody *needs* to be ugly."

Neverfell felt her eyes tingle, and had to swallow hard. "I'm sorry Master Grandible was so rude. If it had been up to me . . ."

"Thank you." There were peacock-colored flecks in Madame Appeline's eyes, as if two green gems had been carefully fractured a hundred times. "I believe you. What was your name again—did Master Grandible call you Neverfell?"

Neverfell nodded.

"Good to meet you, Neverfell. Well, I shall remember that I may have one young friend in these cheese tunnels, even if your master is determined to distrust everyone who belongs to the Court." Madame Appeline glanced back toward the reception room. "Look after him well. He is more vulnerable than he thinks. It is dangerous to lock oneself away and lose track of what is happening outside."

"I wish I could go out into the city and discover things for him," whispered Neverfell. Her reasons were not completely unselfish, though, and she knew the yearning in her voice had betrayed her.

"Do you never leave your master's tunnels?" Madame Appeline's black eyebrows rose gracefully as Neverfell shook her head. Her tone was slightly scandalized. "Never? But why on earth not?"

Neverfell's hands moved defensively back to her mask, and the unloved face it hid.

"Oh." Madame Appeline gave a soft sigh of realization. "Do you really mean to say that he keeps you locked up in here because of your looks? But that is terrible! No wonder you want a new Face!" She reached out one yellow-gloved hand and gently stroked the cheek of Neverfell's mask with a faint rasp of velvet. "Poor child. Well, do not despair. Perhaps you and I will turn out to be friends, and if so perhaps someday I will have a chance to make a Face for you. Would that make you happy?"

Neverfell nodded mutely, her chest full to bursting.

"In the meanwhile," the Facesmith went on, "you can always send a message to me. My tunnels are not far from the Samphire district, where Tytheman's Slink meets the Hurtles."

A bell rang in the reception room, and Neverfell knew that Grandible was becoming impatient. Reluctantly, she unbolted the door again and heaved it open, so that Madame Appeline could drift out.

"Good-bye, Neverfell."

In the fleeting second before the door closed between them, Neverfell glimpsed something that made her heart stumble in its pace. Madame Appeline was watching her with a Face she had never seen before. It was unlike anything from the many Facesmith catalogues Neverfell had treasured over the years, nor was it smooth and beautiful like the other Faces Madame Appeline had worn during her visit. It contained a smile, but one with a world of weariness behind the brightness, and sadness beyond the kindness. There was something a little haggard around the eyes as well that spoke of sleeplessness, patience, and pain.

Next instant the image was gone, and Neverfell was left staring at the door as it clicked to. Her mind was crazed with color and jumbled thoughts. It took her a moment or two before she remembered that she should be throwing all the bolts.

That last extraordinary Face had sent a throb through her very soul, like a breeze shivering the string of a harp, and she could not account for it. Something in her heart cried out that it was familiar. Without knowing why, Neverfell had come very close to flinging the door open again, throwing her arms around the visitor, and bursting into tears.

STIR CRAZY

NEVERFELL REALIZED THAT SHE WAS IN TROUBLE the moment she removed her mask. Grandible's gray gaze settled upon her and hardened like frost.

"What is it?" One of his broad, rough hands cupped her face, while his other raised his lantern so that the greenish trap-light fell upon her cheek. "You are hiding something!"

Faced once again with her master's uncanny ability to guess her thoughts, Neverfell could only stutter and stammer.

"What did you do?" Above all else, it was the hint of fear in Master Grandible's voice that threw Neverfell off balance. "You spoke to her, didn't you?" he demanded hoarsely.

"She . . ."

"Did you take your mask off?"

Neverfell shook her head as best she could with her chin in Grandible's calloused grip. His eyes slid to and fro across her face as though somebody had etched answers there.

"Did you tell her anything about yourself? Anything about me, or the tunnels? Anything at all?"

"No!" squeaked Neverfell, racking her brain to make sure that she had not. No, she had told the beautiful lady almost nothing;

all she had done was ask questions and nod occasionally. "I didn't! All I told her was . . . that I was sorry."

"Sorry? Why sorry?"

Because she was nice and you were rude, thought Neverfell.

"Because she was nice and you were rude," said Neverfell. Then gulped and chewed her lower lip as once again her words galloped away from her.

There was a pause, then her master let out a long sigh and released her chin.

"Why wouldn't you give her what she wanted?" asked Neverfell. Her feet kept up a back-and-forth dance. Timid step backward, impatient step forward. "There's a round of Stackfalter Sturton the size of my fist going spare—the one we set aside so we'd know when the bigger one was ripe. Why don't we give her a crumb or two of that?"

"For the same reason that I do not try to pull a thread free from a cobweb and use it to darn my socks," growled Grandible. "Pull on a thread, and you pull on the whole web. And then out come the spiders . . ."

Even when Master Grandible answered questions, the result was not always very rewarding.

For the next week, Neverfell was a menace. She could concentrate on nothing. She spooned elk's spittle onto a Barkbent round instead of reindeer tears, and it protested with a flood of acid steam, scalding her arm scarlet. She forgot to move the Liquorish Lazars down from the shelf near the cooling pipes, and remembered them only when they started juddering against the wood.

Strange and wonderful Madame Appeline had said that she might be able to devise a Face for Neverfell that would make her less hideous. The thought filled her with a warm surge of hope, but then she remembered the Facesmith's ominous words about the Court and this was replaced by a turbulent and queasy sense of dread. Master Grandible was so stonily immovable, she could no more imagine anything happening to him than she could visualize living without the rocky ceiling that crowned her world. But the Facesmith had hinted that by hiding away from the Court he was putting himself in danger and letting others plot against him. Could it be true? He had not been ready with an answer. Could anybody harm her master in his impregnable dairy castle?

"What's got into you?" Grandible growled.

And Neverfell could give him no answer, for she did not know what had got into her. But into her it had decidedly got, for now in the cooking pot of her thoughts she could feel it simmering, sending up a bubble-string of excitement. She had half an idea, she had a seed of a plan, though perhaps it was untrue to say that she had it, for she felt rather as if it had her. For once, however, she had a wispy thought that she had not confided to Grandible, for the simple reason that she did not quite know what it was or what to say about it.

"You see?" Grandible growled. "One look at that woman's world, one whiff . . . it's an infection. You've a fever now, and you'll be lucky if that's all you get." He did not treat her as an invalid, though, and, in fact, seemed determined to keep Neverfell as busy as possible.

Could Neverfell trust Madame Appeline? Again and again her mind strayed back to the last Face she had seen her wearing, the tired and loving expression without gloss. Try as she might, she could not believe it was nothing but an empty mask.

You couldn't invent a Face like that without feeling it, she told herself.

. . . . .

The thought was still at the forefront of her mind three days later when Erstwhile dropped by to deliver several barrels of fresh milk, a vat of clean dove feathers, and six bottles of lavender water that had been used to wash a dead man's feet. Erstwhile was a scrawny, slightly pockmarked delivery boy, and the most regular visitor to Grandible's tunnels. He was about a year older than Neverfell, although two inches shorter, and was often willing to spend time with her and answer her questions, albeit in a rather lordly way. Neverfell suspected that he rather liked seeing her hanging on his every word and knowing that his visits were important to somebody.

"Erstwhile—what do you know about Madame Appeline?" The question was out almost before he had sat down.

Erstwhile did not have any angry or annoyed expressions. Worker and drudge-class families were never taught such Faces, for it was assumed they did not need them. Nonetheless, Neverfell noticed his shoulders stiffen and sensed that she had offended him. He had arrived full of pride and ready to tell her something, and now she had put his nose out of joint by asking about somebody else. He thawed slightly, however, when she brought him a cup of ginger tea.

"Here—look at this." He brandished something in front of her face for an instant, just long enough for her to see that it was a small, yellowing painting of an overground scene, then hid it back in his coat. "I have to deliver it to a trader in the Crumbles, but I'll let you look at it for three eggs."

When Neverfell brought him three preserved eggs, still in their blue shells, he let her hold the picture. It showed a small house peeping wary-windowed through a veil of trees, with a forest hill rising behind. There was a whitish hole in the sky, brighter than the rest.

"That's the sun, isn't it?" she asked, pointing.

"Yes—that's why there's nobody outdoors in the picture. You know about that, don't you? The sun *burns* people. And lots of them have to go out to work in the fields, but if they're out too long their skin burns red and painful and then it *falls off.* And none of them can ever look up because the sun is too bright, and if they do, it burns their eyes out and they go blind."

He glanced sideways at Neverfell as he unpeeled one of the eggs, revealing the fine, snowflake-like patterns across its caramel-colored surface.

"Look at you, jumpy as a sick rat. You know, it's just as well I come here, or you'd go crazy. Grandible will be sorry someday he's locked you up like this with no company. You'll go proper crazy and kill him."

"Don't say things like that!" squeaked Neverfell, her voice shrill with distress but also a touch of outrage. She had told Erstwhile too much in the past, and thus he knew that occasionally she *did* go crazy. Sometimes it was when she felt particularly trapped or hopeless, or when the tunnels were unusually dark or stuffy, or when she got stuck in a crawl-through. Sometimes it happened for no obvious reason at all. She would feel a terrible panic tightening her chest and giving her heart a queasy lollop, she would be fighting for breath . . . and then she would be recovering somewhere, shuddering and sick, devastation around her and her fingernails broken from clawing at the rock walls and ceilings.

She could remember almost nothing of her fits afterward, except a desperation for light and air. Not greenish trap-lantern light or the dull red drowsing of embers, but a chilly, searing immensity staring down at her from above. Not the ordinary, homey, pungent air of the cheese tunnels, but air that smelled of big and had somewhere to be. Air that jostled and roared.

Erstwhile cackled at her dismay, his good humor restored.

"All right. That's long enough." He took back the picture, tucked it in his jacket, and settled down to cutting his egg in half, exposing its creamy, dark turquoise yolk. "You want to know about Madame Appeline?"

Neverfell nodded.

"Easy. I know all about *her*. She's one of the best-known Facesmiths in Caverna. Probably about seventy years old now, though she hasn't aged in forty years. The other Facesmiths hate her like poison—even more than they hate each other—because she didn't become a Facesmith through a proper apprenticeship like everybody else. About seven years ago she was a nobody, just some back-cave feature-twitcher teaching pretty smiles for pocket money. Then all of a sudden she brought out her Tragedy Range."

"Tragedy Range?" Neverfell's mind flitted to the haggard look she had glimpsed for an instant behind Madame Appeline's smile.

"Yeah. You see, before that everybody used to hire Facesmiths because they wanted to have the newest, brightest smile, or the most lordly glare. The Tragedy Range wasn't like that. It had sad Faces. Hurt Faces. Brave Faces. They weren't always pretty, but they made people look deep and interesting, like they had a secret sorrow. The Court went crazy over them. She's been famous ever since."

"But what's she like? I mean . . . is she nice? Is she trustworthy?"

"Trustworthy?" Erstwhile picked his teeth. "She's a *Facesmith*. Everything about her is fake. And for sale."

"But . . . Faces have to come from somewhere, don't they?" persisted Neverfell. "The feelings behind them, I mean. So . . . perhaps something happened to her seven years ago, something tragic, and that's why she suddenly came up with all these Faces?"

Erstwhile shrugged. He was bored of Madame Appeline.

"I can't sit around nattering all day." He dropped the crushed eggshells into Neverfell's hand. "You shouldn't be sitting around like a great lump either. You've got your precious banquet cheese to prepare, haven't you?"

The approach of a grand banquet always sent a shiver through the tunnels of Caverna. In some parts, masked perfumiers might be letting a single droplet of a pearly fluid fall into a vast aviary to see how many of their canaries swooned with the fumes. Elsewhere, furriers would be carefully skinning dozens of moles to produce gloves from their tiny pelts. A thousand little luxuries were being tested with trepidation to discover which were too ordinary for the Court, and which too exquisite to be survivable.

As far as Grandible and Neverfell were concerned, the banquet meant one thing—the debut of the great Stackfalter Sturton. It was a cheese of monstrous proportions, weighing as much as Neverfell herself. Sturtons were known for the peculiarity of the visions they induced. They had a habit of showing people truths that they knew already but still needed to be told, because they had forgotten them or refused to see them. Sturtons were also notoriously difficult to craft successfully and without fatalities, so Grandible and Neverfell dedicated all their energies to making the Stackfalter Sturton ready for its great moment. It might have been a bride being groomed for a wedding.

Every day the Stackfalter Sturton's dappled white-and-apricot hide had to be painted with a mixture of primrose oil and musk, and its long, fine mosses groomed with a careful brush. More important, the great cheese had to be turned over every 141 minutes, and, since it was about five feet across, this required two people and a great deal of huffing. Every 141 minutes, therefore, both Neverfell and Grandible needed to be awake.

In the sunless world of Caverna there were no days or nights as such, but everybody by mutual consent used the same twenty-five-hour clock. To make sure that there was always somebody awake in the cheese tunnels, Grandible and Neverfell slept different shifts, or "kept different clocks," to use the common phrase. Grandible generally slept from seven until thirteen o'clock, and Neverfell from twenty-one until four. One person, however, could not hope to turn the Sturton alone.

After about three days of sleeping no more than two hours at a time, both of them started to come unsprung. To make matters worse, other orders poured in shortly before the banquet. Those in the highest circles had heard of the great Sturton debut, and suddenly Grandible's wares were fashionable. There were small orders from countless illustrious-sounding ladies, including Madame Appeline, who asked only for a small package of Zephurta's Whim. Even though the lady seemed to have given up on her request for the Sturton, Neverfell clung to hope like a drowner.

"Can't we just send a crumb or two of Sturton to Madame Appeline? Please? Can we? We can send her some of the sample truckle!" Beside the great Sturton sat a smaller replica, like the lumpy egg of some ill-constructed bird. This wheel would be opened before the Sturton was sent out to glory, just to make sure that the paste of the cheese was everything it should be.

"No."

Eventually things reached crisis point. The other cheeses had noticed their attendants' favoritism and started to complain at their neglect. Angry Bries went on an ooze offensive. One Popping Quimp triggered unexpectedly and had bounced and crackled halfway down the tunnel before Neverfell could leap on it with a damp towel and smother the flames. Even Grandible's stolen moments of slumber were interrupted by the sound of Neverfell shrieking for assistance or desperately swatting butter-flies.

"Master, Master, can I take apart the mangle? Because then we can put the cheese between two big serving boards and I can make a crank-handle thingy and it will only take one of us to wind it so it turns over the cheese and so one of us can sleep, Master Grandible. Can I try that?"

And Grandible, who had impatiently batted away a hundred other impractical suggestions, hesitated and scratched at his chin.

"Hmph. Tell me more."

As it turned out, the mangle did not die in vain. There were false starts and nipped fingers, but like many of Neverfell's mechanical experiments the crank-handle cheese-turner eventually worked. When Neverfell demonstrated it at long last, her master watched her with the most acute and belligerent attention, then slowly nodded.

"Go to bed" was all he said. And he ruffled Neverfell's nests of pigtails with a hand so large and rough that the gesture almost felt like a cuff. Neverfell staggered off and dropped into her hammock knowing that, for once, Master Grandible was very pleased with her. Sleep swallowed her like a pond gulping a pebble.

She woke again quite suddenly two hours later, and stared up at the rocky ceiling of the tunnel, eardrums tingling as if somebody had snapped their fingers in front of her face. She knew instantly that it must be twenty-five o'clock, the hour of naught. When the silver-faced clock in Grandible's reception room reached the hour of naught, it gave a dull click as the mechanism reset. For some reason, it was this and not the chimes of other hours that had a habit of waking Neverfell.

Despite her exhaustion this click had jerked her out of sleep once more. She gave a small, beleaguered moan and wrapped herself in a ball, but to no avail. She was drenched in ice-cold wakefulness, and jumpy as a grasshopper.

"Not fair," she whispered as she tumbled out of her hammock. "Not *fair*. Please don't let me be out of clock! Not again!"

Because there was no night or day in Caverna, sometimes people fell "out of clock." Their cycles of sleeping and waking collapsed, and often they could not sleep at all but drifted through endless hazy, miserable hours. Neverfell was particularly prone to this.

Doing, doing, doing. What can I be doing?

Her brain felt like a sponge, and everything looked spangly as she tottered down the passages, checking on the slumbering cheeses. She tried sweeping up, but she kept tripping over pails and leaving little whey prints down the corridors. In the end she hobbled back to the Sturton's boudoir, knowing that Master Grandible would find something for her to do.

There were only a couple of trap-lanterns set in corners of the antechamber. As their lemony light ebbed and glowed, the great cheese almost seemed to swell and contract like a creature breathing in its sleep. Wicked glints slunk along the iron angles of the mangled mangle. Beyond them, seated on the floor with his back to the wall, was Master Grandible, his eyes closed and jaw hanging open.

Neverfell's lungs seemed to empty of air, and she managed only a faint squeak of alarm. For a moment all she could think was that somehow her master had suddenly died. Cheeses turned on you sometimes, even mild-mannered and well-trained cheeses. It was one of the hazards of the profession. And what other alternative explanation was there? In all the years she had known him, Master Grandible had never slipped, never made an error, never forgotten a responsibility. Surely, even with his exhaustion . . .

Master Grandible's jaw wobbled slightly; from his throat issued a reverberating snore. Yes, the impossible had happened. The infallible Master Grandible had fallen asleep on duty, two minutes before the Sturton needed to be turned.

Neverfell tiptoed over to him and put her hand out toward his shoulder, then hesitated and withdrew it. No, why shake him awake? He needed sleep, and she would let him have it. She would take care of the turning for him, and the next one too if he was still asleep then. He would be proud of her. He would have to be.

She counted out the seconds, then silently set about cranking the handle and turning the great cheese. After she had turned the tiny sample Sturton too, by hand, she grinned to herself as she tried out her brand-new and unfamiliar sense of self-satisfaction.

There was no point in trying to sleep until exhaustion kicked in once again, and Neverfell began groggily preparing other orders, the dainties for the market gala, the camel cheese for the eminent chocolatier, and the delivery for Madame Appeline.

Ten minutes before she was due to turn the Sturton again, the bells rang at Grandible's front door. Neverfell tied her mask on crooked and ran to answer it, almost falling afoul of Grandible's various lethal traps in her hurry. Peering through the spyhole she saw a footman displaying a leanness and angularity of jaw usually reserved for lizards.

"Your business?" Neverfell tried to imitate Grandible's brusque tone.

The footman's smile was instantly charming, while suggesting an awareness of his own dignity. His consonants all had a damp sound.

"If you would be so kind, there is a package reserved for Madame Appeline. If it is ready—"

The idea hit Neverfell like a fist. It hit her so hard that she actually rocked back on to her heels, then stood trembling and trying to decide whether to cry. It was a good idea, a brilliant idea, perhaps the best she had ever had, better than the mangle/cheese-turner. But it seemed unfair that it should have occurred to her now, just when she was enjoying the thought of Master Grandible being pleased with her. She deserved to feel that happiness a little longer. But no, now she had the idea and it had her. She gnawed her fingers, and the idea gnawed her, and she knew she was going to do what it wanted.

"One moment!" she squeaked, then sprinted back toward the room where the Stackfalter Sturton lay in state.

At the door she halted, then edged slowly into the room, softening her steps as best she could to avoid waking her master. Not two feet from the great sleeping Sturton nestled the baby sample Sturton, ragged with its feathery white mosses. At Neverfell's belt hung a circular steel cutter, designed so that you could push it in through the rind of a cheese and pull out a tiny cylindrical sample. Hardly daring to breathe, Neverfell reached out and picked up the sample Sturton between finger and thumb, wincing as she felt the tender mosses crush beneath her touch like loose snow.

She pushed her cutter into the base of the little cheese and felt a tingle of fear and excitement as the rind gave way. When she pulled it out with a small round of ripe cheese within it, the exposed paste filled the room with the scent of wildflowers and wet dogs, and for a moment she was afraid that it would tickle Grandible's well-trained nose and wake him. He snored on, however, and she carefully returned the sample to its place, the new hole flush against the shelf so as to conceal her crime and stop the spread of the smell.

She was partly doing this for him, she reminded herself. He needed friends in the Court, and soon he would have Madame Appeline.

Back in the packing room she found the box put aside for Madame Appeline's order, the pearl-gray round of Zephurta's Whim already nestling within in its bed of olive leaves. Neverfell quickly removed the stolen cheese from her cutter and wrapped it in muslin. In a moment of inspiration, she tied the muslin bundle with a piece of black velvet ribbon, so that Madame Appeline would remember the black velvet mask and realize who was responsible.

Out, out, out, said her heart with every beat. *Doing this will get me out of here. Madame Appeline will make me a new Face, and I can go out.*

Grandible had hidden away the front-door keys once again, but there was a small much-bolted hatch beside the door for receiving small deliveries, and Madame Appeline's box was narrow enough to fit through it.

"Here—sign this!" She unbolted the hatch and pushed a receipt through it. Once the footman had signed it, Neverfell thrust the box through the hatch and bolted it again. "There! Take it!" She watched him depart through the spyhole, then leaned gasping against the door.

I can sleep now, I can . . . no, wait! The next Sturton turning!

She sprinted down the corridors to the Sturton room and flung open the door. One sniff of the air told her that she was almost too late. The fumes from the unturned cheese were starting to turn poisonous, and her eyes stung as she staggered forward toward the crank. Grandible was already crawling his way across the floor, jowls shaking as he choked on the now-overpowering smell of wildflowers. Holding her breath and closing her eyes, Neverfell cranked the handle and slowly inverted the Sturton. At last it found itself standing on its head, and began to settle.

"Master Grandible!" Neverfell ran to his side, all else forgotten in her concern. It took a while for his breaths to steady.

"Child . . . I shall forgive you your wakefulness. If I had slept on . . . the cheese would have been *ruined*." This was clearly of far greater horror to him than the prospect of his own demise. "Good . . . good work, Neverfell." His eyes rose to her face. "Why . . . why are you wearing your mask?"

"Oh." Neverfell felt her skin tingle and grow hot as she removed the mask. "I . . . I . . . A footman came for a delivery . . . Madame Appeline . . ."

And, looking into her master's eyes, Neverfell was suddenly sure that he knew absolutely the reason for her stammer and the greasy cutter at her belt. Somehow he could see right through her.

"I wanted to protect you!" she squeaked, giving up all hope of pretense.

"Death's gate," whispered Grandible. His expression was grim and dogged as ever, but suddenly he was ashen pale.

SPYDERS

"WHAT HAVE I DONE? WHAT HAVE I DONE? I have done something terrible—what is it? I just wanted to help! I thought if I sent Madame Appeline what she wanted, it would make friends for you in the Court . . . I just wanted to keep you safe!"

"Safe?" Grandible's face was still that of a statue, frozen and grayish with suppressed emotion. "Safe?" His voice rose to a roar, tiny flecks of Stackfalter Sturton falling out of his eyebrows. Neverfell gave a wordless squeak of apology as she was shaken like a doll and then abruptly thrust away.

Master Grandible stared at her, one hand raised as if he were considering striking her. Then he reached out unsteadily and shoved at her shoulder with the flat of his hand. Neverfell quivered and went nowhere, uncertain whether he wanted her to leave, unsure whether the gesture had been angry or affectionate.

"A person I could trust" was all he said, and gave a small choking sound that she did not immediately recognize as a laugh. "That was what I thought. When I pulled you out of the whey. You were so . . ." He sighed and cupped his hands as if a small, damp kitten were resting its paws on his palms. "What more could

I do? I boarded my doors against every betrayal I could imagine. But there was one I never expected." He rasped his yellowing fingernails through his beard with a sound like a toothbrush war. "Ha. Betrayal for my own good."

"What . . . what does it mean? What have I done?"

"You have woken the spiders."

Master Grandible sometimes had an odd, unbalanced way of saying words that gave them new meanings. When he talked of ordinary spiders of the spindle-legged and spinning variety, the word had its usual ring. But here there was a greater weight on the first syllable, the second dusty and dead, almost inaudible. Spy . . . der.

"Go and fetch the prune gin. Bring it to the reception room."

Neverfell ran off to fetch the bottle, her face burning and her stomach acid. She had gone so fast from lifesaver to betrayer that all her words seemed to have fallen out of her. When she reached the reception room, Master Grandible had dropped into his chair, eyes bloodshot and breath still wheezing. She carried in her tiny tapestry-seat stool and hunched on it at his feet, her knees pulled up to her nose. He took the bottle, sipped, then stared down the neck.

"Neverfell—what do you think the Court is?"

Neverfell could not even shape a sentence. The Court was golden; the Court was glory. It was fair maidens and a thousand new faces and her heart beating fast. It was the world. It was everything that was not here.

"I know you hate it," she said.

Master Grandible leaned forward, and dropped his broad chin down to rest on his fists.

"It is a giant web, Neverfell, full of bright-winged, glistening insects. All of them full of their own poison, all entangled, all struggling to live and to kill. All of them pull the web this way and that to favor themselves or throttle each other. And every motion that one of them makes is felt by all the others."

"But Madame Appeline . . ."

Madame Appeline is different, Neverfell wanted to say. *I saw it in her Face.* But she could hear how foolish it would sound, so she let the sentence drop.

"It sickens me now to say it," Grandible went on, "but as a young man I had a notable place at Court."

"Did you?" Neverfell could not help leaning forward in excitement, even though she knew it was not how her master wanted her to react.

"Nobody else had successfully ripened a Wanepilch Milchmaid in this city without their eyes falling out," Grandible explained, "so when I succeeded, a round of it was sent to the Grand Steward himself. And . . . they say that when he placed the first sliver of it into his mouth, he *actually tasted* it."

"So . . . it is all true what they say of him, then? That he would be blind, deaf, and numb without the very finest luxuries?"

"Not quite. There is nothing wrong with his eyes, ears, nose, skin, or tongue, only the parley they hold with his soul. He can look at a flower and tell you it is blue, but blue means nothing to him. You can put a forkful of meat on his tongue and he will be able to tell you that it is roast beef, the age and stock of the cow, exactly how long it has been cooked, and which type of tree gave the wood for the fire, but it might as well be a pebble for all the flavor means to him. He can analyze it, but he no longer *feels* it.

"But what is to be expected of a man five hundred years old? They say he remembers the days when there was an overground city up on the mountainside, and no Caverna, just a set of caves and cellars where the city stored its luxuries. He has outlived that city, seen it fall into ruin beneath the ravages of war and weather, while its citizens gradually retreated beneath the earth and dug downward.

"For four hundred and twenty of those five hundred years his body has been trying to die. He has sustained himself on every liquor, spice, and unguent known to hold back death, but there is only so long you can drag a bow against a string before it starts to creak. The colors in his soul are fading, and his passions are going out one by one, like stars. That is why the Craftsmen of the City strive, night and day, century in and century out, to steal, create, or invent something that he can feel."

"And you succeeded!"

"Yes. I won the Grand Steward's favor."

There was something in his dark tone that curbed Neverfell's burning desire to know about the benefits of the favor of the Grand Steward. *Did he give you a hat made of gold and a monkey is that where your clock came from did he knight you did you drink pearls dissolved in coffee . . .* These were all questions that Neverfell managed not to ask.

"Some say the favor of the Grand Steward is double-edged. They are wrong. It is all edge, and everybody knows it, and still all the courtiers spend their every waking moment clutching at it and bleeding. The moment you rise to favor, you gain a hundred unseen and envious enemies.

"I was stung too often. No favor was worth it. I decided to pull myself out of the web, and buried myself in these tunnels so that I could not find myself playing the Court games even by accident. Leaving the Court is no easy matter, for one finds oneself entangled—debts, threats, secrets shared, people who know your weaknesses, and people whose weaknesses you know. When I left, many whispered that this was just another move in a more complicated game, one that required me to be out of sight. There were four assassination attempts against me in the first month."

The many locks, the precautions taken for every visitor . . . all of these began to make more sense.

"Eventually they left me alone," continued the cheesemaker, "but only because, year in and year out, I took every care to be completely neutral. No games, no alliances, no biases. I used the same rules for everybody. No exceptions."

"Oh . . ." Neverfell hugged her knees as clarity dawned. "So that's why you didn't want to give Madame Appeline the Sturton when she asked for it? Because that would be making an exception?"

"Yes," Grandible muttered hollowly. "And now everybody will think that I have done so knowingly. At the grand banquet the Sturton will make its debut, and Madame Appeline's client will already have a Face tailor-made to respond to it. It will be obvious that it could not have been prepared without prior knowledge of the cheese. Everybody will see the Face and *know*."

"What . . . what can I do? Can I make it better?"

"No."

There it was. Neverfell felt her stomach turn over. For the hundredth time one of her wild gestures had knocked something over and broken it beyond mending. This time, however, she knew that she had broken something far larger, something that could not be replaced. Her soul burned with self-hate, and she wished that she could break herself into a thousand pieces like a china pot. She buried her nose between her knees and snuffled.

"No," her master repeated. "There is nothing we can do. I shall send a man to try to retrieve the delivery, but I think it is too late."

"But . . . you could tell everybody it was my fault, and that you did nothing wrong! I could tell them what happened! Or maybe you could send me to talk to Madame Appeline! I could explain, and ask her to give us back the Stackfalter Sturton—"

"NO!" For the first time Grandible sounded truly and ferociously angry. Neverfell leaped to her feet and fled.

It was all very well being told that she could do nothing to make things better. Neverfell did not have the kind of mind that could take that quietly. She did not have the kind of mind that could be quiet at all.

In many respects, poor Neverfell's overactive mind had coped with her lonely and cloistered life in the only way it could. It had gone a little mad to avoid going wholly mad. To break up the dreary repetition of the day it had learned to skip unpredictably, to invent and half-believe, to shuffle thoughts until they were surprising and unrecognizable.

Small wonder that when she did find somebody to talk with they barely understood her. She was like a playing piece making "knight moves" when everybody else was obeying checkers rules. Half the time her mind was visiting squares where nobody else ever landed, and even when people understood the position her mind had reached, they could never work out how she had got there.

At the moment, her mind was throwing up ideas and thoughts the way a fountain throws up water drops, most of them foolish on second glance, losing their glitter as they fell.

We can give Stackfalter Sturton samples to everybody! Everybody in the entire Court! Then it'll be fair!

We can swap the big banquet Sturton for another giant cheese that looks exactly the same but tastes a bit different, so that the Face Madame Appeline creates won't match the taste!

We can send an extra cheese to the banquet, one that will split

*and fill the whole room with stinging steam! That way everybody
will have to run away, and nobody will see the Face Madame
Appeline has prepared!*

Fortunately she had just enough common sense to see the
flaws in these plans before presenting them to Cheesemaster
Grandible. There was not enough Sturton to give to everybody
without breaking into the big truckle, there was not enough
time to make and ripen a suitable decoy cheese, and it was
just possible that blinding the Grand Steward and his privileged
nobles with poison cheese steam would not greatly improve
Master Grandible's position.

Among the flood of ideas and imaginings, however, a couple
of thoughts bubbled and bobbed to the surface again and again.
Why had Master Grandible been so angry at her suggestion that
she talk to people and take the blame? He had been frightened
at the idea of her speaking with Madame Appeline from the start.
Was there some secret that her careless words might give away?

By the time she dared to reappear, Master Grandible had staggered
back to tend to the Sturton once more, his racking coughs just
audible in the distance, and Neverfell was reluctant to disturb
him. To judge from the papers on his desk, however, he was
translating all his fears into action. The traps and precautions he
had already laid in place were nothing compared to those he now
seemed to be preparing. To judge by the scrawled maps on his
desk, he was planning a series of heavy doors subdividing his
district, so that if he found himself under siege he could fall back
and fall back, forcing his imagined enemies to break in through
door after door.

The door that stood between his tunnels and the rest of
Caverna was now covered with new padlocks in addition to the

original locks, and as usual there was no sign of the keys. *Are those locks to keep enemies out,* thought Neverfell, *or me in?*

She also found a list of new duties with her name at the top, and gawped in alarm as her eye ran down it. Evidently the fortification project was taking all Grandible's time, so he had passed most of his customary tasks on to her. The scrawled entry "Stckfltr brush rabbt milk once daily" was explained when a small crate arrived at the appointed time containing one quivering, wild-eyed rabbit, not best pleased by Neverfell's inquisitive but innocent decision to shake the box before opening it.

The rabbit's pale coat was patchy, as though it had been pulling out its own fur through nerves or boredom. But when it twitched its buttonhole nostrils at Neverfell, she felt a surge of love for it in the way that only the lonely can. To judge by the long scratches its hind claws left on her forearms when she tried to hug it, however, the feeling was not mutual.

The Sturton had to be brushed with rabbit milk. How did you milk rabbits? Neverfell knew something of the way cows, sheep, and goats were milked. How different could it be?

"Don't— Hold still— Oh, you dratted, pink-eyed . . . Oh, come back, sweetheart! I didn't mean it!"

Neverfell knelt on the stone floor, peering under the long wooden shelf affixed to the wall of the passage. Along the top of the shelf a row of crimson-veined Pulp Cheddars gently perspired. Underneath the shelf, a pale shape flattened itself to the floor like a slumped soufflé, long ears flush to its back, pink eyes dark and empty with fear.

She was not much wiser about how one went about milking a rabbit, but she was considerably wiser when it came to ways not to do it. For example, she was now aware that even though rabbit bellies hung very close to the ground, they were very resistant to being lifted into a croquet-hoop shape so that one could slip a bucket under them. Furthermore, she was now better educated about the power of a rabbit's jump, the sharpness of its claws, and the sheer speed of its mismatched legs.

Unfortunately, as a result of these lessons, the rabbit was loose in the cheese tunnels, probably leaving an invisible trail of shed hair, fleas, and rodent fear in its wake to startle and spoil the delicately reared truckles.

"Here . . . it's all right . . ."

She impulsively reached toward the rabbit, despite the tufted hole that its teeth had ravaged in the shoulder of her doublet. The rabbit scrambled away from her with a chitter of claws, and Neverfell flinched backward, grazing her knuckles on the coarse wood of the shelf.

"Don't . . ." Somehow she had to calm and capture the rabbit again, before the cheesemaker found out. "Is it my face? Look— it's all right, I'm covering it." She tied her velvet mask over her features. "There! Look! Bad face gone away now." The rabbit simply broke into a round-backed bobbing run, and took off down the corridor. "Oh, you little . . ." Neverfell scrambled to her feet and sprinted after it, the tiny pail rattling on her arm.

The rabbit took the first left into the Whistleplatch corridor. It squeezed between the vats as if it were boneless, and lurked behind them until Neverfell poked it out with a broom handle. It kicked a bucket of standing cream, and for a time Neverfell could track the long, pale prints left by its back legs. By throwing herself full length she managed to place a hand upon it, pushing it to the ground, so that it flattened itself again into a quivering, docile dollop of rabbit. Then she tried to pick it up and it transformed into a wild white halo of fur, claw, and tooth.

Cursing and bleeding from a dozen scratches, Neverfell set off in pursuit once more.

Every time the rabbit had a choice between two corridors, it chose the one that sloped upward. *Up, up, up,* its frantic unthinking heart was chanting. *Up means out.* Somehow Neverfell could almost hear it, and as she pursued the rabbit her heart began the same chant.

At last it found a dead end, a parade of mighty cheese presses crushing the whey out of great Gravelhide truckles as rough as a cow's tongue.

"Ha!" Neverfell swung the door shut behind her and fastened it, then gazed up and down the Gravelhide passage. There—a pair of white ears. The rabbit had squeezed behind one of the presses.

"Oh . . . don't make me do this." There was a scrabbling. Silence. Scrabbling. Silence. Silence. "All right, all right!" Neverfell pushed back her hair, then began slowly dragging the nearest press forward.

First press, grindingly, painfully dragged away from the rock wall. No rabbit.

Second press. No rabbit.

Third press. No rabbit. And . . . no wall.

Down through the part of the wall that had been hidden by the presses, there ran a vertical crack some four feet high. At the bottom, the crack opened into a triangular hole, half-filled with rubble. At some long-forgotten time, the rock's great mass must have shifted, so that it cracked and created this narrow fissure. The rows of presses had concealed it.

There were distinct rabbit tracks in the surrounding mortar dust, leading to the hole. Neverfell stared. Lay flat. Clawed the chunks of loose masonry out of the way. Peered.

With her cheek pressed against the ground, Neverfell could see that the aperture continued into the rock for about three yards, and then opened out into a larger space. What was more, there seemed to be a hint of light beyond. With a rush of the blood, she realized that she was on the edge of Master Grandible's district. If that was another tunnel beyond the hole, it was one she had never seen before. Her well-trained cheesemaker's nose twitched as a thousand delicate and unfamiliar smells assailed it.

As an obedient apprentice, she knew she had to warn Master Grandible of the breach in his defenses. If she did that straightaway and in person, however, he would find ways to block this beautiful hole, and she was not ready for that. For the first time that she could remember, the way was open, and the locks on Grandible's door could not hold her in.

She scampered furtively back to Grandible's study, found paper and pen, and dashed out a quick note.

Rabbit escaped through hole in wall behind Gravelhide presses. Gone to find it.

Leaving this note on her master's desk and snatching up her mask, Neverfell scuttled back to the fissure. It was true that she did have an escapee rabbit to retrieve, of course, but that was not her main reason for wriggling through the hole.

I can find Madame Appeline. I can ask her to give back the Stackfalter Sturton. I can make it all better.

She had no solid reason for believing that Madame Appeline would listen to her, and yet she did believe it. Neverfell could not shake the memory of that sad and strangely familiar Face the woman had worn. It was as if there were an invisible cord between them, pulling her along.

With difficulty she dragged herself through the hole and out to the other side, shaking stone dust from her pigtails, almost sick with excitement and terror. The scene before her was only a dusty corridor, but it was a *new* corridor, with dust that tasted different, and walls that had never known the warmth of her hand. It was fascinating, and she was shaking as she scrambled over the debris toward the light of a distant cavern.

Out, was the beat in her heart. *Out, out, out.*

A CROSSING OF PATHS

EVERY INCH OF NEVERFELL SEEMED TO BE throbbing with life. Everything was new, and new was a drug.

She piled some of the rubble back into the hole to conceal it, then ventured slowly forward, trailing her calloused fingers over the corrugated surface of the wall. *New* rock, cleanly chipped, not rough with age or lichen. Split rocks rolled under her shoe soles. Somewhere in the distance there were sounds, jumbled by echo, and she realized that these had been the background music of her world, until this moment muffled to cloud murmurs by the thick stone wall in between. Now she felt as if plugs had been pulled from her ears.

Most confused of all, however, was her nose. Over seven years it had become finely attuned to the overpowering odor of cheese, so that she could have found her way blindfolded through Grandible's tunnels by recognizing each great truckle she passed from its familiar soft, sleeping reek.

Now, there was an eerie nose-silence, followed by a giddy awareness of . . . *not*-cheese smells. Cold, washed-chalk smells of freshly cracked rock, the dank fragrance of unseen plants clinging slickly to life. Warm smells, animal smells. People smells. Feet, sweat, hair grease, fatty soap . . . and yet each fragrance different, personal. It was so overwhelming that Neverfell was glad of her mask, with its familiar scent of musty velvet.

Behind all these, she detected the aroma of scared rabbit. Neverfell followed the scent and found a tiny pyramid of moist brown droppings a little farther up the tunnel. The fugitive had clearly come that way.

She tiptoed to the end of her tiny passage, then crouched and peered out on the largest cavern she ever remembered seeing.

It was some fifty feet high, well-lit, and shaped like half a dome. The rounded walls were ridged with natural ledges and balconies, from which cascaded peach-colored stalactites, and on these nestled great wild flytraps as big as her head, freckled like orchids and glowing creamily as they gaped their finely toothed maws. Neverfell realized this must be a cavern through which many people passed, if the traps were thriving. These glowed brightly, which meant that not long ago they had sensed motion or a released breath.

Opposite the tunnel entrance was a large and ruggedly sheer wall with a number of broad rock shelves, along each of which a thoroughfare seemed to run. The uppermost bore metal tracks, and occasionally man-high trolleys of black steel would rear out of black tunnel mouths, rattle along the rails with their wheels sparking at the corners and their stunted chimneys shuddering with invisible fumes, then plummet into the shadows once more. Other narrower ledges appeared to be for foot traffic, to judge by the railings and the rope ladders that dangled to allow passage between them. The dusty cavern floor itself was striped with wheel ruts. Sheltered as she was, even Neverfell could see that this cavern was a great junction for passageways.

Halfway between Neverfell's hiding place and this wall of

thoroughfares was a ten-foot crater with a raised lip that had filled to become a pool. A series of rusty rings was driven into the rock nearby, and to one of these rings was tethered a gray, four-legged, long-muzzled beast as high as Neverfell herself. From Erstwhile's descriptions, she realized that this must be one of the blind pit ponies that did most of the drag-work in the tunnels. Its muzzle was dipped into the cool of the water, and Neverfell watched with hypnotic fascination the soft puckering and quivering of its nose as it drank, the fine gray hairs and mottle spots between its nostrils, the ripples that raced across the water, the silver bells that festooned its bridle.

Then a strong pale arm reached around to slap at the pony's dusty flank, and Neverfell realized that there was somebody standing behind it. To judge by the shadow thrown on the wall, somebody small and slight. Somebody her size, perhaps her age.

Her heart leaped, but her body did exactly the opposite. Suddenly she found herself flat on the ground, her arms wrapped protectively around her head. She would be seen. The Great Outside would notice her. She was not ready. She had thought she was ready, but she was not.

"Hey!"

Neverfell made about six feet in a backward scuffle-crawl before she heard an answering yell, and realized that the first had not been directed at her. Gingerly, she advanced again and peered into the cavern.

There were no fewer than three people. The nearest was a brown-haired boy of about her own age, tugging at the pony's thick coat with a heavy brush, his blunt features frozen and alert, as if listening to an order. Even when he looked away, the expression hung as if the rocks, the horse, the lanterns were all there to instruct him. It was the sort of Face all drudge-class servants were encouraged to wear.

In a narrow, unpainted wooden cart some small distance beyond were seated two girls, one tall, one short. The pair was talking, but it took a little time for Neverfell to be sure that it was words she was hearing. They prattled the way brooks ran, talking over each other with a speed and ease that left the poor eavesdropper grasping at stray syllables as they flew by. It was a far cry from Grandible and his curt, gravelly utterances. It was even faster than Erstwhile.

". . . well, we have to do something about it quickly, or we are both down the well without a rope. I would love to take care of it all myself, but this time it just isn't possible. I really need you to help with this."

The older girl's high, confident tones were louder than those of her companion. She looked about fifteen, a long, blonde plait gleaming down the shoulder of her gray muslin gown. She had three smiles and was clearly proud of them. On the occasions when she was not speaking, she slid smoothly between them, as regularly as a rota. Warm confidential smile. Narrow speculative smile. Amused expectant smile with a tilt of the head. The drudge workers and errand boys who called on Grandible's domain usually had only one smile. This was clearly a better class of person.

The other girl was shorter, rounder, more hesitant in gesture, her hair tucked under a white coif. When she turned to look over her shoulder, Neverfell caught a glimpse of her rounded baby features. The corner of her mouth was dragged down unnaturally, and one of her eyebrows was raised high, as though the muscles of her face were playing tug-of-war.

The boy meanwhile tethered the horse to the cart once more, and began leading it at a gentle amble toward Neverfell's passage . . . only to pass it and disappear into the next passage.

Close, so close! Neverfell had seen enough to be fascinated. The blonde girl had star-shaped spangles on her sleeves. The pony-boy had a toffee-colored mole on his neck. The little fat girl had short, pink, bitten nails. They were all new and large and real, and Neverfell felt sick at the idea of letting them pass out of her life and vanish.

Peering around the corner after the little cart, Neverfell noticed one other detail that made her feel yet more sick. At the back of the cart was a low-lipped trolley put aside for luggage, and poking up among the chests and boxes she could just make out the tips of two white rabbit ears.

She had a mission, of course, but sooner or later she had to return to Master Grandible. She did not think she could face him without the rabbit.

The three travelers did not notice as a dark-clad figure emerged from the shadowy rubble and edged down the path after them, nothing visible behind its black mask but a fog of red pigtails.

The little cart rumbled down a series of broad passageways and at last vanished into a narrow, rough-hewn tunnel, where the only light was the trap-lantern dangling from the boy's staff. Here the cart's progress slowed, and Neverfell could just see the pony-boy stooping now and then to clear fallen rocks so that the cart could pass. Under cover of the darkness, Neverfell dared to draw closer, and despite the echo was able to make out some of the travelers' conversation.

"Borcas, do you have to keep making those strange Faces while we talk?" the older girl was asking. "It's very distracting."

"Yes—I have an audition today, remember? I have to exercise my muscles!" exclaimed the smaller girl. At least, that was what Neverfell guessed she was trying to say. Her words were a little too slurred and misshapen to be certain, perhaps because of the way one corner of her mouth was tugged down. It sounded a lot more like "Yesh—I ha' un ardishun today, renenber? I ha' to eckshershishe ny nushulsh."

"Right now, dear, it's your brain you should be exercising!" retorted the taller girl. Somehow, her expression and tone remained kindly, if impatient. "Have you forgotten how much trouble we will be in if nothing is done? Madame Appeline caught me looking through her case. Once she finds out that we are close friends, she will work out who smuggled me into that party in the first place. Borcas, Madame Appeline only picks one girl a year from the academy to train as a Putty Girl, and it is hardly likely to be you if she decides she cannot trust you, is it? It won't matter how well you do in the audition."

Borcas, the younger girl, gave a small snuffle of what sounded like concern.

"You 'romished you 'ould take care o' it," she answered reproachfully. "You shaid you could nake her 'orget it all—"

"And I would have done," the blonde girl interrupted smoothly. "I had just the Wine for it and everything. But that plan only works if she is ordering Wine from my family, and she isn't so I can't. So you have to give it to her when you do the audition. All the girls give presents to the Facesmith judging, don't they?"

By now Neverfell was listening intently. She knew that every Facesmith employed a number of "Putty Girls" whom they used to display Faces to potential customers. They were so called because they were trained to keep their faces flexible, like modeling clay. The lucky ones eventually became Facesmiths themselves.

More important, it was clear that the two girls knew Madame Appeline. Perhaps they could help Neverfell, show her where the Facesmith could be found. Of course, that would mean actually having to *talk* to the two girls.

Heart in mouth, Neverfell crept closer to the cart. She tried to think of something calming and cheery to say to them, but her mind was a mass of scribbles. Soon she was close enough to make out the silhouettes of the girls' heads against the light of the lantern, which touched the older girl's long and elegant neck with alabaster and set the stray wisps of Borcas's hair agleam. It made the pair of them look warm, angelic, and fragile.

"Stop trembling." The older girl was wearing her warm, confiding smile, and her voice sounded kind and infinitely sensible. "It'll all be all right as long as you stick with the plan. You don't need to worry about anything. You don't ever need to worry about making decisions. I'll do that for you. I'll always look after you."

She sounded wonderful and big-sisterly, and Neverfell felt a flood of hope. Unguarded as ever, her heart galloped into a sudden wild liking for the two girls, with their scrubbed skin and clever voices. Perhaps everything was going to be all right after all. She *could* talk to them—they would be kind. They were her friends. Of course they did not know that yet, but if she followed them and listened to them and found out all their likings and habits and secrets and if she told them so, they would *have* to like her . . .

These excited thoughts were interrupted by the sight of Borcas stiffening slightly.

"Zouelle! 'ot'sh 'hat?" The younger girl's voice was hushed with fear.

"What?"

Have I been heard? Have I been seen?

"I . . . I can *shnell* shun'hing."

"What? Wait . . . oh yes, so can I. It smells like rot, or maybe . . . cheese?"

Neverfell sniffed, perplexed, for this tunnel smelled less like cheese than anywhere she had ever been. It took a moment for the real explanation to strike her.

"Borcas . . ." Zouelle, the older girl, sounded less than confident for the first time. "I . . . I think you're right. There's something down there behind us. I heard . . . I heard it snuffling."

Quick! I need to make a sound like a . . . a horse!

Neverfell had no idea what a horse really sounded like, only what they looked like they would sound like. Her panic-stricken effort came out as a cross between a yawn and a screech, echoing down the tunnel. The two girls screamed.

The pony-boy, with admirable presence of mind, threw a pebble down the corridor to strike a large, sleeping trap sprouting just behind Neverfell. It flared into a vivid and irritable glow, snapping its combs of fine teeth in search of food. Suddenly she was backlit, and her long, tapering shadow was extending down the tunnel before her.

"There! Look—there it ish!"

"It's got no face!"

"Aaaaaah! Red wormsh for hair!"

The pit pony and cart took off with unprecedented speed, the lantern bouncing and jolting before it.

"Wait! Please! Don't go!" Neverfell's words were lost amid the muffling of the mask and the echoes of the screams and pounding hoofs. She broke into a sprint, struggling as the rocks beneath her feet rolled, crumbled, and barked her shins. She saw both girls twisting around in their seats, mouths stretched in screams as a faceless monster pursued them in a lolloping run, one hand clawing out to take hold of the rear of the cart. Zouelle's features still held the remnants of her smile, and Borcas wore her lopsided "exercise" Face. The shock had been so great they had forgotten to change their expressions.

As Neverfell tried to take hold of the back of the cart and clamber onto the luggage trolley, she felt a blow to her neck. In panic, Zouelle had snatched up a horsewhip by the wrong end and swung it, so that the handle hit Neverfell below the chin. Out of surprise and hurt, Neverfell lost her grip, and then her footing, and tumbled to the ground, jarring her jaw. She could only watch, winded, as the cart rattled away and the light of the lantern faded.

"Please . . . please don't run away from me . . ."

As the cart receded, the newly woken trap decided there was no food to catch after all and slowly dimmed its light. Darkness descended, and the dripping water covered the sound of one solitary figure snuffling into her mask.

The Great Outside that had filled Neverfell's thoughts had noticed her and judged her. It had found her wanting. No, worse than that, it had screamed in horror and disgust and fled from her. Her neck was bruised, but far more painful was the thought of kind big-sister Zouelle hitting out at her.

Wincing a little, she picked herself up and felt for lumps and cuts. Then, still snuffling with misery and pain, she limped off after the cart. Neverfell had never taken rejection well. In fact, despite plenty of practice, she had never learned how to take it at all. Aside from anything else, she still had a rabbit to retrieve.

A few minutes later, her persistence was rewarded by the sound of a deafening crash.

Neverfell ran toward the noise as quickly as her bruises and the near-absence of light would allow. Peering around a corner she glimpsed her quarries' lantern and discovered the cause of the cacophony.

There had been very good reasons for the cart's previous sedate pace. The way was scattered with fallen rocks large and small, and occasional foot-deep potholes just waiting for a careless wheel. To judge by the tilt of the cart, its pell-mell flight had run its left-hand wheel straight into one of these holes.

Both girls had dismounted. The pony-boy, with some hushed verbal instruction from Zouelle, seemed to be trying to heft the cart out of the hole again. Borcas was acting as lookout, which appeared to involve a lot of whimpering and hand-wringing as she gazed back the way they had come.

When Neverfell stepped out, legs trembling, hands raised to show that she was harmless, Borcas gave a wail and pointed at her.

"The demon! It followed ush! It'sh come after ush!"

"Argh!"

A shower of inexpertly thrown rocks clattered around Neverfell, chipping pieces off the walls.

"I . . . Stop it! You nearly—ow! Stop it! I won't hurt you! I don't want to—"

She might have explained in more detail, but at this point the rabbit decided that it had had quite enough of all the screaming, and made a break for a fissure in the wall. Neverfell promptly abandoned her placatory pose and sprinted toward the cart, to the terror of its passengers, and then past it, ending her run with a pounce at full stretch. Her body hit rock, her hands met fur, and she had it, flattened to the ground, terrified, maddened, tensed for action but still. She scrambled to a crouch, held it between her knees, ripped off her doublet, and a few moments later was cuddling a kicking, wild-eyed rabbit bundle.

"I'm sorry," she babbled helplessly, "I'm sorry, I had to get my . . . It kicked the bucket and ran and I squeezed out after it and I'm here . . ."

Her voice sounded so ugly and unused next to theirs, and the welling of tears was making everything worse.

"I won't hurt you." She rose unsteadily, and took a few limping steps back toward the cart.

"What do you want?" Zouelle's voice was strident but tremulous. She was holding the whip out toward Neverfell in a very shaky hand.

"I just . . . I just . . . needed some cheese . . ." Despite herself Neverfell started to sob.

The three strangers observed her rigidly, then exchanged brief sideways glances.

"Does anybody have any cheese?" whispered Zouelle to the others. "If we give it cheese, will it go away?"

"No . . . it's not just any cheese. The . . ." Neverfell collapsed to her knees, hugging the rabbit while it tried to bite her. The conversation had gone wrong. She tried to explain everything, her mistake in sending the cheese to Madame Appeline, her desperate need to recover it, but the words sounded clumsy and stupid even in her ears. When she finished, she was scarcely sure that the others were still there listening. She was in a hell of self-hate, and barely heard the whispers from the cart.

"No," Zouelle was hissing, "*listen* to me. This fits. This *fits*. This girl wants to go and find Madame Appeline. We want somebody to present the Wine to her. So *you* help smuggle her in, by stealing her an invitation or something, and she helps us out. Stop whimpering, now. Put on a clean Face. I'm going to talk to her."

Neverfell only started paying attention again when she heard the crackle of gravel underfoot. She looked up and found that Zouelle was walking toward her, carefully, as if afraid of startling a wild animal. The blonde girl was wearing her amused smile, her eyes twinkling and expectant.

"It's all right," she said, in much the same tone Neverfell had used on the rabbit. "It's all going to be all right. We're going to help you."

Neverfell looked up into her smiling face and thought that she looked like an angel.

THE IMPOSTER

AFTER ALL THE BLOWS AND UPHEAVALS OF THE day, Neverfell was very glad to have found somebody who could make a plan for her. She was even happier to have somebody to understand the plan for her, since try as she might she could not follow the musical fluting of Zouelle's explanation. There was something to do with an audition, and a misunderstanding, and something that had happened to the two girls the day before, but it was explained so rapidly that the details slipped sand-like through the clutches of her dazzled brain.

"Do you understand?" the older girl asked again, yet more slowly and patiently. Once more Neverfell answered by moving her head in a joggle that started in a nod and ended in a shake.

"It doesn't matter," said the older girl in the kindest voice in the world. "Just remember the bits you have to do, and it'll all be fine." She gave a brief but significant glance at her portlier companion before returning her gaze to Neverfell. "So . . . we're going to put you in a new dress. All right? Can you take off that mask?"

Neverfell responded with a muffled screech and a panic-stricken clutch at her mask to hold it to her face. If these girls saw how hideous she was, they would flee again, and she would be back where she started.

"Don't worry," Zouelle cooed soothingly. "That's fine . . . leave it on. Are you burnt or something under there? It doesn't matter—you don't have to tell me. If anybody asks you why you're wearing it, just say that you're protecting your complexion. Now, you will be going up to Madame Appeline's door, and when somebody answers you say that you've been sent by the Beaumoreau Academy, and you're there to audition as a Putty Girl. Can you remember that?"

Neverfell nodded.

"That's *really* good." A beautiful smile. "That should get you inside Madame Appeline's domain. Now, you see this?" A little cut-glass bottle full of seething purple liquid was waved in front of her face for the tenth time. "Do you remember what you do with this?"

"I . . . give it to the servants?"

"That's right. You tell them that it's a gift for Madame Appeline, to thank her for the audition. That's all we need you to do. After that, if you want, you can slip away from the other girls attending the audition, and find your way to the storerooms or wherever she keeps her new deliveries, and take back your cheese. It's not stealing, after all, is it?"

"Shouldn't I just talk to Madame Appeline?" This was the part of the plan that Neverfell was less comfortable about. "She had a nice Face—"

"No, I'm afraid not," Zouelle said gently. "If you do, the plan won't work. She won't give you back your cheese, Neverfell. Why would she? It's useful to her. And if she knows you're not a real candidate, she won't drink the Wine."

Neverfell gazed down at the little bottle. "It won't do anything bad to her?"

"Oh no, of course not!" exclaimed Zouelle. "It's just Wine. Madame Appeline often orders Wine to help her forget something— you know how people do. This will just help her forget an extra memory, that's all. One that might be upsetting to her."

When Zouelle put it like that, it all sounded quite straightforward. Neverfell knew that special Wines could be blended that allowed you to forget specific things or times, and that they were popular among the rich and bored who felt they had seen everything. They cleared out useless or ugly memories the way some threw out cracked china, so that their minds creaked less under the burden of the years.

"Anyway, once you have your cheese back, you sneak back to the other girls and leave with them. Can you do that?"

Neverfell's eye kept straying to the frosted glitter of the taller girl's brooch. It looked like sugar, and Neverfell wondered what it tasted like. Thoughts tried to crowd out of her mouth, but there were too many of them and they jammed in the door. *Of course I will,* she wanted to answer. *You're the kindest person I've ever met and you're calm and wonderful and any minute now I'm going to say something really stupid . . .*

"Your gloves have stripes on!" was what she actually said.

"Ye-e-es. Yes, they do." Zouelle wet her lips. "But you understand what you have to do, don't you?" Neverfell hesitated, then gave a slow, firm nod, and Zouelle's shoulders relaxed a little.

"What are we going to do about . . ." The shorter girl glanced at Neverfell and tapped meaningfully at her own nose. "Everybody will *notice.*"

"Cloves," her friend answered promptly. "Oil of cloves, so everybody thinks she's trying to treat herself for pimples. That should have a strong enough fragrance to mask the . . . problem.

"Now, the most important bit." The taller girl leaned forward, holding Neverfell's gaze. "The *most* important bit is that if you see either of us you have to pretend you don't know us. Whatever happens, you don't know us. Otherwise . . . everything will go badly for everyone. Understand?"

Right at that moment, Neverfell would have given her two new friends the world. She wanted to give them her buttons, or Master Grandible's rabbit, or iridescent ballrooms, or mountains of figs. But what they seemed to want was a nod, so she gave them that instead.

Tucked between the luggage on the back of the cart, Neverfell knew that she was supposed to be completely covered by the blanket, but she could not resist lifting it just enough to give herself an arrow slit of vision out between the great trunks. Passage by passage, lane by lane, the boundaries of her world were pushing back.

After a time, the wheels of the pony cart ceased to bounce and jolt, and she noticed that the tunnels were floored in smooth flagstones. At a glance, she could see that these tunnels were not part of a natural cave system but had been carefully excavated. The walls were regular and square-cornered, and wooden struts helped reinforce the ceiling. Black iron trap-lanterns blazed from brackets, and along the tops of the walls ran hefty, shuddering hot- and cold-water pipes.

Then they entered busier thoroughfares, filled with voices, wheel judders, whinnies, and footfalls that echoed and mingled until they roared like rapids. Neverfell glimpsed swift messenger boys teetering past on unicycles, arms spread for balance. Dusty miners' carts trundled by, filled with rubble. Muscled men heaved on great wheels to haul pearl-colored flying sedans up through shafts in the ceiling. In one of the larger caverns, pony carts for hire clustered grayly around a vast clock set in the rocky wall, so old that it wore a crust of limestone and a frail fringe of stalactites. Stiff-faced pannier-bearers flounced past in dun-colored linen, and Neverfell could smell the grease in their hair, the dirt under their fingernails.

The cart headed off down a quieter, green-lit lane after this, and at last came to a halt before a gilt-handled door with a panel above it that showed a silver heron on a blue background.

A whispered argument ensued.

"Why do I have to steal the invitation?" hissed Borcas.

"Because you already have one of your own," Zouelle responded with an air of patience, "so nobody will suspect you, and you know the other candidates better than I do, so you can get closer to them. Come on—we do not have much time!"

Borcas vanished through the door just long enough for Neverfell to reach a fever pitch of anxiety, and for the rabbit to deposit a heap of soft, distressed droppings on her knee. At last Borcas returned, rather flushed, with a bundle under one arm and a card in one hand.

"Good." Zouelle smiled. "Marden—go!" The cart rattled away again. "Head to the Twirl Stair."

When the rumble of wheels stopped again, Neverfell's blanket was pulled away, and she found that the cart stood in a small cavern some ten feet across, in the ceiling of which was set a broad, rough-hewn shaft. Up the middle of this shaft rose a spiraling stair of black iron.

Borcas's bundle was opened, and, the next thing Neverfell knew, a white muslin gown was being pulled down over her ordinary clothes. Round her waist was tied a blue sash with a silver heron embroidered on it, very much like the one she had seen above the door. Beneath the heron was stitched the words "Beaumoreau Academy." Neverfell's rough pigtails were tucked under a gauzy cap, and an ointment smeared across her neck, hands, and wrists, filling the air with the bitterly piquant smell of cloves.

The card Borcas had brought out was placed in Neverfell's hand, and proved to be a gilt-edged invitation to attend an "Audition in Facial Athletics and Artistry."

"There." Zouelle smoothed Neverfell's cap, tucking in a few stray wisps. "Now, is everybody ready? Take the stair, and when you reach the top the door will be twenty yards to your left. Good luck, both of you!"

"Wha— Aren't you coming?" Borcas sounded as horrified as Neverfell felt.

"Me? Of course not! I can hardly show my face there after yesterday, can I?" Zouelle was climbing back onto the cart. "But I shall be right here waiting for you and looking after the rabbit— and if you two do *exactly* what I told you to do, then everything should go perfectly."

Somewhat crestfallen, Neverfell accompanied Borcas to the foot of the stairway. Borcas was still wearing her strange, lopsided Face, but she smelled a bit like Grandible's rabbit had when it felt cornered.

"You smell like my rabbit," Neverfell whispered.

"Well, you smell like a dead man's pantry," snapped Borcas, "but some of us are too polite to comment."

"Now, Borcas," called Zouelle, "you should go first, and, Neverfell—climb up a few minutes after her. You don't want to arrive together, do you?"

Neverfell obediently let Borcas start climbing first, and only began her own ascent once the other girl was nothing but a dark blot against the skeletal whorls of the staircase above. Neverfell was naturally nimble, but was not used to long skirts, and found that her legs were trembling from excitement. The shaft itself was full of strange gusts and gasps of air, and occasionally solitary bright droplets winked down past her and then vanished into darkness below.

At the top of the stair, she found herself in a long corridor that stretched from left to right. There was no sign of Borcas. To her left, she could see a heavy-looking door set deep in the wall. It was intricately decorated in a tracery of green vines in which gold and purple birds nestled. At the sight of this, the clamp of excitement in Neverfell's stomach tightened and became terror. Her mind was a mad moth, and she could barely keep Zouelle's instructions straight in her head as she reached the door and tugged at the red rope bellpull.

One of the birds painted on the door was a large owl, staring directly out toward Neverfell. She jumped when, without warning, the owl's painted eyes receded with a *shunk*, leaving two round holes, through which a pair of more human eyes could be seen peering a few seconds later.

"Your business?"

"I was sent here . . . by . . . by the Bomo school. For an . . . audition for Putty Girls." Neverfell hesitantly waved her stolen invitation before the gaze of the owl-eye spyholes.

"Name?"

Neverfell goldfished helplessly behind her mask as she fell off the edge of her briefing.

"Name? I . . . I . . . can't remember!" It was an idiotic, panic-stricken thing to say, and escaped Neverfell in a sort of incoherent chirrup.

There was a pause.

"Caramemba," muttered the voice in the slow, careful tone of one writing something down. "Caramemba from the Beaumoreau Academy. You are lucky—the auditions have not started yet."

The human eyes receded into darkness, and the owl's eyes reappeared in their appointed place. After a series of clicks and scrapes the door opened. Somehow, despite her panic, Neverfell had bluffed her way in.

Beyond the door extended a neat hallway, floors patterned in a mosaic of different crystals, walls covered in ornate tapestries depicting woodland scenes from which multicolored animals peered coyly. Disturbingly, there was no sign of Neverfell's interlocutor, so she was left to tiptoe down the corridor alone, watched by the stitched eyes of azure squirrels and purple chamois.

At the far end two wooden doors swung open to reveal a room unlike anything Neverfell had ever seen. From the ceiling hung a large trap-lantern chandelier, so vast that you could barely see the little black-clad boy crouched upon it, puffing hard to keep the traps aglow. The walls were suffocating beneath pastoral tapestries and framed pictures.

In the middle of the room was a long table, covered by a white and gold cloth and an ornate silver tea service. Along its length some dozen girls sat stiff-backed, hands nervously twisted in their laps. One of the girls was Borcas. She met Neverfell's gaze with a bland, disinterested stare, then cleared her throat slightly and looked meaningfully across the room. Following her gaze, Neverfell noticed a servant woman standing next to a little side table where wrapped and beribboned boxes clustered.

Realizing these must be the presents that the girls had brought for the Facesmith, Neverfell timidly approached the servant, bobbed a curtsy, and mutely offered up her bottle to be added to the rest. Relieved of her burden, she gingerly approached the main table and seated herself on the one stool remaining.

Most of the girls seemed to be too self-absorbed for conversation. Many were cupping tiny hand mirrors in their palms to examine their own countenances. Some, like Borcas, were carefully holding grotesque or unnatural distortions of their features. Others were cycling so quickly through different expressions that their faces seemed to be in spasm. Neverfell's bizarre appearance, however, was gradually gaining some attention. Those wearing the same Beaumoreau uniform as herself seemed particularly curious.

Neverfell had delivered the Wine, just as she had promised. Now, according to Zouelle's plan, she should be slipping away from the other girls to look for the piece of the Stackfalter Sturton. But how was she supposed to do that when so many of them were staring at her?

A tall, auburn-haired girl to Neverfell's right scrutinized her for some time before speaking.

"You should probably take off your mask, you know."

"I . . ." Neverfell's mind emptied and her mouth became a desert. "I . . . have pimples!"

"Nobody here minds. And how can you audition with your face covered?"

Neverfell did not answer. How could she, when she could only guess what the audition would involve? She lowered her head and blushed deeply under her mask and got on with clattering her crockery and stirring jam into her tea.

The exchange had apparently sparked off a small forest fire of gossip and surmise. Neverfell could hear whispered snatches from all around her.

". . . must have a special Face that she prepared early and doesn't want us to see . . ."

". . . probably recognize her if we saw her . . . one of the high-ranking Craftsmen houses . . ."

". . . wrong side of the blanket . . ."

". . . notice the smell of cloves? Obviously she's using Perfume and trying to hide it . . ."

Neverfell was almost relieved when another door opened, and Madame Appeline swept into the room, glittering like a dragonfly in pleated emerald satin. Just as the Facesmith's smiling gaze was gliding down the rows of seated girls, Neverfell remembered that Madame Appeline had seen her mask before.

She had wanted more than anything to talk to Madame Appeline, but now everything had changed. She was an imposter, and had lied her way into the house. Overwhelmed by fear and confusion, she feigned a muffled coughing fit and doubled over, quietly lowering her face into her hands and her napkin so that her mask could not be seen.

"My dears, it is a delight to see such a bevy of fresh, fair, and flexible faces." Madame Appeline's voice was just as warm and sweet as Neverfell had remembered. "Your schools have picked you out as particularly exceptional candidates, which is why you are here today.

"Now, first of all I would like you to show me what you can do. In a moment you will be shown through that door and into the light." She waved a hand at the doorway through which she had just entered. "You will see something . . . very unusual. Unique, I like to think, in Caverna. You will then have half an hour to observe what you find there and prepare a selection of five Faces from your personal repertoire that you think are an appropriate response to it."

The door opened, and out of it trooped a string of girls, all a few years older than those seated at the table. These older girls were all dressed in simple, unornamented white gowns, their hair tied back so that their carefully serene faces were entirely visible. Most of them had large, well-spaced eyes, high cheekbones, and broad, flexible mouths, giving the uncanny impression that they were members of the same enormous extended family. Neverfell guessed that these must be Madame Appeline's Putty Girls. Light poured through the door so brightly that it put the chandelier to shame.

Madame Appeline flashed a last smile and departed the room, leaving Neverfell and the other candidates to file awkwardly into the light. And as she emerged, each girl halted in her tracks as if thunderstruck. As Neverfell's eyes adjusted to the scene before her, her heart, which had been jerking like a drowning hare, stopped for a beat.

She was standing in a grove. She had never seen a grove except in pictures, and yet she knew, *knew* that this was what she was seeing. A path weaved between tall and sturdy trunks, ridged and rugged bark gleaming with tiny beads of dew. From above brilliant golden light turned shifting leaves to blades of green fire. A breeze brushed her face, giving a sudden giddying sense of unlimited distance.

A grove. A grove, deep in the sunless tunnels of the city of Caverna.

Only after she had taken a few stumbling steps did Neverfell realize that she was looking not at a miracle but at a masterpiece. For all its brilliant green, the softness beneath her feet was carpet. Somehow she *knew* that real woodland moss should give, slip, and crush more under her weight. The leaves above were chiming softly in the breeze, and she guessed that they must be glass. Spellbound, she reached out a hand to touch one of the dewdrops, and found it was a crystal bead. As her finger traced the surface of the bark, she somehow *knew* that she should be feeling the green down of lichen, and that the bark itself should be crumbling under her touch to reveal pale wood and insects. Somewhere above, hundreds of powerful trap-lanterns must be hanging from the high and unseen ceiling of the cavern to provide the brilliant light.

The great trunks were the pièce de résistance, of course, for she realized that these must be real trees . . . or at least that they must have been real trees uncounted thousands of years ago. Petrified forests were sometimes discovered deep within the rock, places where the earth had drowned and swallowed hundreds of living trees, and then over the millennia had replaced living, sap-filled wood with quartzes and multicolored gemstones, a little at a time.

In this case, instead of mining the trees for the beauty of their pink, gold, and green crystal, the diggers had apparently removed only the rock around them, leaving the trees untouched. This forest of jeweled trees was without decay. Every knothole, every ring was preserved with semiprecious precision. It was infinitely valuable and utterly dead.

For several minutes the audition candidates could only gawp. Then, as one, they glanced at each other, then scattered, mirrors in hand. Nobody wanted to try out sample Faces where another candidate might observe and steal ideas. In a space of seconds, Neverfell found herself entirely alone—which was, she remembered with a jolt, precisely what she wanted.

She would not have long alone. If she was to track down the Sturton fragment, it had to be now.

Eyes closed, she breathed deeply and focused upon the smells. There were traces of a dozen soaps and perfumes, body smells, dried flowers, and of course the oil of cloves in which she was doused . . . but there it was, the faintest pungent hint of cheese, like a familiar voice in a crowd's tumult. Having made sure nobody else was within view, she loosened her mask and pulled it slightly away from her face so that she could smell more easily.

Snuffing like a bloodhound, she made her way through the crystalline forest. At last she came upon a small white stone hut richly carved with images of leaping fish. The faint scent seemed to come from within, so she tried the door. It was locked, but she recognized it as a trick lock of a sort Grandible often used, and soon had it open.

Within she found an odd but elegant pantry. Wide shelves housed a number of crates, little sacks, bottles, and jars. Up on the high shelf was a box that she recognized as the one she had packed for Madame Appeline. She scrambled onto a chair and retrieved it. It did not appear to have been opened, and when she prised off the lid the little crumb of Sturton was still in its hiding place. She plucked it out and hastily crammed the box back in its place, then jumped down from her chair, just in time to hear the door unlock from the outside.

There was no time for a plan. As the door began to open, Neverfell threw herself at the gap, doubled over in the hope of pushing past the new arrival's legs. In the end, her non-plan very nearly worked. She plunged forward, headbutted the thigh of the manservant at the door, and her momentum carried her on past him . . . or would have done had he not reached out reflexively and grabbed her collar.

She fought and flailed, but he managed to hook his spare arm round her waist, and suddenly she was no longer touching the ground. Her loosened mask fell to the ground. She was caught. She was done for.

But, came the wild thought, *I can still save Master Grandible. I can still undo what I did.*

And so, before her arms could be pinned, Neverfell crammed the crumb of Sturton in her mouth. She felt it crumble and melt on her tongue, and this was the last thing she knew before the world exploded.

It burst apart, and it turned out that it had always been made of music. Not music for the ear, but notes of pure soul and haunting memory. She had no body, and yet she sensed that her nose was a cathedral where a choir was singing full-throatedly, and her mouth a nation with its own history and legends of staggering beauty.

And then she had a body again, or so it seemed, and she was staggering through a woodland where trees wept soft sap and whispered, and light pooled and puddled like honey, and her ankles tangled in lush stems and a mist of blue flowers that reached up to her waist. All the while there was a warming sense of a presence beside her.

Then the vision was gone. She was back in Madame Appeline's grove, and hanging limp from the grip of the man who had captured her. Her mask lay at her feet. In the false woodland all around her stood the other auditioners, the Putty Girls, and Madame Appeline herself. They wore a wide range of expressions, but none of them meant anything. Their Faces were frozen, forgotten, as they all stared at Neverfell's exposed face.

LIES AND BARE FACES

IT WAS TOO MUCH. THE EYES WERE TOO MUCH. Neverfell was not used to being looked at, let alone by so many all at once. She clenched her own eyes tight, but she could still feel the stares, cold and hard against her skin like a wall of marble. The stunned silence was dissolving now, and from all sides she could hear cries of alarm and desperate, frightened questions.

"Cover its face!" came a scream. "Stop it from doing that!"

"Impossible!" somebody else croaked, in tones of utter shock. "Impossible!" It sounded a little like Madame Appeline.

From all around came the sour smell of fear, and it filled her like a gas, searing away her self-control. Like the rabbit she had tried so hard to catch, she went limp for a moment in the grip of her captor. The next instant she flung herself into desperate, thrashing, unthinking struggles. Through a fog of terror she heard a yelp of surprise, and felt raked skin under her fingernails.

"Quick, wrap it in this!" The breath was knocked out of Neverfell as she was wrestled to the ground, legs flailing. Something soft and heavy was flapped on top of her, smothering her face and pinning her arms. It took her maddened mind a second or two to realize that somebody was rolling her up in some of the moss carpet that covered the floor of the grove. Fear of unforgiving gazes immediately gave way to a much more practical fear of suffocation.

Neverfell wanted to beg, to apologize, to scream at them to stop, but she was beyond words, and nobody could have heard her through her mouthful of carpet. She was manhandled and hefted until she was sagging, doubled up over something, probably the shoulder of one of her captors. Only fragments of words reached her.

". . . in the world is it?"

". . . how did it get in?"

". . . how was it doing that?"

". . . the Enquiry—"

". . . Enquiry will deal with it—"

Whoever was carrying her was running, and his shoulder jogged into her stomach with every step until she thought she would throw up. She was flung onto something flat that lurched and creaked to the clopping of a horse's hoofs. She screeched, whimpered, and struggled pointlessly, trying to crane back her head enough to give herself a bit more air. The life, breath, and wits were being smothered out of her, and terror rose up like a black fountain and swallowed her whole.

For a long time, there was no thought, no sanity, only rough screams bottlenecking in her throat, and panic like a white fire in the blood. Then a numb darkness fell around her. When she came to, she was lying sprawled, her cheek pressed against something cold and hard. Terror had left her mind as empty as a scooped gourd.

What had happened? Why? Where? She could not remember. Perhaps she had broken cheeses. Perhaps Master Grandible would be angry.

Neverfell sat up groggily and knocked her head against something hard-edged. She steadied it with her hand, and it proved to be a slowly swaying trap-lantern with a sullen glow within. She breathed on it a few times to give it air. It quickly flushed into full radiance, showing where she was.

Neverfell was in an onion-shaped cage of black iron some five feet across, with bars that bulged outward at the sides and met at the top. A tin chamber pot and a wooden bowl of water sat beside her. The trap-lantern hung from the ceiling of the cage, and the cage itself hung suspended from a barely visible pulley by a long, thick chain. A couple of feet below the grill of the floor, she could make out the glimmer of black, rippleless water. The cage was suspended above a subterranean canal flanked by two high walls. Running along the wall farthest from her was a wooden jetty a foot or so above the level of the water.

She was in more than trouble, she realized hazily. She was in prison. What had she done to bring her here? A stubborn little spark suddenly flared up in her, and told her that whatever she had done had not been bad enough for *this*.

Her cage was revolving very slowly in response to her motions, and she could see that to her left and right there were other cages hanging above the water. Most of them were empty, but in a few she could see stirring bundles of cloth and life. One offered a long, low, despairing bleat that sounded barely human. Another was just a round of sullen back and straggling hair. At either end of the jetty she could just make out what looked like a purple-clad guard standing to attention with a halberd.

"Hello?" Her voice was tiny and hoarse. "Hello?"

She heard a murmur of conversation, then a door set in the wall opened and three figures stepped out onto the jetty, all clad in deep amethyst tones. Two were men, but the foremost was a woman with steel-gray hair. She had a stern jaw, a surprisingly athletic stride, and a Face that combined austerity, authority, and cold scrutiny. *Nothing escapes my all-penetrating eye,* said the Face, and Neverfell hastily bowed her head.

"Do you know who I am?" The woman had a voice like a cheesewire. Neverfell shook her head, keeping her hands raised to hide her own hideousness. "I am Enquirer Treble. You have been placed under Enquiry. Do you understand me?"

Neverfell gave a whimper as memory of her misadventures finally began to seep back into her head. This was no ordinary arrest. The Enquirers were the Grand Steward's special law enforcers for peculiar or dangerous cases.

"If you wish to live—if you wish to *wish* to live—you must answer our questions truthfully. Now—how did you get in? Are there any more of you?"

"Any more . . ." *Any more of what?* "No, there's . . . only me. I just went to an audition. They gave me a dress—"

"Gave you a dress? Who?"

Neverfell's skin burned. She thought of Zouelle's beautiful smile and Borcas's soft, pink nervousness. She couldn't bring herself to betray them, but did not know how to lie. She hid her face in her hands.

"Come now! It is obvious what you are and where you come from. Who are your masters?"

She could not reveal that either. What danger would she bring to Master Grandible if she did?

"Tell me! Who let you into Caverna? How many of you are there? Why were you infiltrating Madame Appeline's auditions? What is your name? Whose assassin are you?"

Neverfell continued numbly shaking her head. Half the questions meant nothing to her. At the word "assassin," however, her breath caught in her throat. Overcome with fear and outrage she jumped to her feet and clutched at the bars, no longer concerned with covering her face.

"I'm not an assassin! I never wanted to hurt anybody! Never!"

The effect on the Enquirer was instantaneous and striking. There was no change of expression, but the woman leaped backward with such energy that her back collided with the wall. For a few moments she stared rigidly at Neverfell, then fumbled a purple handkerchief free from a pocket and began dabbing at her own forehead.

"How dare you?" she exclaimed. "Stop doing that! Put on something more appropriate! Immediately!"

"What?"

"Stop it!" It sounded as if the Enquirer were on the verge of losing control.

"Stop what?" Neverfell demanded helplessly.

Enquirer Treble bristled for a couple of seconds, then made a gesture. One of the men who had entered with her stepped toward the wall, where Neverfell could just make out a large crank handle. He began turning the handle, and almost immediately Neverfell's cage began a jolting descent.

"Unless you cooperate—"

"Stop it!" shrieked Neverfell as the bottom of the cage dipped into the surface of the canal and water started spilling in between the bars. She scrambled up the lantern chain to pull herself out of the water, clinging to the top of the cage.

The cage, however, continued its jerky descent into the canal, and Neverfell's clamberings availed her nothing. Icy water claimed her feet, her calves, her knees, her thighs. When it finally ceased its descent, the cage was all but submerged. With her head pressed against the roof, Neverfell's chin was only just above the water.

"One more turn of this handle—" called out the Enquirer.

"I don't understand!" Neverfell erupted, through sheer desperation. "I don't understand what you're talking about! I don't understand why I'm here! I don't understand what I've done or what I'm doing! So how am I supposed to stop it?"

While she sobbed and shivered, Neverfell could just about make out parts of a murmured discussion taking place on the jetty.

". . . how can we hold a sensible interrogation with something that looks like . . ."

". . . a face like glass . . ."

". . . mask back, perhaps?"

". . . no, we cannot study this properly if it is covered . . ."

After a long pause, Neverfell heard the sound of the crank handle being turned once again. To her numb relief, however, the cage did not descend but was hauled up to its previous position, water streaming out between its bars.

Enquirer Treble disappeared through the nearest door, then emerged once more and clipped sharply over, gripping what looked like a frying pan with a nine-foot handle.

"Here. Take this." Refusing to look at Neverfell directly, the woman extended the pan until it was touching against the bars of Neverfell's cage. Looking down, Neverfell saw that something dark and square was resting in the pan. She lifted it out carefully with slick and shaking hands. "Take some time to put yourself in order. When you have a Face fit to be seen, I will come back and speak with you again."

The pan withdrew, and the Enquirer retreated behind her door once more. Neverfell was left staring at the object in her wet hands. It had a wooden border. The side currently uppermost was covered in dark brown felt, but she could feel that the underside had the cold smoothness of glass. Her fingers started to tremble as she realized what she had been given.

Neverfell was holding a mirror. If she turned it over, she would see at last the horror that Master Grandible had decided to hide from the world. She would see the face that made people break into a sweat and flee.

She recalled the phrase she had heard muttered on the jetty. *A face like glass.* What did that mean? Perhaps her skin was transparent. Perhaps anybody looking at her could see the pulsing of her blood vessels, and the grin of her skull, and her eyeballs through the lids. Perhaps that was why everybody ran away.

She couldn't look. She wouldn't look. She watched with a fascinated sense of helplessness as her hands slowly, tremulously turned over the mirror to present her for the first time with her reflection.

For a little age she stood staring at the image in the glass. The hungry traplight beside her brightened, but she barely registered that it was doing so only because she was heaving in breath after rapid breath. The reflection in the glass moved a little, and she flinched from head to foot. Then she gave a scream that seemed to tear right up through her like a thumbnail through a blade of grass.

The mirror shattered when it struck the floor, but that was not enough. The lantern struck sparks off the bars and then swung wildly, its light and shadow tipping giddily, the little trap snapping blindly at the air as its world tilted. The barred door rattled and jumped under a torrent of kicks.

Only when she was exhausted did Neverfell drop to her knees, the dancing traplight glinting on the tiny shards of glass that now starred the puddled floor.

The skin of the face she had seen in the mirror had been pale, with a dappling of faint freckles like those across Neverfell's hands. A long face with a full and tremulous lower lip, downy pale red eyebrows, large and light-colored eyes. It had been wearing a Face. Neverfell had not expected that, for she did not remember ever having learned any. It had been an unfamiliar Face, but it had looked just the way she felt. Then the reflection had changed Face, and the way it had done so had been strange. It had slid into a new expression in a curious, liquid way she had never seen before. But it was not this strangeness that had made her break the mirror.

Staring at the new Face, she had been able to read the thoughts behind it, even while they echoed in her own head.

You locked me away, said the expression. *You locked me away for seven* years, *Master Grandible. For* nothing.

The face in the mirror was not beautiful, nor was it ugly. It was not scarred, burnt, or disfigured. Aside from the curious shifting of its Faces, there was nothing wrong with it at all.

Neverfell had expected the Enquirers to come running after this uproar, perhaps with cudgels and chains, but they did not. Instead, she was left to herself, shivering in her darkened cage as it creaked slowly to and fro, specks of glass crunching under her each time she moved, drips falling into the canal below.

She tried calling out, but her voice was a mere mouse squeak in the well of darkness. She had plenty of questions now, but nobody to answer them. *If there's nothing wrong with my face, why does everybody keep running away? And why am I here? All I did was steal a tiny piece of cheese that shouldn't have been sent in the first place. What am I doing under Enquiry?*

Shivering, Neverfell sank into a sort of torpor, in which after a time she could hardly feel the cold of her limbs. Despite everything she drowsed, and so later she could not say precisely when it was that the next visitation occurred.

With a dreamy faintness, she heard the door open and close once more, and the jetty creak under careful steps. But it did not matter because her drowsy fear was receding, leaving her filled instead with a warm and sleepy sense of well-being and safety. She knew that somebody had come whom she could trust. At the same time, the faintest trace of a pleasant fragrance seeped into Neverfell's awareness, whispering of rosemary, silver, and sweet sleep. She could relax now, the smell told her, slide into slumber.

Neverfell felt the scent stroke across her mind and soul like a peacock feather . . . and flinched in recoil, banging her head against the bars. Something told her that one's mind should not be touched like that. Now that she was shocked awake, her trained nose told her that there was an undercurrent to the smell, something wrong and ugly.

In a flash, she remembered Grandible telling her over and over to sniff visitors through the vent before admitting them within his tunnels, to check for mind-enslaving Perfume.

You'll know it when you smell it. You're a cheesemaker. We have a nose for something rotten, even if nobody else has.

She pinched her nose shut, and instantly the feeling of trust drained out of her.

Someone was standing on the jetty. It was hard to make out

the figure, and Neverfell realized that the lanterns had been hooded. The figure stepped to the wall, and with a freezing of the blood Neverfell heard the metallic protest of the crank handle once again.

"No!" she bellowed at the top of her lungs. "Stop! Stop!" Her scream echoed to and fro between the walls, like a bird banging around inside a flue. There was a rushing rattle, and the cage plunged into the water, this time with a splash, and sank within seconds, taking Neverfell down with it. She had just enough presence of mind to take a deep breath before she was dragged down beneath the black, freezing water, her sodden clothes tangling around her limbs as she flailed. She heard the muffled, watery clang of the cage hitting the rocky canal bed.

This is death was all she could think. *This is death, cold and alone and trapped, with no way of calling to anybody.*

And then, just as her lungs were aching for breath, the cage she clung to righted itself again. There was a submerged *cling-cling-cling* of metal striking metal, and then her face surfaced once more, allowing her a rippling, lopsided view of the jetty. The cage was being hauled up out of the water again. The hoods on the lanterns had been removed. Treble was standing on the jetty now, as were a number of other Enquirers, one of whom was cranking the wall handle as fast as possible. Once the water had trickled out of Neverfell's ears, she realized that Treble was shouting.

"What the devil happened? Who dropped this cage?" She strode to the jetty's edge and glared out toward Neverfell. "Did you see who it was? Did you see who released the mechanism?"

All Neverfell could do was numbly shake her head as she started to understand what had happened. Somebody had tried to kill her, and not on the Enquiry's orders.

· · · · ·

From that point forth, a guard watched her cage from the shadows all the time. There was no clock, no change in light, no way of marking the passing of time but by the arrival of food and water, delivered to the cage through the frying pan. Neverfell could not tell how long she had been catnapping in her cage when she was woken by a small, polite cough.

On the jetty stood an unfamiliar lanky figure, looking intently toward her. This man, however, did not hold himself with the stiffness of authority but was leaning back against the wall as if he had paused mid-stroll. His lantern was dangling from his hand, so she could make out little of him but his shoes.

"Let's see you, then." His voice was not unkind.

Neverfell obediently breathed on her lantern until it flared and showed her face properly. The stranger regarded her steadily for a long while. His lean figure showed no tremor.

"So it's true," he said quietly after a long pause. "That's . . . genuinely remarkable. Oh—wait a second—this isn't very fair, is it? One moment." He raised his own lantern to his face and blew on it until it gleamed, illuminating his own figure. "That evens things out a bit, doesn't it?"

The lantern showed her a long face with a narrow black beard that looked as if it had been painted on. He had deep, watchful eyes and a complicated mouth, a hiding place for secret smiles. He was wearing a Face that combined self-assurance, readiness to be amused, and a tiny hint of pity. It was the friendliest Face Neverfell had seen since her arrest.

He was just over average height and unusually thin, but everything he wore served to make him look taller and thinner. The fingers of his gloves had been extended and padded so that they looked longer and more elegant. His trailing coat of burgundy-colored moleskin was striped with long, vertical furrows.

"You're terrified," he said, studying Neverfell carefully. "You're bewildered, you're fighting down a sense of unfairness and betrayal, and you really don't have any idea what's going on at all, do you?" He shook his head and gave a small, grim smile. "Idiots," he muttered. "Hiding out and jabbering about the way you 'keep putting on terrible Faces.' What were they expecting, with you dangling over Wrath's Descent like this?"

"I'm not putting on Faces!" Neverfell shouted in desperation. "I don't even know how I *have* Faces—I don't remember learning any! And I don't know why they change the way they do! I never even saw a mirror before I came here! And now somebody in here is trying to kill me, and I don't know why! You have to believe me!"

"Yes. Yes, I really *do* have to believe you." Again the small, dark smile. "Oh dear. We're going to have to do something about you, aren't we?" He kicked his heel against the wall thoughtfully. "Do you want to get out of here?"

Neverfell gripped the bars, nodded furiously, and managed the world's smallest, mousiest "yes."

"Then I will see what I can do. But you will have to trust me. What have you told the Enquiry so far?"

Neverfell racked her brain. "Not really anything—they haven't really asked me much since I broke the mirror they gave me."

"Well, you will need to talk to them about your history." He raised a hand to hold off Neverfell's protest. "I can see that you are trying to protect somebody. However, let me tell you what the Enquirers *already* know.

"They know that your name is Neverfell, and that you are the apprentice of Cheesemaster Grandible. After the canal water washed the oil of cloves off you, there was nothing to disguise the smell of cheese, and they deduced your trade in one sniff. After that, it was only a matter of time before that black velvet mask of yours was identified by couriers who had visited the various cheese tunnels."

"Is Master Grandible in trouble?" Neverfell's heart plummeted. She had tried so hard to protect him, and now it seemed the very scent of her clothes and skin had betrayed him.

"I am afraid so."

"But none of this is his fault! He didn't even know I was out of his tunnels!" Bitter as the shock of the mirror had been, Neverfell could not bear to think of her master taking the blame for her actions.

"That's not the problem. He's in danger of arrest for hiding and harboring you all these years."

"Why?" The cold iron of the bars bit into Neverfell's fingers as she clutched at them, and the most important question burst from her. *"What's wrong with me?"*

"You really don't know, do you?" The stranger contemplated her for a few seconds with his head on one side, long enough that Neverfell started to feel a creeping horror of hearing the answer to her question. "Do you want to know?"

She nodded.

"Nothing," he answered. "Nothing's wrong with you, except that *you don't have Faces*. What you have on the front of your head has the usual eyes, nose, mouth, that sort of thing, but your expressions are a sort of . . . window. They show exactly what you're thinking and feeling. In detail.

"Nobody in Caverna is supposed to look like that. Nobody. Even outsiders can usually manage a few clumsy Faces, though their own emotions tend to leak through. But you? Every time a thought crosses your mind, it crosses your face at speed, like a wild pony. That's why the Enquirers can't bear to look at you.

Right now you're upset to the point of shattering, and your expression is too painful for them to see."

"So . . . they think I'm an *outsider*?"

"Yes, of course they do. That's what you are. Aren't you?"

"I . . . don't know." Neverfell had lost all her moorings. Was she an outsider? Could she have known another world during her first forgotten years of life? A thousand little details and unspoken thoughts started singing together, and her ears filled with a rush. "I don't remember anything before I turned up in Master Grandible's tunnels, about seven years ago."

"Nothing at all? Nothing about your life, or how you came to Caverna, or who smuggled you in?"

Neverfell shook her head slowly. Was it true? Could she really be an outsider?

All at once she found herself recalling the curious vision the Stackfalter Sturton had given her, the dappled woodland scene.

The flowers came up to my waist, as if I were very small. And Sturtons tell you things you know but still need to be told, because you won't face up to them, or because you've forgotten them. Is it possible that I did once walk through that woodland, long ago, when I was much younger? Or was it just a dream, and nothing to do with my past?

She could not be sure, but what she *did* know was that for seven years Cheesemaster Grandible had hidden her from the world. If she were an outsider, and if Grandible had always known it, then that might explain why he had always been so determined to conceal her face. But whom had he been trying to protect, Neverfell or himself?

"What's going to happen to Master Grandible?" she asked.

"As things stand, it does not look good. There are strict rules against bringing in or harboring outsiders—there is the risk of disease and overcrowding, after all. And he must have known at a glance what you were, even if you didn't. The Enquiry cannot exile him. He is a fully trained cheesemaker, knowledgeable in a hundred rites of dairymancy, and Caverna must protect her secrets. So . . . imprisonment, probably. Or indentured servitude. Perhaps even execution."

"Execution?" squeaked Neverfell in horror.

"You really want to protect him, don't you?"

Neverfell hesitated, then nodded vigorously.

"All right. There might be a way. Here's what you should do. Tell the Enquirers that you wish to take full responsibility for your own presence in Caverna, so that nobody else will be punished but you, under clause 149 of the Masques and Infiltration Act. Then tell them everything you can remember about your background. Then tell them how you came to be in Madame Appeline's arbor—but do not reveal the identity of any accomplices who helped you. Explain that they were chance acquaintances and you take responsibility for their actions as well as your own. It is the only way you can protect everybody—and yourself."

"Will they really let me do that?" asked Neverfell, hardly daring to hope.

"In this particular case, I think they will," answered the stranger. "I do not think that they are looking forward to arresting Cheesemaster Grandible. It would be just like him to refuse to come out and be arrested, you see, which means they would have to besiege him in his lair, which would be . . . messy. But if they let you take on the whole of the punishment, then they can indenture you instead, put you up for sale, and actually make good money out of this whole business."

"But I don't want to be for sale!" Indentured servants were little better than slaves, and there were terrible tales of them being used as test subjects for wild Wines and perilous pomades.

"Do not worry. Once you are for sale, *I* will buy you. I am Maxim Childersin, head of the Childersin vintner family, and I pity anyone who pits his purse against mine."

Childersin. That was a name Neverfell knew; indeed, there was not a soul in Caverna who did not know it. The Childersin dynasty had been making Wine for more than three hundred years, and had vineyards all over the overground world. They were masters of memory, its loss and recovery. They could brew Wine that would make you remember the face of your dead love so clearly you could count her eyelashes, or that would make you forget specific chapters of a book so that you could read them again with pleasure.

Neverfell felt a swell of relief and hope. Being owned by a vintner family certainly sounded better than dangling in a cage and waiting to be murdered. However, there were still a lot of parts of the plan that she did not really understand.

"But . . . if your family makes Wine, why do you want to buy a cheesemaker's apprentice?"

"Because you are by far the most interesting thing I have seen in many years. Leaving you to rot in prison or wander the overground deserts would be a terrible waste of potential. For that matter, locking you away for all these years in a glorified cheese pantry was a downright crime, and I do not intend to let it happen again. Do you understand what I am saying? I will write to let Master

Grandible know you are safe, but I cannot let you return to his care. I am sorry."

I cannot go home. Neverfell could barely understand the words. She could only begin to comprehend the concept a piece at a time. *Good-bye, blue-silver clock. Good-bye, hammock between the shelves. Good-bye, passageways I would know blind. Good-bye, scrawled ledgers.*

Good-bye, Master Grandible.

But the last was too large, and her mind could not manage it. And if she had been brought face to face with Cheesemaster Grandible at that moment, she could not say what would have been written in her expression.

FAMILY

AS IT TURNED OUT, MAXIM CHILDERSIN WAS right about everything. Within half an hour, Neverfell was seated in the back of Childersin's jolting carriage, watching the bobbing heads of the two broad-backed sorrel-colored ponies ahead. Her hands kept creeping up to touch her face, to find out what it was doing. Right now, she could feel her mouth stretching outward into an enormous grin as her spirits, ever volatile, rose uncontrollably like bubbles. Whatever else these transactions meant, they meant no longer being in a cage. Better yet, they meant saving Zouelle and Borcas from trouble, and Grandible from an executioner's block.

There was so much to see and hear that she started to feel drunk. Every carriage in the thoroughfare was roofless, to avoid sticking in low-ceilinged tunnels, and thus Neverfell could easily make out the well-dressed occupants of every passing vehicle. As the carriage rattled along sandstone colonnades, then down rose-marble avenues dappled like raspberry ice cream, she found herself passing ever grander carriages with better-decorated people within. She was struck by how tall many of them were, taller than the throngs in the common thoroughfares, or the servants that surrounded them, even a little taller than the intimidating

Enquirers from whom she had so recently been rescued. These were clearly courtiers, and Neverfell could scarcely resist leaning out to stare.

Another abrupt corner, and she found herself staring down a strange, straight avenue fifty feet long. The walls were about thirty feet high, and were painted to resemble a row of lavish town houses, of the sort she had sometimes seen in pictures. The pastel paint of the "houses" had a soft and sugary twinkle. They were studded with doors and glowing windows, and even had wooden balconies, from which hung paper lanterns like multicolored moons.

"Here we are," declared Childersin. Neverfell was helped down from the carriage, and stood gawping in the street. Beneath her feet were cobbles. The ceiling above had been smoothed with plaster, and painted deep blue like a night sky. Not far away, figures strolled beneath canopies carried by attendants, or lounged in tasseled wooden swing-seats.

"It's warm!" Neverfell gaped her mouth and breathed out slowly, but could not summon the slightest hint of visible vapor. "How is it so warm?" She barely listened as Childersin began a patient explanation about embers under the floor.

As Neverfell plunged into the crowd, more than one pedestrian flinched away, clutching a scented handkerchief to their nose, before looking at her properly and examining her with real fascination. Neverfell sensed that she was a smudged and ugly word on a page of perfect calligraphy, yet everything around her was so beautiful she could not bring herself to care. Suddenly she was herself again, a skinny bundle of fidget with limbs and fingers that wanted to be everywhere at once.

"Look! Monkey!"

"Er, no, Neverfell, that is just a short servant with a stoop."

"That man's moustache is fake yellow!"

"How nice. Now, Neverfell, if you'll come with—"

"Why do the houses look like they're covered in sugar?"

"Because they . . . Neverfell, I do not think you are supposed to climb those. No—no, Neverfell! No licking the walls! This way."

Only the firm hand on Neverfell's collar prevented her from running off inquisitively through the crowd, and with some difficulty she was led to one of the town houses. The door opened at Childersin's approach, and then Neverfell's wits were bewildered as a torrent of servants swept over them. Ready hands removed their boots, and slippers were laid out for them to step into. The door closed behind them, and trap-lanterns surged into life. Childersin's coat was taken, and warm cups of mulled cider were placed in their hands. All this seemed to happen without either Neverfell or Childersin even breaking stride.

Neverfell had not been sure what to expect, and had walked in braced for a broom to be thrust immediately into her hands, followed by a list of chores. As she sipped her spiced cider, Neverfell could not help feeling that life as an indentured servant was looking up.

"First things first," declared Childersin, while Neverfell was still staring around her at the neatly chiseled, square-cornered, carpeted room, with its lack of rugged walls, stalagmites, or gravel. "There is somebody here who will be very glad to see you, Neverfell." He marched her through another door, and Neverfell gave a whoop.

"Zouelle!"

It was indeed the mysterious blonde girl, looking to Neverfell's mind more angelic than ever. Better yet, she still appeared to be looking after the rabbit that Neverfell had given her to guard. Since then somebody had bathed it and placed it in a small cage with a handle on top. There was a pink bow tied round its neck, though it had made some progress on lacerating this with its hind claws.

Zouelle ran forward, hesitated, then gave Neverfell a careful hug, despite the sodden disarray of the younger girl's clothes. Like everybody else, she had trouble taking her eyes off Neverfell's face, but she kept her smile in place. It was smile number one, warm and confidential.

"Zouelle Paractaca Childersin, one of my favorite nieces," introduced Childersin. "Zouelle—you already know Neverfell."

Neverfell noticed that for all her brave Face the older girl was very pale. She recalled suddenly her part in Zouelle's plan, the part that had gone so badly awry. Next moment she remembered her own promise never to admit to knowing Zouelle and Borcas.

"Oh no! Did I just . . . ?" She tailed off, aware that finishing the sentence was unlikely to make things better. "Are you all right? I mean, you're not in trouble, are you?"

"Not anymore," Childersin answered promptly. "You saved her when you signed these papers. That was one of the reasons I was so happy to help you, by the way. If you were willing to go out on a limb to protect a girl you barely knew, I thought the least I could do was return the favor."

Neverfell grinned at everybody, and even poked her finger toward the rabbit, which made a determined attempt to bite it.

"Oh—but the rabbit belongs to Master Grandible! Can we send it back to him, and can I write a note to go with it? Just so I can tell him where I am and that everything is all right."

"Of course," consented Maxim Childersin with a smile. "Now, I have some matters to discuss with Zouelle, but I will leave you in good hands. Miss Howlick!" At his call a middle-aged woman appeared in the door. "This is the young lady I was telling you about, the one who will be staying with us from now on. She requires pen and paper so that she may write to her previous guardian. After that, I have a task for you. She has had a very trying few days, and will need a hot bath and some new clothes. Twenty-five hours from now, I wish to see her fit for the highest circles. The *highest*."

Neverfell was dizzy with love for everybody. She pushed back her grimy pigtails, and beamed into the round, moist, carefully impassive face of Miss Howlick.

"Your face is like a great big bun!" Neverfell told her happily.

Childersin and Miss Howlick exchanged glances.

"Do what you can," conceded Childersin.

Zouelle prided herself on always being ready with a plan. When catastrophe hit, she was a little more cool-headed than her fellows, a little quicker to turn a problem to advantage.

Right now, however, she was anything but cool. As she followed her uncle through his town house, she mentally flicked through her repertoire of smiles with increasing desperation. She could not be certain, even now, how angry her uncle really was, but she was sure that she could not afford to look amused, or flippant, or little-girly, or complacent. It was too late to be warm and winning. She had to be something new, and she did not have a Face for it.

Her uncle was actually her great-great-great-uncle. Like many of his peers, Maxim Childersin had taken the necessary measures to prevent his body from falling into old age. He had a youthful air and a talent for putting people at ease, but Zouelle was always aware of him watching the world through old, old eyes and noting every detail. She had enemies in the family but until now had held her head high, knowing that she wore Maxim

Childersin's approval and expectations across her brow like an invisible crown. Even now she could not be sure whether that crown had been dashed from her head.

"Come on into my laboratory. We are less likely to be disturbed."

As usual the room was dimly lit, to avoid exciting the more volatile Wines. With care, Zouelle picked her way between the crowded tables covered in glass bottles, scales, and trap-masks sealed in case of poison gas clouds.

Every member of the family of sufficient age and skill to be trusted with the handling of Wines had their own laboratory, including Zouelle herself. The blending of True Wines was a dangerous business, particularly when they had conflicting personalities. In Maxim Childersin's laboratory, a sigil-covered white barrel of Smogwreath currently sighed in one corner, while in the center of the room a set of concentric salt circles confined a restlessly creaking vat of Addlemeau. The two Wines were not yet ready to blend. The Addlemeau still needed to develop its undertones of vanilla, and the Smogwreath had not overcome its fear of strangers. Both, if disturbed, were quite capable of tearing strips off a man's soul like bark from a tree.

Childersin dropped himself into a large and comfortable chair, and spent a few moments studying his great-great-great-niece. She had by this time settled upon No. 65, The Pupil Waits in Eagerness for Instruction, as the most inoffensive Face at her disposal.

"Well, well. How grown-up you look. I like to think I'm quite a good uncle, but then it turns out I haven't been watching my favorite niece closely enough. I take my eye off you for a moment—and you decide to become an adult while I'm not looking."

These almost sounded like words of approval, but they made Zouelle more nervous and not less. She had developed a talent for sensing which of Uncle Maxim's mild statements were the first rattle of an imminent rockfall.

"I have an eye for talent and promise," he went on, "and I've always seen potential in you. Do you know why I sent you to the Beaumoreau Academy? Because I thought it would give you a chance to cut your teeth. All those daughters of prominent families, ambitious and clever enough to give you a run for your money . . . a perfect playground for you to practice your arts of intrigue and manipulation, so that you'd be ready for the Great Game of Court when you were older.

"But you got impatient, didn't you?"

Zouelle swallowed and bowed her head.

"You wanted to join in the grown-up games," Childersin continued. "When Madame Appeline visited your school to talk to the headmistress about the potential Putty Girls, you decided to sneak a look through the papers in her valise."

"I . . . am so very sorry." Zouelle managed to keep her voice level. "I was arrogant and . . . thought I could help. I knew that Madame Appeline was not a friend of our family, so I thought if I could find out something incriminating it might be useful . . ."

"Useful?" asked Childersin softly. "*You got caught.* How useful is that? And then, instead of coming to the family to admit what had happened, you tried to cover it up. You decided you could trick the Facesmith into drinking Wine that would make her forget the last month, so that she would never remember you rifling through her bag. And when Neverfell blundered across your path you roped her into the plan. Correct?"

Zouelle maintained a calmly respectful expression. She could not let herself tremble, for that would be a timid appeal for pity and would disappoint the man before her. Instead, she simply nodded, mouth dry.

"You have quite a good eye, Zouelle. Look at the bottle on the table in front of you. What can you tell me about it?"

Zouelle cleared her throat, took a few moments to still the tremble in her hands, then examined the label.

"It is a Permonniac—sixty-two years old, about a year from its prime. Very rare. Very valuable."

"And if I was asked which I value most, this bottle or yourself, what do you think I would answer?"

Zouelle felt her heart plummet. What answer could he possibly expect her to give? "It is a very valuable Wine. I . . ."

Childersin chuckled. "Don't be silly. In terms of what I value, there is no competition. There is nothing more important to me than family. No bottle of Wine matters more to me than you do."

Zouelle did not relax. The conversation was not over. She could feel it.

"So. Answer me a second question. Suppose right now I had to choose between saving you and saving this bottle. Which do you think I would pick?"

Zouelle looked up into the face of the man she admired most in the world, and could not muster a voice. She mouthed an answer, but lacked enough certainty to give it sound.

Me?

Childersin leaned forward and rested his elbows on his knees. "That would have been a very easy question to answer a few days ago," he said. "Today it is much harder. As I say, nothing means as much to me as this family. Nothing. Everything I do is to ensure the strength, safety, and future of its members. This bottle"—he tapped the cork very gently—"is an asset that can help me do that, so that I can strengthen our position and protect everyone. A few days ago, I thought of you as another asset, a seed for a bright future. Well, your little games just put the family at risk. Should I really protect something that endangers everybody else here?"

Zouelle shook her head. Try as she might, she could not prevent herself from shaking. Despite her great-great-great-uncle's gentle tone, she felt as if she were being systematically stripped of her armor and skin. "If there is anything I can do to make things better . . ."

"Why? Do you have another plan, my dear? Like the one that left us entangled with cases of burglary, fraud, attempted memory-theft, and consorting with an outsider?"

"Did the Enquiry say—"

"—anything about you? No. Neverfell still hadn't told them anything useful when I arrived. Of course, they would have forced the truth out of her sooner or later if she had remained in their hands. The only way I could prevent that was to arrange her indenture and purchase her, at considerable expense. Buying Madame Appeline's silence and forbearance will be much more difficult and costly, I fear, but I have contacted her and it seems she is at least willing to discuss the matter with me."

Hesitantly, the weight on Zouelle's chest started to lift. Ever since the failure of her plan she had been haunted by thoughts of being dragged away by the Enquiry, interrogated in their black halls, and left to rot in some bat-infested hell-cage. Her uncle had saved her. That had to mean that he still valued her, despite the trouble she had brought.

"Thank you," she whispered. "I promise I will not interfere in Court business again."

"Oh yes, you will."

Zouelle looked up to see her uncle regarding her with a sad little smile.

"You decided that you were ready to start meddling in the Great Game. I really hope you were right, Zouelle, because once you start playing it you can never leave.

"You are in the game now, my dear. There is no going back."

Neverfell had never had the luxury of a bath with hot water and bubbles before, and over the next six hours she made up for lost time in no uncertain terms. Her pigtails were matted so densely they were almost like wood, but Miss Howlick battled them with oils and teased them with spindles until Neverfell had hair, slippery clinging hair that got in her eyes, and floated in the water, and slid over her shoulders like dark red paint.

Neverfell's long-ingrained smell of cheese was the great enemy, and Miss Howlick fought it with thyme oil and with saffron, with sandalwood and with pumice stones. Most of all, she fought it with pot after pot of piping hot water, until Neverfell's fingers were wrinkled and her foot soles were bleached. When all that remained was a faint, phantom Stilton whiff that all but the sharpest of noses would miss, Miss Howlick sent a serving girl to fetch Miss Metella.

When Miss Metella arrived, Neverfell took one look at her and then tried to hide under the soap suds. Miss Metella was an elderly, apple-cheeked woman with a calming voice, the effect being spoiled by the fact that she wore two skin-pink silken eye patches, each with a picture of a wide, blue eye embroidered on it.

She was obviously a perfumier, for all perfumiers had their eyes removed when they became apprentices. Perfumiers were notorious for disliking cheesemakers, whose reek offended their elegant noses and who also had an annoying knack of noticing the use of Perfume when others did not. However, her air of calm and common sense eventually lured Neverfell out.

"Don't you worry, dear," she said, beaming, adding the tiniest drop from a pipette into Neverfell's bath. "We're both friends of the Childersin family, so we've got nothing to quarrel about."

It was a very different Neverfell who confronted herself in a mirror seven hours later. Indeed, it took several minutes of flapping her arms like a penguin to convince her that she really was regarding her own reflection. The new Neverfell had softly glossy dark red hair that hung to her shoulders, and wore a simple green dress with white fur trim at the collar and cuffs. She had crochet gloves ornamented with small bobbles that her fingers itched to twiddle. Her green boots were fur-lined as well. Her face looked flushed beneath its freckles, surprised, and gleeful.

She had just started to experiment, pinching and pulling at her face to make it do things, when she noticed Zouelle in the reflection behind her. To her surprise, the older girl pushed forward and folded the mirror shut with a click.

"Miss Howlick should not have given you that," Zouelle said, a little tartly. "I will have to speak to her about it."

"What? Why not?" Neverfell stared nonplussed at the closed mirror.

"Your face will spoil if you keep staring at it like that. Anyway, if you can remember what you just saw, you do not really need a mirror anymore, do you?" Zouelle's tone was confident and big-sisterly again. Her smile was even.

"What's wrong?" Just for a moment Neverfell felt as if there were an invisible wire pulled to razor tautness between her and the other girl, humming tension into the room. If she blundered toward it, it might snap or cut her, and yet she half wished it would, so that she knew where it was. "Is it something I did?"

"What did you tell the Enquiry?" Zouelle was still wearing her warm and confidential Face, but the eyes no longer matched it, frantically scanning Neverfell's own features. "Uncle Maxim says you didn't tell them anything. That isn't true, is it?"

"But it is! I mean . . . I told them bits of your plan, but I didn't say who was in it except me. I never told them about you."

"That makes no sense." Zouelle kept slipping Face between her confidential smile and a look of polite concern as if uncertain what to use. "Of course you told them. Why wouldn't you tell them?"

Neverfell stared at her. "They would have put you in a cage like mine! I couldn't let them do that! After all, you were just trying to help me, weren't you? You're my friend!"

It was Zouelle's turn to stare. At least that seemed to be what her eyes were doing. The rest of her face was still politely concerned. And then she looked away, and gave an utterly charming little laugh.

"That's right," she said in her usual tone. "I'm your friend. And I'm going to look after you, Neverfell. Uncle has asked me to help you with everything. What to wear, how to talk, how to act in good company. My uncle has . . . great plans for you."

Neverfell's spirits skyrocketed again. "So everything's all right?"

"Yes, Neverfell. Everything's fine."

Of course it was. Neverfell was just being nervous and stupid. She could see that now. Zouelle did not resist Neverfell's hug, but there was something stiff about the way she returned it, and her hands felt cold.

THE MORNING ROOM

DRAINED, DIZZY, AND BONE-TIRED AFTER THE events of the day, Neverfell was shown to a beautiful little room in the Childersin town house and told it was hers. She loved it, then spent eight hours failing to sleep in it. The small four-poster bed had soft golden covers and strokeable curtains, but she was used to her rough hammock, and the flat mattress left her squirming. The air smelled of dried violets instead of slumbering cheeses, and all the soft sounds around her were wrong. Besides this, the day had stuffed her head so full of new thoughts and sights that it hurt, and now her mind whirled and whirled and would not shut down.

Then there was the cockerel-shaped clock on her dressing table. It had a weird face in which the numbers only went up to twelve, and its tick was loud and unfamiliar, but worst of all it did not chime. Every time it struck the hour she would be startled alert by the lack of chime. In the end she got up, sat down with the cockerel, and did what she always did when she was "out of clock" and needed to calm her mind.

At some point she must have fallen asleep at the dressing table, since when a sharp rap at the door woke her she was lolling across its surface, her cheek pressed against a heap of cogs. She started awake and staggered to the door to find Zouelle waiting for her in a white dress.

"You're not dressed! Didn't your cockerel wake you an hour ago?" Zouelle peered past Neverfell, and her gaze lighted upon a gleaming, half-dismantled shape, its beaked head missing and several of its cogs scattered across the table doilies. "Neverfell! Did you take the cockerel-clock to pieces?"

"I was fixing it!" stammered Neverfell. "I wanted to make it chime! They said everything in here was mine, so I thought nobody would mind—"

"You can't just take things apart! Everything in this room is yours to use, if you use them the right way, but you can't just do whatever you like with them." Zouelle took a deep breath and stroked one hand over her blonde hair. "Never mind, Neverfell. Get dressed quickly, or we'll be late for breakfast."

Having dressed and rejoined Zouelle in the corridor, Neverfell was somewhat surprised to find the whole family also in the process of rising.

"Why is everybody getting up at the same time?" whispered Neverfell. "Surely you don't all keep the same clock? Don't you sleep different shifts so somebody is always awake?" It seemed a very strange and impractical way of doing things.

Zouelle shook her head. "We always eat breakfast together in the Morning Room," she answered. "Uncle Maxim insists upon it—he is a great believer in family, and says that we should all sit down together for at least one meal each day. Apparently people do that in the overground, and he is determined that we will do the same. Uncle Maxim has quite the passion for the overground. He even has us living by overground clocks."

She gestured to the wall, and Neverfell realized that they were passing another outlandish twelve-hour clock, like her cockerel. It looked quite bare and bald with so few numbers painted on its face.

"But . . . then . . . aren't your clocks telling totally different times from everybody else's nearly all the time?" asked Neverfell, feeling that her life was about to get very confusing.

"Oh yes," agreed Zouelle. "But one simply does not say no to Uncle Maxim, and he is usually right about everything. We started living by overground time back when I was seven, and do you know something? Nobody in the family has been out of clock since."

Neverfell wondered if that was why the Childersins all seemed so gleamingly healthy and full of life. You could spot people who spent a lot of their time out of clock. They were quite often overweight, soapily pale, and unhealthy-looking. The Childersins, on the contrary, all appeared to be clear-skinned, clear-eyed, and alert.

It soon became apparent that the Morning Room was not even part of the main house. Instead, the whole family had to walk through a back door and along a private tunnel for half an hour. It was bizarre to watch the extended Childersin clan strolling out resolutely, the ladies carrying paradribbles, the tasseled umbrellas that protected one from cave drips, and the babes pushed along in silken carriages. They were a particularly tall and statuesque family, and it made for an impressive parade. The servants following after them with steaming urns and silver trays of croissants looked stunted in comparison.

"Uncle Maxim found a room he liked in another district," Zouelle explained in an undertone. "Refreshing atmosphere, he said. So he walled it in and had a passage built to it from our house. That's always the way it is. When he finds something that pleases him, he just buys it, and the rest of us adapt."

"Is that what he did with me?" whispered Neverfell. Zouelle did not seem to hear.

The Morning Room was a fine square room with a walnut-wood table in the middle. In an alcove, two bronze clockwork birds sang jerkily, twisting their heads to and fro. In the center of the ceiling was set a large glass orb, clearly some kind of lantern, and it was from this that the room's light poured. However, instead of the usual yellow or greenish light, this was blue-white.

The blueness made Neverfell feel shocked and alive, as if she had been rinsed out with crystal-cold water. She did not know why. The Childersins, however, seemed to think nothing of it, and settled themselves around the table. Seeing the whole family all at once, Neverfell was again struck by how much brighter, healthier, taller, and more elegant they seemed than anybody else she had ever met. For once, at least, she did not feel too lanky and overgrown.

"Ah, Neverfell." Maxim Childersin beckoned to her, and to her relief, Neverfell found that she was to be seated between Maxim Childersin and Zouelle. "Everybody, this is Neverfell. Please treat her gently. After all, I have only just bought her, and she was very expensive."

Meals had always been something Neverfell gobbled alone between tasks. Now suddenly there seemed to be rules. Even the eggs sat up in little china cups, and people made a point of tapping their way in through the tops instead of just peeling off the murky shells. Neverfell watched everybody else with a sort of awe, breaking bread in her lap and sneaking pieces into her mouth like a thief. They even seemed to know when to laugh, how to laugh, and when to stop, and every witticism was met by a gust of perfectly synchronized mirth, which everybody except Neverfell ceased at exactly the same instant. To her relief, though, they did not spend the whole meal staring at her, sparing her only occasional, smiling glances.

"Zouelle—are those your parents?" whispered Neverfell, casting a glance at the two adults sitting on the blonde girl's other side.

"No, that is one of my uncles and his wife," Zouelle whispered back. "My parents were devoured by a corked bottle of Sardonny when I was two years old." She sounded so unconcerned and offhand that Neverfell hesitated to offer condolences for fear of sounding silly.

The family gossiped quietly, mostly about the most recent thefts of the infamous and anonymous Kleptomancer. As usual they were daring, incomprehensible, and appeared designed to cause as much annoyance as possible. His last act had been to purloin a great waterwheel powered by one of the underground rivers. It had been discovered later on its side in an abandoned quarry cave, with a giant tablecloth across it and seventeen places set for dinner.

Neverfell could not concentrate on the brilliant tinkle of conversation. The blue got in the way. The blue wanted to tell her about wild, wide spaces beyond the numb place in her mind. She reached for her cup, but the gleam on the porcelain made her blink, and just for a moment her mind filled with the image of an expanse of water so bright that it seemed to be seething with diamonds. She could almost see it. She wanted to see it.

Water! She needed water. There was some in a big jug, just within reach. And . . . there! A bowl. Tipping out its cargo of pears and apples only took a moment. Fill it up with water. No, still not quite right. But if she splashed the water around, made the surface sparkle . . .

"Neverfell," hissed Zouelle between motionless lips, "what are you doing?"

Neverfell slowly withdrew her fingers from the great bowl. Everybody was staring at her. Some of them now had damp flecks on their shirtfronts.

"I . . ." Neverfell looked abashed at her wet fingers. "There's water. Lots of water. As far as I can . . . water right to the edge of . . . with light on it. Bright light. Blue light, like . . ." She looked up at the glass bulb in the ceiling. "I . . . it's like the blue I keep remembering."

She sat down slowly, and silently thanked the Childersins from her heart when they hesitantly resumed their conversations. After a moment or two, however, she realized that Maxim Childersin was still observing her, quite motionless, his spoon halfway through decapitating his egg.

"'The blue I keep remembering,'" he repeated softly, then laid down his spoon, greasy with blue yolk. "I dislike inconsistencies, Neverfell. The last time we spoke about your memory, you told me that you remembered nothing of your earliest years." There was a hint of something new in his voice, something that could become hardness if it chose.

"But I don't really remember anything!" Neverfell exclaimed hastily. "Just tiny pieces, sometimes. Feelings. And I don't even know if they're real memories or things I made up. It's like when you wake up and can't remember the dream, but there's still something in your head."

"What kind of something?"

Neverfell shrugged. "A sort of a . . . smear, a feeling you can't put into words. I can't remember anything properly, but sometimes I know when things are wrong. Like your birds over there." She glanced over at the bronze birds with their jerking beaks. "They're wrong. They sing like beautiful music boxes, and real birds don't. I just know that."

"Interesting." Master Childersin's scrutiny was becoming somewhat unnerving.

"And . . . there's something that I thought might be a memory. Or it might not." Hesitantly, Neverfell related the Stackfalter Sturton vision of the bluebell wood, then trailed off, gnawing her lip. "Master Childersin, I wanted to ask something. How do you know if True Wine has been used to make you forget things? Is there a way you can tell?"

"Yes, Neverfell. There are certain signs." Maxim Childersin folded his napkin. "I think this is a subject that merits a long and private discussion. Come to my study after breakfast."

"Look at the paintings, Neverfell." Settling his angular form in the large damask armchair in his study, Childersin folded his arms and observed her. "Tell me what you feel when you look at them. Tell me if they stir your memories."

Neverfell walked slowly around the room, running her fingers over the curls and whorls of the gilded picture frames that covered every inch of the walls. Half the paintings were detailed and realistic pictures of luscious-looking grapevines. There were no fresh grapes in Caverna, of course, but Neverfell had encountered enough pictures of them to recognize what these must be. The other half were landscapes. Above sleek and ragged horizons glowed dozens of painted skies, some marked with a pale, flaky blob for a sun. Neverfell had never seen so many overground landscapes in one place.

"Where are all these places?" Neverfell peered into the nearest landscape.

"They are mine," answered Childersin. "My overground vineyards in Vronkoti, Chateau Bellamaire, and a dozen other countries besides."

"What's this one?" The small picture before her showed yellow hills, dusty and wild under their fleece of gray cloud.

"My estate in Tadaraca," answered Childersin, walking over to join her. "Does it look familiar?"

"No, but I feel like I should know what those are." She pointed hesitantly to a V-shape of dots in the painted sky. The almost-knowing was an ache. She shrugged, then looked up at Childersin. "What are they?"

"I have no idea." Childersin smiled down at her bafflement. "I have never seen the sky, Neverfell. I have never left Caverna. Why do you think I must hire the very best artists to paint my vineyards and grapes?"

He gestured toward a beautifully rendered picture of a vine heavy with pale gold grapes. These fruit looked real enough to pluck, some dusky with shadow, some honey-bright with the sun, cold lights in the dewdrops that beaded the leaves.

"It looks like I could crawl right into it and eat them," Neverfell thought aloud.

"Please don't try." Childersin laughed, then sighed with every sign of true wistfulness. "Overground vintners can wander down to their vineyards, pinch their grapes for plumpness, smell them ripening in the sun. Alas, I have to work from pictures, detailed reports, maps, soil samples, raisins, and send thousands of minute instructions back to the vineyards."

"But you're so powerful! If you really wanted to go there, couldn't you arrange something?"

"Nobody is permitted to leave Caverna, particularly those who are masters of their Craft, and for excellent reasons. Our trade secrets must be protected. If overgrounders learned how to make True Delicacies the way we do, then we would lose our power in the world, and camel trains would no longer trudge the deserts to bring us provisions." Childersin shook his head, and gave Neverfell a small and complicated smile. "And even if I could leave Caverna for a time I would not do so. Too dangerous. The games of Court are fast and subtle, and if I were absent even for a little while I would miss moves in the game. I would probably return to find my family murdered, strangers living in this house, and my cellars in the hands of my rivals.

"And what then? My power base would be broken, and one of the other vintner families would find ways to take over my vineyards and distant castles. Seeing my estates at Tadaraca would mean losing them . . . and everything else."

"But what's the point of owning them if you never see them?" burst out Neverfell. She blinked, and for a moment it seemed to her the V of painted freckles was flickering slightly, wavering in formation.

"What's the point of seeing them if I don't own them?" was Childersin's rejoinder.

Neverfell barely heard him, her gaze still entranced by the painted images of a world that was lost to her. "Master Childersin, could you bring my memory back? Wine can help people remember things, can't it?"

"Possibly. But is that what you want?" Childersin held up an admonishing hand as Neverfell opened her mouth to give a hasty yes. "No, think carefully before you answer. Aside from the fact that True Wine can be very perilous to those who are not used to it, have you considered the other dangers?

"If your earliest memories *were* removed using True Wine, then somebody has gone to considerable trouble and expense to keep a secret. The use of such a luxury suggests somebody at Court, that is to say, somebody with power and influence. Thanks to your amnesia, you are no threat to them. If they think you are starting to remember, on the other hand, you will be in a great deal of danger. Your thoughts can be read in your face. Once you can remember the guilty parties, you will not be able to hide it from them."

"But somebody's already trying to kill me!" Neverfell gave a gabbled account of her near-drowning in the Enquiry cell. "So whoever ordered that is probably the same person who wiped my memory, isn't it? They already want me dead. Wouldn't it be safer for me to know who they are?"

"Not necessarily." Childersin steepled his fingers and mused. "And you should also consider that forgetfulness can be a blessing. I believe there may be dark matters in your past—matters that you may not be happy to remember."

Neverfell said nothing. Her throat felt tight. Suddenly her mind was full of the image of Zouelle slamming the folding mirror shut.

"You're trembling," Childersin remarked.

"Yes." Neverfell twisted her hands, but they kept on shaking. "I don't know why."

"I do. Do you want to know what I glimpsed in your face just now, for the briefest moment? Rage. I saw the same look flash through your expression this morning when you were filling the bowl with water. You're shaking because you're very, very angry."

"But I'm not! I'm not angry! Am I?"

"Hmm. Well, somebody is." Childersin retreated into contemplation for a moment, and his next question surprised her. "Tell me, Neverfell, do you ever do things without knowing why?"

"Oh yes—all the time! But . . . that's just because I'm a bit mad."

"Maybe not. Maybe your memories are locked away but not destroyed. Maybe that younger you is still trapped deep inside, remembering everything and just now and then giving you an unexpected nudge in certain directions. I have known such things to happen.

"I suspect that there is another Neverfell caged inside you, and that she is burning with rage. Anger at something she remembers, perhaps. Anger at being locked away for so long. She may even be angry with *you*."

Neverfell moved her hands up to her chest, and almost wondered whether she would feel a second heartbeat from a hidden self. The idea frightened her, as if ordinary Neverfell were an egg that might crack open and let out something stronger.

She had lived seven years without knowing about her past. Did she really need her memory, or could she get on quite well without it?

"I can't!" she exploded. "I can't go on like this forever! I feel like I'm running around with a hole in the back of my head, with things falling out or crawling in without warning! If I don't find out who I am, then I'll always just be oh-don't-mind-Neverfell-she's-a-bit-mad, and nothing will ever make any sense. I have to know, Master Childersin! I *want* to know."

"Good," answered Childersin, suddenly crisp and matter-of-fact. "I had to point out the risks, but I myself am deeply curious about the secret somebody has been so desperate to hide. Wait here."

He absented himself for a short time, then returned with a single glass goblet in his hand, a tiny splash of Wine in the base.

"The most powerful reprise Wine in my cellars," he said as he put it into her hand. Neverfell knew that Wines with "reprises" could sting faded memories to life, so that one experienced them afresh. "If this cannot force the lock of your caged memories, nothing can. After this, one way or the other, we will know if they are lost to you."

A rich, strange, and entrancing smell tickled at Neverfell's nostrils. She hesitated a moment, remembering stories of those who drank Wines too strong for them and went mad, or forgot everything except their birthdays. Then she fought down the spasm of fear, dipped her mouth, and sipped.

For a while it felt as though she were rising, or the world were dropping away. There was no room, there was no stool. She was suspended above a nothingness as she had been in her cage, but this gulf was full of light instead of darkness. It seemed to her that a torrent of moths surged up and past her, fanning her with their burgundy-colored wings as they went. The flavors were not flavors; they were ruby and purple lights that coruscated about her.

And then, with a shock like a faller's impact, she found herself in darkness and being pulled in two. Somebody much larger had an arm around her middle and was trying to drag her away, but she clung to a hand, a hand twice the size of her own. She could not let go, they could not make her let go, she would never let go. The hand was gripping hers too, as tightly as it could. That other hand was everything she had, everything she loved. But there were too many of the dark shapes pulling them apart, and they were too big and too strong. Her fingers slipped from the other grasp, and she heard a scream from the owner of the other hand. The sound tore through her. It was her fault. It was all her fault. She had failed to hold on. Her fingers had weakened.

The scene faded. She was floating in the ruby radiance again, and it gave a dark pulse with each beat of her heart. There was a vast purple voice all around that thundered questions at her, and she tried to answer but could barely hear her own voice.

"What else?" The reddish haze was ebbing, and the voice resolving into something more human, less deafening. "What else do you remember?"

Neverfell opened her eyes. She was still seated in her chair, the goblet gripped in one shaking hand. Childersin was standing over her, everything in his posture suggesting urgent and intense concentration. Something was tickling her cheek, and when she reached up to brush at it she found it was a tear.

"Nothing. Just that one memory. Being dragged away from . . . somebody." She racked her brain, but the great locked doors of her memory stared back at her. "Nothing else." There was a long pause during which Childersin continued to examine her, and then he slowly exhaled.

"I see." Childersin's voice was calm and kind. "Then I am sorry, Neverfell, but the Wine that took your memories must have been too powerful to be removed safely."

"But . . . I saw something from the past!" Neverfell could have wept with disappointment, and this no doubt showed in her face. "If we tried again . . ."

"If we tried a hundred times we would get nothing more," responded Childersin pensively, "and Wine this strong would destroy your health long before that. No, you glimpsed this memory only because it was particularly powerful and had left its mark on your mind.

"If we are to find out about your past, we must try other methods. I have taken you at your word, Neverfell. You say that you wish to know the truth at any cost. So I have a plan to propose. A risky plan.

"Tomorrow my family will be attending the banquet of the Grand Steward. Now, you were signed over to me as an indentured servant, but the papers also effectively make you my ward. If I can argue that you are an honorary member of my family, then I would be entirely within my rights to bring you to the banquet."

Neverfell did not know what her face was saying, but she could feel it growing hot and cold in turns.

"As far as the hoi polloi are concerned," continued Childersin, "I would be bringing you along as a novelty, an oddity to invite stares. The more astute would be told that you were there to use your fine cheesemaker's nose to detect anybody trying to use Perfume against me or my family.

"Only you and I would know why you were really there. Anybody who is anybody will be at that banquet, so you would have a first-rate opportunity to cast your eye over them and see whether any of them stir those lost memories of yours. And even if the memories are too deeply buried for you to recognize anybody from your past, it is possible that somebody might recognize *you,* and give themselves away with their reaction.

"Do you think you are brave enough for that, Neverfell? I know you are not used to big crowds yet, and the Court has frightened braver men than I. It is not a safe place. One may make a deadly enemy by meeting the wrong gaze or wearing a tactless shade of purple."

"Will I have to get forks right and drink out of goblets made of ice with live fish within?"

Childersin laughed under his breath. "Is that a yes?"

Neverfell thought for a moment. "Yes. Yes, it is."

"Very well. I had not planned for you to make your debut so soon, but this is too good an opportunity to miss. However, please remember—this plan is hazardous for more than just yourself. I will be staking the good name and safety of my family on your behavior, and there is nothing I care about more than my family.

"You will be at the banquet to see and be seen. Please try not to . . . *do* anything."

"I'll try, Master Childersin."

"Bravo, Neverfell."

The Stackfalter Sturton was making its Court debut in less than a day, and it seemed that so was she.

DEATH BY DELICACY

WHEN NEVERFELL WOKE THE NEXT DAY AFTER nine blissful hours of deep sleep, she no longer felt out of clock. Her mind was clearer than it had been for weeks.

Almost immediately, she noticed that the mood of the Childersin house had changed. She could not pin down what had altered or why, but she sensed a bristling tension, and noted the way conversations died when she entered the room.

Zouelle found her quickly, and commandeered her arm.

"Come on!" she said firmly. "We have a lot to get through and not much time." Her smile was charming and rather motherly. Her grip on Neverfell's arm was fierce as a vise.

Before she knew it, Neverfell was neck-deep in an exhausting crash course in basic etiquette. Her brain cramped in the face of countless people waving what looked like elegant torture instruments in front of her face, while slowly and patiently explaining exactly what food each was meant to dissect. Try as she might, she could not tell the difference between the spoon for tadpole pâté and the one for tamarind jam. She was shown two dozen times how to spread her napkin on her lap, and copied the gestures as exactly as she could, but still everybody flinched when she did so and exchanged glances.

The more she focused, the worse her nerves and the clumsier her gestures. She was wondering how everybody else managed to stay so calm when Zouelle gave a wordless noise in her throat and strode from the room.

"Zouelle?" Neverfell pattered after the older girl and found her leaning against the wall, both hands in fists, showing every sign of controlling herself with difficulty.

"Do you have any idea," Zouelle asked in a tight little voice, "how much danger you could put us all in if you get things wrong? Even the tiniest mistake could anger the Grand Steward, or put us at war with another house!" She closed her eyes and raised trembling hands to her cheeks. "Nobody *ever* goes to one of these banquets without years of training. Some of us have been rehearsing for our first banquet since we were old enough to stand!"

"I . . . I'm sorry!" stammered Neverfell. "I didn't know!" Then the true import of Zouelle's words sank in. "You . . . you mean this is your first banquet too?"

Zouelle's smile remained perfectly sweet-tempered and encouraging, even as she released a long and bitter sigh through it. "It was going to be my debut," she murmured. "And now . . ."

Now you've spoiled everything.

"I won't go, then," Neverfell answered hastily. "I'll tell Master Childersin I've changed my mind—that I'm ill . . ."

"No!" Zouelle's voice was sharp with alarm. "If you try to back out after talking to me, he'll blame me! It's too late once he's set his mind on something. And because he's put me in charge of you, everything you do wrong at the banquet will be my fault as well."

Uncertainly, Neverfell reached out and squeezed one of Zouelle's hands. It lay there in her grasp, cool and inert as a bar of soap.

"I won't get you in trouble at the banquet—I'll just copy you all the time. Or sit on my hands and look at people and do nothing. Just like a parrot in a cage. But with no gnawing or squawking. I'll only do what you tell me, I promise."

Seconds passed during which Zouelle stared down at their clasped hands, her face as serene as a porcelain angel.

"All right, then," she said at last, sounding calm again, almost bored. "As long as you don't . . . *do* anything, perhaps I can get you through this. Come on, let's go back. Forget about the napkin for now. We have so many other things to teach you . . ."

There was a long list of prohibitions. *Don't sneeze, don't point at anybody with your little finger, don't scratch your left eyebrow, don't angle your knife so that it reflects light in somebody's eyes unless you're challenging them to a duel . . .*

There were briefings on even more alarming issues as well. Neverfell was given a rundown of various strange or innocent-seeming symptoms she might experience, and the poisons that caused them. Her fingers were loaded with rings, each containing a secret cavity with a different antidote.

"And it's important that you know what to do if Uncle Maxim gives any of the emergency signals. Remember, we won't be able to bring any of our retinue and guards into the actual banquet to protect us from assassins. It is terribly bad form to *admit* to being terrified for one's life, but nobody in their right mind would go to a Court banquet without making preparations. One must have the right costume, the right Faces, and at least eighty-two ways of avoiding assassination."

Neverfell looked about her, with the expression of somebody suddenly expecting to be assassinated in eighty-two different ways. The rings were heavy on her fingers.

Everything is really something else in disguise. Of course she was no exception, she reminded herself. Everybody would assume she was there as the Childersins' novelty pet, or as a Perfume detector. Nobody would guess she was there to look for the person who had stolen her history.

By the time the hour arrived for departure, Neverfell was feeling sick and suffering from second thoughts, and for that matter third, fourth, and fifth thoughts. The die was cast, however, and even if she had wanted to flee she did not think the heels on her green satin shoes would have let her. Her green dress was simple, thankfully, and a wreath of silk ivy leaves had been twined in her hair. Zouelle herself had a new smile that she had been learning and saving specially for this banquet. It made Neverfell think of a shimmer of silver, and went well with the blonde girl's elegant jewelry.

Both had short capes of white fur, but Neverfell found herself shivering nonetheless. As they were walking down the street, Zouelle noticed and slipped a hand into hers. Her grasp was warm and firm, her gaze steady, and Neverfell had no idea what her smile meant.

The flying sedans at the end of the street were beautifully ornamented boxes hanging from ropes with dark shafts above and below them. Muscular-looking men stood by great turnstiles, waiting to haul the sedan up through the ceiling or down through the floor as required.

Childersin dropped coins into waiting hands. "Down," he instructed. "The Lagoon."

Taking their leave of their servants, the Childersins climbed into the waiting damask-covered sedans. Neverfell obediently seated herself next to Zouelle. As the sedan juddered into life, however, and began its rocky descent, she lurched out of her seat again.

"Neverfell!"

Neverfell could not resist leaning far out of the door, so that she could peer up the shaft and watch the ropes as they vibrated with the strain. She had just about made out where they fed into pulleys, and how those connected to the surrounding wheels and spindles, when she was pulled back into the sedan by Zouelle.

"Sorry," Neverfell whispered apologetically as she dropped into her seat again. "I just . . . wanted to see how it worked."

Zouelle sighed, and mouthed an answer. *Don't. Do. Anything. Remember?*

Neverfell hung her head and kicked her heels for a while. Then the sedan reached their destination, and all other thoughts dropped out of Neverfell's mind.

The cavern facing them was not high, but it was broader than any Neverfell had ever seen. The lantern-studded ceiling was rugged and rough-hewn, rising here into cathedral-like domes, then dropping into jagged, menacing, downward spikes. At first the floor seemed just as tumultuous, a perilous landscape of spikes and ravines. The next moment a tiny ripple slid across this image, disrupting it, and Neverfell realized that she was looking not at the floor, but at the ceiling reflected in the mirror-smooth surface of a large, dark lagoon.

Neverfell and the other passengers stepped out of the sedan, taking great care not to fall down the shaft that continued to descend below it. On the nearside shore of the lagoon, a company of white gondolas was waiting, white-clad gondoliers standing at their prows, all wearing the same poetically pensive Face.

It took a small convoy of the gondolas to transport the Childersin family. Neverfell could not concentrate on their conversations. Here and there the ceiling dipped almost into the water, and she watched fascinated as the gondoliers sidled their boats through without getting their poles wedged. Once Neverfell thought she heard a splash and saw a small, dark rodent head swimming away from them.

At last the ceiling started to rise, and the cavern opened out. And out, and out, and out. Neverfell dropped her jaw, craned back her head, and stared around at the largest cave she had ever seen.

It was about two hundred feet across and roughly circular, with a high domed ceiling, the uppermost reaches of which were lost in darkness. From the walls tumbled countless tiny, silver waterfalls, which trickled into the waters of the lagoon. In the middle of the cave a broad, low island rose from the waters, and it was toward this that the gondolas were steering. Four great vaulted pillars rose from the edges of this island to the high ceiling, presumably to support it and stop the cavern from caving in.

The gondolas came to a halt at the shore, their hulls crunching against submerged gravel, and the passengers alighted. Neverfell felt the ground give a little under her tread, and looked down to find that it was made of a fine white powder, now lightly dusting her shoes.

Sand, said Neverfell's head, recollecting accounts of distant lands. *Not sand,* said some stubborn instinct. *Too fine. Too white.*

Everything's too white, she thought suddenly, heart banging. *Everything's just waiting for me to stain it or break it somehow.*

Staring about her, Neverfell could see large tables set up around the edge of the island. However, each was surrounded by a fence of what looked a bit like gauze. The figures seated within were distinctly visible, but it was like looking at them through a fine film of mist. From the center of each table rose a little tree fashioned from metal, and in the branches of these nestled lanterns with peach- and cream-colored trap-lanterns. On the far side of the island, a little wooden bridge ran from the island to the wall of the cavern, where it met a pair of swinging doors. Through these flowed a stream of serving staff bearing napkins, glasses of water, and so forth.

Two footmen appeared, each wearing the same white doublet and mournfully restrained Face. They showed the Childersin party to an unoccupied table. When the footmen held the gauze open for the new arrivals to enter, it gave a faint tinkle, and Neverfell realized that it was actually made up of thousands of very fine metallic links, like diaphanous chain mail. Another precaution to protect the guests from one another, she suspected.

Neverfell settled uneasily into her chair next to Zouelle. On either side of her place setting was laid out a terrifying range of bizarre cutlery. There were seven different glasses, and a small bowl full of white, feathery biscuits in the shape of moths.

Do nothing. Do nothing do nothing do nothing. Neverfell's face burned with self-consciousness, and keeping her limbs still took agonizing effort. But this was her chance, she realized. She was there to be seen . . . and to see.

Gripping her seat to keep her hands still, Neverfell dared to peer across at the other tables and let her dazzled eye slide over unfamiliar faces and figures. She was still not used to seeing so many *tall* people. Courtiers simply seemed to be taller and healthier-looking than the servants and all the drudge messengers she had ever seen. The Childersins, however, tended to be taller, clearer-skinned, and brighter-eyed than the rest. In particular, the younger members of the family had a definite height advantage over their counterparts at other tables.

A faint breeze rippled the silvery gauze around the other tables, so that the distant diners shimmered in and out of sight, and briefly Neverfell thought she glimpsed a hazy but familiar figure on the far side with an elegantly tiny waist, brilliant green feathers quivering in its coiffure.

"That looks like Madame Appeline!" Without thinking, Neverfell started to raise one hand, but Zouelle caught at her wrist and prevented her.

"Stop!" she hissed. "Neverfell, what are you doing? If you wave, you will look as if you are mocking her! You must *think* of these things!"

The common sense in Zouelle's words hit Neverfell like a slingshot. The last time Neverfell had appeared before Madame Appeline, it had been in the role of captured thief, and the Facesmith had duly handed Neverfell over to the authorities. If there had been any chance of friendship between them, Neverfell's actions had probably killed it dead.

"Besides," Zouelle continued, "our family has as little to do with Madame Appeline as possible."

"Really?" Neverfell rubbed at her forehead as the world became even more complicated. "Why? What has she done wrong?"

"Well, I don't know all the details," Zouelle admitted, "but Uncle has always made it very clear that she is not a friend to our family."

Crestfallen, Neverfell stared across at the distant figure. She had secretly hoped for another chance to talk to Madame Appeline so that she could explain everything. Instead, she found herself on the far side of the banquet and, worse still, surrounded by a family of the Facesmith's enemies.

Before she could devote much time to moping, however, her highly trained nose was tantalized by a delicious smell that left hunger softly raking her stomach. A few minutes later, the white-clad servants swooped in with the first course. It was a glazed peacock filled with pineapple marinated in orange brandy. Disturbingly, the bird's head and neck had been stuffed and reattached to the roasted body, and its luxuriant tail feathers sprouted from the back. Its silvery, shocked-looking glass eyes seemed to be looking directly at Neverfell, and her brain promptly became a battleground.

It looks like it's alive . . . I wonder if its eyes would be squishy if I poked them with my— no— mustn't do anything— but the meat looks like it's been varnished— I could just reach out and— no — mustn't do anything— it smells good; can I eat it now? What about now? No! Mustn't do anything! She only became aware that she was bouncing on her chair when she noticed the Childersins' gazes resting on her.

Grand Steward banquets were designed with great care, so as to allow the guests to enjoy as many True Delicacies as possible without actually dying. Thus they alternated between courses that were merely excellent and those that were dangerously extraordinary. The peacock was one of the former.

Everybody else behaved as if the servants were invisible, but Neverfell could not help marveling at the silent grace with which they moved as one, filling each glass to precisely the same level and setting dishes down with feather softness.

"They're like wonderful mice!" she whispered to Zouelle.

"They need to be," Zouelle murmured back, out of the corner of her smile. "Only the best are allowed to serve at these banquets— it's a great honor and a great responsibility. Making the slightest error would shame the Grand Steward, and that would be worth more than their lives."

"So which one *is* the Grand Steward?" Neverfell glanced around the tables, trying to see if any of them were larger and grander than the others. She suddenly realized that she had no idea what he looked like.

"Oh, he isn't down here with us," Zouelle corrected her. "He always has somewhere set aside where he can watch us without being seen. I think he's probably up there." She let her eyes flick up for a moment to point halfway up the opposite wall of the vast cavern. Following her gaze, Neverfell saw one waterfall that was larger than the rest and fell like a silver curtain before a dark recess. "They will be particularly careful now, of course. After what happened three days ago."

"What did happen?"

"Oh, yet another of his food tasters died." Zouelle folded her napkin into a simple flower shape before using one corner to dab at the corner of her mouth. "His favorite one, this time. Poison, doubtless meant for the Grand Steward himself. People do try it from time to time. I hear the Enquiry has already caught the poisoner, but it will make the Grand Steward wary."

Banquets were sounding so horribly dangerous that Neverfell was starting to wonder why anybody ever went to them. Then she took her first mouthful of the peacock, and decided that she had found at least one good reason to take the risk. Between mouthfuls, however, she could not help leaning over to Zouelle with questions.

"Who are those?" Neverfell realized that there was one table that had been set up on a separate little island away from the main gathering. The gaggle of men and women seated at it did not seem to be dressed for the occasion, or, in fact, any occasion that Neverfell could easily imagine. Several wore lantern hats of the sort many donned when wandering deep and obscure caves where the traps seldom grew. A couple of them had pushed aside their cutlery so that they could set down a device that looked a lot like a huge steel trifle, covered in whirring dials. To her chagrin, Neverfell was too far away to deduce the fascinating device's purpose, but to judge by the zeal with which the strange men were beating it with hammers, it was not doing what it should. "What's wrong with them? And why aren't they doing etiquette?"

"Oh, the rules are different for them," answered Zouelle. "They're Cartographers."

"They look a bit mad," whispered Neverfell.

"Oh no," Zouelle corrected her. "They're very, *very* mad. All Cartographers and mapmakers are."

"Why?"

"Well, the way Uncle puts it, mapmaking is all very well if you're dealing with somewhere flat, like an overground landscape. The problem with Caverna is that it isn't flat. It goes up and down and slants and narrows and spirals round itself and bursts into huge caverns and meets itself going the other way. So—you know the crinkly edible bit inside a walnut? Well, suppose you had to draw a flat picture of the surface of that."

There was a small pause while Neverfell went cross-eyed trying to imagine it.

"And now," continued Zouelle relentlessly, "imagine that you are trying to map the biggest, crinkliest, most complicated walnut in the world—that's Caverna. Cartographers have to twist their brains a certain way to understand even part of it, and afterward their brains don't untwist. The maddest ones spend half the time pot-holing and the rest of it squeaking like bats. There are a few slightly saner ones you can talk to, but it's not a good idea."

"Why?"

"Because if you talk to them long enough, you start to

understand them, and then after a short while you don't really understand anything else. You run off to be a Cartographer and next thing you know, you're bat-squeaking."

"So, if they're mad and dangerous, why are they here?"

"Because the Grand Steward invites everybody important to his banquets, and Cartographers *are* important. Essential, really. They're the only people who can tell you where it's safe to dig new tunnels, where you'll end up when you do, and if the existing tunnels are in danger of falling down. Now sit up straight, Neverfell; people are staring."

Following Zouelle's gaze, Neverfell realized that here and there among the crowded tables she could make out a faint star of light. With a frisson, she realized that each of them was trap-light winking off opera glasses and lorgnettes, all apparently pointed toward her. For some reason, she did indeed seem to be attracting attention.

"Quick, here comes the next course!" Zouelle told her. "This is the first real course, a True Delicacy. Make sure you eat one of the moth biscuits first to clean away the taste of the last course."

The moth biscuits tasted a bit dusty and mothy, and made Neverfell want to sneeze so badly she only stopped herself by gripping her own nose firmly with one napkin-covered hand. Afterward, she couldn't taste anything at all.

The newly arrived True Delicacy was a pale gold jelly in the shape of a tiny castle, complete with turrets. Embedded in it were what looked like beautifully crafted models of tiny birds with jewel-colored plumage and long beaks. Neverfell was leaning forward to peer when she saw one twitch slightly, sending a quiver through the jelly.

"Zouelle!" she gasped in horror. "That one's alive!" The jelly on the table began shivering from head to foot as more and more tiny wings tried to flutter. "Oh, they're all alive! We have to get them out!" She had to be pulled down into her chair by Zouelle's restraining hand.

"Don't! They'll be out in a moment, I promise! If you try to spoon them out you'll wake them up too quickly and they'll choke. Wait and see—they'll be fine."

It was all Neverfell could do to stay in her seat, her mind full of how horrible it must be to have one's eyes and ears and beak full of jelly, and to have one's wings not work without knowing why. But as she watched, something altered in the jelly castle. It started to soften and subside, and the birds' wing trembles grew more determined, and then, as one, all the little birds burst free, leaving ragged holes in the quivering mass, their wings beaded with sticky gold.

Neverfell followed them with her eyes. "I hope they get out," she muttered. "I hope the trap-lanterns don't eat them."

A tiny spoonful of the jelly was placed on her plate. Gingerly, she dipped the tip of her tongue into it. The taste was a sound, a thin ribbon of blue-silver sounds blended together into a single melody so loud and vivid that she looked around for the orchestra. The tune was the most haunting she had ever encountered, and she thought she heard in it a song of loss, confusion, and remembered skies.

She could hear the rest of the family talking about the jelly.

". . . wonderful, how the birds remain unharmed . . ."

". . . have to steep them in the jelly for a year and a day so it absorbs their song, then it takes another year to reorder the notes into real music . . ."

Tiny bird-shapes with long beaks were just visible, flitting about the corners of the cavern, their wings a whirr and their shadows thrown large and rippled on the wall. They uttered not a chirrup, trill, or keen. The spoon trembled in Neverfell's hand.

It was at this point that her attention was distracted by the peculiar behavior of a richly dressed, gray-haired man on another table. In the middle of a conversation, his head wobbled comically, and he opened his mouth wide as if preparing to bellow something across the table. Instead of doing so, however, he rocked back and then made a determined attempt to plant his face in his jelly. He was thwarted in this at the last moment by the two guests next to him, who placed hurried hands on his shoulders and caught him just before his beard grazed the plate.

The whole thing was so clownish that Neverfell could not suppress a snort of mirth. Fortunately this was covered by a slightly louder laugh from Maxim Childersin, who was looking the same way.

"Oh, that is quite beautiful. Masterful. I did wonder if something like that would happen."

It seemed that the man was being helped out of his chair, and carried back to his boat, his arms over the shoulders of two of his companions. His head lolled forward, and his dragging toes left matching grooves in the sand. The laughter inside Neverfell died a death.

"Is that man all right?"

"Oh goodness, no. Did you see the bird flitting around near his ear just before he collapsed? Somebody who knew about the jelly course in advance must have bought and trained a bird of the same sort before the banquet, then released it mid-course. It would have been primed to hunt down a particular person and jab them with its beak. With so many birds flitting around, nobody would notice an extra one, or wonder whether it had poison on its beak."

"Somebody hired the Zookeeper, you think?" suggested one of the other Childersin uncles.

"It certainly looks like his work," agreed Maxim Childersin. "Trained animals, poison . . . yes, I think so. Very elegant."

Neverfell could think of lots of other words to describe such a murder, and she had a horrible feeling that all of them were printed across her face. And yet although she understood in her head that she had just watched a man die, she could not really believe it. It had all seemed like something from a pantomime, and everybody around her was so calm and amused.

"Why didn't his friends do anything? Why did they just quietly carry him away?" she whispered.

"Making a fuss would be far more disastrous. The death will look like a heart attack, and they cannot suggest it is anything else without casting aspersions on the Grand Steward's birds."

As Neverfell digested this, she realized that her reaction had not gone unnoticed. Seated a few tables away were two women well dressed in peach and gold brocade. One of them was desperately peering across at Neverfell with a sketchbook in her hand. The other seemed to be suffering some kind of apoplexy.

"Zouelle, who are those women?"

"Facesmiths," whispered Zouelle, and spared Neverfell a confidential smirk. "Poor dears. They've never seen anyone who can—oh! Neverfell! Hands in your lap, back straight, here comes the next course!"

And the next was followed by the next and then the next, each heralded by a different captivating scent. A quail-and-cranberry pie led to a cordial of cloud and elderberry and then a huge tureen of turtle and thyme soup. With trepidation Neverfell realized that the time of the Stackfalter Sturton's debut was arriving. She knew she should be more worried about her own grand introduction to Court society, but when she thought of the trouble that had gone into the great cheese she felt a bit like a mother whose child is about to step onto the stage in front of hundreds of onlookers.

"They will be bringing out a True Wine to suit it and prepare the palate," Zouelle murmured as she reached for another moth biscuit. "Not one of ours, I'm afraid. Something from the Ganderblack family, who have not been seeing eye to eye with us *at all*. And Ganderblack Wines are always so treacherous and aggressive."

Tiny crystal goblets were placed before each person, and the carvers were swiftly replaced by bottle-bearers. The liquid within each bottle was a deep and stormy mauve. Only when the corks were eased free did Neverfell start to understand what Zouelle meant. The Wine did not slop around like ordinary liquid but moved smokily and stealthily, coiling up the inside of the bottle and trying to snake over the lip. The waiters managed to keep it in the bottle through a set of amazingly agile twists, jerks, tilts, and arm waggles. Once tipped into the goblets it seemed to become calmer.

Neverfell was just marveling at the skill of the young male servant who had succeeded in pouring the prowling Wine into her goblet, when a single rebellious drop slipped from the mouth and down the neck of the bottle. It fell to the pure white cloth, leaving a brilliant purple splotch.

The young man froze, staring at the spot. His blandly polite expression did not waver, but Neverfell heard him give a tiny, ragged gasp of pure horror and mortal terror. Immediately she remembered Zouelle saying that making the smallest mistake was worth more than a servant's life.

It didn't even feel like a decision. There was a thing to do and Neverfell did it. She flicked the back of her hand at her goblet, knocking it over, so that the Wine flooded out across the tablecloth, swamping and hiding the spilled drop before anybody else could see it.

The *thonk* of the goblet hitting the table was muted and yet terribly loud. Her knuckles still stinging from the chill of the crystal, Neverfell felt silence flood from that one sound through the feast, like the purple tide across the cloth. The next moment, awareness of what she had just done hit her like a bucketful of ice water.

Neverfell's gaze crept up to the faces of Zouelle and the other Childersins. All of them had frozen and were staring paralyzed at the spreading stain. Half of them had apparently forgotten how to breathe. The servants halted mid-motion, then as one they melted away from the table.

All over the island, conversation had been replaced by an eerie hush. From every table, frozen Faces watched entranced as the priceless Wine dripped off the edge of the table. Forgotten forks hovered where they had halted halfway to open mouths.

They know. They all know it wasn't an accident. They can see it in my face.

Fearfully, Neverfell glanced across at Maxim Childersin. He still wore a wryly attentive smile, but it meant nothing. He was not looking in Neverfell's direction. Instead, he was gazing out with unblinking watchfulness toward the distant waterfall that Neverfell had been told hid the Grand Steward. Following his gaze, Neverfell thought for a moment that she glimpsed traces of movement behind the curtain of water, perhaps even the silhouette of a human shape.

"Neverfell, take the gondola back to the sedan. The servants will see you home." Childersin's order was too quiet and too calm to be questioned for an instant.

Shaky with shock and mortification, Neverfell rose, not daring to look at Zouelle, and fled back toward the boat, her head bowed and her green satin shoes hobbling awkwardly on the false sand. She could not bring herself to look back as the gondola carried her away, until the stalactites hid the scene of her crime from view.

Thus it was that Neverfell did not see what happened next.

The servants were in instant, voiceless motion. The strange girl's action had torn a hole in the beautifully woven fabric of the banquet, a hole in a dozen conversations. The hole had to be filled. The Stackfalter Sturton had to be brought in early. Half a dozen men ran out to the little icehouse where the great cheese was waiting, to collect it and bring it in. The two guards placed to watch it blinked at them in mute confusion when they arrived, but there was no time for explanation. The door was opened, and the great covered dish heaved onto its trolley and wheeled out across the little bridge onto the dining island.

As the trolley emerged, light gleaming on the four-foot-wide silver dish cover, dozens of courtiers braced themselves, ready to don what they hoped would be suitable Faces for such a masterpiece. Rumor had spread of underhanded attempts to steal parts of it, and that had just increased its fame.

There was a pause, and then the great dish cover was tweaked away.

Nobody was ever quite sure what to expect from a True Cheese. What they definitely did not expect, however, was the sight of a short and stocky figure, clad from head to foot in slatted metal scales, which raised a goggled head, leaped from the dish, and sprinted across the island. Sheer shock froze the guards for an all-important second, and by the time they were racing to intercept the strange figure, it had dived cleanly into the water of the lagoon. No bubbles rose to the surface and neither did the stranger.

After a few seconds most watchers realized that even a True Cheese was very unlikely to do that. In the ensuing gondola search, no sign could be found of the bizarre figure. Furthermore, there was no sign of the Sturton, except for a few crumbs of rind and strands of moss. At last the truth dawned.

The Kleptomancer had struck again, and this time had stolen from the Grand Steward himself.

DESPERATE DEEDS

NOBODY SAID ANYTHING TO CHIDE NEVERFELL
when she arrived back at the Childersin house, but she noticed
the fraction of a second each servant paused in surprise before
rushing to take her coat and gloves. She was not expected back
yet. An early return could only mean disgrace.

She fled to her room, but the very sight of it was a reproach
to her, a reminder of the Childersins' kindness. Instead, she crept
down and found a hiding place in a little storeroom just off the
main hall. There she hunched amid the brooms and grub-sacks,
limp with self-disgust. Nobody seemed to be hunting for her,
no doubt supposing her still in her room, so she was left in the
unkind company of her thoughts.

Stupid, so stupid! So much for her promises to do nothing.
Had she really thought that the Childersins could make something
new of her, just by combing her hair and putting her in a nice
dress? No, she was still Neverfell, gangling around like a crane
fly and breaking everything. Not only had she failed to learn
anything about her own history but she had brought trouble on
the very people who had tried to help her.

The only form of disgrace Neverfell really knew was Grandible's anger, which blew over if you hid for long enough or let him rage. But this was not a crisis that would burn itself out or get distracted by Stilton. Worse still, she was still not sure what exactly she had done, nor what it would mean. How much trouble had she created for herself? For Zouelle? For the Childersin family?

The open chink of the storeroom door gave her a view of the hall, and thus she was in a good position to watch when, two hours later, the Childersin group returned. Neverfell glimpsed Zouelle's blonde plait and pale face passing by, and did not know how she could face the other girl. Even worse, however, was the thought of having to explain herself to Maxim Childersin.

She braced herself and waited for him to pass her hiding place, in the hope that she could read something—anything—in his manner. Face after face passed, however, until the faces ran out, and she felt a creeping dawn of horror. She had been ready to see him brisk, or striding, or taciturn, or wearing a dangerous mask of good humor. She had not been prepared to find him missing. The Childersins had returned, but they had done so without their patriarch.

What have I done? Oh no — what have I done?

As it turned out, Neverfell had found herself a hiding hole well placed for hearing answers to that question.

The front door was barely shut before the Childersins erupted into argument, for all the world as if they were responding to an agreed signal. They still wore their banquet clothes and their polite-dinner Faces, but their voices were so savagely bitter that Neverfell barely knew them.

"Quiet!" One voice gained ascendancy for a moment. Neverfell thought it belonged to Maxim Childersin's oldest adult nephew. "We need to make plans *right now*. Do you really think Maxim will be coming back from that 'private audience with the Grand

Steward'? He won't. He's gone, and unless we act fast the rest of us will be next for the blade. Do you remember the last time somebody showed contempt for the Grand Steward's hospitality, by dropping a fig on the floor? That was the end of the whole Jeroboam clan."

"So what do we do?" snapped one of Zouelle's aunts. "Nobody is going to believe that little cheese-girl spilled the Ganderblack Wine of her own accord. And even if they did, we're still responsible for her actions." There was a furor of agreement, disagreement, recriminations.

"Everybody quiet!" shouted the oldest nephew again. "Listen! Unless we do something drastic, the Childersin dynasty comes to an end tonight. So I have just now sent emissaries to the Grand Steward and the Ganderblacks, suggesting that the Ganderblack family take over the whole Childersin legacy as compensation."

"What?" A chorus of outrage.

"It's the only way to keep the whole inheritance together. It will be run as a vassal concern, but we'll be alive."

There was a thoughtful silence.

Neverfell did not understand everything she was hearing, but the important parts were all too clear. Maxim Childersin was not coming back. Her one simple, silly action had murdered him. And now one of his nephews was selling out the family to a rival vintner family.

"The Ganderblacks won't take that mildly." Another of Zouelle's aunts, sounding uncertain. "They hate us—they'll want their pound of flesh."

"If they want a sacrificial lamb, we'll give them one," replied the nephew with a tone of smug malice. "What about Maxim's maddening little pet? It's all her fault, after all."

Neverfell gasped silently. Yes, the whole thing was her fault, but it was a different matter to hear somebody else say so, and with such chill poison in their tone. Worse still, there was a murmur of consent from the others.

"Agreed, then," declared the eldest nephew. "Clapperfland, lock the silly blonde brat in her room. We don't want to lose track of our lamb."

It took a few heartbeats for Neverfell to understand what she had heard. They were not talking about her at all. They were speaking of Zouelle. It had never occurred to Neverfell that charming, clever, beautiful Zouelle might not be loved by everybody. In fact, it had not really occurred to her at all that the denizens of the good-natured, brilliant Childersin household might not all have one another's best interests at heart.

She heard small cries of protest. Pushing the storeroom door a little farther open and peering around the corner, she saw Zouelle being manhandled down the passageway by one of her uncles.

"Wait." It was the sharp-voiced aunt once more. "When you wrote to the Ganderblacks, who did you say would be running this vassal Childersin concern for them? Not *you*, by any chance?"

The brief truce collapsed. Most of the Childersins surged for the front door, nearly bursting it off its hinges in their haste to get out, so that they could head to the Ganderblacks and make their own claim before the others. A moment later yells, horse whinnies, and the clang of blades could be heard from the street. To judge by the words shouted, the Childersins were fighting over the available horses.

It was at this point, with the door still hanging open, that Neverfell took her courage in one hand and a bucket in the other, then sprinted from cover.

The uncle dragging Zouelle down the passage was not expecting to be hit on the back of the head with a bucket. The blow was not heavy or well-aimed, but it startled him enough that he lost his grip on Zouelle's wrists. Neverfell seized the moment and one of Zouelle's hands, then sprinted for the open door, dragging the blonde girl with her into the street.

"Hey!"

Neverfell did not look back to discover which of the Childersin aunts and uncles were now in pursuit. She continued to run, hearing Zouelle's ragged breaths behind her, and wishing she had her old boots back instead of satin shoes.

It took her a moment or two to realize that there was an errand boy running alongside them, his bare feet keeping pace with her easily.

"Turn left!" snapped a familiar voice, and Neverfell obeyed. "Now right! Now duck down here through the crack!" A dozen or so turns later, he finally slowed in a small, craggy alley, halted, and listened.

"Lost 'em," he muttered, and turned at last to face Neverfell.

The errand boy was Erstwhile.

And how had Erstwhile happened to be in this particular illustrious street? The truth was he had been there, on and off, for some time. He had known that his loitering would not be remarked upon. His betters had seen only his drudge clothes, his messenger satchel, and his fly-pouch, and had known he was only a tool. They had noticed nothing else about him.

He had known Neverfell was within the house, and when at last she had erupted onto the street there had been no mistaking the red of the hair, the rapid, ungainly run. Now as they recovered their breath beside a wild trap-lantern, however, Erstwhile saw her properly for the first time.

There was no mask. There was no mask at all. Even after

hearing the rumors Erstwhile had not been prepared. *Eyes too big, too many freckles,* that was his first thought. Then Neverfell's features did things and went places, and he nearly fell over from the shock.

Across her features, anxiety, resolution, and remorse were being swamped by a surge of recognition, affection, and surprise. Seeing her smile was like being hit in the face with a big, gold gong. Then, almost immediately, he saw the smile fade a little, become diluted by hurt. She was looking for some reaction from him, some sign that he was as pleased to see her.

Erstwhile had exactly five expressions. Polite but stony calm with eyes lowered, for slipping discreetly past his betters. Respectful attentiveness for receiving orders. Keen alertness when expecting or inviting orders. Humble remorse and fearfulness for receiving criticism or punishment. And just one smile, for those times when an employer had a right to expect a show of gratitude.

This was not a day for smiles, and none of the others would fit. So he stared at her, with a blank, respectfully attentive Face, and could give her nothing more. It made him feel shabby, stupid, and angry.

Neverfell's blonde companion had dropped down to sit on a boulder, lowering her face into her shaking hands. Erstwhile cast a suspicious glance over her burgundy court dress, then took Neverfell by the arm and dragged her out of the other girl's earshot.

"So. It's true, then." It sounded like an accusation. "About your face." He could hardly bear to look at her. Her expressions changed so fast they made him feel sick. They shimmered and shifted and shone through one another. It was broken, it was all wrong.

Furthermore, the unquestioning faith and respect in Neverfell's face when she looked at him made him self-conscious. It was like seeing his own shadow stretching away from him sized out of all proportion, like that of a giant. *So that's what I look like in Neverfell's world. A giant.*

"Yes . . . I . . . Listen, Erstwhile—"

"You never told me your face could do that," he muttered fiercely. "I listened to your nattering for hours. For years. And the one interesting thing about you? You never mentioned it. Not once. Didn't you trust me?" He found that he was really angry. Neverfell wasn't supposed to have Faces! Just that one velvet mask-Face, which had always made him feel better about only having five.

"I didn't know!" protested Neverfell. "Master Grandible never told me—there weren't any mirrors—how was I to know I wasn't just wearing a mask because I was ugly?"

"Dropped me fast enough, though, didn't you? All these years, I been making myself late for my other errands, hanging around your parlor answering your dopey bloody questions, 'cos I felt sorry for you, and knew you were lonely and a bit crazy. But the moment you got yourself some Craftsmen friends you can't spare two minutes to talk to me, even when I've got an urgent message. No, then it's 'Miss Neverfell sends her regrets, but has an engagement and is busy with her toilette.'"

"What? You . . . you came to the house to see me?"

"They didn't tell you?" Erstwhile sighed. "No. I should have guessed."

In the kaleidoscope that was Neverfell's face, he could see her thoughts dance with shocking vividness. *The Childersins hid things from me. Oh, no, they can't have done. Perhaps they forgot to tell me about— But they are all different from what I thought . . . Perhaps they really . . . Oh no, no, I can't believe it . . .*

"Oh, shut up and believe it!" he hissed, answering the unspoken thought. "They been keeping you in a box, and the last thing they want is you getting messages from old man Grandible! That's why they kept sending me away!"

"You've brought a message from—"

"Yeah, Master Grandible's been worried sick about you. Been writing to the Enquiry to overturn the indenture and get you back as his apprentice."

"No!" Neverfell twisted her hands together. "Tell him he can't! I did something terrible at the banquet, and I'll just bring trouble on anybody in charge of me! Maxim Childersin was kind to me and now he's probably being executed, and Zouelle over there was going to be a sacrificial lamb, and now the rest of the family is turning on one another. Erstwhile, I don't need rescuing! Everybody needs rescuing from me!"

"Stop!" Erstwhile took hold of Neverfell's shoulders and did his best to meet her eye, while her expressions moved like flames. "You listen to me. This is what's *really* happening. Everybody in Caverna has heard about you knocking over that Wine, and everybody's trying to guess who got you to do it. Most of them think it was a distraction to help the Kleptomancer steal the Stackfalter Sturton."

"*What?*"

"Didn't you know? Yeah, he found a way to steal every crumb. But nobody blames *you*. Because that would be like blaming a hat. Or a stick. Or a chess piece. To them, you're just a thing. A new thing that's got everybody talking. And you know what? Right now half the Court is quarreling about who gets to *buy* you if the Childersins go under."

"But it *is* my fault." Again Neverfell's face became painful to watch as her thoughts started their crazy carousel again. *Faces shouldn't do that,* thought Erstwhile furiously. *You're supposed to see 'em, not feel 'em.* "Nobody told me to spill the Wine. *I* brought all this trouble on them. Just me."

"You sure? You don't know what Court folk are like." Erstwhile gave up and dropped his gaze. Looking at Neverfell was just too jarring. "They pull people about like puppets. Particularly the older ones. Don't trust anybody over a hundred and fifty years old, particularly if they look thirty. Anybody who gets that old in Caverna loses something, and they don't get it back. They can't feel properly anymore. They're hollow inside, and all they got left is a hunger—a hunger to feel. They're like . . . great big trap-lanterns, all blind gaping need, and thousands of teeth, with decades to come up with tricks and schemes.

"That goes for your precious Master Childersin too. You think he took you in out of kindness? He didn't. I don't know what he's playing at, but he's playing, mark my words. Nobody here is being kind to you. *Nobody.*" He could not help glancing across at the blonde girl just out of earshot. "You got to get clear of 'em *all,* then cut and run. Head back to Grandible. Or hole up somewhere, and send a message to me at Sallow's Elbow if you find yourself in a spot."

"Erstwhile." Neverfell's voice was very small. "I can't. I . . . I have to go to the palace. So I can save Master Childersin."

"Have you gone Cartographic?" exploded Erstwhile. "If you go to the palace, they'll have your head on a block! Who came up with that plan—the Childersin girl?"

"No. It's my idea." Neverfell's voice sounded somewhat tremulous. "Listen—I can tell the Grand Steward that Master Childersin had nothing to do with me spilling the Wine. And everybody will have to believe me, won't they? Because my face shows what I'm thinking. I can't lie. And then Master Childersin can go home and stop his family from tearing one another apart—"

"Stop it!" spat Erstwhile. "You don't owe this Childersin family anything, don't you understand that? It's their own juice they're stewing in. Have you listened to a word I've said? What's wrong with you? Don't you believe me?"

"I . . . I do . . . I know you wouldn't lie to me." Neverfell sounded miserable and distressed. "All these years . . . you've been my best friend. My only friend."

Erstwhile heard the sad, numb little confession, and dug his fingernails into his palms.

"Don't be such a puddle-head," he snapped. "I've lied to you. Lots of times. You asked me about things I didn't know and I made things up. I made things up about me too. Hundreds of them. And you got no idea which bits were the lies, have you?

"I lied to you and it was easy, because you believe everybody means what they say. Everyone's lying to you, Neverfell. Everyone. And you can't tell, because you're just not very bright when it comes to people. Brighten up fast, or you're done for."

He did not look at her. He did not need to. Over the years she had built a special palace of the mind for him, and he had helped lay every brick. Now he could feel its golden walls tumbling. If he looked into her face, he would see hurt, bewilderment, and the painful, necessary birth of doubt.

He turned away before she could answer, and was soon running off down the labyrinth of tunnels. Drudge boy running an errand, eyes obediently lowered.

Of course I lied to you all these years, he told Neverfell in his head. *For the same reason I had to tell you the truth just now.*

You're the only real friend I've ever had, you stupid little hen.

. . . . .

In the heart of Caverna, the thronging thoroughfares at last yielded to a broad avenue of marble, flanked by well-guarded colonnades. At the far end of this could be glimpsed a vast door with matching portcullis, the only entrance into the elite labyrinth of courtyards and pleasure rooms that formed the Grand Steward's palace.

Toward this portcullis walked two girls, one a straight-backed blonde girl in a torn burgundy dress, the other red-haired, jittery, and fretting at her green silk sleeves.

"Are you ready?" asked Zouelle in an undertone. She seemed to be having some trouble meeting Neverfell's eye.

"What if they show me in to see the Grand Steward?" whispered Neverfell.

"They won't," Zouelle declared, and then hesitated. "And if they do . . . call him 'Your Excellency.' Remember that if the Grand Steward's right eye is open, he will be cold but fair, but if his left eye is open, that is a time when people fall in or out of favor. If both eyes are open, then you are of special interest to him."

Neverfell's knees felt like custard and her heart galloped as they approached one of the white-clad palace guards. He turned a cold and uninviting Face upon her.

"Excuse . . . excuse me? My name is Neverfell. I . . . I knocked over the Ganderblack Wine at the banquet. I need to give evidence—I've come to turn myself in."

HALF-LIFE

THE GRAND STEWARD WAS DYING.

There was nothing precisely wrong with his body. It was, in fact, unusually healthy and strong, though it had become strange over time. His heart beat slowly and steadily, strengthened by the juice of a hundred carefully chosen herbs that flowed with his blood. No, the problem was his mind, or more accurately his soul. Try as he might, he could not stop the life gradually seeping from it and leaving it grayly numb.

His senses had never faded with age. On the contrary, over the years he had used specific spices to sharpen them. He could gaze upon a particular deep shade of green and pick out every nuance of the color. *Zeluppian Fern Green,* his mind would inform him.

Gray, said his soul. *Just a shade of gray with a greenish name.*

His well-trained tongue could pick out every flavor of a sweetmeat. *Honey from bees fed only cowslip nectar,* his mind would tell him, *with cherries marinated for twenty-one years in peach-and-saffron brandy.*

Ash, said his soul. *Ash and dust.*

Even the continual battle to stay alive, to avoid assassination by the hungry and ambitious, no longer made him feel alive as it once had. The danger no longer gave him a thrill; the battle of wits offered no surge of the blood. Now there was only a cold and heavy dread that death would bring not release but an eternity of greater monotony, that he would find himself trapped in a lifeless body, with a mind that was fading mote by mote, blind, deaf, dumb, numb, and powerless against the march of the gray.

And yet, yesterday, he had almost felt something. He had sat behind the crystal curtain of the waterfall, his sharp ears catching every sordid whisper at every table, each a tiresome scribble across the marble of his mind. Then the tedium had been broken, a goblet had been tipped over, and his attention had been dragged to the figure of a girl who had jumped to her feet as purple Wine spread across the table before her. He could not now recall what she had looked like, but he remembered the torrent of feelings that had blazed, ached, and flickered across her face. Shock, guilt, regret, horror, self-consciousness—for a moment he had almost remembered what it was like to feel these things. His mind had flinched from the flame of the Real.

And now the Enquiry told him that this very girl had turned herself in at the gate. He would send for her, and perhaps he would find that her facial antics had all been a cunning piece of theatrics, a natural-looking montage of Faces prepared by some clever Facesmith to impress and deceive everyone. Yes, it was probably so. Nothing in Caverna happened naturally or without planning.

Despite this, as he waited in his marble-tiled reception chamber, he felt something sluggish stirring in his soul, something that in another heart might have been hope.

Flanked by guards, Neverfell walked through the palace down corridors of malachite. For hours she had been kept in an antechamber, her mind a snowstorm, and now that she had been summoned forth without explanation she did not know whether to be terrified or relieved.

The events of the last day had flung open great doors in her head, and now big windy thoughts were blowing in from all directions and throwing everything into a mess. Strangely, the thoughts that had haunted her most were the images of Erstwhile storming off stony-faced, and Master Grandible sitting alone in his reeking tunnels.

At the end of the corridor were twinned doors, flanked by two figures dressed in black and dark green. Their black silk blindfolds revealed them to be perfumiers. Neverfell's eye traveled perplexed over the twinned swords at the belt of each. As she approached, they held up a hand to halt her and sniffed, slowly and carefully. Apparently satisfied, they then stepped back and pulled open the doors. She walked through, and heard the doors close behind her.

The dimness of the room she had entered made it seem even larger than it was. The ceiling was high-vaulted, intricately carved arches rising from twin rows of pale pillars; the apex was lost in gloom. The only light came from a chandelier that hung over a desk at the far end of the room. Behind the desk sat three figures, a woman and two men. Most of their faces were in shadow, the lanterns above them making bright slabs of their foreheads and upper cheeks.

"Come forward."

Neverfell could not even be sure which of the three had spoken. The floor between her and the waiting figures had a glossy shimmer and slithered under her shoe soles. There were mother-of-pearl pictures inlaid in the pale stone of the pillars, and as Neverfell passed them the light seemed to shiver across them, as if in apprehension. In the shadow cast by the pillars, she thought she saw motionless figures standing flush against the wall and watching her every motion.

She could see the mist of her breath as she drew closer to the desk. Above, two of the chandelier traps stirred with restless hunger, flickering and flashing as they snapped at each other. In the gloom behind the threesome a vast banner sagged against the wall. Beneath it lurked a white marble throne, on which was seated the pale gray statue of a man, his pensive gaze half turned away.

"Do you know how long it takes to prepare a perfect Cardlespray Wine?"

Neverfell jumped, and tried to scrabble a handful of her wits. Amid the chill silence she had almost started to feel that she was the only living thing in the room. It was the middlemost figure who had spoken, a man whose eyes were mere sparks in deep diamond-shaped hollows, and whose hair had thinned to a gauze of well-combed wisps. Was this the Grand Steward? His voice had an irritable bite to it, as if Neverfell were a vexing scrap caught between his teeth.

"I . . . no . . ."

"One hundred and three years." The woman's voice was like molten chocolate, dark and warm, but there was no emotion in it. "The grapes spoil if they are exposed to loud noises, so they are tended by a silent order of monks, and all the local birds are killed. The fruit can be harvested only at night during the new moon, and must be crushed by the feet of orphans. The barrels are stored deep in the earth, and only the softest, sweetest music is played to them, continually, for over a century. And after all this, the Wine is fit to be drunk . . . unless somebody throws it over a table."

"I . . ." There was nothing Neverfell could say. She could not promise to reharvest the grapes, trample them into Wine by moonlight, and then play harp music to it for a century.

"Do you know why a vandal is worse than a thief?" asked the man on the right, in a soft growl. "A thief steals a treasure from its owner. A vandal steals it from the world."

"I didn't . . ." She trailed off. *I didn't mean to.* But she had meant to.

"Who is your master?" demanded the central man. "Whose orders were you following?"

"Nobody! There weren't any orders!"

During the icy silence, Neverfell could almost see the barrage of questions arcing in a dark cloud toward her. Next moment they fell thick and fast as arrows.

"What did the Childersin family promise you if you did this?"

"Nothing! They didn't . . . They—"

"What was the rest of the plan?"

"There wasn't any—nobody planned it—*I* didn't plan—I just—"

"You just what? Why? You spilled the Cardlespray knowingly, deliberately. Why?"

Neverfell's mouth fell open, but she could not seem to breathe. There was a pain in her eyes and throat that wanted to become tears. The panel would see through any lie she told, and this was the one question she could not answer truthfully, not without giving away the servant whose error she had risked everything to hide.

The only good thing about the spilled Wine is that maybe I saved that man. And if I tell them about it now, even that will be undone.

"I'm sorry." Neverfell gulped. Her eyes felt warm, and tears tumbled helplessly over her cheeks.

"What was that? Louder!"

"I'm . . . I'm sorry. But I can't tell you."

"What?"

The floodgates broke open. All three interrogators were on their feet and bellowing. Neverfell flinched and twitched as bellowed questions struck and sliced at her. She clutched her hands to the sides of her head to steady herself, shaking like a leaf. The craziness of panic was only a few gasps away.

"You're wrong!" she screamed, desperation making her bold. "You're all wrong! Nobody told me to do it—nobody did anything but me! And I didn't plan it—it just happened, and I can't tell you why! I just can't!"

While she stood panting, the statue of the man on the throne moved his head slightly, and in the darkness beneath his brow a frost-spark of light glimmered in a human eye.

It was no statue. It was a living man. His stillness and lack of color had led Neverfell to mistake him for stone. As she watched, the middlemost of her interrogators cast a glance over his shoulder, as if for instruction, and saw the throned man's left hand move very slightly, the little finger executing a tiny gesture. The interrogator's demeanor changed, and when he turned to face Neverfell once more his face was calmly inscrutable.

"Come closer," he said.

Everything changed before Neverfell's eyes. The threesome at the desk were still forbidding and fearsome, but now she saw them for what they were—cat's-paws, mouthpieces, a curtain between her and the true source of power. As she drew nearer to the desk, she could not stop her eye from straying to the figure on the throne.

His skin was smooth, unwrinkled, and bluish white, but even from a distance Neverfell could make out a faint network of glistening lines all over it, as though he were inlaid with pearly patterns like the pillars. From a distance his long hair had looked white, but as she got closer she realized that each strand was like a thread of glass. His fingernails had an iridescent mother-of-pearl sheen.

He was seated at an angle on his throne, so that the left-hand side of his body and face were turned toward the room. It was his left eye that watched her with frosted, unblinking tenacity. What she could see of his features was set in an expression both slumberous and attentive, as if he were listening to cunningly played music of great beauty.

The right half of his face and body was largely obscured by shadow and the angle. However, in the darkness beneath his right brow she glimpsed the pale curve of a closed lid. His right eye was shut.

If his left eye is open, Zouelle had told her, *that is a time when people fall in or out of favor.*

Could this still be a trick?

The Grand Steward stared at the red-haired girl, who trembled like a harp string, face still flushed from the shock of her own shouting.

In her face he saw terror. Evasion. Defiance. Outrage. Desperation. She looked at him, and the green mirrors of her eyes showed him his own silvery strangeness, his fierce lifelessness. Fear. Curiosity. Recoil.

Could somebody really have schooled her to blunder in with such expressions, clumsy and unwelcome as mud on a puppy's paws? And could any Facesmith really have supplied her with this blinding torrent of Faces?

He saw her with one eye and with half his mind. Surrounded by deceit and conspiracy as he was, the Grand Steward could not afford to lower his guard, and so a hundred years before, he had given up on sleep. Since then he had only allowed the right and left sides of his mind to slumber in turn.

Today it was the right half of his mind that was awake. Due to some strange alchemy of the body that still baffled him, this meant that it was the left half of his body that he could feel and move, the left eye he could train upon the oddity before him. Most of his underlings did not understand such subtleties, of course. They knew only that he had two aspects, and quietly referred to them as Left-Eye and Right-Eye among themselves.

Because the Grand Steward was Left-Eye today, he could not remember the girl's name, nor could he have put what he saw into sentences. Only Right-Eye could truly manage language, and when he fell asleep words simply fell apart, scattering their letters like the beads of broken necklaces. Left-Eye, however, could see patterns behind details. It saw the expression behind the features, the music behind the notes, the conspiracy behind the odd details and coincidences.

And yes, there was conspiracy here. Everything that had brought this girl before him today was part of somebody's game. He could almost see it arching away behind her like a poison rainbow.

But did she know? Was she genuine or a fraud? He had given the signal, and soon he would find out.

Neverfell stiffened. Somewhere behind her, she thought she heard the faintest of sounds, like a squeak of a hasty step on the glass floor. She spun around. There was nobody behind her, though she thought she saw a figure slip back into the shadow of the nearest pillar.

A few yards away from her, however, sat a chest of tortoiseshell wood, its catch toward her.

Neverfell turned to face the desk once more, hoping for guidance, but the threesome seated behind it had settled into an eerie stillness, all wearing the same stony, immovable Face. Again, Neverfell had the uncanny feeling that she was the only living thing in the room.

"Do you want me to open it?"

There was no response. Warily she tiptoed over to it and dropped to her knees. The latch was cold beneath her fingertips. Her shadow lolled over the chest's lid. And she knew, as she always knew such things, that she had to open it, whether she liked it or not. Even now that dark oblong of the unknown within it was tugging at her hands.

She clicked the catch back and opened the chest. It was dark within, but seemed to be empty. Then she glimpsed movement inside, a dark, frail scuttle. She shuffled to one side to let the light from behind her fall on the chest, just in time to see two long, eyelash-thin wisps appear above the rim, waving in a questing, predatory fashion. The next instant the owner of these wisps leaped onto the back of her hand.

"Ow!" A vicious stab of pain shot through Neverfell's wrist. It was a full-grown cavern spider, large enough to span her hand with its legs, and it had bitten her just where her glove ended. She dashed the spider off reflexively with her other hand, and was repelled to see two crushed legs left behind. A warning tickle in her collar sent her slapping at her neck and shoulders, only to feel another bite on her ankle. Another spider on her skirt, another on her right arm, and more crawling out of the box.

Neverfell staggered away from the chest, swatting, slapping, and shaking herself, yelping each time the spiders got inside her clothes and their mandibles found flesh. It was a good five minutes before she slumped exhausted near the foot of one of the pillars, covered with bites but at last satisfied that she was free from her many-legged attackers.

Recovering her breath, she looked up toward the seated threesome and the unspeaking figure behind them.

On the desk before the woman sat something on a bone-china plate. It was squat, round, and marble white, with little pleats and plumes of pink icing.

"Do you like cake?" asked the woman, still in her deep, molten voice. "This has raspberries in it."

Neverfell stared at it with uncertainty and dread. Somehow the cake was more confusing and alarming than the spiders. *Yes, ma'am, I like raspberry cake, only I like it better with no poison or scorpions in it.*

"It is just cake," the woman reassured her. "You can choose to take it. Or . . ."

Or?

Slowly, Neverfell turned her head, and found that the spider chest had gone. At some point while she had been freeing herself of their scuttling forms, it had been removed and replaced with a smaller box of red teak, carved with zigzag patterns.

If it's really just cake, then it's safe. Why would she lie? If they want me dead, they can just have me executed. All I need to do is take the cake.

And yet somehow Neverfell found herself edging hesitantly toward the chest. She rubbed her hands down her dress to wipe the sweat from her palms, then reached trembling fingers to unfasten the mysterious box.

The lid flipped back, and a silver snake slithered out with dainty menace. Neverfell sprang to her feet and sprinted away.

There was a low whistle from a darkened corner of the room, and the escapee turned about and skimmed its way toward the sound in a silent slalom.

When it showed no sign of returning, Neverfell dared to peer out from behind the pillar where she had been hiding.

The raspberry cake still sat before the motionless interrogators. In the place of the snake box was a finely carved ivory cask. Nobody said a word. The question hung in the air. The cake . . . or . . .

I don't want to see what's in it, I don't want to, I don't, I . . . oh no.

The third cask was filled with grayish crystals that flared into searing flame as soon as she opened the box, followed by a sour and choking smoke that sandpapered her throat and left her sightless for ten minutes afterward.

The fourth box held what looked a lot like human eyes.

The fifth box was empty, but covered in a glistening moist veneer that soaked through her gloves and burned her skin when she touched it, and left her fingers swelling even after she tore off her gloves.

The sixth was a music box that started playing once open, each note making a different tooth vibrate so painfully she thought they might shatter.

An hour later, Neverfell was hunched on the floor, tear-streaked, stung, bitten, singed, and nauseous, shoulders jumping with sob after sob. She was still having trouble seeing, particularly through her right eye. Once again, she was in the deathly hush between boxes. Soon she would have to brace herself, look up, and see the next box . . .

There was no box. The cake had vanished from the table as well. All three of the interrogators had turned their heads and were regarding the stony figure on the throne. Now the silence had a waiting air, like the flex of a cavern spider's legs before its leap.

The girl was genuine. The Grand Steward no longer had any doubt.

Every time she reached for a box he had seen the fizzling of indecision, the war of fear with optimism, the tremors of compulsion, and the insatiable hunger of curiosity. And it seemed unlikely that any Facesmith had primed her with an expression appropriate for situations like dodging a Skimberslithe Whip-Adder while being offered cake.

However, her face had shown him far more than this. Watching her expression, he could almost feel the cold of the tiles through the soles of her satin shoes. As her nervous gaze flitted around the antechamber, for the first time in centuries he noticed his own pearly frescoes and saw them through fresh eyes. The incense in the air suddenly had a smell, and as her gaze traveled the room, colors bloomed for a second through the gray.

Possibilities flooded his mind. If he kept her close by, how many more things could he see through her eyes, hear through her ears, experience through her taste buds?

And this was exactly what somebody wanted him to think and feel. It was too tempting. It was too neat, this strange creature falling into his path mere days after the death of his favorite food taster. Somebody was counting on his inability to resist. The coldly logical Right-Eye would not have hesitated in the face of suspicions. One small signal to the guards, and Neverfell's story would have reached a smothered end in seconds.

But it was Left-Eye who was awake at this moment, and he found reasons to delay. Over the centuries he had used the test of the boxes a few times. You could tell a lot about a person from noting when they gave up and stopped opening boxes. Ordinary people opened the first and then no more. Optimists and slow learners might open three or four. Those who thought it might be a test of hardiness sometimes opened five or six. But all of them had stopped opening boxes eventually. All but one.

What sort of person would keep on opening boxes until they ran out? An idiot, obviously, but a special kind of idiot.

The girl seemed to sense the wavering of the invisible scales in which her destiny hung. It was painful to look at her, and it had been a while since he had known pain. The world prickled with pins and needles as if the blood were flowing back into it. She watched him with mute terror as he gave a series of small gestures, and the guards clipped neatly forward to take her away.

As soon as he had made the decision, he felt a sting of doubt. It seemed for a moment that he tasted something bittersweet on his tongue, as if he had just sipped something pleasant but poisonous.

"Where are we going?"

The guards would not answer Neverfell's questions but escorted her through ornamental corridor after ornamental corridor, her eyes and mind too bleary to appreciate them. She was not dead yet, but perhaps they had a special execution ground for people who turned down the Grand Steward's cake.

What's wrong with me? Why didn't I take the cake?

Because I knew I needed a miracle to get out of all this alive. Cake is nice, but it isn't a miracle. And so I had to hope that the whole box game wasn't a cruel joke with no right answers, and that maybe, just maybe, one of those boxes had a miracle in it, a way out. I just had to hope.

Ahead of her, the guard rapped on a gilded door, which was opened by a woman with faded features.

"Food tasters' quarters?" The guard passed the woman a scroll, which she read with a Face of polite surprise. "New recruit for you."

Conversation took place around Neverfell, and some remarks were even addressed to her, but the sentences might as well have been birdsong for all the sense she could make of them. All she could think of was two of the words she had just heard.

New recruit. Being recruited meant not being killed. That was all she knew or needed to know. Numbly she shook hands that were offered to her, and let palace servants in white show her down a narrow passage to a little box-like chamber where a small canopy bed awaited her.

Left alone in the room, she let herself drop full length onto the bed, only to find this a considerably less comfortable experience than she was expecting. There was something angular under the covers, and even as she pulled them back she knew what she would find.

Nestled upon the sheet was a small box, tiled in ivory and ebony. Neverfell crumpled and buried her face in the pillow, shaking with sobs.

It was all a trick, she thought in despair. *They wanted me to think they'd decided not to execute me, but the box test is still going on, and there will just be more and more boxes forever until one of them kills me or I go mad, or . . .*

She sat up and snatched the box, meaning to throw it away from her, but the impulse to open it was too strong. *This time it might not be snakes. If I just open enough boxes, one of them might be different . . .*

The catch gave a small click as she unfastened it. It was almost entirely empty but for a small roll of paper that fell out onto the sheet. Neverfell unrolled it and read the writing upon it.

You have won favor with Left-Eye, but Right-Eye will be harder to convince. Never joke with Right-Eye. Never waste words. Never try to lie to him. Never look like a fool.

Good luck,

A friend

CURIOSITY AND
THE CAT BURGLAR

AT ONE O'CLOCK, THE EVER-LOGICAL RIGHT-EYE
Grand Steward woke up to discover that during his sleep his
left-eyed counterpart had executed three of his advisors for
treason, ordered the creation of a new carp pool, and banned
limericks. Worse still, no progress had been made in tracking
down the Kleptomancer, and of the two people believed to be his
accomplices, both had been released from prison and one had
been appointed food taster. Right-Eye was not amused. He had
known for centuries that he could trust nobody but himself. Now
he was seriously starting to wonder about himself.

Left-Eye Grand Steward always did things for reasons, and
Right-Eye could usually even remember what they were, but they
made no sense to him. It was like trying to decipher pictures
scrawled by a madman. This girl Neverfell had been made a food
taster because . . . something to do with a poison rainbow? A
firework? A spiderweb turned inside out? It was as if the two
halves of his mind were drifting farther apart with time and losing
any ability to understand each other. Nowadays, on those rare
occasions when both were awake, it felt as if there were two

people crammed into his skull, and his left hand sometimes made strange gestures without explanation.

He called for his spymasters and asked for their report on the investigation into the theft of the Stackfalter Sturton. The results were disappointing. Somewhere between the kitchens and the banqueting hall, the cheese had simply vanished from beneath its silver dish cover, despite the armed guard placed around it.

"We will have more information soon" was the promise.

"When? When he steals the very beards from your chins? You will have information soon? It is 'soon' *now*. Very soon it will be 'later.'"

But even these words were an effort for him. He could make these grim men tremble so easily, but what was the point? The failure of others was tiring, too tiring to be worth words. Nowadays he said little but sat coldly watching his underlings fail, and fail, until he felt driven to execute them through utter weariness and disgust.

He would need to involve himself in the investigation. Until now this thief had not dared to steal from the Grand Steward or trespass upon his property. He had been a distraction for the courtiers, a bogey to keep them on edge. This latest theft had changed everything. The Kleptomancer had successfully slipped through all the defenses of a grand banquet, and stolen a dish from the Grand Steward's personal store in the most ostentatious manner possible.

The culprit had to be found, and quickly. If not, someday he might infiltrate the palace, this time in the role of assassin. Besides, the Grand Steward could never afford to be made to look foolish or weak, or the rest of the Court would start sniffing like hounds at a blood trail.

"Cancel all my audiences for the day—I shall be changing my schedule. Have my sedan made ready. Also my traveling mask, twenty guards, Master Calmnus, and a food taster." He hesitated. Memories of the previous day floated back to him murkily, like images seen through smudged and distorting glass. "The newest food taster."

Neverfell was rattled out of bed by a thunderous knocking after what felt like only an hour's sleep. Unfamiliar bed, unfamiliar room. She pulled an unfamiliar dress over her head and staggered to the door. It opened to an unfamiliar corridor full of unfamiliar and very animated people.

"She's awake!" Strange hands grabbed her by the collar, dragged her to a long, low breakfast room, dropped a bowl of lentil soup in front of her, and pushed a spoon in her hand. Somebody else started tugging a brush painfully through her hair.

"You've been summoned by the Grand Steward. We have five minutes to get you ready." Seated next to her on the bench was a lean, hollow-eyed woman with a trace of moustache, who smelled of scented smoke. Neverfell vaguely remembered her being introduced the previous day as Food Taster-in-Chief Leodora. "I hadn't expected you to be called to attend on him so soon—I'll have to go through the rules with you quickly. Are you listening?"

Neverfell nodded, albeit at an angle because the brusher was battling a particularly stubborn tangle. Fragments of the previous day were drifting back to her limp, shocked brain. She was in the tasters' quarters. These people hurrying her shoes on her feet and knotting her brown sash of office too tightly round her waist were her colleagues. Most of them were wearing Faces of careful unconcern, belied by the urgency of their actions and the way their eyes strayed again and again to her face.

I'm not executed, she thought with dazed curiosity and surprise. *Look. Look at all my limbs, all still stuck on.*

"Don't speak in his presence unless you're asked a question and he gives you permission. If you talk to him, call him 'Your Excellency.' Keep your eyes lowered. Take only a tiny piece when you're tasting, and never use your fingers, always the pins or forks they give you, so they can see for sure you've put it in your mouth.

"Don't go wandering off or talking to people. Try to avoid making friends with anybody who is not a food taster. Lots of people at Court will try to win you over, but it does not look good if you seem to be taking sides.

"The most important thing to remember is this: The food we receive in this dining hall has been checked by the Chancery of Safety. Apart from the food and drink you test for the Grand Steward when you are on duty, you must eat and drink *nothing* that does not come from this hall. Don't even drink the water from the fountains."

Neverfell swallowed her mouthful of soup. "In case . . . it contains poison?" she hazarded.

Leodora shook her head. "In case it contains a poison antidote. It is an old way of tricking a lord into thinking that food is safe when it is not. A food taster eats something without ill effect, so the lord eats it . . . and dies." The older woman reached out and pulled Neverfell's hand away from her mouth, stopping her from anxiously nibbling at her own fingertips. "Don't bite your nails. Sometimes they even try to slip antidotes into the water we use to wash our hands."

The full extent of Neverfell's new responsibilities suddenly yawned open before her. Life and death. As her eye crept across the ranks of the other tasters it crossed her mind that all of them looked rather ill, and none of them looked very old.

The butterflies returned only as Neverfell was being hurried out to a colonnade where a large sedan stood waiting, flanked by six bearers and a dozen armed guards.

She assumed that she would be walking along behind the sedan, but instead the door was opened for her. Gingerly she climbed in. She was almost surprised to find that the person inside was man-sized. Her imagination had distorted the Grand Steward overnight, so that she remembered him as a monumental shadow with one coldly gazing silver eye.

Once again she found herself caught in the icy light of the Grand Steward's gaze. Today, however, it was the right eye that regarded her. His face was divided neatly down the middle, the left side covered by a close-fitting white velvet mask. His glassy hair poured over the collar of his bear-fur coat.

With a jolt, Neverfell remembered the warning in the mysterious note she had read the night before.

Never joke with Right-Eye. Never waste words. Never try to lie to him. Never look like a fool.

Easier said than done. Neverfell was just deciding that the only way to obey these instructions was to say nothing when the Grand Steward spoke, and destroyed that plan entirely.

"The view bores my eye." His voice was a low, creaking note, and Neverfell had a sense of great effort, as if each word were a vast bell that had to be hauled and swung to be sounded. "Look out for me, and tell me of anything interesting that we pass."

The Grand Steward was seated to Neverfell's left, his open eye angled toward her. The window on his side was firmly shuttered, while hers was open.

The sedan shambled into motion, and she tried to describe what she saw, stumbling where she did not know the words. She tried all the time to keep her speech plain. *Never waste words.* As time passed, however, she could not be sure whether he was even listening.

Neverfell started to understand. *She* was the view. She was the window on the world. Through her and with her he saw cobbled fords through underground streams, ossuary doorways decorated with a thousand human bones, ladies pausing to have stone dust brushed out of their coats. She knew that she was making the golds bright, the shadows black, the reds vivid, and she could feel his gaze like a draft.

"Your questions bother me," he snapped at one point.

"I haven't asked any!" exclaimed Neverfell in panic.

"No, and I see them loitering like peddlers behind the door. Ask them and be rid of them. Quickly!"

"What's happened to Master Childersin?" It was the foremost question in Neverfell's mind.

"Acquitted of disrupting the banquet on purpose, in light of your evidence. Found guilty, however, of introducing a disruptive individual into the proceedings. Given a chance to save his skin by passing ownership of you to me, an opportunity he did not allow to go stale. Freed for now, sent home, told that there is a rope round his neck that can be pulled taut if he stumbles."

Neverfell felt some of her anxiety melt into relief. Her rash and desperate gamble had not been in vain after all. "And his family—are they still in trouble?" Zouelle's pale face was vivid in her memory.

"There are heavy black marks against their name," the Grand Steward answered coolly, "and another small slip will damn them, but they will be safe enough if they are not fools."

"And they haven't been taken over by the Ganderblacks?"

"No. Next question!"

The Childersins were out of immediate danger, and Maxim had returned to his family, which surely meant that the persecution of Zouelle would be brought to a halt. Neverfell let out a breath, and at last could turn her mind to her own situation.

"Where are we going?" she asked.

"Today we are hunting for the Kleptomancer, and those who can help us find him. Enough questions—we arrive."

Peering out through the window, Neverfell realized that she was back in the long lagoon cavern where the banquet had taken place. The sedan was very carefully lowered into a boat, which was sculled across to the island. A number of figures were waiting on the other side, and Neverfell felt her skin crawl as she recognized the purple garments that marked them out as Enquirers. Their leader hurried to the sedan to give her report, and to her horror Neverfell recognized Enquirer Treble, who had been her interrogator back at the hanging cells. Today the Enquirer was wearing Face No. 312, A Guardian at the Gray Gates, a grave and impressive expression designed to make her look formidable, reliable, and respectful all at once.

"We have a clearer picture of the crime now, Your Excellency." Enquirer Treble was doing an excellent job of keeping her eye from straying to Neverfell, which was probably just as well. "The only time the Stackfalter Sturton was unwatched was while it was locked away in an ice room mere yards from this cavern, so as to lower it to the perfect temperature for consumption. The door was guarded, so it was believed to be safe.

"It would seem the thief tunneled down into the ice room from a little-used store cave directly above it. In the storeroom we found these." She held up some grimy beakers and a tiny, fragile pair of apothecary's scales. "Whoever he is, he knows his Edible Alchemy. We think he mixed some cunning combination of Gnat-wine, Crathepepper, and Shrieking Bladdercheese. Whatever it was, it ate through two yards of stone like boiling water through chocolate.

"We also found this down in the ice room." She held up a slender metal implement with fork prongs at one end and a handle four feet long. "We believe he cut the Sturton up into pieces, and then used this fork to push them up through the hole. No doubt when this was done he was planning to climb back up himself and make away with his prize."

"So why did he change his plans?"

"We think he had no choice." The Enquirer cast a glance across at Neverfell. "After . . . somebody spilled the Ganderblack Wine, the servants panicked and decided to bring in the Sturton half an hour earlier than planned. The thief must have heard somebody unlocking the door, and realized that the only place he could hide in time was under the Sturton's dish cover."

"Then . . . it wasn't my fault!" Neverfell interrupted jubilantly. "I didn't help the Kleptomancer's plan—I interrupted it!"

"So it would seem," conceded Enquirer Treble, with a good deal of reluctance.

"Have you discovered how this thief managed to infiltrate the storerooms in the first place?" inquired the Grand Steward. "Or, for that matter, how he managed to escape after diving into the lagoon?"

"The Cartographers have been looking into it," Treble answered promptly, "and we have summoned Master Harpsicalian to explain their findings. He is not . . . safe, but he is better than most of the others. He awaits the honor of your attention."

"Have him brought here."

There was a rattle, and Neverfell saw another sedan chair being hefted unsteadily toward them. It was unlike the one in which she sat in almost every way. For one thing, it had no windows, and its door was covered in heavy-looking bolts and padlocks, so that it looked more like a giant strongbox than a means of transport. Even the dark wood from which it was made had a gleaming solidity to it. Even more curious, on the frame next to the door an hourglass was affixed on a central pivot.

"You have another question," the Grand Steward prompted her, as one of his men began pulling back the bolts.

"Who's in the box?" Neverfell was trying hard not to bite her nails.

"A Cartographer."

Neverfell recollected Zouelle's warning at the banquet. Cartographers suffered from a contagious insanity. They were useful, many of them brilliant, but anybody who talked to them ran the risk of going bogglingly insane.

The door opened, and the guard immediately stepped to one side and revolved the hourglass on its pivot so that sand started to pour down through its narrow heart.

A man stepped out, swaying and bobbing in a frenzy of courtesy. Immediately there was a sniff of the wrong about him, and Neverfell felt herself tensing. She could see all the guards doing the same. His tea-colored eyes were unusually large and seemed to wobble slightly in their sockets. His belt bristled with strange gadgets, and a device strapped to his head gave a resounding click every ten seconds, causing him to jerk slightly.

He was wearing Face No. 33, Acknowledgment of Gallantry,

a mild smile suitable when one had been passed the sugar at important functions. It did not fit the situation, and that made Neverfell nervous, just as it would have if he had been wearing his jacket backward or socks on his hands.

"Master Harpsicalian, I wish to know all you have discovered about the late infiltration into the storerooms over there," declared the Grand Steward without preamble. "I want to know how the intruder got in, where he came from, and where he escaped to." His eye was on the timer, and he spoke with a new harsh urgency. "Speak! Be quick!"

"Ahhh." The strange figure let out a long breath, let in a long breath, and then started to speak in a surprisingly crisp and sane-sounding tone. "Well, of course I am summarizing the findings of my more skilled peers, but I understand from Peckletter that for some time"—jerk—"there's been a waterlogged channel in the granitelanes . . ."

He had a wonderfully crystalline way of talking. His voice rose and fell and took you with it, up spiral staircases you did not know were there and down sudden shafts and into unsuspected corridors until you lost track of time and—

". . . batwise scutterblack so we hadn't time to wind up properly with elbow-mandator before we could gauge the reverberation and the earth-hiccups—"

"Time's up!" shouted the guard as the last grains of the hourglass tumbled into the base. The Cartographer was still talking, but the guard pushed him firmly back through the door and closed it behind him.

There was a small pause while eighteen people recovered their breath and started untwisting their brains, a curiously painful process.

The Cartographer had been talking for five minutes. For the last three of those, Neverfell now realized, he had been

174

saying very little that made ordinary sense. Worryingly, at the time, she had felt that she understood him perfectly. Her mind had been pulled out from the shores of sanity by the current of the Cartographer's words, and hauling herself back was a wrench.

Even now there was a lurking feeling that she had, for a moment, been shown something wonderful, a hint to a colossal puzzle that would unravel and help her understand the world. She still had a sense of how rock felt, what it meant to have silver and copper in your veins. She could feel the tug of the unseen caves, the urge to leave her prints in caverns never before trodden by man . . .

Now it was obvious why there was an hourglass outside the Cartographer's door. More than five minutes' conversation with him was just too dangerous.

"So." The Grand Steward startled her out of her own thoughts. "How much of that did you understand?"

Neverfell struggled to answer, remembering the importance of not seeming a fool. So many of the Cartographer's phrases, which had seemed so lucid, now collapsed into nonsense under the cold light of sanity. Neverfell no longer understood what "melancholy basalt" was, or why it was important to "sing three degrees of silver." However, parts of his speech lingered, and made some murky sense.

"Er . . . the Cartographers have been searching the area with . . . with weasels and spoon meters . . ." Neverfell creased her brow. "And now they think the only way he could have got in was up a . . . waste chute?"

"That was also my understanding of Master Harpsicalian's words." Enquirer Treble was resting her fingertips on her forehead, as if trying to keep the contents steady.

"And mine," muttered the Grand Steward, as incredulously as if the Kleptomancer had been accused of crawling out of a teapot spout. "I see. So our thief squeezed his way up two hundred feet of sheer shaft, slithery with every kind of rot and foulness, despite all the downward-pointing metal spikes designed to stop anybody or anything doing exactly that. And since the fumes of those places are deadly and no trap-lanterns will grow there, he presumably did it without needing to breathe."

"My apologies, Your Excellency." Enquirer Treble seemed wary of rising too far out of a bow. "But it would seem that the Cartographers have found no other way that he can have entered."

"And his escape seems equally implausible," continued the Grand Steward. "If I have understood Master Harpsicalian's babblings, the criminal escaped through an underwater tunnel leading from the lagoon. An escape route that would require him to hold his breath for ten minutes, then dive down through a forty-foot waterfall into a fast-moving river."

There was a long pause.

"I am rather assuming that nobody here seriously thinks the man drowned in that river," the Grand Steward remarked.

"Not unless his ghost returned later to recover the cheese pieces from the storeroom where he had hidden them," answered Enquirer Treble. "There is no sign of them now. As for drowning, we suspect his suit was probably airtight, perhaps even equipped with its own air supply. Some of the Cartographers have developed suits a lot like that for exploring caves filled with water."

"That is interesting." The Grand Steward's single eye did not precisely change expression, but something in its pale fire brightened and intensified. "Treble, this man may be a Cartographer. It might explain his knowledge of hidden ways. Make discreet inquiries, but the Cartographers themselves must not know of our suspicion, or word may reach our thief."

When Treble had bowed and departed to pass on orders, Neverfell spent a few moments biting back a question, until as usual it escaped her.

"What's wrong with the Cartographer? There's something upsetting him, isn't there? Like there's an itch he can't scratch."

The Grand Steward turned his cold eye upon her, then gave a curt but approving nod. "The Cartographers are restless of late," he confirmed. "Excitable. Unpredictable. They have not been this bad since the madness over the Undiscovered Passage."

"Undiscovered Passage?"

"An obsession of theirs. You know, I suppose, that some Cartographers deliberately learn to squeak and hear like bats— they believe that they can use the squeak echoes to tell the shape of tunnels all around them, the way bats do but with much greater accuracy. About seven years ago all these bat-squeakers became convinced that they had sensed a new tunnel, one that had never been noticed before.

"They seemed to believe it ran deep into the heart of Caverna, and yet was on no map. No wider than three feet, straight as a harp string, and very, very long. They insisted that there was something wrong with it—that it only had one end. And then, before they could work out where it was, it vanished again. The obsession filtered through to the rest of the Cartographers, like smoke seeping under a door, and they went demented, hunting it for a time. They calmed after a while but never completely gave up their search for it."

"Could that passage be the way the Kleptomancer sneaked in and out?"

"The Cartographers think not. And perhaps it does not even exist outside of their delusions."

"So if they never found any new trace of the tunnel, why are they restless now?"

"Nobody knows. Perhaps they do not know themselves."

Neverfell contemplated this while the Grand Steward continued talking to Enquirer Treble, who had returned from her errand.

"So what else do we know of this man?"

"The thief is short," she answered, "but not a child—he has been operating for a long time. His activities were first reported ten years ago, but he became notorious only seven years ago, when a very sizeable reward was offered for his capture. Anonymously, it would seem. We also have a list of all the thefts for which he is believed to be responsible. There . . . does not seem to be any pattern, Your Excellency."

"See if you can find out who offered that reward," instructed the Grand Steward. "What else can we deduce about him? This is a thief who will risk his life to steal a truckle of Stackfalter Sturton. What does this tell us?"

"He really likes cheese?" Neverfell suggested, then clapped both hands over her mouth when everybody glared at her.

"Spoken like a cheesemaker," responded the Enquirer with cool disdain.

"But . . ." Neverfell could not suppress her thoughts. "But he must *know* a little about cheese. Or about this cheese, anyway. You see, when a Sturton is ripening it's very important to turn it often, but after it's ripe and sliced, you have to poke it with a gold needle regularly to let it vent. So he must be doing that, at the very least."

"What makes you so sure?" snapped the Enquirer.

"Um . . . well, if he hadn't, I think somebody would have heard the explosion," Neverfell explained meekly.

"He may have let them detonate in the wild tunnels, where none would hear them," the Enquirer responded dismissively. "It is plain from our records that the Kleptomancer cares little for the things he steals. Most of the time he destroys them or casts them aside as soon as he has them. The theft is all that matters to him. The disruption he causes. The notoriety it gains him. The challenge."

"Why don't you challenge him to steal something, then? You could lie in wait and grab him." Neverfell looked round, and found that the Grand Steward's cold right eye was fixed upon her. "Oh! Um . . . I mean . . . why don't you challenge him to steal something, *Your Excellency.*"

The Enquirer froze her with a glance of weary contempt. "If the man is clever enough to mix luxuries without blowing off his own head, then he is intelligent enough to spot such an obvious trap."

"Yes, of course." Neverfell paused, trying to organize the squirrel-dance of her thoughts. "But people do walk into traps, don't they? When it's the right bait. They just can't help it, even when they know it's a trap."

"Not everybody opens a box when they know it will blow up in their face," the Enquirer suggested icily, and Neverfell reddened.

"You are wrong, Treble," said the Grand Steward speculatively, his eye still on Neverfell. "Everybody has a box they cannot help but open, even if they are almost certain it is a trap. Everybody has something they cannot resist. It is just a matter of finding the right box and the right bait for each person. And for this thief I think we must bait the trap with something odd enough to pique his sense of theater, something unique.

"Our next stop will be the Cabinet of Curiosities."

The Grand Steward's sedan was carried through the Avenue of Marvels, where ancient fossilized fish with narrow snouts grinned toothily from the rock of the wall, and down the Street of Dry Tears, where solitary drop-shaped crystals hung suspended from nigh-invisible threads. At last they came to two green doors, just wide enough when open for the sedan to be carried within.

The Cabinet of Curiosities was, in fact, a set of rooms filled with wonders of the world. The Grand Steward's hunger for anything that would break his boredom was well-known in the overground world, and so explorers would travel distant lands and take deadly risks just to bring him back something extraordinary enough to amuse him for a little while. Small wonder, for any man who could deliver a novelty worthy of the Grand Steward's notice was paid a king's ransom.

Each object within had, at one time, stirred in his mind some spark of curiosity, and a fleeting sense that the world was marvelous and not always predictable. Each time, however, the interest had burned itself out, leaving only the bland gray ashes of boredom, and the new novelty was sent to join its fellows in the Cabinet of Curiosities. Every addition had made it ever more a testament to the Grand Steward's all-consuming, all-annihilating boredom, and he had not set foot in it for more than fifty years.

Now, however, everything was different, for he had his strange young food taster by his side. She had never seen such marvels before, and under her eye the curiosities came to life again. He saw anew the mummified body of King Arupet with gems the size of dove's eggs in his eye sockets; the horn of a giant narwhal; a dragonfly the length of a man's arm trapped in amber; the stuffed corpse of a three-headed calf; the skeleton of a man so holy that tiny wings had grown from his shoulders; a singed round rock said to be a thunderbolt. She seemed particularly fascinated by the pale plaster death masks of famous poets, their eyes closed and cheeks slack. He saw her curiosity building, like a geyser waiting to erupt.

The curator of the Cabinet nearly crippled himself in his haste to approach the Grand Steward and offer his trembling bows.

"Yes, yes," the Grand Steward responded wearily. "Keep that girl out of my way and answer her questions, will you?"

The girl was insatiable, capering about like a mad monkey, peering into the cases at rocs' eggs and rhino hides. Then she halted, gaped, and moved slowly to stand before the lean, towering figure of a stuffed animal some eighteen feet tall. She stared transfixed at its tawny fur and tortoiseshell blotches, its soft horn-stubs and handlebar ears, its stilt legs and the mane-fringe down the back of its telescope neck.

"What have you done to this horse?" Her voice was audible to the Grand Steward even from the other side of the room. "Did it die from having its neck stretched too far?"

"Ah, no, miss, that is a cameleopard, our newest acquisition, a quite remarkable creature from the sun-baked plains . . ." The curator began his explanation, but Neverfell seemed to be paying little attention to his words. She was stooping to peer at the turnip-bulges of the cameleopard's ankles, and sniff at its broad, dark, cloven hoofs. The Grand Steward suddenly realized that she was trying to find the smell of grass on its feet.

"So why is it that tall, then?" Neverfell's voice floated relentlessly across the dark, attic-like room. "Does the sun make animals grow, the way it makes plants grow? Are there other creatures as tall as that up there? What about people? Does it make them grow too? Is that why I'm tall for my age?"

"Ahem . . ." The curator sounded somewhat out of his depth. "No, no, I scarcely think so . . . by all accounts sunlight is a withering and dangerous business. I . . . I believe the cameleopard's neck is stretched by, ah, reaching for high leaves . . ."

"So is it born with a short neck, and does it just get longer from stretching? If I kept stretching up to bite leaves, would my neck get longer? I always reach for things with my right hand—why isn't my right arm longer than my left one? That doesn't make sense!"

Contrary to the curator's hopes, she was showing no obvious sign of running out of questions. Instead, she was scampering over to peer at several towering suits of armor from distant lands, sometimes holding out an arm to compare its length to an enameled gauntlet.

"And look! These *do* look like they were made for giants. So perhaps the sun really does make all overground people extra large!"

The Grand Steward managed to drag his eye from the caperings of his new taster. He was, after all, there for a reason.

"Take a note." One of his scribes rushed to his side with pen and paper. "Let it be known that the Stewardship of Caverna has challenged the so-called Kleptomancer to demonstrate his skill and courage by stealing one of the Grand Steward's Curiosities before three days pass. Let it also be known that a space will be put aside for the stuffed and mounted remains of said Kleptomancer, so that the gentles of Court may gawp at him after his inevitable arrest and execution."

But which Curiosity should he challenge the Kleptomancer to steal? How should he bait the trap? His eye wandered back to the cameleopard that had so fascinated Neverfell. Tall, unwieldy, difficult for a thief to maneuver down chutes at speed . . .

"Change that a little," he muttered to his scribe. "Instead of 'one of the Curiosities,' write 'the Latest and Greatest Curiosity to come into the Grand Steward's possession.'"

The Kleptomancer would need to ask questions in order to find out which was the last item in the Cabinet to be presented to the Grand Steward, and perhaps he could be caught doing so. And even if that trap failed, the mysterious thief would still be faced with the task of stealing a rigid, eighteen-foot-tall monstrosity.

In his icy soul, the Grand Steward felt a tiny quiver of mirth.

EVERYTHING WE NEED

BY THE TIME NEVERFELL RETURNED TO THE tasters' halls, she was starving. The Grand Steward had eaten nothing in five hours except a small plate of olives, a candied pomegranate, and some quail eggs. Neverfell, of course, had been given only a very tiny portion of each. Already she was starting to see one of the downsides of being a food taster. Originally she had worried about dying of poison. Now she was more worried about starvation. Worse still, the pomegranate had contained some spice that widened her field of vision, which was very distracting and made her feel a bit like an owl.

Once Neverfell had gobbled enough refreshingly ordinary porridge that she lost the queasy emptiness and the dizzy ache behind her eyes, Leodora swept her off on a slightly calmer tour of the tasters' quarters, while filling her in on the rules.

"This whole area is set aside for us," explained Leodora. "One entrance, carefully guarded, so that nobody can get in except tasters and the palace servants." There was indeed the usual supply of soft-paced, flitting servants, all wearing white palace liveries and Faces like very polite sleepwalkers.

"This is where you will be spending most of your time when you are not on duty." Leodora opened a door to a pleasant antechamber where six or so people relaxed on cushions reading, gossiping, and playing board games. The second door swung back to reveal a narrow room, dark with crimson hangings, where several figures laid out on mattresses smoked great, glittering hookahs as high as Neverfell herself. The room was filled with the same scented smoke that seemed to follow Leodora around. Something caught in the back of Neverfell's throat, and she recoiled, gripping her nose.

"That's Perfume! There's Perfume in the air!"

"It is all right," Leodora reassured her. "They add a trace of it to the hookah smoke. We find it calming, that is all. Some people have difficulty sleeping at first, and the pipes help."

Neverfell stubbornly held her nose until the door was shut, and only then gingerly released her grip. Being calm was all very nice, but she didn't want to be *forced* to be calm. Then again, she reflected, perhaps she hadn't been living in fear as long as the other tasters.

Even with the door shut, the air still held the cloying smell of the smoke. Neverfell looked at Leodora's pale fingernails and glossy gaze and suddenly wanted to breathe something cleaner. The recreation rooms were pretty and comfortable, but there was something stale about them, like hutches for pets that are never allowed out to run.

"Can I go out?"

"Out?" Leodora sounded rather taken aback. "Well, yes, in theory. These rooms are within the palace. Technically you are allowed to roam around most of the palace's public courts and pleasure halls—it should be fairly clear which parts are off limits—

but why would you wish to do that? Here we have everything we need, and it is much, much safer."

"But I can go out if I want to?" persisted Neverfell. "If I'm back in time for my shifts?"

Leodora hesitated before nodding. "You can. But I would advise against it. Particularly in your case. It is not just a matter of ordinary dangers. You do not want to *see* too much." Neverfell gawped in incomprehension, so Leodora sighed and continued. "Neverfell, your face is your fortune. It is the reason you're still alive. You know that?"

Neverfell nodded, her mood sobering.

"Well, what do you think would happen to your face if you found out something you couldn't forget? Something terrible that changed the way you thought, and would show through your expressions forever?" Leodora leaned forward and spoke in a low, gentle tone. "Your face would be spoiled. And then there would be no point to you anymore. I am sorry, but your neck is on the line, and you have to understand this."

Neverfell was overwhelmed by this notion, and recovered her wits only as Leodora was walking away.

"Wait—Mistress Leodora—can I at least have paper and ink? I want to write to Cheesemaster Grandible and Vintner Childersin."

"That is not really encouraged," Leodora told her blandly. "We hear so much in our profession that they do not really like us writing letters."

"But I have to know whether Master Grandible is all right!" Neverfell tried and failed to swallow down her frustration. "And there's my friend Zouelle Childersin . . . I want to make sure nothing bad has happened to her—"

"Neverfell," Leodora interrupted with a sigh, "let me ask you this. Do you want the Enquiry reading your letters, and the responses that come back? Because they will." Neverfell drooped despite herself. The mention of the Enquiry still sent a cold shiver through her marrow. "Do not worry, everybody who tried to stake a claim of ownership over you has been sent a message to let them know your new position. Master Grandible, the Childersins, and Madame Appeline have all been told that you are alive, well, and serving as part of His Excellency's household."

Neverfell's heart gave a little broken-winged soar. It touched her immensely to think of Cheesemaster Grandible still trying to recover her, just the way Erstwhile had claimed. Then she realized what Leodora had just said.

"Did you say Madame Appeline? Madame Appeline wanted me as well?"

"Did you not know? Yes—it would seem that after your first arrest she tried to insist that you should be indentured to her, but by then it was too late, and you were already serving Maxim Childersin. She tried to register another claim after the banquet but was overruled."

"But—"

"Politics. All politics. Have as little to do with it as you can. Take my advice. Rest, relax, and forget about it all."

Neverfell tottered back to the recreation room, and lost at chess repeatedly while she tried to organize her thoughts. In the end she gave up and returned to her private room to be alone.

Madame Appeline had attempted to have Neverfell delivered into her care. But was it her care or her custody? Had she wanted to capture Neverfell or protect her?

"Somebody tried to drown me," Neverfell reminded herself, pressing her palms against the side of her head to stop her thoughts from bouncing around. Who had known that she was in the Enquiry cell? The Enquirers, of course, and the Childersins . . . and Madame Appeline.

Into Neverfell's mind flashed the feline face of Madame Appeline, the slanting green eyes flashing like colored glass, the mouth a perfect, cold jewel. The next instant this picture was dashed aside by the memory of Madame Appeline wearing the saddened, loving Face that Neverfell had glimpsed on their first meeting. Neverfell's thoughts about the Facesmith were a jumble of broken splinters, and they did not seem to fit together.

There was a connection between herself and the Facesmith— she knew it. She had sensed it ever since seeing that weary, kindly Face that had spoken to her soul in a way that nothing else ever had. It had filled her with trust, sympathy, yearning, and an ache of the familiar, as if somebody had reached straight into her heart. Strange coincidences buzzed through Neverfell's mind.

Madame Appeline's Tragedy Range came out seven years ago. That's when I appeared from nowhere in the cheese tunnels. Did something really terrible and sad happen to Madame Appeline back then, so that all her new Faces were filled with suffering? And did it have anything to do with me?

Could Madame Appeline be a figure from Neverfell's lost past? The first time they had met, the Facesmith had shown no sign of recognition, but then again Neverfell's face had been covered. And when Neverfell had been shamefully unmasked, she was sure she had heard Madame Appeline exclaiming in tones of deepest shock. *Impossible* was all she had said, *impossible.*

Was she just saying that because my face was so weird and frightening? Or . . . did she recognize me? Is that what shocked her so badly?

Again Neverfell considered the Face she had glimpsed at the cheese-tunnel door, the look of tired tenderness in the emerald-green eyes . . .

Madame Appeline's eyes are green. So are mine. Does that mean something?

There was one possible explanation that might answer all these questions. However, whenever she tried to think about it, her stomach lurched up and then down, like a giddy little boat with a monstrous wave passing beneath it. A lurch, dark water, and a fear of looking down.

Maxim Childersin had promised to help Neverfell investigate her past, but now she had been taken beyond his reach. She had seen the confident and powerful vintner patriarch come within an ant's step of disgrace and execution, all because of her own actions. She could not expect him to take more risks on her behalf, even supposing he still wished to do so.

If she wanted to discover the secrets of her past, she would have to do so without Maxim Childersin. She was alone. Or was she? Suddenly she remembered the mysterious note from the day before.

On an impulse of optimism she ran to her bed and pulled back the counterpane. There was no sign of the little box she had discovered previously. Instead, a bottle of ink had been concealed there, along with five pieces of clean paper. There was also a note, which read as follows:

Hide ink, spare paper, and completed letters under mattress. Letters will be delivered safely and unopened. Any letters sent in reply will be left for you in the same place.

If you must go out, avoid the Court of Snipes, Melamourse

Colonnade, and the Hall of the Harps, since all three are prowling
grounds for assassins.
We will keep our eyes open but can do only so much.

Neverfell hardly knew what to feel first. Such a prompt appearance of paper and ink could not be coincidence. Either Leodora had had a change of heart, or their conversation had been overheard, and her anonymous benefactor had somehow learned of her wishes. It made her feel spied upon and was both eerie and reassuring, like being caught mid-stumble by an invisible hand.

The first mysterious letter had been signed "a friend." This second note spoke of "we." Whoever her mysterious contact was, it seemed there was more than one of them.

Neverfell knew that it could be a trap but could not bear to waste the opportunity. Snatching up the loose paper, Neverfell wrote long, scruffy letters to both Master Grandible and Master Childersin, telling them everything that had happened to her. The only parts she left out were those relating to the Kleptomancer trap, since she was fairly sure that was deadly secret. After folding up the letters, she hesitated, and then wrote one last note.

> *Dear Friend,*
> *Thank you.*
> *Who are you?*

She tucked the letters and the notes under the mattress as instructed, then sat on the bed, rocking back and forth and staring the crowds of questions in the eye.

"Oh, I'm not going to find out anything in here, and I can't just sit here waiting to be murdered!" Neverfell exclaimed aloud. "Somebody wants me dead. And if I don't find out why, one day I'll wake up and I *will* be."

The sentries who stood at the archway that led to the tasters' district had very detailed orders, nearly all of which involved preventing non-tasters entering the area. None of them reacted at all when the youngest and newest of the food tasters slipped past them and out into the public courtyards of the Grand Steward's palace, where the favored elite of the Court met, mingled, and conspired.

She was not unobserved, however. As she ventured out, one gaze settled upon her with a carefully feigned disinterest. The owner of this gaze let her pass out of sight without giving her a second glance, then coolly turned to follow her.

BEAUTY AND THE BEASTS

LEAVING THE TASTERS' CHAMBERS WAS A GOOD
deal like entering a dream, and after a few paces into the courtyard
beyond Neverfell was gazing around her with a dream-like lack
of fear. A corridor lined in midnight-blue velvet, studded with
pearls for stars, led to a broad tunnel colored in dull, predawn
violet. This opened out to a set of rooms where dawn-like streaks
of pink and gold ribboned the ceiling, followed by courtyards that
glittered with gilt, quartz, and tiny crystal mirrors, illuminated by
hundreds of gold-painted lanterns decorated with stylized suns.
The Grand Steward is the sun, it seemed to be saying. *When you
walk toward the heart of the palace, you walk into the day.*

She was just stepping out into a courtyard when something
jumped onto her shoulder, tickling her face with fur and curling
a rough but delicate tail round her throat. She gave a squeal of
shock, and turned her head to find her nose almost touching a
tiny, pinkish, flattened face, framed by wild white hair.

"Monkey!" she squeaked in glee as much as surprise. "A real
monkey!" It was no bigger than a small cat, and wore a blue
sequined jacket and a tiny black velvet cap with a trailing blue
feather. Neverfell instantly loved its clever black fingers and the

mournful puckering of its pale brows. When it doffed its cap and turned its lips inside out in a broad, fearless grin, she burst out laughing.

"You startled me! Oh no, no, thank you!" Neverfell had to put up a hand to dissuade it from pushing half a meringue into her mouth with its spare hand. "No, I can't, sorry! I'm not allowed to eat strange cake. Where did you come from, anyway?" Looking around her, she could see no sign of the monkey's owner. Her small passenger decided that her moment of distraction was a good time to clamber over her face. "Stop that!" hissed Neverfell, through laughter and fur. "I'm on a secret mission, and there are enough people staring at me without monkeys pushing meringue in my ear . . . OW!"

The monkey leaped down from Neverfell's shoulder and bounded away into the darkness, one of its fists still gripping the few red hairs that it had yanked without warning from her head.

"Fine!" she called after it. "That's the last time you get to ride on my shoulder!"

Unsurprisingly there was no answer, and Neverfell decided to hurry on before anything else jumped on her and pulled her hair out.

This was a world full of strange, lofty, and gorgeous denizens. Ladies drifted by in ermine, with damask trains six feet long. A pair of Cartographers capered unsteadily past wearing earmuffs and padlocked gags, occasionally miming to each other or waving weird structures made of wire. Now and then Neverfell pinched her nose hard as some statuesque lady or lord drifted past trailing a subtle reek of Perfume. One glittering lady emitted a faint buzz as she passed, which confused Neverfell until she realized that her black-and-gold hair ornaments were made of live wasps, their stings removed.

Many of the courtiers, she noticed now, had their own monkeys with them, usually dressed in their household's livery. Watching a white-backed monkey teeter by with a silver tray of tiny cakes, Neverfell remembered Zouelle telling her that since courtiers were allowed no servants inside the palace, for fear of them bringing in their own assassins and soldiers, many instead brought monkeys that had been trained to act as small, hairy attendants.

Neverfell was not blind to the way she was gathering gazes like spider threads. Time and again richly dressed figures glided coolly past her, only for the clop of their tread and swish of their clothes to cease a few paces later, a tingle on the back of Neverfell's neck telling her that they had halted to watch her go. Ruff rustled against ruff as heads drew close to whisper. Neverfell was surprised to find herself thinking wistfully of her mask. Nonetheless, she took care to peer at every beautifully presented Face that passed.

Sooner or later she would see a Face that stirred her heart strangely, in the way that Madame Appeline's haggard smile had. Any courtier wearing a Face from the Tragedy Range would be a customer of Madame Appeline, and might know where the Facesmith could be found.

Following Neverfell should have been easy. She was distinctive, undisguised, and guileless, and since she kept glancing over her shoulder at the wonders of the Court her unsuspected shadow had ample opportunity to observe her thoughts and intentions writ large across her face.

Soon, however, he was learning an important lesson. Being able to read somebody's thoughts is all very well, but if they have the attention span of a summer-addled gnat, this does not necessarily help you guess what they will do next.

Neverfell's face could be read like a book, and what the book said was this:

Wonder where this corridor goes . . . I'd probably better keep an eye out for any sign of danger . . . Ooh, look at the llama! Let's run across and stare at its knees! Actually, llamas are scary, so let's back off—everybody's watching me and maybe I should go and talk to the stringy-looking woman with the warts on her— Wait a minute, are those dates on the table? Mmm, dates. But I'm not allowed to eat them. So I'll climb up onto this balcony instead!

Her zigzags were tantalizing. Sometimes it seemed that she was about to veer off into the lonelier corridors where a cry could be muffled with ease, but a moment later she would gallop back into the thick of the throngs. Still he followed and remained alert, for experience had taught him that opportunities could come suddenly, and patience was usually rewarded.

At last Neverfell discovered a courtyard that seemed on first glance to be thronged with giants. The great figures were evenly spaced and some twelve feet tall, heads bowed as they strained to bear the weight of the ceiling on their shoulders. On closer inspection these proved to be cunningly carved and decorated pillars running from floor to ceiling, faces set in grimaces as if they really were struggling to hold up the tons of rock above.

Shorter human figures drifted among them, admiring the painted canvases leaning against the walls, listening to the musicians who plied their instruments softly in corners, spending a moment here and there to hear the efforts of a poet. Although Neverfell did not know it, this was a place where artists, musicians, and providers of more curious services gathered in the hope of earning themselves powerful patrons.

Two dozen heads turned as she broke into an impulsive sprint. By the time she halted in front of a silver-clad noblewoman, both of the latter's male companions had their hands on their sword hilts.

"Excuse me! I—that's such a lovely Face you were wearing just then. It was so sad and strange and . . . like one of those paintings of the moon or something." Neverfell saw the lady's shoulders relax very slightly, her eyes moving rapidly and with interest over Neverfell's own face. "I just wanted to ask where it came from. Is it one of Madame Appeline's?"

"How clever of you!" The silver-painted mouth of the woman smiled. She stepped forward, and the chain-mail mesh of her long dress chimed as she did so. Bodkins glittered in her hair. "Yes, a sweet little Face from the Tragedy Range, but tweaked to suit me. I can never bear to take a Face from a range without having it adjusted." She drifted closer, and curled a gray-gloved hand companionably but firmly through Neverfell's arm. "You must be His Excellency's new food taster, am I right?"

Neverfell nodded, a little daunted to find her fame so well established.

"Then we simply must take a little promenade. I'll tell you where I get all my Faces, but you really must share your Face secrets with me in return." The lady raised her paradribble, and held it over both Neverfell's head and her own. "How did you manage such extraordinary effects? Is it true that you're an outsider?"

"I . . . I think so." Neverfell answered hesitantly. "I don't really remember. I'm sorry, I don't have any Face secrets, just runaway features. I can't control them. But I really want to talk to Madame Appeline. Do you know where I could find her?"

"No." Her companion gave a speculative silver smile. "No, but if you are looking for Facesmiths I can do better than that."

Neverfell was led to two women seated by an obsidian fountain that spewed crystal arcs of rose water into a star-shaped pool. As soon as they noticed her approach, both women started to their feet, one dropping her sketch pad. Neverfell recognized them instantly as the two Facesmiths who had been staring at her during the banquet.

Introductions were made. The silvery lady, Lady Adamant, belonged to a celebrated chocolate family. The two Facesmiths were sisters, Simpria and Snia de Meina. Lady Adamant gave the sisters a meaningful smile as she took her leave, and was rewarded by an equally meaningful nod of acknowledgment.

"How very charming it is to meet you!" Snia was dumpier than her sister, with wide, watery eyes and a thick voice that made Neverfell think of fudge. She was wearing a Face that looked sleek and expensive, the warmth of her smile tempered with a regal dreaminess. "We were just talking about you today . . ."

". . . and wondering who we needed to bribe to get to meet you . . ." interjected tall, hoarse, red-faced Simpria with a laugh. Her Face was also clearly top of the range, but more experimental than her sister's, a daring mixture of magnanimity, wry confidence, and peckishness.

". . . but here you are. Now, you probably didn't notice us, but at the last banquet . . ."

"Yes!" Neverfell beamed. "You were both staring at me! And then *you* drew lots of pictures of me, and *you* went purple and fell over!"

The sister's faces froze for the merest second before they managed an indulgent laugh.

"Well, since you mention the drawings, my dear, do you mind if I . . . ?" Snia recovered her sketch pad from the ground, and hovered her pencil hopefully above it. "Just while we are talking."

"I don't mind at all."

Snia's pencil began skating furiously across the page, while her watery eyes flitted over Neverfell's face.

"So." Simpria took over the conversation. "Lady Adamant said that you wanted to speak to a Facesmith."

"Well, yes," admitted Neverfell. "I asked her about Madame Appeline."

"Vesperta Appeline? Why did you want to speak to her?" There was an edge to Simpria's voice, and Neverfell remembered that Erstwhile had told her all the other Facesmiths hated Madame Appeline.

"Um . . ." Neverfell spent a whole second trying to think of a good story, then gave up. "I met her in the cheese tunnels, and she seemed kind, but then I broke into her house and now I don't know if she's angry, and I wanted to talk to her to find out more about her. Is it true that you and all the other Facesmiths hate her?"

"Oh, dear me!" Simpria laughed, a little too merrily. "Hate indeed! What a term. No, no. Nobody would waste hate on that upstart! After all, nobody comes from nowhere. If she does not speak of her past, then she has a past that does not bear speaking of." She nodded knowingly. "And one can make guesses."

Neverfell felt a throb of excitement. "You know something about her past?"

Beside her, Snia was making occasional tutting noises, and Neverfell was vaguely aware that the ground around their feet was now littered with torn-out, half-finished sketches.

"Nothing has ever been proven against her," Simpria admitted, "but there are one or two things I *do* know. She used to live in the Doldrums, a terrible district full of grub-driers, fossil-glossers, and cut-price Cartographers, where nobody asks any questions." She leaned forward, a confiding smile on her radish-red face. "Well, over the year before she brought out her Tragedy Range, she ran up debts. Odd debts. For one thing, she was buying more food than she needed for herself and her one Putty Girl. Then there were all the tiny samples of Delicacies she kept buying— particularly Wine."

It crossed Neverfell's mind that Madame Simpria must have done quite a lot of running around interrogating tradesmen to find out so much about somebody "beneath her notice."

"And then there were the dresses."

"Dresses?"

"Yes. Little dresses for a girl so high." Simpria held out her hand some three and a half feet above the ground. "Far too small for her Putty Girl. Do you see what that means?"

Neverfell stared at her wide-eyed as the tall Facesmith leaned forward confidentially.

"Somewhere in the dingy mole hole of hers," whispered Simpria, "she must have been hiding a child."

Neverfell felt as if her world were exploding. Again the fantastical explanation, the impossible possibility, glimmered at her through the gloom, this time brighter than before.

". . . and if she was hiding it," Simpria continued, "there must have been something shameful about it. Perhaps it was a child from some forbidden and disgraceful love, or a clandestine marriage. The father was probably a criminal, or the lowest sort of drudge. Or, worse still, perhaps the child was *ugly*." Her mouth spread in a smile. "Can you imagine the disgrace of that? A Facesmith with a child whose face was beyond the power of her art to rescue."

Snia gave a muffled sound of anguish and frustration as she ripped out yet another page from her sketch pad. "My dear child," she said through clenched teeth, "do you think that you could try to hold the same expression for more than half a second?"

Neverfell barely heard her. "What happened to the little girl?"

"Nobody knows." Simpria arched her brows. "By the time Vesperta Appeline moved to her rich new apartments near the Court, there was no such child in her household. But I suppose the poor thing might have died in the influenza epidemic."

"Influenza? But that's a disease, isn't it?" Neverfell was perplexed. "Aren't we supposed to be safe from diseases in Caverna? Isn't that one of the reasons outsiders aren't allowed in?"

"Oh indeed!" agreed Simpria. "There were no end of investigations| afterward to find out how the influenza entered Caverna, but they never found an answer. In the end, they walled off the whole district, with the sick inside. To this day, nobody is allowed to dig their way into the Doldrums in case the disease is still lurking inside."

Neverfell felt a queasy horror at the thought of the influenza sufferers, sealed into homes that had become tombs, waiting for their water to run out and their trap-lanterns to fail.

"Those in the Doldrums who remained well were quarantined," Simpria went on, "until everyone was certain they were not infected. By then, however, a lot of people had died. Vesperta

Appeline's own Putty Girl was one of the first to go. Alas! Such a pretty girl, only sixteen. Green eyes. Madame Appeline always chooses Putty Girls with green eyes like her own when she can."

Green eyes. Green eyes like hers. Green eyes like mine. Could it really be? Could Madame Appeline be my . . .

But I'm an outsider and she isn't! It doesn't make sense! Unless . . .

"You said Madame Appeline came from nowhere, didn't you? Could she . . . could she have come from outside Caverna?"

She turned to find that the two sisters were no longer listening to her. They were both stooped over the scattered sketches, each directing the occasional, rapid glance at Neverfell.

"No, no, no use at all, all the changes far too fast to capture . . ."

". . . like a butterfly's wing . . ."

". . . yes, just as much chance of preserving . . ."

Both halted as if struck by the same thought, then locked gazes for a few seconds. Slowly they turned back toward Neverfell, wearing identical motherly, reassuring smiles.

"Ye-e-es," purred Simpria. "I think perhaps . . ." She straightened, and reached out a curious hand to touch Neverfell's jawline. "About here, would you say?"

"It would have to be done ve-e-ery carefully." Snia spoke softly as if Neverfell were an animal they were wary of frightening away. Something about her tone sent a tingle through Neverfell's legs and clouded her head with thoughts of running. "Mounted on a corkboard, do you think?"

"And then we could find out how it all functions," murmured Simpria, tilting her head on her long neck to regard Neverfell's forehead. "Why it is so different. What makes it jump and change so . . ."

Neverfell flinched away from their reaching fingers and leaped to her feet.

"You want to peel my face off to find out how it works!" she shrilled.

Both sisters rose, carefully and slowly, perhaps still hoping they could calm Neverfell into sitting with them. Neverfell was suddenly aware of the folds in Snia's toad-like neck, and the strong look of Simpria's large hands.

"Oh, tish, tosh, tiddle," wheezed Simpria gently. "Not now. Not while you have a use for it. Not while you're alive."

"Get away from me!" Neverfell backed off and dodged behind one of the great, man-shaped pillars.

"We could do so much for you," wheedled Snia, edging softly forward. "All we want in return is a signature on a piece of paper, leaving your remains to us when you die. Not even the whole body. Just one little head . . ."

Glancing round the pillar, Neverfell could see that the shouting had drawn the attention of Lady Adamant and her two male companions, and that all three were gliding in at speed, the lady's dress chiming like a war of tiny cymbals.

Neverfell ran. She took a wild zigzag from pillar to pillar, and heard the pursuers curse as they slithered on the smooth flags, trying to change direction. She darted, dodged, skidded then sprinted flat out for the arch, ignoring the screeches of bewildered monkeys. Just as she reached it there was a sibilant tinkle to her left, and she dodged just in time as Lady Adamant leaped out with cobra-like speed and made a snatch at her sleeve. The silver glove closed on nothing, and Neverfell made it through the arch.

Neverfell careered down the nearest arcade, saw a fountain too late and splashed through it before sprinting on her way, leaving great damp prints behind her. Too late, she realized that she had just made herself incredibly easy to follow. Panic added to her speed but left her even more clumsy.

"Aargh! Sorry! I'm so sorry!" She accidentally jostled a passing servant, knocking his bowl of dried damsons to the floor. Neverfell faltered, but could not stop. A few steps later she stumbled, rucking a rug and nearly losing her footing. At the next archway she set a collection of wind chimes ringing and startled a caged cockatoo into a screaming fit.

She could not stop to correct anything. There was no time. She continued to run, her heart beating in her head like pursuing steps.

Unbeknownst to Neverfell, however, something magical was happening in her wake. By the time Lady Adamant and her colleagues arrived half a minute later, there was no sign of the chaos Neverfell had caused. The mosaic floor was dry, the spilled food gone without trace. The rug was immaculate. The chimes were still, the cockatoo was silently and happily chewing upon a rusk, and the only sound was the meek lapping of the fountain's disturbed water. Furthermore, the corridor seemed to be a dead end. The far arch was curtained, and a couple of food tables placed before it.

Lady Adamant summoned a white-clad servant over with an imperious silver finger. "I am looking for a friend of mine," she explained, letting her features ease into Face No. 96, Slow Dawn Seen Through a Glass of Honeydew. "Could you tell me if a young red-haired girl in a taster's sash ran through here just now? I am afraid she might get lost."

"I am sorry, ma'am, but there has been nobody here of that description. Could I assist you with anything else?" The servant looked up at her with the same Face that all his fellows wore, bland and blank as a clean napkin. Lady Adamant dismissed him with a wave of her hand and stalked off, only the fierce rapidity of her steps giving away her annoyance.

A short while later, however, a different set of feet trod that same corridor, more slowly and carefully than Lady Adamant had done. A different set of eyes slid over every detail, noticing the motion of the water, the cockatoo's dropped feathers in the cage, the slight crookedness of the hastily placed tables.

The girl had passed this way, and somehow the way had closed behind her. No matter. He had arranged for something to be stolen from her, something that could be used to reach her, and she had already forgotten its loss.

THE HUNT

THERE WERE MANY WHO CALLED THE COURT a jungle, and with good reason. It had a jungle's lush and glittering beauty. The people who dwelt in it, in their turn, were not unlike jungle creatures. Some were like iridescent birds and long-tailed butterflies dripping with color, lavish, selfish, and beautiful. Others labored tirelessly, diligent and unnoticed, like great ants bearing hulking burdens across the leafy floor. Then there were bush babies and lemurs, hugging branches, their bulging night-eyes missing nothing.

There are many dangers in the jungle, but perhaps the greatest is forgetting that one is not the only hunter, and that one is probably not the largest.

The guards at the tasters' quarters made no comment at seeing the youngest taster tear in past them, her sash loose and her face as red as her hair from running.

Dashing back to her own chamber, Neverfell locked herself in, then sagged into a chair with a long release of breath. Remembering her letters to Grandible and Childersin, Neverfell pulled back the mattress and found, to her satisfaction, that they had gone. All that remained was a single folded note, which she opened with some excitement.

We cannot tell you who we are. If we did, your face might reveal it to everybody else and put us in danger.

Be careful. You were followed during your walk today. We believe the man to be an assassin.

Neverfell spent a full minute staring at the word "assassin." She had thought she was being careful in the courtyards, and had tried to keep an eye out for anybody following her. She had noticed a lot of stares but had observed nobody shadowing her. She felt a pang of cold in the soles of her feet, as if belatedly sensing the assassin's tread following in her own tracks.

Worse still, she could not even be sure why this particular killer had dogged her steps. Perhaps he had been sent by someone from her past who feared that she might remember some terrible secret. For all she knew, though, he might be in the pay of the family whose Wine she had spilled, or somebody else she had unintentionally offended.

Every step she took seemed to show her a new danger. Talking to strangers could kill her. Failing to remember table etiquette could kill her. Ignorance could kill her. And now it seemed that stepping outside the tasters' chambers for a stroll could kill her.

But it didn't, answered the newly rebellious part of her mind. *I went out to investigate, and I discovered things. For once I did something that was my idea — just mine — and it worked.*

She sat up and considered everything she had learned during her outing. If Simpria and Snia were to be believed, about seven years ago Madame Appeline had been buying clothes for a little girl. Perhaps the child had been a niece or the daughter of a friend, but then why would she need to be so secretive about it? And why would the Facesmith spend money she could not afford on nice dresses unless they were for her own child, her very own secret daughter?

She must have loved her very much. If the de Meina sisters had meant to make Neverfell think less of their rival by telling the story of the dresses, they had failed. On the contrary, the tale had filled Neverfell with sympathy, curiosity, and hope.

Despite all her fears, Neverfell could not help wiggling her feet in her satin shoes, as silver caterpillars of excitement writhed around each other in her stomach. She ran her fingertips over her own face. *Do I look like Madame Appeline?* She could still recall her reflection in the mirror. *Not much,* she conceded. *I'm not beautiful like her. I'm tall for my age, too, and she's quite short for hers. But we both have green eyes.*

There was that influenza outbreak. Perhaps that happened because an outsider broke into Caverna somehow and brought it in with him. Perhaps he was my father, and he came to the Doldrums, and he met Madame Appeline and they fell in love, and . . .

Neverfell's imagination stumbled mid-gallop. *No, that doesn't make sense, because then the little girl would have to be born after the outbreak, wouldn't she? And she wasn't; she was already at least five years old by then and having dresses bought for her. So . . . perhaps Madame Appeline sneaked out of Caverna somehow, secretly got married and had a baby, and then later sneaked back in again with her daughter . . . But how?*

Neverfell hesitated then frowned, biting her lip. She was trying to force her theory to make sense, but there were some annoying knobbly facts getting in the way. She had the uneasy feeling that she was thumping mismatched jigsaw pieces together to make them fit.

Neverfell needed more information, and with an assassin waiting for her in the courtyards it would be madness to run out there alone again. She needed an ally fast. Snatching up a piece of blank paper, Neverfell sat down and penned another note.

Dear Zouelle,

Please write and let me know that you are well and if your family has stopped trying to stab each other and lock you up. I am fine and I do not think anybody wants to arrest me at the moment, which is a nice change.

Can you come to the palace? I really want to talk to you about some things I found out about Madame Appeline. You know much more about Court than me, and you are good at coming up with plans. Also, do you know anything about a place called the Doldrums?

Only send letters back to me through this messenger or the Enquiry will get them.

Neverfell

Once the letter was tucked under her mattress, Neverfell hugged her knees once more and sat in thought. There were new ideas in her head and new feelings. For the first time, she was not hidden in a corner or fleeing from one emergency to the next. This time she was the hunter, tracking down the past . . . and Madame Appeline.

. . . . .

It was a very different hunt that was being discussed all over Caverna. The Kleptomancer's scandalous theft of the Stackfalter Sturton and the Grand Steward's challenge were the gossip on every level of the labyrinthine city. Perfumiers brought out novelty fragrances called "Thief of Hearts" and "Stealth of the Cat." Artists drew up a hundred imagined figures of the Kleptomancer, most of them tall, suave, caped, and absolutely nothing like the stumpy, begoggled, metal-suited figure that had last been seen leaping off a cheese plate and diving into a lagoon.

Meanwhile, a hundred measures were afoot to catch the scurrilous Stackfalter-snatcher. Such a powerful and prodigious cheese generally had a powerful and prodigious smell, and this was no exception. Perfumiers who worked for the Enquiry were stalking the caverns, scenting the air for the slightest hint of its mossy aroma. Others were scouring the tunnels using harnessed glisserblinds, in the hope that the tiny blind snakes' miraculous sense of smell would detect a trace even the perfumiers had missed.

The Cabinet of Curiosities now drew more curiosity than ever before. Hundreds flocked to survey the oddities there, in particular the lanky cameleopard. The visitors noted the increase in guards, but there were many new security measures that they did not see. They were oblivious to the unseen watchers who peered through hidden slits in the walls, their senses sharpened with spices.

In the hope of finding out how the theft would take place, one Enquirer even decided to turn to cheese. Despite all warnings, he risked taking several small nibbles of the infamous Whispermole Mumblecheddar, famous for revealing flashes of the future and also for tasting like rotting slug juice on fire. Cheeses, however, are not meek and slavish foods, and their visions not so easily commanded. The Enquirer did indeed see glimpses of his own future but learned only that his second son would be born with a squint, that his own nose would someday be broken by a penguin-shaped paperweight, and that he would spend the rest of the day being miserably ill due to eating food far too rich for him.

The Grand Steward, meanwhile, had designed the guarding of the Cabinet with extreme care. He had done everything in his power to make sure that the protection surrounding it was almost impenetrable. Almost. That "almost" was critical. He had ensured that there was one tiny chink in the armor that only a very careful and brilliant thief would spot, a route through the main palace water pipe that only a madman or a prince of audacity would even consider. He had no doubt that the Kleptomancer *would* spot the flaw in the defenses, and hoped that he would mistake it for an oversight on the part of the guards. If it worked, if the Kleptomancer did try to worm his way in through the prepared chink, the Grand Steward's forces would be ready and waiting for him.

And if the trap failed? The Grand Steward smiled. If it failed, there were other traps ready and waiting. He thought it all too likely that the Kleptomancer's strange, all-covering metallic suit would protect him from darts, poison fumes, and Perfumes, but he had asked for something special to be designed for the occasion. The stuffed body of the cameleopard itself was no longer as safe as it had been when Neverfell put her arms round it. Mixed with its sawdust there was now a powerful blend of ominous powders, ready to release their vapors if the cameleopard was jogged or manhandled.

These vapors would not choke away the breath or addle the mind, but they had the virtue of rusting metal with supernatural speed. The Grand Steward felt a thrill of scientific interest as he waited to see the results. He doubted that the Kleptomancer would be quite so spry and speedy with every slat of his armor rusted solid.

Across the room, a venturesome spider swung from a gleaming thread, its legs curling and fiddling against each other like the fingers of a hand, every motion illuminated by the garish green light immediately below. It lowered itself an inch and another inch, tempted by the slick bead of the dead fly below, laid out on its glowing cushion. It dropped one more inch and then suddenly vanished as the jaws of the waiting trap-lantern snapped shut around it, fine teeth meshing and allowing no escape.

In the dreaded Hall of the Harps swaggered a small figure, chattering and chirruping softly to itself. Now and then it glanced about, the whites showed at the edges of its wise, sad, cocoa-colored eyes, but it did not seem unduly alarmed. Meringue crumbs clung to its pink, jutting pout. In the very center of the hall where a little light pooled unwillingly, it settled comfortably on its haunches to sniff at the red hairs it still gripped in its clever little hands, tweaking and plucking at them like a housewife teasing out wool threads for her spinning wheel.

At last it pushed out its lips like an old man drinking soup, then raised itself up and continued its casual lollop to the far wall, where it tugged back the edge of a tapestry to reveal a tiny rope ladder. It began to climb, only a rising bulge in the tapestry revealing its position. At the top of the ladder it reached a tiny arched window, concealed by the tapestry, and clambered through.

The room on the other side was somewhat lighter, and filled with a rather different music from the Hall of the Harps, mostly snores and chitters. The monkey drew itself up and tottered daintily across the tabletop with both hands raised and spread like a fastidious duchess, past a cage with a snoring wolverine, a glass case of cave spiders, and a tank of fish humbug-striped in crimson and cream, dozens of banded, spine-like fins floating around them in a halo. It ignored them all, and instead leaped upon an arm, then scrambled up to a shoulder, and pouted coyly as a finger scritched the fur next to its jaw.

"Bravo, Marcel." The fistful of red hairs was gently taken from its grasp and held up to the light. Marcel accepted a shelled Brazil nut, turning it over and over in his tiny hands before pushing it into his cheek and chewing on it. "Well done."

Meanwhile, his master took the frail red hairs over to a box next to a lantern. The box was fashioned from the finest mesh, for its occupants would have been quite capable of sliding out through the holes in any ordinary cage. Within, it was just possible to see a slick, slate-gray tangle that now and then stirred sluggishly, like a long-abandoned knot trying to undo itself.

Marcel's master picked up a wooden object resembling a pepper grinder. Holding it over the cage he gave it a few turns, with the confident care of an expert chef seasoning a stew, and from it fell a fine pinkish dust. This was not pepper, however, but finely ground Tommyreek, a spice famous for sharpening the sense of smell. At once the knot inside the cage gave a start. Blind tapering heads raised themselves, and mouths opened to taste the air.

Gripping one of the hairs with a pair of tongs, he lowered it until it spooled in through one of the holes in the mesh. The blind mass within began to writhe in good earnest, shivers of electric blue shimmering down the glossy, slender forms as they strove against each other. The solitary hair was tugged from the tongs, pulled away by a dozen small, snapping mouths, which then gaped again, looking for more.

Marcel pulled back his lips in a grin like a yellow zip.

BLIND SIDE

TO PASS SAFELY THROUGH A JUNGLE, ONE MUST walk either with stealth or with confidence.

Zouelle recited this mantra of her uncle Maxim as she trod the intricate mosaics of the Court for the first time. She had made her debut and been a guest at one of the Grand Steward's banquets, and thus had now won the right to enter the public walks of the palace, but she knew that rights alone would not keep her skin whole. If she flinched or showed a hint of uncertainty, others would notice her and start to see her as a victim or an opportunity.

Even with the three palace guards accompanying her, she was sure to keep her stride steady, her face locked in a smile of radiant smugness and anticipation. She counted in her head, forcing herself to breathe slowly. One, two, three, in, four, five, six, out. *I am a Childersin,* she told herself. *I am a Childersin. I am one whisker on a great lion. When they look at me, they see the lion.*

I can do this. I can do all of this. I'm the best actress in the Beaumoreau Academy.

They had reached an arched door, presumably the entrance to the tasters' quarters, and to her surprise Zouelle found her apprehension increasing instead of diminishing.

This is silly! It's Neverfell, remember? Just Neverfell. But . . . so much has happened now. What do I say to her? And what have other people been saying to her? Does she realize she's the talk of the Court?

Zouelle was sure that many courtiers were already bargaining and battling for introductions to the Grand Steward's notorious and fascinating new food taster. Neverfell was not only elevated, she was fashionable, and there was much status to be gained just by being seen with her. Zouelle had a head start on her rivals since Neverfell already regarded her as a friend, but if she did not press that advantage she would doubtless be crowded out as others jostled their way into Neverfell's warm and impressionable heart.

When Zouelle had shown Neverfell's letter to her uncle Maxim, he had made it clear that his niece *should* press her advantage. *Yes, you should go and see Neverfell, or she will turn to others with her problems and questions. Be a friend to her. A confidante. When she looks for somebody to trust, we want her to come to us.* Zouelle thought she understood why. The Childersin family had rocked on its pedestal recently and nearly tumbled. At this moment it needed to increase its influence, and in her new position Neverfell could be a useful contact.

"If you would not mind waiting, my lady," murmured the nearest guard. Zouelle gave a small nod of consent, and the man disappeared through the door, leaving her attended by the other two. So she was "my lady" now, not "miss." That was what she had always wanted, wasn't it? Why did the words chill her? There was something so cold and final about it, like the click of a door closing behind her. Her childhood was over, and now there was only her place in the Great Game, and whatever role Uncle Maxim had chosen for her. There was no going back.

The door before her burst open barely a minute later.

"Zouelle!"

The blonde girl was nearly thrown backward off her feet by a high-speed redheaded hug. "You're alive and not locked in anywhere! Is the rest of your family safe? Are they here?" Evidently Neverfell's etiquette training had only achieved so much. One reunion, and everything she had been taught about proper greetings had fallen from her mind, like precariously placed trunks from a runaway cart.

"Steady! No, it's just me here." With difficulty Zouelle extricated herself, and held Neverfell by the shoulders to examine her at arm's length. "Uncle Maxim sends his regards, but thought it would look less suspicious if I came alone. And don't worry, the family is all fine. We're all . . . fine. It . . . your plan worked." Remembering Neverfell's suicidal, hell-for-leather gallop into custody to save the Childersin family, Zouelle could not help letting her gaze drop for a moment. "And you, how are you?" Neverfell's grin was like an explosion, and at first it was hard to see anything past it. However, when Zouelle looked the younger girl up and down, she noticed swellings, bruises, reddened punctures raked by scratch-marks. "You look . . . Has it been bad? What did they do when they questioned you? Did they hurt you?"

"Oh." Neverfell rubbed ruefully at a spider bite on her neck and shrugged. "Well, they set spiders and snakes on me for a bit and blew me up and there was this really scary cake, but it's mostly all right now, I think. Except I don't ever want any more cake. Look!" Neverfell held up her hands to show the steel thimbles on the edge of each of her fingers. "I have to wear these so I don't bite my fingernails. I don't really mind, but they clink on my teeth a bit."

"But the Grand Steward?" Zouelle made a desperate grab at the trailing rein of the conversation before it could run away again. "You have his favor? His protection?"

"Sort of." Neverfell bit her lip and leaned forward to whisper in Zouelle's ear. "His left eye seems to like me, anyway."

"Good." Zouelle glanced about, aware that many at Court took Paprickle spice to help them eavesdrop. "We should sit down somewhere quiet and talk."

Zouelle was not allowed into the main tasters' quarters, but there was a little secluded parlor set aside for visitors, so they retired there to speak in private. The ubiquitous palace servants opened the door for Neverfell as she approached, and Zouelle was suddenly stung by the thought of the guards perhaps calling Neverfell "my lady" the same way they had addressed her. Immediately the honor of that title cheapened in her mind, like a piece of tinsel that had adorned the neck of a puppy or piglet.

Once they were alone, Zouelle came straight to the point.

"Neverfell, it's not enough to be favored by Left-Eye. You urgently need to win over Right-Eye."

"Urgently? Why?"

"Because Right-Eye looks kindly on the Enquiry, and the Enquiry is not on your side. I know for a fact that Enquirer Treble distrusts you and has suggested to His Excellency more than once that her people should be allowed to put you to the question. Neverfell, on no account let yourself fall into the hands of the Enquiry, or you will be tortured into confessing all kinds of things."

"But I thought they'd finished with me!" Neverfell looked distraught. "How do you know all this?"

"Because our family has spies among the Enquirers," Zouelle responded smoothly, then laughed at Neverfell's expression.

"Don't look so shocked! Anybody who is anybody at Court has agents in the Enquiry. They're riddled with infiltrators. That's why it's so hard to work out who tried to have you killed in the Enquiry cells. It was probably an Enquirer, but they could have been secretly working for *anybody*."

Neverfell was full of questions about the Childersins' welfare, so Zouelle hastened to bring her up to date. Mere hours after Neverfell had been taken into the Grand Steward's custody, Maxim Childersin had returned to his town house, somewhat haggard but unharmed. He had effortlessly seized the reins of the family once again, just in time to stop his relations from tearing one another apart.

"And since then we have all been pretending none of it ever happened." Zouelle gave a small breathless laugh as Neverfell boggled at her. "How else could we face one another over the breakfast table every day? Uncle Maxim will punish some of the family for the things they did when they thought he was dead, but he won't do it openly, and he won't do it yet. Everybody knows that."

As Zouelle expected, Neverfell's face went into a whirligig of surprise, consternation, disbelief. This time, however, these did not ebb into confused acceptance. Like a monkey with a nut, Neverfell was turning over a thought, holding it to her eye, testing her teeth against its shell. Zouelle suspected that she was thinking hard about Maxim Childersin, perhaps trying for the first time to see him clearly past the golden glow of her own loyalty and gratitude.

"You've changed," Zouelle said, inadvertently speaking her thought aloud.

"Have I?"

"I think so. A little. Your expressions . . . they're bolder.

And less . . ." Zouelle fought back the word "half-witted." "Less dazzled-looking."

"I think you're right. I feel different."

"So what is all of this about? I got your letter—why all this interest in Madame Appeline?" In truth, Madame Appeline was the last subject Zouelle wanted to discuss, so soon after the disastrous audition plan. Her very name was a reminder of Zouelle's own mistakes, Uncle Maxim's quiet displeasure, and the price he had probably paid to persuade the Facesmith not to pursue the matter.

As it was, Zouelle was forced to listen as Neverfell launched into a rambling, badly ordered explanation. She talked of a strange feeling of connection to Madame Appeline, a mysterious Face that had tugged at her heart, a moment when she thought the Facesmith might have recognized her, a vision she had experienced after Maxim Childersin's Wine, and finally information gleaned from the de Meina sisters. Zouelle had forgotten how tiring it was listening to Neverfell at full pace, like being bludgeoned with exclamation marks. One bit of the explanation caught her attention.

"You went out into the palace walks by yourself? Neverfell—do you have any idea how dangerous that was?" Zouelle was torn between horror at Neverfell's recklessness and a sense of acute unfairness. Somebody as clumsy and clueless as Neverfell should not have wandered around the Court and escaped unscathed. Somehow the younger girl rampaged about, more like a young animal than a human being, and survived things that would see anybody else dead.

On the positive side, it sounded as if some other courtiers had tried to establish an acquaintance with Neverfell and mishandled it badly. With luck, this might make Neverfell wary of such overtures, and more inclined to turn to the Childersins instead.

"But I had to find out about Madame Appeline!" protested Neverfell. "I think I might be . . . related to her. A . . . a close relation." There was another word that Neverfell clearly could not quite bring herself to use, but it might as well have been written on the air between them.

"Oh dear." Zouelle could not help sighing at the pathetic hopefulness of it all. "Neverfell, you really haven't thought this through at all, have you? *Of course* you felt a sense of connection when you saw that Face at the cheese-tunnel door. You felt what you were meant to feel. There is a set of motherly Faces from the Tragedy Range that Madame Appeline wears all the time when she's dealing with her Putty Girls, because it wins them over and leaves them doting on her. She wanted to get you on her side, so she used one of them on you.

"Besides, all you recognized was the Face she was wearing, Neverfell. Not her, just the Face. And seven years ago the Tragedy Range was all the rage. Scores of people were wearing them. Well, maybe when you were little you did know somebody who was good to you and who wore that Face, but that doesn't mean it was Madame Appeline."

Neverfell's face fell, but did not stay fallen. Her brow puckered, and her lip protruded mulishly. A previously unsuspected pot of stubbornness was simmering away there, Zouelle realized, and in its depths she glimpsed, just for a moment, a startling little diamond splinter of anger.

"There's a link," Neverfell said, a little defensively. "There's a link between me and Madame Appeline. I know it, and I know that doesn't make any sense. Something in me woke up when I saw her. Everything started to move, to break open. It's as if all these years there have been things waiting to happen, like a machine ready for somebody to pull the first lever. And that first lever was me seeing her. I know her, Zouelle. And I know I have to push on until I remember why."

The red-haired girl did seem more awake. The nervous energy that had previously been stuttering out of her in fidgets and frets appeared more focused now. If anything she seemed less tame, less manageable.

Zouelle took a deep breath and then released it. "All right, then. I'll help you push." Neverfell, who had obviously been bracing for an argument, looked at her in surprise, and Zouelle gave a small, elegant shrug. "Well, I had better—if only to stop you from running around the palace by yourself." She smiled, deciding upon Face No. 57, The Willow Bows Before the Gale.

Out came the blinding Neverfell grin again, and next thing Zouelle knew she was being hugged so hard that she had to beg the younger girl to stop.

"Anyway, I asked a few questions about the Doldrums, since you seemed so interested in them," Zouelle went on, once she had recovered her breath. "Apparently the whole district is still walled up and sealed off, even after all these years. Back before the epidemic it was a bit of a slum, by all accounts. Dingy and dripping. Worst of all, seven years ago there was a lot of excavation going on all around it—at that time they were still digging out the tunnels that became the Samphire district and the Octopus. The sounds of mining and drilling were deafening, so nobody of quality was interested in living there."

Neverfell rubbed at her temples.

"I can't remember. You would think I'd remember something like that, wouldn't you?"

"What it does mean," Zouelle continued patiently, "is that pretty much anything could have happened down there, and none of the neighbors would have heard a thing."

"What about Madame Appeline? What do you know about her? You said that your family doesn't get on with her. Why not?"

"I don't really know. I think she and Uncle Maxim just fell out over something years ago." Zouelle shrugged. "Her feud with my family does make it rather hard for me to get close to her without causing suspicion. Don't worry, though, I have a better idea.

"Do you remember Borcas? Well, she passed the audition, and she's working for Madame Appeline now. I suppose Madame Appeline never *did* find out that she was a close friend of mine, otherwise I don't think she would have taken her on. Of course, Borcas has been avoiding me like the plague ever since the audition, to make sure her employer never *does* connect us, but I'm sure I can talk her into helping."

"What about me?" asked Neverfell. "What can I do?"

Zouelle took hold of both her hands and looked her straight in the eye.

"Stay safe," she said in her best firm, big-sister voice. "Oh, Neverfell, you're just not made for undercover work. You can't lie, my dear, and I can. Leave Madame Appeline and the Doldrums to me. Stay here and keep your head down."

"I . . . I don't know if that'll help," said Neverfell hesitantly. "Even here. Zouelle . . . I keep feeling like I'm being watched."

"Neverfell, you *are* being watched. All the time. By everybody. Haven't you noticed? You're the latest spectacle."

"But there was this note that told me . . ."

Zouelle could see that the younger girl was hovering on the edge of telling her something. *I can trust Zouelle* was written across her face as clearly as on any page. *Oh, but I probably shouldn't tell anybody. And there's no harm in keeping it a secret.* By the looks of things, Neverfell was trying to protect somebody again, so there was no point in trying to wrestle the truth from her. No doubt it would come out in time.

"Wait!" A new thought had evidently paralyzed Neverfell. "If there's a killer out there who doesn't want people looking into my past . . . won't investigating put you in danger?"

"Don't worry. I'm a Childersin. I'm very good at covering my tracks. Because even when I do make a mistake, I remove it."

"Remove it?"

"If nobody remembers a mistake, it never happened. So wherever I go I carry this." Zouelle delved into her pocket and drew out a small corked vial. "If I do or say anything really regrettable and there's a witness, I just slip this into their drink, and they forget the last hour. I've used it dozens of times."

The younger girl did not look exactly reassured. "You'll be careful, though, won't you?" demanded Neverfell.

"Of course! And I'll be back soon, when I've found out more."

Neverfell's wide-eyed look of consternation stayed with Zouelle as she left the tasters' quarters and began her tense glide back to the exit of the palace. Did Neverfell even remember from one moment to the next that she herself, and not Zouelle, was the assassin's target? Neverfell was a blundering puppy, blind to all the dangers, blind to the offense she caused with every step.

No, nobody would ever call Neverfell "my lady." She was still a "miss" all the way—misunderstanding, making mistakes, getting into misadventures. Zouelle swallowed down an unexpected surge of envy and tried to focus her mind, to think like a Childersin.

That went well. Neverfell still trusts me more than she does anybody else. None of the other Court factions have won her over yet. I'm in a game against the big players now, and when they notice me they'll start making moves against me, but at the moment I'm winning.

I can do this. I can do all of this. I'm the best actress in the Beaumoreau Academy.

All over Caverna clocks were ticking, each earning more than the usual share of glances. If the Kleptomancer were to meet the Grand Steward's challenge, he had a mere three hours to do so. It was decades since the Court had known such excitement.

In secret, wagers were made on his success or failure. The errand boys made a thriving business hotfooting to and from the Cabinet of Curiosities to report on whether a daring theft had taken place. Some nobles who had been particularly bored over the last century decided upon a vigil, and could be seen picnicking in their palanquins in the neighboring courtyards, their monkeys running to and fro laden down with silver plates of crystallized fruit.

The Grand Steward refused to join them, all too aware that this would give far too much opportunity for assassins while his security forces were focused upon seizing the ingenious and notorious thief. Besides, a personal appearance would only inflate the Kleptomancer's reputation and ego.

Most of the tasters were immune to the general excitement, drugged by the soothing smoke of their long pipes. Neverfell, however, lay painfully awake in her bed. Her trap-lantern was still grumpily snapping at the scoopful of grubs she had brought it from the fresh barrel in the corridor, but even when it quieted, Neverfell's thoughts still ground and sparked.

More than anything else, Neverfell knew that she needed to sleep. She had slept badly the previous night, and tomorrow she would be attending upon the changeable Grand Steward for eight hours. Which would it be, Right-Eye, exacting, intolerant, waiting for her to make a slip? Or Left-Eye, mad, silent, and unguessable? Either way, she needed to be as alert as possible. She also needed to be sharp enough to watch out for assassins seeking her blood.

She lay there with her eyes closed, as if sleep were a shy creature that might venture out if she played dead. But every time it seemed to be drawing closer, some loud thought would crash and blunder through the undergrowth, putting it to flight.

And then there was the Kleptomancer. It was only two hours until the final moment of the Grand Steward's challenge. Would the plan work? And if it didn't, what would become of her? It was partly her idea, after all.

She was so tired she could have cried. At last she sat up and glared down at the relentless flatness of her mattress. How did people sleep on these things? Too soft and too hard at the same time. Something tickled her forehead and made her start, but when she looked up she saw nothing threatening, only the fringed tassels hanging from the upper frame and the swell of the cloth canopy that hung like a little ceiling over the bed.

An idea came to her. Everything would be all right. She would be able to sleep after all.

It was forty minutes until the hour of naught.

In a cobbled square not far from the tasters' quarters, a great clock told out each minute with ponderous disdain. Beneath the clock quailed a man whom nobody was inclined to see. He was fairly tall and of middling years, but he stooped slightly like an old man, perhaps from the weight of the briefcase in his hand. His heavy jowls wobbled when he blew his nose, and he squinted at the world through Face No. 92, The Lamb Before the Butcher, an expression of pained pleading. Every time somebody passed through the square he called out to them in quavering tones and hobbled toward them a few steps.

"Ah, great ladies, I wonder whether I might call upon your gentle assistance . . . or perhaps you, sir, there is a plea that I would wish to be placed before the Grand Steward . . ." The ladies' fans opened with cracks like pistol shots and were held up to block the stranger from view. The men invariably snapped on the most aloof Faces in their repertoire and strode firmly past, leaving him bowing in their wake. He was obviously just another pathetic, fallen courtier, desperately trying to find friends to help him claw his way back into favor. Nobody would look at such a man in case the disfavor he suffered was contagious.

This was, in some respects, something of a pity. Had anybody actually taken the trouble to examine the man with any care, they might have noticed a number of oddities. First of all, while he often proffered his briefcase toward promising-looking parties, he never opened it. Second, every few minutes he cast an eye on the clock behind him. Third, when he hobbled forward, his feet did not make the slightest sound on the mosaic floor.

Now the trickle of passersby had slowed to almost nothing. After all, it was now thirty minutes until the hour of naught. Outside the Cabinet of Curiosities, the crowds would be swelling. Here there was almost nobody, except the pleader and a few guards. Here there was hardly a sound, except for the ticking of the clock, the echo of voices from the direction of the Cabinet, and the faint sounds that were always present in Caverna, the dim reverberation of gongs far below, the faint, tinny sound of water pipes, and, behind it all, the hollow boom of vast, unseen winds above playing the mountain like a flute.

Suddenly, just for a moment, the far corner of the square dimmed and flickered. It brightened, but then just as quickly dimmed again. A faint papery chittering was audible, and it soon became clear that it was coming from the trap in the corner lantern. The trap itself was gaping, and seemed to be suffering a fit. It was covered with what looked like a fine white snow, which fell away as it convulsed, revealing steaming black patches.

One guard cautiously approached the afflicted trap with his sword drawn, and dared to reach out and poke the lantern with the tip of his blade. Just as he did so, the trap snapped shut its jaws. With a *whump* like the slamming of a felt-lined door, it exploded, so that the corner it had lit was plunged into darkness. The guard reeled back, blinking and coughing, his face and clothes dusted with a fine white powder. More flour-like powder had spattered the nearest walls and could be heard raining with a soft hiss onto the polished floor, the ornaments, the other lanterns, and everything else.

The guards were well-trained and immediately covered their noses and mouths with their handkerchiefs, for fear of inhaling something poisonous.

"What in the name of peril—"

Again, there was a faint sound from the empty side of the courtyard, the same papery chittering, but this time louder and more insistent. Three other trap-lanterns had been rained upon by the explosive white dust, and the traps within each were starting to quiver and palpitate, dimming as their glowing flesh seethed and frothed with a white and powdery snow.

Whump. Whump whump. All three quietly exploded, one after the other, and as they did so darkness swallowed more and more of the courtyard in great hungry gulps. Only half the courtyard was lit now, and it was hazy with fine, drifting powder, slowly descending to settle on the gaping guards, the remaining lanterns . . .

"Cover the lamps!" One guard, more quick-witted than the rest, lurched forward in an attempt to throw his cape over the nearest lantern and shield it from the falling powder. He was too late. Even as the other guards followed his cue, the tiny plants were starting to quiver, chitter, and froth.

Whump. Whump. Whump. The square was claimed by shadow. *Whump whump whump whump whump.* The darkness chased its way down the corridor that led to the tasters' quarters, as the traps along it burst one after the other.

One guard was standing next to the stooping courtier when the final lantern failed. During that last gasp of light, he saw the courtier straighten from his stoop and cast off his pleading posture. He no longer squinted, and the irises of his eyes were utterly black and perfectly lightless. This much the guard saw as darkness swallowed all. He did not call to alert his comrades, for he was given no time. The only warning he gave was the muffled sound of his lifeless body hitting the floor.

The guards tried to defend themselves, but they had a foe who could see in the dark where they could not. They tried to flee, but their foe could run faster and more silently than they.

We are under attack, they tried to call out as they were cut down. *Bring more men, bring light, bring a trap-lantern . . .*

Their cries were too brief and faint, and nobody was close enough to hear them. The word "trap" echoed plaintively through the empty lazuli halls as a fine and delicate mist of powder seeped and billowed under the door leading to the tasters' quarters.

There was nobody in the main corridor of the tasters' retreat, nobody to see as each of the traps hanging from the walls started to shiver and blister white. Now they were shedding white flakes like dandruff, now their light was sallowing, now there was a string of woolly detonations, filling the air with the spores of their destruction.

The sounds were too quiet to disturb the happy haze of those in the smoking room, or those sleeping in their chambers. In the recreation room, however, several looked up from chess or cards to peer quizzically at the door and notice a bitter taste in the air. One stood to open the door, and gaped uncomprehendingly into the void beyond.

Only when the lamps in the room itself frenzied, frothed, and failed did the tasters wake up to their danger. Like most such awakenings, it arrived too late.

Darkness, they were in darkness! It was one of the greatest fears of all those in Caverna. To be in darkness meant to be without trap-lanterns. No traps sooner or later meant suffocating in stale air. In their panic, the tasters forgot that the fresh air in the rooms would last for hours yet. They seemed already to feel a harshness like dust in their lungs and a choking in their throats. Their only thought was to get out, to run through the palace until they found light.

They forgot all about their comrades in their private chambers and in the smoking room. Scrambling over one another, trying to claw each other out of the way, they blundered to the door that led to the rest of the palace, and yanked back the bolts that had been thrown to keep them safe. They surged into the courtyard, choking and calling out, and the few palace servants in attendance scrambled after them, following the sounds of their voices. Neither group noticed somebody slipping past them the other way, into the tasters' quarters.

Those in the smoking room were roused by the sounds of chaos outside, and found themselves staring up into a chilling and sobering blackness. The Perfume in the hookah smoke, however, lulled them back into their daze. *There is nothing to worry about,* it told them. *You do not need light. You do not need breath. You need only me.* They lolled back onto their divans, and let the Perfume pull their dreams over them once more like a golden counterpane.

Meanwhile, the unseen stranger stopped in the middle of the now-empty corridor. To his midnight-colored eyes there was no darkness. Dead matter like the walls and floor was murky and colorless but visible. Life was luminous. His spice-sharpened vision showed him his own body as a glowing, man-shaped phantasm. Even now the whole scene was softly gilded with the dust from the newly dead traps, the powdery glow fading as the last traces of vitality ebbed away.

The assassin smiled, knowing that he had the mysterious Kleptomancer to thank for the sparseness of guards in this area. Right now, most of the armed men in the palace would be waiting to ambush the master thief in the Cabinet of Curiosities.

He set down his briefcase in the middle of the hallway, and opened it. For him, the contents were alive with shimmering, squirming light. Sinuous slivers of this light broke off from the main tangle, slithering out of the case and onto the floor. They seethed and skimmed over the corridor, following their own blind instincts and their extraordinary sense of smell.

Here! They found a footprint with the scent they sought, and they clicked to tell one another, a cold sound like pebbles rapped together. They coiled and writhed in the unseen print, until the watcher could almost make out its outline. There—a few slivers flowed on ahead of the rest, and they found another print. Another, another, and now they were seething at the base of a door.

So this was the chamber of his quarry. Stooping, the man scooped up the twisting slivers with his gloved hands, and fed them in through the keyhole.

On the other side, the slivers tumbled down to the floor, retracting into coils from the shock of their fall, then recovering and tasting the air with their tiny gaping mouths.

The slivers themselves were not disturbed by the darkness, for they had never known anything else. Theirs was a world of brightly colored scents, sounds felt through their bellies and the tremors of the ground, and the sinuous touch of one another's scales. Hours before, their narrow mouths had closed upon strands of hair that smelled of something young and living. Now they thought of nothing but that scent. It blazed in their minds, russet gold, and drew them on. There was no excitement, only cool, mindless hunger.

They silently seethed over the carpet, discovering ruffled indentations recently pressed by feet, a trail drawing them farther and farther into the room. The frontrunners touched their noses against something soft and slippery smooth, something that smelled of the russet gold. It was a discarded satin shoe, and their tiny shapes poured in between its straps, drunk with the smell. Narrow mouths sought and bit, lithe bodies boiled in a mass, and within seconds there was nothing left of the shoe but its sole, and scattered fragments of silk, some melting with a hiss as venom ate into the tender fabric.

The slivers were abroad again. One found the carved wooden foot of a bed, and gave three rapid clicks. Its siblings heard, and joined it in twining up the leg, sliding over the knobbles and grooves in the ornate carvings.

Their tiny bodies barely dented the pillow as they slid out

upon it, exploring the valley in its center, strewn with occasional fine hairs. They weaved down the pillow's slope, found the crumpled edge of a blanket, and slipped neatly under it, in search of animal warmth.

They found none, only cool sheet and rough blanket. Their quarry's scent was everywhere. Their quarry was nowhere. Where was she?

Up above them, lying on the thick brocade canopy stretched over the frame of the bed, Neverfell crouched in darkness and held her breath.

The idea of sleeping on the bed's canopy had come to her all of a sudden. It looked a little like her own dear, much-missed hammock, and so she had scrambled up, using the ornate carvings of the bedposts for footholds. Sleep had indeed been waiting for her there, and as soon as she had stretched out on the canopy her eyelids had drooped and her mind had tumbled into sweet fog.

There it might have remained if it had not been for her sharp cheesemaker's nose. It had twitched in sleep as the fine powder crept under her door, and when her own trap blew itself apart she was woken, not by the sound but by the smell. And there, staring up into darkness and listening to the sounds of receding screams, she had heard something or things quietly slithering and rasping their way through her keyhole. There were alien things in her room. They smelled the way cold stone felt. The blackness was absolute, and she could tell where they were only from the clicks.

Click. Click click. They were directly below her, and Neverfell knew they were in her bed.

She also had a keen idea what they were. Only glisserblinds clicked that way, and only when they were hunting as a pack.

She listened intensely, trying to work out if any of the clicks were getting closer. She dared not move, for fear of creaking the bed frame. Their hearing was better than hers, their sense of smell more acute. They were blind, of course, but for the moment so was she.

It was while she was listening that she became aware that the thick brocade beneath her was starting to shift and stretch imperceptibly under her unaccustomed weight.

From somewhere beyond Neverfell's feet came a short, sharp *tac* noise, the unmistakable sound of a thread snapping. There was a silence and then a frenzy of clicks below, clicks answering, clicks rising, getting closer. They had heard, they knew, they were writhing up the bedposts to get to her.

Neverfell struggled into a sitting position, the bed frame groaning as she did so. With a staccato *tac-tac-tac-tac,* a seam somewhere gave way, and the canopy beneath her lurched, throwing her off balance. Frantic, Neverfell hauled herself upright again and swung her legs over the edge of the frame. Just as she was bracing for the jump, she felt something cold as a fish slither over the back of her hand.

With a squawk of sheer panic, she gave a violent jerk of her hand and flung the unseen something across the room, she knew not where. Then she hurled herself forward into the waiting darkness.

She could not see the floor to judge the jump, and landed with a crash, her knee jolting into her face. There was no time to sob over her bruised hip or wrenched ankle, however. The glisserblinds would have heard the crash of her landing. Even now they would be sliding back down the bedposts, or falling from the canopy to the carpet like a deadly rain.

Neverfell stumbled to her feet and hobbled as fast as her tortured ankle would let her, in what she hoped was the direction of the table. She succeeded in finding the corner painfully with her hip, and swept a desperate hand across it until she located the key. Feeling her way along the wall, she reached the door, fearing every moment to feel something underfoot that squirmed and bit.

She found the lock, fumbled the key into it somehow, turned it. A click sounded mere feet behind her. Flinging the door open, Neverfell leaped through it. Before she could slam the door behind her, however, her injured ankle gave way.

She slumped abruptly to the floor. And it was for this reason alone that, a moment later, the thing that had been waiting to happen to Neverfell ended up happening an inch above her head instead.

All she heard was the faint silken sound of something slicing the air above her, and then the reverberating thud of metal striking into wood. Her stomach exploded with tingles, as if it sensed that it had been the unseen blade's intended destination. Somewhere in front of her, somebody was breathing.

With all her strength, Neverfell flung herself into a backward roll and rose unsteadily to her feet. Turning, she hurtled away down the corridor at the fastest limp-sprint she could manage.

The killer had not expected her to reach the door alive. He had heard her cry out and had thought that the glisserblinds' work was done. Thus he had been halfway back down the corridor when he heard the key turn, and had been caught off guard. His misjudged swing, furthermore, had left his sword embedded in the wooden paneling of the wall.

Another tug and it was free. He sprinted after the fleeing girl on feet that made no sound. Ahead of him, her frail, luminous form blundered moth-like against walls, and he gained quickly. As she was passing the ember chute, she stumbled over the prone form of a dead guard and fell sprawling with a yelp.

Now was the moment. He leaped forward, sword raised. Or now would have been the moment if another gleaming figure had not, at this very instant, erupted without warning from the gaping blackness of the ember chute.

It was a foot shorter than the killer, but stocky and surprisingly agile. It parried the descending blade with a forearm, and the killer was surprised to hear a metallic clang instead of a shriek of pain. The next moment the odd figure had punched the assassin in the face with shocking force and accuracy, and the assassin realized that it too could see in the dark.

The blow knocked him back a couple of feet, and then he saw the stocky figure lift one arm and level it at him. There seemed to be something bulky jutting from its hand. Reflexively, the killer raised his sword and lunged forward to attack.

During the long second of his lunge, the assassin thought he saw his own body and that of his new enemy grow brighter still, as if both were living more fiercely in that lethal moment. Before his sword could bite anything but air, a supernova went off in his chest, and suddenly he found he was not leaping forward anymore. The floor hit him in the back hard. Then the world and all its lightless lights went out quietly and left him to darkness, like a dying trap-lantern.

Meanwhile, the stocky figure paid no attention to his fallen attacker. Instead, he flung a broad, metal-clad arm round the injured girl as she struggled to her feet, and tumbled backward into the darkness of the ember chute, dragging her with him.

There was a descending and fading scream from the chute. The ember-chute doors, which had flung back on their hinges, swung slowly to and clicked against each other. And then, all over Caverna, the clocks gave a hiccup of their cogs as they chimelessly chimed the hour of naught.

A DROP OF MADNESS

WHEN NEVERFELL CAME AROUND, SHE FOUND
that she was shivering. She was lying on something hard and
flat, and for some reason she seemed to be wet. Her hair was
plastered to her face, and chill dribbles had run in at the collar of
her pajamas.

The memory of her kidnap returned to her, like an army
of soldiers marching out of mist. The glisserblinds, the pursuit
through the dark, chaotic sounds around her, being gripped
around her middle, and plummeting through a choking blackness
that smelled like ash . . . Gingerly she opened her eyes a crack
and peered out between the damp strands of her hair.

She appeared to be lying on a large table, against the wall of a
reasonably sizeable cavern. The ceiling was low and strung with
hooks, from which hung a veritable forest of tools, flasks, baskets,
and sacks, so that her view of the far wall was obstructed. From
one hook hung an armored suit made up of tiny diamond-shaped
scales, and farther off she could just make out the hanging swell of
a tattered hammock of thick wool and sacking. On another table
not far away was what looked like a set of alchemist's equipment,

a huddle of bulge-bellied glass flasks, and flimsy scales loaded with gold and scarlet powders.

From the other side of the room Neverfell could hear faint squeaks and creaks. Her teeth were chattering, but her curiosity was stronger than anything else. As quietly as she could, she lowered herself down from the table and crept slowly in the direction of the sounds, taking care not to nudge the hanging tools and sacks or put too much weight on her injured ankle.

Just ahead, she could see a lantern resting on the ground. Somebody was standing next to it, the upper half of his body concealed behind a rack of hanging grain sacks and cooking pots. She could just make out gloved hands unfastening the clasps on a metal suit, prising the armor apart and letting it fall to the floor, to reveal surprisingly drab brown workaday clothes underneath. Then something large and round was lowered to the ground, where it rang like a gong, rolled a little, and glared up at her with two droplet-spattered goggles.

She recognized it in an instant from description. It was the Kleptomancer's helmet.

His hands, now ungloved, were pulling something out of a pocket with a tremulous eagerness. It was a letter, sealed with a strange and elaborate design in purple wax. The figure crouched, holding the letter close to the lantern, and Neverfell saw the Kleptomancer properly for the first time.

She had been braced for a headless man. She would not have been surprised by searing eyes, aquiline mockery, or twitching insanity. In fact, she had been ready for anything except ordinariness.

The face upward-lit by the measly trap was wide-jawed and clean-shaven, with a high forehead so that the eyes, nose, and mouth seemed crowded in the lower part of it. His eyes were small, his nose short and blunt, his hair nut-brown and close-cropped. It was not a face that would stand out from a crowd. Indeed, given his height, most crowds would have swallowed him altogether.

His expression was perfectly blank. Perhaps there was something a little too even about the central line of his mouth. There were no rises, falls, curls, and valleys, just a perfectly straight line. It was not cruel or hard but level as the surface of still water.

The only remarkable feature was his eyes, the irises of which were black and lightless. As she watched, Neverfell saw him squint at the letter and rub impatiently at his eyes with the heel of his hand.

The dead black irises had to mean that he had been taking Nocteric to help him see in the dark. Neverfell had never used it but knew a little about it. One of the common aftereffects was snow-freckle, a symptom that flecked your eyes with white and left you with half-blind, mottled sight for an hour or so. If she was right, the Kleptomancer was squinting because his eyes were starting to freckle. Perhaps this could work in her favor.

Stealthily she approached, taking pains to stay outside the lantern's halo of light. As she watched, he pulled out a pair of tinted spectacles with triangular lenses and tried peering through them at the letter, then gave a short hiss of annoyance. Slapping his letter down on the floor, he ventured uncertainly into the darkness, one arm raised to protect his head from the hanging tools. Ducking to peer, Neverfell could just see him rummaging in a distant bag, pulling out several pairs of curious-looking goggles.

Neverfell had planned to wait until the Kleptomancer's sight had thickened further before making her move, but the sight of the unattended letter was too much for her. Holding her breath, she slipped forward as quietly as possible, snatched up the letter, and limped stealthily back into the shadows.

A few seconds later she heard a crash. Then there came the sound of hurried, blundering steps and a cacophony of jangling tools as if someone was pushing through them at speed.

Neverfell pulled herself up into the hammock in the nick of time and hung silently in its belly as the Kleptomancer pushed past, in the direction of the table where he had left her. A moment later, she heard his voice for the first time.

"Where are you?" It was a shout, but a strangely passionless one, and his voice had a slight roughness, as if it had gathered fluff through lack of use. "I know you have my letter."

She had to wait. If she could only wait, his sight would dim further, and she would have a chance of making her escape.

The light where she lay was very poor, but with difficulty she could just make out the words written on the front of the envelope.

To be opened after the successful completion of Operation M331.

Stealthily she broke the seal and peered at the contents until her eyes ached:

Immediately imbibe blend 4ZZ to erase days 17670 to 17691 and blend 8HH to revive day 35839. Discover all you can from item. Observe rupture for two days. Once all information gleaned, return item exactly as found. Next letter will arrive in three days' time.

Elsewhere in the room, she could still hear the Kleptomancer crashing around, looking for her. As she listened, however, the attempts seemed to grow more sluggish and desultory. Perhaps he was giving up. Perhaps the snow-freckle was setting in. Perhaps this was her chance to try to escape.

Very gingerly, she let herself down from her hammock and began edging along the wall, looking for a way out. After a short while she was rewarded by the sight of two double doors. From behind them issued a steady, soulless roar. A taut, thick wire entered the room through the crack where the doors met, and slanted down to tether to an iron ring fixed to the floor. The floor around it was glossy with puddles.

Now or never. She pulled the doors open. The roar became deafening, and a fine spray frosted the skin of Neverfell's face. Her heart plummeted. She was staring at a solid wall of mashing, white water, a waterfall that could demolish her as easily as a hippopotamus stepping on an ant. There was no escape that way.

She closed the doors again and spun round, only to find that the Kleptomancer had emerged from the hanging clutter behind her. Perhaps he had heard the waterfall's roar suddenly grow louder as she opened the door.

"Give me my letter." His voice matched the steady line of his mouth, level as still water. Still water wasn't cruel and wasn't kind. It didn't care whether you swam or drowned.

"These are orders, aren't they?" Neverfell tried to snatch back her wits and courage. "Somebody's giving you orders! Somebody sent you to murder me with snakes—or steal me—or kidnap me! Tell me what's going on or . . . or I'll eat the letter!"

The Kleptomancer took a step forward, and Neverfell stuffed the letter into her mouth.

"'Et 'ack!'" she shouted, somewhat unclearly. "I'll shtart chewin'!" There was a pause, and then to her enormous relief he receded a few steps. Slowly, heart pounding, Neverfell prised the now slightly damp letter out of her mouth. The thief's face was still as blank as stone, and Neverfell's world lurched as she suddenly realized how much danger she was in. She had seen the true and secret face of the Kleptomancer. How could he afford to let her live to speak of it?

Then, all at once, one of the strange phrases in the letter leaped to her mind and began to make sense.

"*Return item exactly as found.* The letter says *return item exactly as found!* The item's me, isn't it? You have to return me as found! So, if you hurt me, you'll get into trouble with your master!" She dodged a sudden snatch by the Kleptomancer, and darted away at a high-speed lollop. Yes, his aim was now clearly suffering.

"I'm not trying to hurt you!" he shouted after her. "I just saved your life! Now stop all this . . . running!"

Glancing back at the thief, Neverfell could see him standing in the lantern light, his expression still blank as new slate, one hand rubbing, bemused, at the back of his neck. For the first time it occurred to Neverfell that perhaps he did not know what to do with stolen goods that did not stay where he put them but instead screamed, ran around, and threatened to eat his correspondence. Perhaps he did not really know what to do with people at all.

"You put glisserblinds through my keyhole!" she squeaked. "What kind of saving is that?"

"That was the assassin, not me. He was about to kill you— until I stole you."

Now that Neverfell thought about it, she did remember a scuffle just before she had been dragged down the chute, something that might have been a struggle between two people.

"Prove it!" she shrilled.

"Think about it!" he shouted back. "If I wanted you dead, why are you still alive? I have had plenty of chances to kill you."

He had rather a good point. Neverfell hesitated still, daunted by the Kleptomancer's chillingly stony countenance, and then her mind cleared and she understood the reason for it. It was not an attempt to snub or intimidate her at all. She had seen that very Face dozens of times, each time linked to the memory of quiet but busy brooms, bowed heads, soft and attentive treads, hands held out for coins . . .

For once, Neverfell managed to bite back an exclamation of surprise. The famous Kleptomancer, subject of a hundred paintings and poems, was a drudge. He had been wearing a stonily implacable face because it was one of the very few his caste was allowed.

"How did you know the assassin was coming for me?" she asked instead, still wary of approaching.

"Two days ago you went for a walk through the palace." He was scanning the shadows, trying to work out where she was. "I was following you. So was he. I saw him. He didn't see me. I started following him and his monkey instead to see if he had a good plan for reaching you. He did. So . . . I let him go ahead with it. I let him put out the lights, deal with the guards, and get everybody out of the way for me."

"He nearly killed me!" squeaked Neverfell. "How did you know I would still be alive when you got there?"

The Kleptomancer gave a small shrug. "Alive, preferable. Dead . . . easier to carry. And not as loud," he added with a hint of real feeling.

Neverfell did not feel reassured. "Why did you steal me? Who sent you?"

"Read me the letter," the thief responded levelly. "I need to know what it says. Be careful—if you change a word of it I will know. But if you read it truly we can trade questions and answers in turn, and I will tell you everything you want to know. If the letter says what you claim, I won't have a reason not to."

Neverfell hesitated. "And you give your word that you're going to return me, then, like the letter says? Without hurting or killing me?"

"You have my word."

Neverfell felt unhappy putting her faith in the word of a thief, but she was very much aware that there was only so long she could run around holding his letter at toothpoint.

"All right, then."

She read out the letter truthfully, and the Kleptomancer listened intently, silently mouthing the numbers under his breath. Then he turned and felt his way to a corner of the room, where he unlocked a strongbox that proved to be full of tiny vials. He ran his finger along the rows, evidently counting, and pulled out two vials, perhaps the "blends" the letter had told him to "imbibe" immediately.

He uncorked them, and Neverfell saw the liquid within stirring in a stealthy, smoky fashion that could only mean they were True Wines. One after the other he drank them down.

She remembered the strange wording of the letter. One blend to erase some days, another blend to revive a day . . . For whatever mysterious reason, the Kleptomancer was adjusting his own memory, suppressing some recollections and reviving others in a peculiarly orderly way.

For a few seconds the Kleptomancer stared into empty space, blinking slowly, and the sinuous smell of the Wine gently filled the room.

"Hmm," he said at last. "Interesting." He slid down the wall and settled on his haunches, staring into nothingness and clicking his thumbnail against the vials.

"You have to answer my questions now—you promised!" Neverfell dared to venture to the very edge of the circle of lantern light. "Who are you working for? Who wrote that letter?"

"Mmm. The letter." Peering forward, Neverfell thought she actually could see speckles of white on the thief's eyes. "*I* wrote it. I do not remember when or why, but I know I had my reasons. *I* sent myself to steal you. *I* issue my orders."

"What?"

All her life, Neverfell had suffered the dull, embarrassed ache of the knowledge that she was always the maddest person in the room. Funnily enough, the realization that this was probably no longer the case did not make her feel better at all.

"You asked me earlier why I stole you. Until I drank the Wine just now, I thought I did so to meet the Grand Steward's challenge, but it turns out I didn't. That was just what I wanted me to think for the moment, so I would act as if it were the real reason."

"The challenge?" Neverfell desperately scrabbled for understanding. "But . . . but I'm not a cameleopard!"

"No." The Kleptomancer did not smile, though for a moment he sounded as if he might be thinking about it. "But you are arguably the Latest and Greatest of the Grand Steward's Curiosities. So now everybody will think that's why I stole you."

"But it wasn't?"

"No. I made myself forget the real reason. The Wine has helped me remember it again. I stole you because I need to work out what you're *for*."

"What I'm for?" Somehow everybody always seemed to end up talking about her as if she were an object.

"Yes." He was studying her with his head on one side, and something about his body language reminded her of her own concentration when examining a new clock. Neverfell was suddenly afraid he might take her apart to find out how she worked. "Things are on the move in Caverna. Big things. Strange things that don't seem to be connected to one another, but must be. I keep following threads of oddity, and many of them lead back to . . . you. Somebody is playing a hand, and you are one of their most important cards. Somebody has been maneuvering you into position. And I want to know why.

"My turn to ask a question. Why *did* you knock over the Ganderblack Wine at the banquet? Did you know it would interfere with my plans, or were you just trying to attract the Grand Steward's attention?"

"No! Neither! Oh, peat and mortar!" Neverfell wondered if she would spend her whole life with those questions at her heels like hounds. "It wasn't a plan, and it wasn't orders! I didn't think about it, I just did it! I just do things! Doesn't anybody else just do things?"

"No."

"Well . . . *I* do. I don't have a big plan, and nobody tells me anything in case it marks my face. If you wanted to find things out, I'm afraid you've kidnapped the wrong person."

"I think not."

"What do you mean?"

There was a silence, and glancing across at the thief Neverfell saw him with his head resting back against the wall, his speckled eyes closed. For a moment she thought he had gone to sleep.

"Have you ever seen an anthill?" he said at last. "A machine of tiny marchers. Too much motion, you cannot make out the *aims* in it. But take something away from that anthill—a stone, a leaf, a dead caterpillar—and the ants scurry. You see which ones you have sabotaged, which ones are disturbed and scuttling to prop something in its place.

"That is what I do. That is kleptomancy. Divination by theft. Find something that is important, something on which you suspect many plans rely, and remove it. Then sit and watch. That's why stealing you will help, even if you know nothing. Right now, the people who want to use you and the people who want you dead will be in a race to find you before the others do. People in a hurry often show their hand by mistake."

It was madness, and yet it made a certain sense to Neverfell, or at least the part of her that liked to take things apart to see how they worked, how they fitted together.

"Another question," continued the thief. "Why *was* an assassin after you?"

"I don't really know." Neverfell shepherded her herd of frightened, woolly suspicions. "I think it's something to do with my past. I turned up in a vat of curds when I was five with no memories. We think perhaps I have buried memories, something somebody doesn't want me to remember." Somehow she found herself giving a thumbnail sketch of her early life and her dim, retrieved memories, even her attacks of madness and panic. "It's not the first time somebody has tried to kill me, anyway. When I was in an Enquiry hanging cage, it dropped into the water and would have drowned me if the guards hadn't come back."

"And how did you survive the glisserblinds in your room?"

"What? Oh. I . . . wasn't sleeping in my bed. I was up in the canopy . . . I often can't sleep . . . It looked comfortable . . ." She trailed off, made uneasy by the way he was staring at her. "I just . . . do things," she repeated. "It's the way I am. A bit mad." *Though not as mad as some,* she thought, and was relieved that her companion was too mottle-sighted to read her mind in her face. "My turn. Why are you doing all this? Why are you hiding behind waterfalls, and poking holes in your memories, and leaving yourself notes and . . ."

. . . and being crazy, she mentally finished the sentence.

"When I was ten," answered the thief, "I talked to a Cartographer for six minutes. And then I forgot about my family and ran off with a big coil of string and some chalk, to live in the unmarked tunnels, eating rats, and half-dead with yellow-eye and scrambler's knee. I learned how to squeak as the bats do to sense the shape of the tunnels, and gulped down Paprickle until my ears were big as saucers."

"What was it like?" Neverfell's question was out of turn, but she could not help herself.

"Cartography?" The Kleptomancer smiled. It was just a drudge smile, a "thank you, miss, happy to serve" smile, but she could sense another smile behind it. With a pang of empathy, Neverfell guessed that he had little chance to speak so freely. If there was anything she understood, it was loneliness and the desire to talk. "Yes. I will tell you if you like. You must understand one thing first. Ordinary maps cannot work in Caverna, and that is not just because the city is not flat. Directions do not always work as they should. Compasses spin uncontrollably or shiver into fragments. I know a few places—not many, but they exist— from which you can climb a ladder for half an hour and end up where you started. Things link impossibly, turn themselves inside out, double back.

"It draws you in. You twist your mind into new shapes. You start to understand Caverna . . . and you fall in love with her. Imagine the most beautiful woman in the world, but with tunnels as her long, tangled, snake-like hair. Her skin is dappled in trap-lantern gold and velvety black, like a tropical frog. Her eyes are cavern lagoons, bottomless and full of hunger. When she smiles, she has diamonds and sapphires for teeth, thousands of them, needle-thin."

"But that sounds like a monster!"

"She is. Caverna is terrifying. This is love, not liking. You fear her, but she is all you can think about. That is what it means to be a Cartographer. That was my life for fifteen years.

"And then one day I left it all behind me. You see, I had been exploring the tunnels of my own mind, and my greatest idea had come to me."

"What was it?" Neverfell was fascinated.

"I do not know," the Kleptomancer answered, perfectly phlegmatically. "But I am sure I will let myself know when the time is right. You see, anybody who chases a plan, however secretively and indirectly, gives themselves away. After a while you can predict them, work out what they want. So I decided the only way to avoid this was not to know what the plan was, or even the parts of the plan, until I needed them. Nobody could predict me, because I could not predict myself. Nobody could work out what I wanted, because *I* did not know what I wanted.

"The whole thing needed planning. Years of careful planning. So I had to be sane. I swam across the torrent of my madness, and pulled myself upon the shore of a new and better sanity."

There was an uncomfortable pause, during which Neverfell tried in vain to bite her tongue into silence.

"I don't want to be rude, but . . . has it ever occurred to you that maybe you're actually still mad? That you've always been mad? That perhaps you're the maddest person in the city?"

"Yes," said the Kleptomancer. "But I don't think so." He contemplated Neverfell for a few moments through his freckling eyes. "Has it ever occurred to you that maybe you're sane? That you've always been sane? That perhaps you're the sanest person in the city?"

"I hope not," whispered Neverfell. "Because, if I'm sane, then there's something wrong with Caverna, something horrible and sick, and nobody else has noticed. If I'm sane, then we shouldn't be sitting around talking—we should all be clawing our way out as fast as we can."

"Oh, I don't think she'd like that," the Kleptomancer remarked, with a hint of affection in his voice. "She needs us. Without us, there is no her, after all. She is the *city*, not the tunnels, and so she does everything she can to keep us down here. Sometimes I even wonder whether it is only possible to create True Delicacies here because she gives them their power, as a bribe to stop us from leaving. When the Grand Steward declared that nobody was allowed to enter or leave the city, I believe he became her chosen beloved. I will tell you something else, though I cannot prove it. The city grows, and not just through the effort of pick and shovel. She has been stretching, spreading, and contorting to make room for us all, and I think that is why geography no longer makes sense."

The thief's tone was different when he spoke of Caverna, and Neverfell felt as if she had glimpsed something shadowy and vast under the still water.

"You still sound like a Cartographer," she thought aloud.

"I am no longer one of them," answered the Kleptomancer, and in his tone there was a strange mixture of pride, resolution, and loss. "I no longer draw up maps—and maps are a Cartographer's love letters to Caverna, his way of serving and worshipping her. She is in my thoughts all the time, but I am no longer her slave."

"Then you still . . . love her?" asked Neverfell, struggling with the notion.

"More than ever," her companion answered softly.

It occurred to Neverfell that just in case her sanity was at risk, she had better stop him from talking about geography.

"You said there were big things happening in Caverna, and trails leading back to me. What did you mean?"

"There are strands," answered the Kleptomancer, "and I cannot yet see the pattern they form. There has been a string of murders in the Undercity. Drudges killing their nearest and dearest without warning, their parent, child, husband, wife, for no sane reason.

"Alliances at Court are shifting. The Enquiry is favored by Right-Eye, and so they have been building their power. But there is a league quietly forming against them, a large and loose alliance with no obvious leader.

"A food taster dies, and three days later there you are at the banquet for everybody to see, just in time to take her place.

"And . . . the Cartographers are restless. Usually they are just bothered by the Undiscovered Passage, but now a lot of them believe that Caverna herself is getting ready to grow or shift again, which means that everything is about to change. These are the threads I am following for now, though I cannot have anybody knowing that."

"But . . ." Neverfell bit her own tongue but could not stop the words from escaping. "But if it's so secret, why did you just tell me all about it?"

"That will not be a problem," came the response. "I am to return you exactly as I found you . . . which means I will be erasing your memories of the last three hours as soon as I have some more True Wine."

THE WORKS

"WHAT?" NEVERFELL WAS HORRIFIED AND RATHER hurt. She had started to feel a strange camaraderie with her curious kidnapper during their answer-bartering. He was, after all, perhaps the only person in Caverna who was more of an outsider than she was. And now, quite suddenly, he had reminded her that she had no rights. She was a possession of the Grand Steward. Even her memories were not her own. They were just grime to be wiped away from a borrowed possession.

"I cannot send you back knowing what you know. And it is better for you if you do not. If you know too much, it will show on your face. The less you know, the longer you will live."

"But . . . I want to remember this conversation! I want to understand! I don't want to be a toy! I don't want to be a thing! I want to know how everything works! And I'm not supposed to eat or drink anything anyway! I'll get in trouble if I drink the Wine!"

He gazed at her unblinking with his stony drudge face, and Neverfell had no idea whether he felt sympathy or contempt, or whether he had even heard her. He said not another word more but returned to his metal suit and began methodically donning it.

Once back in his armor, he picked up his helmet, strode to the double doors, and opened them to reveal the bellowing waterfall.

Ignoring Neverfell's protests, he fastened a clip on his belt to the wire, then took out a small crank handle, fixed it to the front of the clip, and wound it vigorously for several minutes. He then swung back, so that he was hanging below the wire, suspended by his belt, and looked across at Neverfell.

"You're thinking of trying to escape," he said. It was a statement, not a question. "Forget that idea. Even if the waterfall didn't kill you, you'd be lost in Drudgery. It's not a safe place for the clueless, and besides, that's where the people who want you dead will be looking for you first. When I return, I will make sure you are left somewhere safe."

Then he screwed on his helmet, kicked off from the floor, and pulled a lever on the hand crank. Instantly, with a *wwhhrrzzjj* noise, he raced backward out of the room along the wire, despite its upward slope. As he reached the waterfall, the falling deluge made an umbrella shape of splatter as it struck him. The next moment he was gone.

Neverfell stared out at the vast waterfall, and her spirits sank. She could feel the cold of it on her face and hands, and its voice was all but deafening. But the Kleptomancer had passed out through it and survived. She did not know how he had managed to slide back up the wire . . . but if he could do it perhaps so could she.

What I need is a belt clip like his. And he has another suit.

Neverfell scampered to the place where she had seen the other armored suit hanging. The fish-shaped scales had a shimmer that made them look watery and light, but when she unhooked it from the ceiling her arms almost gave under its weight. It was lined with leather and smelled of oil and wax.

Hanging beside it was a matching goggled helmet, with a tube leading from the mouth of the mask to a backpack. Curious, Neverfell opened the pack and discovered within a solitary trap-lantern, dull gray and inert. It woke up as the air touched it and managed a hopeful amber gleam.

"Hello, little yellow," she whispered, as the trap snapped blearily around itself, sensing the draft. "So *that's* how he survived swimming so long underwater after the banquet! He had you in an airtight pack, didn't he? Giving him air."

To her excitement, Neverfell found that this other suit also had a belt clip, with a hole in the front for the kind of crank handle the Kleptomancer had wound up before leaving. The handle itself, however, was missing, and her spirits tumbled again. Perhaps it had been too much to hope that the thief would leave her with such an easy means of escape.

She scoured the room, without much hope, but could find no sign of the missing handle. Perhaps he had only one. Or perhaps he had two, but had taken them both with him.

Neverfell found a grub and fed it to the little trap in the pack. "I'm just going to have to do things the hard way, aren't I?" she muttered to it. If her apprenticeship had taught her anything, it was how to jury-rig something in an emergency on no sleep.

One thing that the room did not lack was tools; indeed, many of them were better than any that Neverfell had ever owned. The casing of the belt clip itself was welded shut, so she could not open it and examine the workings. However, she could learn a fair amount by peering into the handle socket and prodding it with a spindle. Then it was a matter of cobbling together something the right shape to act as a makeshift crank handle. After an hour of prodding, hammering, sawing, trial and error, she had an ugly-looking portion of a chair leg with a few nails jutting from one end, which could just about be slotted into the socket and rotated using a cross-shaft. With each turn, a promising *click-click-click-click* issued from within the mechanism.

She stopped only when she was out of breath and the mechanism could be wound no further. The weight of the suit made it very hard to put on, but she managed by laying it on the ground, opening it, wriggling her way in, and fastening the clasps. Once she was standing up in it, everything became a lot easier. Fortunately the Kleptomancer was only a little taller than she was, so there were only a few places where the scales were rucked like concertina wrinkles. She could just about lever her hands into the big leather gloves at the end, though the fingers were clumsy and unwieldy.

Neverfell was just considering putting on the helmet when she heard a familiar sound from beyond the waterfall. It was a high metallic whine, the distinctive whirr of wire passing through a belt clip. Far sooner than she had expected, the Kleptomancer was returning.

Neverfell lurched forward and flung herself against the wall near the opening, so that one of the open shutters would hide her from view. Holding her breath, she saw the goggled figure land dripping in the doorway and unclip his belt from the wire. She let him take two paces into the room before she lurched out with a pair of heavy shears under one arm, fumbled her belt clip onto the wire, and swung out beneath it, the way he had.

"Hey!"

The Kleptomancer turned in time to see her flipping the lever on the clip. The next moment the clip gave a fierce, grating, keening noise, and the ground was gone from beneath her feet. The thief made a snatch at her ankle, and his finger just brushed her armored toes. The next moment the icy power of the waterfall axed down upon her, knocking out her wits. Then she was out the other side and still rising, gasping for air, half-deafened from the shock, her eyes full of wet hair.

Her heart caught in her throat as she looked down and saw the falling water cascading down a hundred feet or more into smokily indistinct spray clouds. Then she was skimming up toward the opposite wall of the great shaft, where her feet shakily found purchase on a waiting ledge. She unclipped her belt mechanism from the wire, and it released its remaining tension in a high-pitched buzz.

The Kleptomancer would not be slow to pursue. With her shears, she sawed at the thick wire that spanned the river until it gave with a *spung* noise and whiplashed back on itself, rebounding off the cliff-face on the other side of the sheer drop.

I hope I haven't stranded him there forever so he starves. No, he's ever so clever. I'm sure he'll think of something.

There was a crawl-through beside her, so Neverfell ducked into it and scrambled away, her armored scales rasping against the gritty floor, water sloshing inside her suit. Only when she reached proper tunnels did she dare unclasp and peel off the heavy suit. She left it sitting up in a dark corner, its arms folded across its stomach as if it had enjoyed a good meal.

Despite the burning pain in her ankle she forced herself to run and run, letting herself slow to a limp only when the roar of the waterfall had faded behind her and she became aware of other noises. The ground shook with a rhythmic shunt and clatter, like that from an enormous machine, distorted by echo. Now and then a gong rang out, trailing its brassy echo after it like a comet tail. She hobbled toward the sounds, for the sounds meant people.

Everywhere a thick gray dust coated the floor, and soon it coated her feet like mouse fur and created a roughness in her throat. The passages here were all low, and squirmed around and over one another like a basket of eels. She was hobbling along one such corridor when it opened out unexpectedly. Fortunately she managed to stop an inch or two before the floor did.

Her passage had ended in an arched aperture set in a cliff-like wall, and she was looking down into a broad crevasse. Far below, she could see the treacherous white flare of a raging river. Half-submerged in the water were monstrous waterwheels of black wood, each the height of ten men, their slatted blades streaming as they rose from the water. Their spindles vanished into the walls of the crevasse on either side, and Neverfell could just make out the edges of great millstones, revolving inch by grudging inch, the unseen mill machinery groaning and roaring like enslaved leviathans.

Set in the sheer walls that flanked either side of the crevasse were countless other archways and openings like the one at which she had just appeared, rope ladders dangling beneath each one. The walls themselves were pocked and etched with ledges barely a hand's span wide, and metal spokes to serve as foot supports and handholds. With the aid of these, hundreds of people were scrambling up and down the cliffs, despite the steepness.

Many of those climbing upward bore wooden yokes with bags or buckets dangling from them, yet did not seem to be thrown off balance by the extra weight. There were bulging burlap flour sacks, fine-weave bags of snuff, even rolls of newly milled paper. Some of those struggling up the cliff-face with such loads were children of Neverfell's age and even younger. Even from a distance, Neverfell could see that the climbing figures were short, the adults probably not much taller than she was. At many of the archways, she could see carts and pit ponies waiting to take the goods away.

The entire crevasse was startlingly bright. Hundreds of greenish wild trap-lanterns glowed and pulsed in the cliff-face, thriving on the air breathed out by the clambering multitude. Some of the traps were large enough to have swallowed a cow. Without really thinking about it, Neverfell had always supposed that the Drudgery would be murky and dark, but of course that made no sense. Dense crowds meant more traps meant brighter light.

Neverfell stared, fascinated. In her head she knew that what she was watching must be backbreaking and dangerous, and yet somehow it was hard to feel anything for the workers. They just seemed so dogged, placid, and docile, a hundred heads all with the same Face. Watching them, it was hard to believe that they had individual thoughts and feelings, that they were not just contented cogs in a giant machine, like those turned by the waterwheels below.

Then Neverfell saw one of the cogs falter and miss a notch. On the far wall of the crevasse, a girl who looked nine or ten years old lost her footing for a moment. She regained it the next instant, but not before her yoke teetered dangerously, so that a bag of snuff fell out of one of the buckets. When she finally reached the top, Neverfell could see a man in a dark red coat counting out the bags in her bucket and turning to berate her. He was obviously shouting, but the roar of water and machinery drowned his voice, and Neverfell could only watch the action play out in dumb show. To judge by his greater height and use of fine Faces, this man was not a drudge but a foreman of some sort.

He pointed down the crevasse, and the girl leaned over to peer, her face still perfectly calm. Following their gaze, Neverfell could just about see a dark blue blob that might be the fallen bag, caught on a jutting prong of rock teased by the river's white mane. Neverfell watched horrified as the girl began her descent, still stone-faced but with hints of tremor in her legs.

When she reached the lowermost ledge and continued to clamber downward onto the more perilous, water-darkened crags, this was noticed by the other climbers. Some of them scrambled swiftly up to the foreman's ledge. Soon there was a horseshoe of figures around the foreman, pointing down at the girl, talking all at once. The foreman responded with bellowing and wild gestures of his gnarled cane. For a moment it looked as if one or two of the drudges over whom he towered might hold their ground, but then they exchanged glances with each other and gradually pulled back, heads bowed in surrender.

The girl below was reaching down from an overhang, trying to snatch at the bag beneath her. *No, don't!* begged Neverfell in her head, as she watched more and more of the younger girl's weight leaning over the drop. *Don't! Please don't! It's just a bag of snuff! A stupid bag of snuff!*

Neverfell blinked and missed the crucial instant. As her lids were closing there was a girl still on the ledge, fingertips just brushing the bag. By the time her eyes were open again, the ledge was empty. There was no sign of her in the water. The river had swallowed her like a white wolf and rushed on.

The other drudges showed no display of emotion. They stared for a long time down into the pitiless millrace, then glanced at one another, picked up their yokes, and returned to their work. The foreman lifted a long-handled wooden hammer and began beating on what looked like a great stone xylophone, great slabs of slate providing the different notes. He played a simple sequence of notes repeatedly, and after a while a new boy arrived, picked up the lost girl's yoke, and began clambering down the sheer face.

"What's wrong with you all?" Neverfell wailed, aloud and unheard. "You saw what happened! Why don't any of you care?"

And then, quite suddenly, everything changed before her eyes. The figures on the wall ceased to be ants and became people. Suddenly she could imagine the strain on their shoulders, their broken nails, the chill of spray, the stomach-twisting awareness of the hungry drop below. How had she been stupid enough to think that these people were not grief-stricken, or cold, or weary, or angry? They just did not have the Faces to show any of these things. They had always been denied such expressions, and now, at last, Neverfell was starting to understand why.

How could the drudges rise up against bullies like the foreman? Rebels needed to look at one another and see their own anger reflected, and know that their feeling was part of a greater tide. But any drudge who glanced at his fellows would see only calm, tame Faces waiting for orders.

Neverfell could feel the muscles of her face tighten and move. There was a tingling sensation in her skin and a buzzing feeling in her chest. Yes, she knew what this was. She remembered Childersin talking to her, telling her that she was . . . angry.

Neverfell found a large, dank piece of sacking and wrapped it around herself to conceal her pajamas and shroud her hair and face. Only then did she dare the narrow tunnels, where she soon found herself stifled and bruised by a mass of hurrying, pressing, unwashed bodies.

The reek of rot and the chamber pot was overwhelming, and she soon realized why. Occasional grills beneath her feet looked down into caverns full of heaped waste of all sorts, being shoveled by masked drudges into a ravine where yet another river rushed, presumably so that it could be carried out of Caverna. Amid the waste stood fine mesh cages the height of a man, their insides boiling and crawling with motion. Thousands of moths and grubs gorged and fattened on dung, not knowing they were destined to feed the lanterns of Caverna.

Through narrow arches, she saw long, low dormitories crammed with sleeping figures and soaked with glaring green light from the unshaded trap-lanterns. She glimpsed crèches where babies were laid out a dozen to a bed, while among them strode the crèche nurses, wearing masks of the docile Faces the infants were permitted to learn. Everybody around her was short, a lot of the adults not much taller than she was. Many of the children walked oddly, their legs buckling inward so that their knees knocked, and they shook with coughs that seemed too large for them.

You wanted to know how everything worked, said the relentless voice in Neverfell's head. *And now you do.*

She felt as if she were looking at a river, a flood of brown and gray clothes, seething with matching foam-pale faces. And that was how everybody else saw the drudges, as one great mindless force of nature that could be harnessed to turn treadmills and bear away rubbish and nourish the whole city.

And yet there was a life to this Undercity, she realized, a life belied by the drab monotony of the naked stone and blank faces. As the air shook with the thunder of grinding millstones, lunging pump pistons, and rattling treadmills, sometimes she heard strains of song trained to follow their rhythm, like man-size footsteps scampering between the long strides of giants. She started to hear the differences in the tunes of the stone xylophones with their coded signals, some urgent, some leisurely, some almost jaunty.

She began to notice the subtle hand mimes the drudges used to communicate over the din, the way they clasped hands in greeting, barely bothering to glance at one another's immobile faces.

In among the dun-colored river of drudges, she saw a flash of purple. Reflexively, she flattened herself against a wall and peered through the crowd. Yes, there was a figure ahead, dressed in the unmistakable colors of an Enquirer. He was standing in the very middle of the corridor, so that the human river was forced to part to pass him, and appeared to be scanning the flow. Now and then he reached out and casually caught at an arm, forcing somebody to stop. Those he halted were nearly all girls of Neverfell's build and height.

Neverfell caught fragments of sentences.

". . . girl with red hair . . . a face like glass . . ."

The Enquiry had moved fast. They must have realized that Neverfell had been spirited down the ember chute and had started searching Drudgery.

Neverfell knotted her fingers, thinking hard. There was nothing to stop her from striding forward right now to demand that the Enquiry take her back to the Grand Steward's palace. Nothing, that is, but the memory of plunging into icy water while in an Enquiry cage, and the warning that Zouelle had given her.

Neverfell, on no account let yourself fall into the hands of the Enquiry, or you will be tortured into confessing all kinds of things.

Somebody in the Enquiry had tried to kill her, and for all she knew it might be the man in front of her. If she placed herself in his custody down here in Drudgery, it would be child's play for him to dispose of her and cover his tracks. And even if he did hand her over to his superiors alive, what then? She would be in the power of Enquirer Treble, who distrusted her and wanted to torture the "truth" out of her.

Keeping close to the wall to avoid notice, Neverfell turned about and headed back along the corridor. Seeing a dented and discarded pail, she picked it up, hoping it would make her look as if she were heading somewhere on an errand. It was full of a greenish slime, the lingering trace of stagnant water, so she scooped up handfuls of it and used it to daub her hair and conceal its bright color.

Where could she go? Who could she turn to now?

Erstwhile. She had to find Erstwhile.

Erstwhile had told her that he lived in Sallow's Elbow. There were no passage signs or signposts, so when Neverfell was at some distance from the Enquirer she dared to ask for directions. She was afraid that doing so might show her up as one unfamiliar to the Undercity, but she had no choice, and tugged at a drudge woman's sleeve.

"Sallow's Elbow?" She made her voice a hoarse whisper, to disguise it.

"Third left to the crossways, follow the ladder straight up, carry on straight ahead over three bridges, cross the scoot slope and the lock," came the whispered answer. The woman did not look at her, but gave Neverfell a couple of quick and companionable pats on the arm before passing on.

When Neverfell found Sallow's Elbow, she could not mistake it. The passage had broadened, and at a certain point it twisted sharply back on itself. In the crook of the elbow, she noticed that the wall was pocked with hollows about three or four feet across, each of which had a blanket or piece of loose fabric roughly pinned over it like a curtain. In some cases she could see a grubby hand or unshod foot dangling out from beneath the cloth.

As she reached the elbow, one of the curtains was pulled aside, and a boy of about her own age groggily scrambled out.

"Excuse me!" She caught at his sleeve before he could disappear into the people-river. "I'm looking for Erstwhile."

He turned and slapped at a black-and-white checkered rag that hung in front of one of the hollows.

"Rise and shine, Erstwhile. Your girlfriend's come to take you to the opera," he called, before disappearing off down the tunnel.

The cloth was snatched back, and Erstwhile stared up at Neverfell, his face flushed with sleep and creased from resting against his collar. His expression deadened and took on the polite blank look so many other drudges wore, and Neverfell's heart sank.

"What the sickness are you doing here?"

"You told me to come here! You said I could if I was in trouble—"

"I told you to send messages here, not come yourself! This isn't a place for you!" He scrambled out and stood defensively in front of his curtained chamber, trying to pull the rag across surreptitiously to protect it from sight. It was hopeless, and he gave up and pulled the cloth back. "Well, go on, then, have a good goggle! Enjoying your tour of Drudgery, are you?"

The hollow behind the curtain was barely two feet deep. The only objects inside were a tin cup, a worn and lumpy satchel, some clothes folded to serve as a pillow, and his precious unicycle. Far too late, she saw the reason for his stony anger. He had not wanted her to see that he lived like this, perched in a wall dimple like a glowworm.

Neverfell wanted to burst into tears. "I didn't *decide* to come here! I was stolen by the Kleptomancer and had to escape using one of his suits. And now Drudgery is crawling with Enquirers, and if they catch me their leader will want to torture me. I can't let them find me, Erstwhile!

"I came looking for you because it was that or give up. You're the only person in Drudgery I can trust. You're one of the few people in the whole of Caverna I can trust."

Erstwhile's expression changed to a look of keen alertness, as if he were expecting her to say more. Neverfell guessed that it was not what he was feeling but was as close as he could get. In any case, at least he was no longer stonily ground-gazing.

"You stupid little hen," he muttered. "Didn't I tell you you were out of your depth? Didn't I say you'd end up neck-deep in trouble if you went to Court? Stolen by the Kleptomancer—how did you manage that?"

"Oh . . . he's mad, and it's all about ruptures and threads and ants . . . and everyone thought it was the cameleopard . . ."

"Still crazy as a squirrel, aren't you?" Erstwhile threw a glance up and down the tunnel, then tugged a ragged cloth out of his "pillow" and handed it to Neverfell. "Wrap that around your head, and pull it forward so it hangs down over your face. Now, come on, follow me! Sharpish!"

Following Erstwhile, Neverfell was almost glad she had not been eating well. He thought nothing of squeezing through fissures she had barely noticed before, or wriggling fish-like through the narrowest of holes.

"This is the route I always take up out of the Undercity when I'm— Oh, pepper it!" Erstwhile halted abruptly. "Back! Into the crevice! They've got an Enquirer waiting at the bottom of the ladders!" They scrambled back the way they had come, until there was no purple in sight.

"Is there another way up out of Drudgery?" whispered Neverfell.

"Only a handful. And if they're blocking this route they'll be doing the same with the others. No, they're cordoning off Drudgery. And they're doing all this to find you?"

"I think so. Or maybe the Kleptomancer."

"Enquirers in Drudgery. That's always bad." Erstwhile gave her a brief sideways glance. "We only see 'em when they think somebody they're after is hiding down here. And then they do everything they can to make us dig him out and hand him over. Beatings, disappearances. And if that doesn't work . . . they cut off everybody's eggs."

Neverfell gaped. "They cut off everybody's legs?"

"No! Eggs! *Eggs!*" As Neverfell gave a relieved snort, Erstwhile glanced at her, his expression becoming briefly stony once more. "It's all right for you to smirk; you've always had as many eggs as you want. Don't you know that if you don't get enough eggs down here, you grow up bow-legged and stunted, with lungs like two old socks?"

Stunned, Neverfell recalled all the times that Erstwhile had asked for favors to be repaid in eggs. She had assumed he just liked them.

"I didn't know," she said very quietly.

"It's not the way it is up there," Erstwhile continued bitterly. "When Enquirers turn up in Drudgery, it's never to protect *us*. When they're chasing something that affects the courtiers and makers, then we see them here beating down doors. But not when drudges get murdered, no, then we can go rot. You don't see them roaming the streets after rehearsals."

"Rehearsals?" There was something menacing in the very blandness and innocence of the word.

"We call 'em that. It's a little joke of ours." Erstwhile's voice was about as humorous as a rockfall. "See, Court assassinations are important business. Wouldn't want to mess up your lines on the night, would you? So courtiers come down here to practice, because they know nobody misses drudges. Nobody except other drudges, and they don't count. They try out new poisons, let would-be assassins show off what they can do, practice blade moves or group tactics."

"They kill people? They just kill them? Innocent people?"

"Just drudges," Erstwhile said, the nonchalance of his tone heavy and hollow as a two-ton bell. "We can usually spot 'em— a run of weird murders all alike, or suicides, or accidents, or sometimes a 'disease outbreak' where everybody dies the same way. That's what goes down on the paperwork, but *we* know.

"It's been happening again, just lately. 'Domestic murders,' drudges killing drudges—that's what the record says. Me? I say somebody's rehearsing. I can feel it in my bones."

Neverfell had no answer. In her mind she looked out across the tangled vista of the Undercity and felt only numb. There was too much to feel strongly about, she was stretched too thin, so she could not quite feel anything about anything.

Erstwhile glanced at her as they passed a trap-lantern, then paused to peer.

"I guess you're not such a fuzzy baby bird anymore," he murmured gruffly. "Got something in your head now, have you? Seen some things?"

Neverfell nodded. "You can see that? I've . . . changed? How bad is it?"

"Yes, you've changed, all right. Your eyes look deeper. Is that bad? I don't think that's bad. Don't know that your owners will agree, though. You're planning to run back to them again, aren't you? Instead of going back to Grandible?"

Neverfell paused, then slowly nodded. "I think I have to. There are things I need to know, about myself and my past. And I can't go back to that life with Grandible. It's like a baby shoe. It doesn't fit me anymore. In fact, I don't think it really fitted me for a very long time, and I was getting all scrunched up living inside it."

Erstwhile gave a vaguely dismissive sound in his throat, but did not argue. "It's going to be ticklish as lice getting you back up there, if we can't go through the Enquiry," he muttered. "But let's think."

As they talked, it became clear that getting into Drudgery was rather easier than getting out of it. Plummeting down an ember or waste chute from the upper strata of Caverna was easy enough. Climbing back up them was all but impossible, if one did not happen to be the Kleptomancer.

"Dozens of shafts," muttered Erstwhile, "but they're all *down* shafts. Nothing is really expected to travel *up* from Drudgery except drudges. Once we've washed our hands."

"Oh." Neverfell felt her eyes grow large. "Erstwhile . . . all the water in Caverna comes from the rivers down in Drudgery, doesn't it? It's taken up to big tanks near the surface, and half of it is heated, and then they pour it down into the hot- and cold-water pipes for everybody to use. Isn't that right?"

"Yes. Why?"

"How does it get all the way up from the rivers to the tanks?"

"This plan is ten kinds of mad," whispered Erstwhile.

A long, dark, and convoluted route had brought them to a domed storage bay full of crates and barrels, beside one of the narrow, murky canals. Before them she could see where the canal reached its final sluice gates, and beyond them the river into which it was yearning to tumble. This, however, was not a roaring, white-bearded monster or a sludge-filled trickle but broad, glassy, muscular, and purposeful, its water lucid. The reflections of the wild traps above quivered and flexed in its surface.

A little farther upstream, Neverfell could see a huge treadmill like a giant wooden hamster wheel, a dozen or so drudges within it pacing to make it turn. This treadmill in turn seemed to be moving a vast belt-and-pulley system. The belt ran from a shaft in the ceiling down to the pulley, and then back up the shaft. A series of broad oblong buckets four feet across were attached to the belt at intervals. As the treadmill turned, the belt was drawn round the pulley, dipping empty buckets into the river in turn, and then bearing them back up the shaft.

"You ready?" growled Erstwhile. "Wait for the gong!"

The gong signaled the end of one working shift and the start of another. For a brief time, supervisors and workers alike were distracted as chits were delivered, attendance books marked, and everybody took care that the wheel's rhythm was not broken as one set of feet replaced the last.

"Now!" hissed Erstwhile, giving Neverfell a rough shove in the back.

She took advantage of the moment's distraction to lollop over to the river's edge.

The Kleptomancer had it right, she reflected in the half second it took her. Nobody was ever ready to stop you from doing things that nobody sensible would even try. Mad things. Like jumping into a river, grabbing the nearest bucket, and letting it haul you up a shaft not designed for human passage.

The water was so icy as to be literally breathtaking. Her clothes soaked almost instantly and became heavy, dragging and tangling her legs. She paddled helplessly, clinging to the bank. A bucket hit her painfully in the shin, and as it rose she lunged at it, and managed to get the top half of her body into it. It lifted, dripping, with her hung over it by her middle, legs frantically cycling.

If anybody looked up, they would see her and stop the treadmill. But the creaking complaints of the bucket did not catch their attention. She wriggled forward and managed to tumble into the bucket with a slopping splash, and the belt carried her up into the darkness of the shaft.

After crouching in the icy, pitching bucket for what seemed like hours, she glimpsed a hint of light above, something larger than the shaft's occasional glowing traps. Yes, there seemed to be some sort of a square hatch floating down to meet her. Perhaps she could leap for it. *I have to be high enough now,* she thought as she readied her numb and shaking limbs. *I must be out of Drudgery.*

The bucket reared angrily beneath her as she rose to her hands and feet, then bucked as she jumped, tumbling through the hatch to land in a sodden sprawl. She seemed to be in a small workshop with rough-hewn walls, and two men in overalls were staring down at her in frozen-faced shock. Their alarm and surprise was apparently not diminished by the sight of Neverfell's face when she pushed back her hair.

"Hello! I . . . I'm sorry about the puddle. I'm Neverfell the food taster, and I belong to the Grand Steward. He . . . he might want to know where I am. Oh! And perhaps you'd better tell people not to drink water from the bucket that went past just now—I've been sitting in it . . ."

A LOSS OF FACE

THE NEXT TWO HOURS WENT BY AS SOMETHING of a whirl, and Neverfell's feet barely seemed to touch the ground. She was handed back to members of the Grand Steward's household, who interrogated her about the Kleptomancer and his lair until her brain ached. She told them all she knew about the mysterious thief. Although she had felt a strange camaraderie during her conversation with him, his willingness to wipe her memory had left her feeling disappointed and betrayed. Besides, she suspected she would be pushing her luck too far if her interrogators saw her trying to protect the very man the Grand Steward wished to see arrested. The Grand Steward might even hand her over to the Enquiry to have answers dragged out of her.

After these questions, she was bathed, checked for any lice or ticks she might have picked up in the Undercity, given fresh clothes and a new set of finger-thimbles, and then examined and her injured ankle tended.

Finally, a set of physicians and perfumiers examined her more carefully, looking for any sign that she had consumed either poison or antidote. In the end, it was her protestations that she had eaten and drunk nothing at all that seemed to carry the most weight. More and more people were coming to accept the fact that she could not lie. Just to be on the safe side, however, they gave her bitter-tasting drinks that made her vomit and left her feeling even more shaky and miserable. Then they stamped a document and declared her "undamaged and fit for Court."

She was not undamaged, however, and she knew it. No food or drink had passed her lips, but she had drunk deep of the Truth, and now it could not be flushed out of her system with bitter cordials, or washed from her skin, or picked out of her hair. Her suspicions were borne out when she was bundled back to the tasters' quarters and fell under the eye of Leodora, who instantly went chalk-pale.

"Oh no," she murmured, gripping Neverfell's chin and peering into her face. "Oh, fire and falling! This is not good, not good at all."

The other tasters crowded around and craned to have a look, filling Neverfell's view with the large, pink, staring collage of their faces. She knew then that Erstwhile had been right. She had changed. The things she had seen had marked her, and now she was carrying them on her face.

"The scrubbing brush! The scouring powder!"

"No use!" Leodora managed to prevent a mass scamper for cleaning goods. "This isn't grime—it's knowledge. She has seen too much. No! Put that away! Scrubbing her eyes will not help!"

Neverfell, whose mind had been full of the plight of the drudges, suddenly remembered that her own existence was precarious in the extreme.

"What . . . what do I look like? What can you see?"

"Disillusionment." Leodora tutted under her breath. "Like a great mud spot on your face. It's all over your brow, and the corners of your mouth . . . I don't think this is coming out. Where did you get all this?"

"The Undercity . . . I was lost in Drudgery . . . I saw the way they treat the drudges . . ."

"Well, couldn't you have kept your eyes shut?" Leodora gripped both of Neverfell's hands with the fierceness of desperation, and stared into her eyes. "Listen—the Grand Steward has asked for you to attend upon him as soon as you are dressed for Court. Whatever it is you saw down in the Undercity, you have to put it out of your mind. You have to learn not to care about such things, and you have to learn it very, very fast. Just try putting everything you saw down there in a room in your mind, then closing the door and locking it."

She was so fervent that Neverfell nodded. As she changed back into her dress and sash, and while she was being walked through the palace by the white-clad attendants, she tried to imagine closing the door on her memories of the Undercity. She made it a heavy, metal-bound oaken door, like the one Grandible used to lock out the world. As she stepped into the audience chamber, however, and saw the Grand Steward, she could feel that imaginary door buckling and bursting into flinders.

His right eye was open, she noticed, and even now it was fixing on her face, her shamefully altered face. What frightened her most was the fact that she did not feel ashamed. She did not know what she should say, but worse still, she did not know what she *might* say. Her mind was filled with one thought: that this was the man who held Caverna in his hand, the man who for centuries had been pampered with the city's finest luxuries while thousands below broke their backs hefting sacks of rocks, or waded the city's sewage to breed moths, or slept in heaps like discarded eggshells. There was no way to hide her feelings, short of putting a lantern shade over her head.

The Grand Steward stared at her for a long moment, and she could not help but stare back, while something in her chest galloped heavy-hoofed circuits of her ribs.

Neverfell's expression was a mirror, and in it Right-Eye saw a clear image of himself, as she saw him.

He saw his own strangeness and age. He saw how life and color had leached out of him an inch at a time, leaving him dead and as precious as the quartz trunks of the petrified trees. He saw the sag of cruelty through apathy at the corner of his jaw. He saw the emptiness of his one open eye. He was a beach of gems where the living tide had gone out, never to return. He was a pearly shell left by a long-dead creature.

Nobody in four hundred years had dared to look at him with such disappointment and saddened anger. If she was seen to do so, boldly and without repercussions, then it would make him seem weak before the courtiers. To seem weak was to bleed into piranha-infested waters. At that very moment, had she not been the only person capable of identifying the Kleptomancer, he might have ordered her thrown back down the ember chute.

"Is this," he croaked at last, "somebody's idea of a joke? Who has done this?" There was the deathly silence of a dozen people hoping that a question was meant for somebody else. "Girl! What Face is this? Explain yourself!" With frustration, he saw her freeze up in panic. "Call Maxim Childersin!"

When the angular master vintner hurried in, the Grand Steward simply waved an impatient hand toward Neverfell. Childersin cast an eye over her face, then drew in a breath through his teeth.

"Definitely disillusionment," answered Childersin. "Doubtless something she saw in Drudgery—"

"When I summon a clockmaker," the Grand Steward commented icily, "I do not expect a lecture on the mechanism. I expect him to set my clock going. This"—he gestured toward Neverfell—"is currently broken. Fix it. If she is disillusioned, re-illusion her. Find out what she has seen to make her look this way, and use Wine to remove her memory of it."

"No!" exploded the girl, face white and aghast. "I don't want to forget! Everybody forgets the drudges!" She stood there quivering with terror at her own temerity, staring around in the silence she had made for herself.

"I saw how the city works," she whispered. "How the embers tumble down and the water gets hoisted up and the waste is washed out, and where the moths come from, and everything else. And it's really clever. Caverna's an amazing machine . . . but now, when I think of it, all I can see is this giant waterwheel, and the river turning it is made of drudge sweat and drudge blood. I scrunch my eyes up tight, but I can still hear it, I can still smell it.

"They sleep all piled up like dirty washing, and their children have legs like hoops and have to carry great sacks up cliffs, and the tunnels are so tight it feels like you're under a rockfall all the time, and everything smells sick or stale, and I saw this girl drop into the river and drown, and nobody stopped to look for the body, and they can't even show what they feel because they have no proper Faces, only stupid ones that make them look like they only care about their next job! And sometimes people come down and kill them for no good reason! Court people steal down to try out poisons and practice murders before they do them for real up here—"

"*What?*" interrupted Right-Eye.

"It's true! The drudges call them 'rehearsals.' There's been another set of them just lately, but nobody bothers looking into it properly, so they're just recorded as drudges killing other drudges, but there's a pattern and nobody's paying attention!"

She was wrong. Right-Eye was now paying the most acute attention to her every word. He had spent centuries scanning the Court for signs of imminent assassination attempts, and in all that time it had never once occurred to him to look for those warning signs in the Undercity. If what this girl said was true, then henceforth the drudge districts could become his early warning system, the crystal ball in which he saw the murder plots against him while they were in the planning stages.

"Is that so?" he muttered. "Things are about to change. These murders will be investigated. Immediately."

In Neverfell's face the clouds broke, and her smile came out like the sun. She could not read his mind as he could read hers. She clearly had no idea of the calculations behind his decision. He could see that she believed he had been overcome by the injustice of the situation and instantly decided to right it. He felt a shock, as if her faith were a golden axe and had struck right through his dusty husk of a heart. The heart did not bleed, however, and in the next moment its dry fibers were closing and knitting back together again.

"Your Excellency," Childersin cut in quickly, "it would be possible to blend a Wine tailored to remove only this child's memories of Drudgery, but it would take time—weeks, in fact. We could tackle the matter more clumsily and give her a Wine guaranteed to erase her memories of a specific time period, but then we would run a high risk of wiping her recollection of the Kleptomancer. After all, we do not know the precise time that she left her kidnapper's lair. If I may make a suggestion, fixing her features may be a task for a Facesmith."

Right-Eye was suddenly bitterly weary of Childersin's suave explanations. "You have seven hours to fix this child's face, by whatever means you see fit. At nineteen o'clock several grand confections and desserts will reach perfection, and will be brought to me for a grand tasting. If the girl's face is not mended by that time . . ." The unspoken end of his threat hung in the air like freezing fog.

As the child Neverfell was led from the room, Right-Eye felt as though the wave of life had gone out again, leaving him once more a beach of dead gems.

It was a long time since he had felt so awake. The girl's smile of unfeigned admiration and joy had thrown into shadow centuries of carefully tailored compliments and flattering portraits. *Perhaps, whenever things grow painfully dull, I could do something to summon that look in her face again. Little concessions for the drudges, maybe? A package of extra food now and then? Or safety ropes for the younger climbers?*

While he was considering this, Enquirer Treble arrived, her Face a mixture of self-importance, deference, and bulldog watchfulness, to report on the latest findings in the Kleptomancer case.

"My people have located the lair described by the girl," she explained. "It was abandoned." Neither Treble nor the Grand Steward pretended surprise at the master thief's escape. "At least now we may have some insight into the workings of his mind . . . providing Neverfell's story is true." Like everybody else at Court, the Enquiry had originally assumed that Neverfell had been stolen in response to the Grand Steward's challenge. They were still coming to grips with the notion of "divination by theft."

"Does her account hold water?"

"So far. It certainly explains what we found in and around the tasters' quarters. Aside from the dead guards, there was the corpse by the ember chute. A lean man with Nocteric-stained eyes and a large crossbow bolt through his chest—perhaps the glisserblind assassin she describes. He has been identified as Tybalt Prane, otherwise known in certain circles as . . . the Zookeeper."

"A killer for hire," muttered Right-Eye, "and whoever paid him still lives. Somebody wants that girl dead. And I cannot permit her to die, not while she is our best chance of identifying the Kleptomancer. No, nobody can be allowed to end her life yet, not even myself. Treble, do you remember our previous conversations on the subject of my . . . counterpart?"

"Yes, Your Excellency."

Although it would be an overstatement to say that Right-Eye liked Treble, he did not completely dislike her. In her he saw some of his own impatience with failure, and the gleaming rails of a ruthless and well-ordered mind. Even her brute ambition had something healthy and direct about it. Her standing at Court was always far lower when Left-Eye was in control.

"My other self is . . . unpredictable." The Grand Steward unhooked a pouch from his belt and passed it to the Enquirer. The contents were harmless, but its scent so violently invigorating that it would wake all but the dead. "If there should come an emergency—should my counterpart make a decision in which you believe I would wish to be involved—throw the pouch to the floor and I will wake. For example, should he decide on impulse to execute the child Neverfell, whom I have very good reasons for keeping alive, I should be woken. You understand?"

"Perfectly, Your Excellency," answered Treble, dropping a low bow. She did not dare to look up at the slack and sleeping left half of her master, turned away and obscured by shadow. She had the uncanny feeling it might be listening, with inscrutable but mischievous intent.

Neverfell was tired, so very tired. While she was waiting in her room to learn of her fate, her mind kept dropping away into sleep for numb instants no longer than a blink. Next moment her thoughts would jar her awake again, thrashing and crashing and clattering like a monstrous waterwheel, turning and turning without end or purpose. She jerked and stared and barely knew where she was, dream pieces floating like iceberg shards across her half-waking mind.

Neverfell had pushed through to the other side of ordinary tiredness, and now she was too tired to fall asleep properly. She was out of clock, maybe further out of clock than she had ever been before. She could feel her mind pulling loose like knitting, the neat stitches of her artificial days unraveling to become one mangled thread.

It was almost a relief when at last she received a knock on the door and was told that Zouelle Childersin was waiting in the parlor to speak to her.

When Neverfell entered, Zouelle rose immediately and put her arms round her in a big-sister hug. The kindness of the gesture was too much. Neverfell wanted to cry, but everything that had happened made a big awkward lump in her throat, and all that came out were small frog-like noises. Then, when she recovered her voice, she found herself gabbling out the whole tale of the attempted glisserblind murder, the kidnap by the Kleptomancer, and her adventures in the Undercity. Zouelle listened all the while, wearing the warm and comforting Face No. 334, A Placid Glow in a Homey Hearth.

"And now my face is spoiled, Zouelle!" Neverfell finished. "And if nobody mends it the Grand Steward will execute us all! I don't know what to do! I don't want them to take away my memories—"

"Shhh." Zouelle squeezed her hand. "Now, listen to me. Nobody's going to take your memories away. You're going to be taught a bit of face control, that's all, just to smooth out the disillusionment. Uncle Maxim has sent me to take you to a Facesmith, and I've persuaded him to let me choose which one.

"Get ready as fast as you can, Neverfell. We're going to see Madame Appeline."

It was half past thirteen. In the audience chamber a silence born of tension settled. The Grand Steward eased back in his great throne, his right eye turning this way and that, making a last-minute inspection of the hall. Then, slowly, almost reluctantly, his right eyelid drooped and closed.

The instant lid touched lid, his left eye sprang open. The servants were too well-trained to flinch, but many of them felt a cold clutch at their heart every time they witnessed the Grand Steward changing his internal guard. He moved his left shoulder slightly, easing out stiffness from twelve and a half hours of inaction, then stretched his left arm and flexed his left fingers.

All around him, the chamber was now in motion. Advisors whom Right-Eye valued were retreating, many carrying scrolls bearing newly stamped orders. Passing them in the doorway were Left-Eye's favored attendants, those who had dedicated long decades to interpreting his tiny gestures, and those whom he had chosen for his own inscrutable, peculiar reasons.

Right-Eye had left his thoughts and conclusions neatly ordered at the front of his mind, ready for his alter ego, like so many carefully written pages. As usual, Left-Eye tore through them like a breeze, scattering and discarding most as irrelevant, and chasing a few that interested him.

The "rehearsals" did not bother him as they had his counterpart. Nothing interested him but the new information about the Kleptomancer.

Left-Eye had an uncanny gift for guessing at the secret schemes of others. He noticed a thousand little signs and self-betrayals and saw the pattern behind them, like a fortune-teller reading shapes in tea leaves.

But, if the girl was to be believed, this Kleptomancer had made an art of confusing such tea-leaf reading. He created false patterns, scattered misleading clues. He deceived himself in order to deceive others. How could you detect the opposite of a pattern? Left-Eye's mind flinched from the idea, but then began compulsively trying to turn itself inside out in an attempt to understand the Kleptomancer.

The Kleptomancer, the Kleptomancer. Like a needle stitching over and over in the same place, Left-Eye's mind struggled with the problem, knotting and tangling itself as it went.

In another cavern room, a note sat snugly in a hidden pocket. It had already been read and reread many times.

My dearest comrade,

I hate repeating myself, and this is the last time I shall do so. You will oblige me by instantly ceasing all attempts against the life of young Neverfell. Please do not bore me with denials or explanations. Simply desist. You are quite aware of the value I place on that young person, and the plans that her murder would jeopardize. Rest assured, the memories of her early life are buried too deep to surface and threaten you.

We have much to discuss. An opportunity has arisen that we cannot afford to waste, one that will open the door for all our plans. I will need your help, however, if we are to take advantage of it. Delay is now a luxury we cannot afford. An investigation has been launched into certain curious murders in Drudgery, and it would be unfortunate if it were given time to discover anything important.

Regards,

Your respectful friend

It was dangerous to think about Caverna, but he did so anyway, lying on the rocky ledge that tonight served him as a bed, with his hands clasped behind his head. As he tried to corral all the information he had gathered, he almost imagined that he could see Caverna's needle-toothed smile hanging in the darkness.

"What are you preparing for, my love?" he asked aloud. "What is it that you know? Something is about to happen. You are excited. I can tell."

His goggled suit sat beside him like a sentry, and he glanced at it now and then to remind himself who he was. Trying to understand Caverna was an invitation to madness, and he needed all his strength to resist it. Again and again he felt Cartographic thoughts breaking against his mind like waves, trying to find weaknesses in his defenses and seep inside.

For three hours he had been staring at the opposite wall of the cavern in which he lay. The change in its appearance had been very slow, so slow that a normal man would have missed it, but he was sure that the central crack had widened, the ceiling risen, and some of the stalactites reduced in size, like claws retracted into a cat's paw.

The Cartographers were right. Caverna was readying herself to move, to grow.

Then map me, came the relentless voice in his head. *Draw up the changes in all their glory. Worship me.*

No, my love, he answered silently. *I will find out what you are doing without scattering my wits on the ground for you to trample. I will not bow to you.*

TEARS ON ALABASTER

ZOUELLE AND NEVERFELL WERE ESCORTED OUT through the great palace gates to a smart little low-slung carriage pulled by two short but stocky white horses, belled and tasseled. Zouelle put a white fur wrap around Neverfell's shoulders.

"You're trembling like a moth's wing," she remarked as the carriage set off.

"I'm really out of clock," Neverfell explained. "It often leaves me feeling cold—I don't know why. And hungry." Everything had an unreal look, and sometimes voices seemed to be floating past her, rather than passing through her ears and into her brain. The bobbing of the horses' heads threatened to hypnotize her. "Does that ever happen to you?"

"Not really," confessed Zouelle. "I'm a Childersin. We're never out of clock, remember?"

"But I guess I'm frightened too," went on Neverfell. "I don't know what to say to Madame Appeline. Won't she be angry with me for breaking into her storeroom?"

"I don't think so." Zouelle narrowed her eyes speculatively. "There isn't a Facesmith in Caverna who wouldn't give a hundred smiles for the chance to study your face in their own time. No, I think she'll welcome us in . . . which means that while she's fixing your face we'll have a chance to talk to her and her girls, and find out more about her, won't we?"

When they finally reached the door to Madame Appeline's abode, however, Neverfell felt a few flutters of apprehension fluttering in her stomach. She was almost glad of her tiredness, which numbed the edge of her anxiety.

They were clearly expected. The door swung open as they approached. On the other side of the door was a Putty Girl a little older than Zouelle, who smiled sweetly but blandly, took their wraps, and showed them into the reception room with the table and chandelier, and through the opposite door into the grove.

The brightness stung Neverfell's eyes. For a moment her senses swam, and she seemed to hear a drone of insects and smell fresh sap. When she blinked her vision clear again, before her stood Madame Appeline.

The Facesmith was dressed in a delicate spring green, with long and flowing sleeves and a gauzy shawl over her hair and shoulders. The fiercely glittering jewelry was gone, and her waist looked less splinter-thin. Even her usually elaborate hair had been released to fall in smooth but orderly waves on either side of her face, making her look younger and a little mermaid-like.

Madame Appeline looked Neverfell up and down, and her heart-shaped face melted into a small bow of a smile.

"Neverfell," she said. "It really *is* you, isn't it? The little cheesemaking girl. The one in the mask. Come on, sit down, both of you." They obeyed, blinking the false sunlight out of their eyes. "Now . . . yes, I *do* see the problem. An unwanted emotion pushing through and staining your expression, is it? Well, that is rather out of my usual line, and obviously I cannot teach you

Faces in the usual sense, but I can give you some exercises that might help relax your features."

Neverfell mumbled something that she hoped sounded grateful.

"Neelia!" called Madame Appeline. A Putty Girl a little older than Zouelle appeared from among the trees, wearing a very pretty Face, No. 301, Dewdrops Regarded in a Spirit of Hope. "Will you show Miss Childersin to the refreshments, and then give her a tour of our latest Faces as discussed?"

"That is most generous, but really not necessary," Zouelle countered swiftly. "And Neverfell is shy when she is completely surrounded by strangers."

"Ah, but Neverfell and I are not strangers. This is our . . . third meeting?"

The memory of the ignominious second meeting sent Neverfell into mortified blushing.

"I promised Neverfell that I would stay with her," Zouelle replied calmly.

"How sweet!" Madame Appeline's smile was suddenly perfectly feline. "Where would Neverfell be if she had never met you?" Although both her companions seemed to be trying to compete in the sweetness of their smiles, Neverfell had the distinct feeling that the atmosphere was frosting over. "Please, I must insist! You will be terribly bored sitting here while we talk Faces." There was a brief silence, and Neverfell felt a sting of frustration that she alone was unable to tell who was winning the battle of wills.

"Do you know, Miss Childersin," Madame Appeline continued slowly, "you have a slight tendency to *flutter*. You waver rapidly between two or more Faces, because none of them are really what you want or need."

Zouelle did not appear to have an answer. Now that it had been mentioned, Neverfell realized that she had more than once seen Zouelle do exactly that. In fact, she was doing it now, helplessly fluttering between two smiles, one less confident than the other.

"I know how it is," Madame Appeline said, narrowing her slanting eyes slightly over her ice-cream smile. "There is a feeling deep down inside you, isn't there? All the time. It bothers you. You don't really know what it is, or how to describe it. You do not have a Face for it. And so you scan all the Face catalogues, and ask for Faces for every birthday because perhaps, just perhaps, if you had the right Face, you might understand what you are feeling. You need to find that Face." She leaned forward slightly. "*Do* go and look at our exhibition rooms, Miss Childersin."

"Zouelle, it's all right." Neverfell could not bear the chill in the air. "I really will be fine."

After a long pause it was Zouelle who lowered her gaze and somewhat hesitantly stood.

"I will not be far away," she whispered, then turned and followed Neelia to disappear among the trees. Neverfell watched her depart, and instantly regretted asking her to do so. What was she supposed to do now? She had not really thought about it, but she had assumed that Zouelle would be doing most of the clever talking.

Three other Putty Girls were watching from nearby, their green eyes fixed on Neverfell's face. She was touched to see how confused and worried they looked, until she realized that they were on hand to watch and imitate her expressions for the Facesmith to use later. The expressions she was seeing on their faces were a semblance of her own.

Neverfell swallowed. "Madame Appeline? Can I . . . can I talk to you privately for a moment?"

As soon as they were alone, Neverfell gave up and jumped straight into the abyss, mouth-first.

"I'm so sorry!" she burst out. "I'm sorry about everything that happened last time! I put a tiny bit of the Stackfalter Sturton with the other things you ordered—I thought it would help you, and that you would help Master Grandible—but then I found it would just cause trouble so I had to try to get it back, and really I just wanted to find you and talk to you about it . . . but then everything happened so fast, and next thing I knew I was in your house in disguise with memory-destroying Wine trying to steal the cheese back . . . and then I was arrested before I could explain."

"Ahh . . ." Madame Appeline tipped her head back and studied Neverfell through careful green slits. "I begin to see. You found yourself tangled up in somebody else's plans?" Her eye drifted briefly in the direction that Zouelle had departed.

Neverfell felt herself crimson. Somehow she had betrayed Zouelle with her expression, and had learned nothing in return. She could find no purchase on the older woman's marble-smooth countenance. There were no cracks to give her a view into her soul.

"I can't tell if you're angry!" she exclaimed helplessly. "I just hoped if we talked everything would make sense, but nothing ever does. I can't tell who's feeling anything."

"I am not angry. Not with you, anyway. But I do think you should choose your friends more carefully, my dear." Neverfell felt her own brow furrow, and Madame Appeline smiled. "Oh, now I have made you uncomfortable. You are delightfully loyal . . . but you really have very little sense of when you are being mistreated or used, do you? You probably still feel loyal to Cheesemaster Grandible, even after he imprisoned and lied to you, don't you?"

"No! Well, yes . . . I . . . Please don't say things like that!" The Facesmith's words were like a giant spoon, stirring up all the uncomfortable, stinging feelings in Neverfell's stomach.

"As you wish."

"Madame Appeline," Neverfell plunged on impulsively, "if I can choose my friends, can I choose you? I felt . . . when we met the first time, back in the cheese tunnels . . . I . . ." She lost her nerve. "I just wanted us to be friends," she ended, a bit limply.

"Oh, I was quite the same." Madame Appeline's smile was dazzling. "I felt we had an instant understanding. A sort of natural trust."

"Yes! In fact, I . . . did you ever feel that we were sort of . . . alike?"

"In what way?"

The question cut Neverfell short, and she had no idea how to continue. "I don't know," she said miserably, frustrated with her own fear and confusion. "Just a sort of connection. Like we . . . like we knew each other already."

"It can feel a little like that sometimes," answered Madame Appeline, "when you meet somebody with whom you have a rapport." Her tone was warm, but it seemed to Neverfell that it was not a warmth from the core. Neverfell could only assume that she had said something wrong, and she had no idea what or how.

Where was that sense of connection now?

"Can I see your Tragedy Range?" she asked desperately, snatching at the first thought foolish enough to enter her head.

"What?" No, Neverfell was not mistaken. Madame Appeline's beautiful, subtle, mobile countenance had frozen for just a split second, and when she spoke her voice was a little too rapid. "Why the Tragedy Range? It is not really intended for wearers as young as yourself. Now, if you wanted to see the Lambs' Tails Range, or the Brook's Source—"

"Please! I don't want to wear the Tragedy Range! I just want to see it!" Without thinking, Neverfell reached out toward the long, bejeweled hand of the Facesmith. To her shock, Madame Appeline's hand jerked away from hers, as if from the touch of a nettle. "I'm sorry! What did I do?"

"Nothing." Madame Appeline dropped her eyes for a moment, and when she raised them her smile was impeccable once more. With great deliberation, she reached out and patted at Neverfell's hand. "If you want to see the Tragedy Range, see it you shall. Are you happy to see it in an exhibition room, or would you like the girls to display the Faces?"

"Um . . . whatever you think best?"

"The exhibition room is easier and faster. Come!"

Madame Appeline rose and led Neverfell back out of the grove, and into a long, narrow, vaulted room. It took a few seconds for the lanterns near the door to sense their breath and struggle into life. Slowly the room became visible, and Neverfell's heart missed a beat.

Her first impression was of two dozen floating, snow-white faces, arranged in two lines facing each other across the width of the room. As the traps pulsed more brightly, she caught sight of the black stands that supported the alabaster masks, almost camouflaged against the black-painted walls. Every mask showed a heart-shaped face, hairless and neckless, with slanting green eyes and high cheekbones. Two dozen Madame Appelines hovering in the void, each bearing a different expression, all loaded with sorrow and solemn power.

Neverfell's jaw dropped as she walked slowly down the room, each Face she passed setting off an avalanche in her soul. The first had a faraway look, as if it were burying a thought far too painful, just long enough to tell somebody else a bedtime story. The second was alert, agonized but undaunted, as if it were looking down a long, long dark tunnel toward some terrible thing, but refusing to flinch or lower its eyes. The third was smiling, the tear-touched smile of somebody regarding something incredibly precious but fragile, a bird's egg in a jungle of thrashing thorns.

Neverfell felt something tickle her cheek. Putting up her hand, she found there was a tear running down her face. Here it was, here was the connection she had sensed before. She felt a mad desire to throw her arms around the nearest mask, make it feel better. She put out a hand to it, as if to wipe tears from its cheek.

Her palm met cold, unyielding alabaster, and her hand jerked away of its own volition. *This is wrong,* screamed a voice in her blood and from beyond the locked door in her head. *This is wrong. Everything is wrong.*

"You shouldn't touch them," said Madame Appeline, just behind her. "They mark easily."

Suddenly frightened and confused, Neverfell looked over her shoulder at the woman behind her. The Facesmith's smile was perfectly kind and patient, but it was like a wall that Neverfell could not penetrate.

"You . . . you must have been very unhappy . . . when you designed these. Weren't you?" Why wasn't Zouelle here? Zouelle who was good at this, who could always think of the right thing to say. "I mean . . . you must have felt all these things." Neverfell flapped an arm at the floating masks. "Didn't you?"

"Why do you say that? That is like saying you must know how a cheese feels to make good cheese. No. You just know all the things you need to do to produce a cheese that has the right effect. It is just something you make."

"But Faces aren't the same! They can't be!" Neverfell was moving too far now, but too fast to stop. "You *were* unhappy, I know it! The Doldrums, you were in the Doldrums. And there was a child . . ."

Too far. The expression in Madame Appeline's eyes did not change, but suddenly Neverfell felt as if the Facesmith had withdrawn a thousand miles away. She almost felt she could see the older woman receding away from her, and could feel a cold gust as the cavern air was dragged after her.

"There was a child," Neverfell whispered, twisting her fingers together so hard they hurt. "You lost a child. Didn't you?"

Without a word, Madame Appeline turned and strode back out of the room, disappearing through the door at the far end. Neverfell was left staring after her, while on either side the lanterns dimmed slightly, making the masks even more spectral in appearance.

A few minutes later, Zouelle found Neverfell there, rubbing one tear-stained cheek against one of the masks.

"Neverfell!" she hissed from the doorway. Neverfell pulled back abashed, leaving a trickle of dampness down the cheek of the mask.

"I spoiled everything!" wailed Neverfell. "You weren't there and I didn't know what to say, and . . . and then I was so stupid! I blurted out questions about the Doldrums, and whether she'd had a child . . . and she marched off without a word!"

"Did she now?" Zouelle answered, in a tone that suggested excitement rather than concern. "Then she *did* have a secret in the Doldrums."

"I don't think she's ever going to speak to me again."

"Oh, of course she will! But never mind that now. Let me tell you what *I* found out from talking to the Putty Girls. Apparently they're allowed into all the rooms and galleries in Madame Appeline's tunnels so that they can sweep and feed the traps— all rooms bar one. There's a hidden door somewhere in here, painted over so that it is hard to see. It is always kept locked, and nobody but Madame herself is allowed to go in there. The Putty Girls are not even supposed to speak of it."

Curiosity filled Neverfell's mind like pain, as if somebody had pressed a burning fingertip against her thoughts. It was not enough to clear the fog in her mind, though. She blinked, then started awake again as she wobbled, Zouelle's steadying hand on her arm.

"Neverfell, you really are exhausted, aren't you?" Zouelle's eyes were large and concerned. "You can't learn face-calming tricks in this state. You need to sleep, even if it's only for an hour. We'll ask if they have a guest room."

Neverfell felt a rush of relief, which was cut short when Zouelle took her by the shoulders and met her gaze earnestly.

"But if they do, Neverfell, make sure it's one with a lock or bolt, and make sure you secure the door from the inside. We're in a nest of secrets here. Don't let down your guard."

The guest room was small, round, and slightly domed, with a little postless bed in the middle and a cut-glass lantern on the side table. Remembering Zouelle's instructions, Neverfell bolted the door behind her, then put a chair against it. Was it really necessary? She did not know.

Neverfell did not even bother kicking off her shoes. The bed was soft and forgiving, and for once it scarcely mattered that it was not a hammock. Her mind slipped gratefully out of wakefulness like a fish from a net.

Afterward, trying to remember the dream was like wandering in the dark and feeling ribbons of a tattered curtain trailing across one's face. There were pieces, hints, nothing more.

She was climbing a ladder made of black vines up to a golden balcony, looking for a hidden door. Although she was frightened, at least she had a monkey with her who knew the way and would guide her.

Her companion opened a door, and suddenly Neverfell was alone in a darkened hall, facing a single white mask with green eyes. Neverfell reached toward it, but as her fingers touched the mask it began to quiver and crack, the expression changing to one of pain and terror.

"What did you do to her?" it screamed as its lips shattered and its mouth became a ragged hole. "Why did nobody tell me what would happen?" It was a young voice, younger than the face. Its eyes became cobwebbed with fine cracks, then crumbled away leaving dark sockets. "If I had known, I would never . . . I would never . . ."

At first she tried to hold the mask together, but that only crushed it further, and the screaming took on a horrible ragged sound. In the end, mad with terror and pity, she started flailing at it, beating it to powder with her fists and forearms, anything to make the screaming stop. At last the voice died with a croak, and there was nothing but loose china dust leaking between her fingers.

A violent sneeze shook Neverfell awake and left her flailing, bewildered, in the strange bed for a few seconds. Even after her heartbeat slowed, it still seemed to her that her fists and forearms were tender from pounding on the terrible mask.

Somebody was banging on the door. Neverfell raked her fingers through her hair, managed to find all but one of her thimbles, and pulled her shoes back on. Unbolting the door, she found a Putty Girl outside, wearing a Face of polite concern.

"Madame Appeline will be very glad to hear that you are awake! Please, follow me—quickly!"

In the grove, a veritable clan of Putty Girls was waiting. At the heart of the group stood Madame Appeline, wasp-waisted and perfectly coiffured, with not a hint of dismay or discomposure. A yard or two from them sat Zouelle, her eyes remaining downcast even as Neverfell approached.

"Ah!" exclaimed Madame Appeline. "Neverfell, settle yourself in this chair. Now, we do not have a great deal of time, so we shall have to try all these methods quickly. Poppya! The signature points, if you please."

Neverfell tried not to flinch as a girl set about gently tapping places on her face with an extremely delicate silver hammer, and regarding the results intensely. Next there was a girl with a bowl of unguent, who rubbed something into Neverfell's brow that smelled like horseradish. Then there was a velvet-lined metal headband that strapped round the head and pulled the skin of the forehead up slightly "to tug against the frown." To judge by the haste with which each of these was abandoned, none of them were achieving the desired effects.

"The problem is internal, as we feared." Madame Appeline sighed. "Let us return to the mind."

Half a dozen books were hastily opened. Neverfell listened, baffled, as she was read stories and poems, some fanciful, some mournful, many joyful. Some of them were quite pretty and probably very good, but it was hard to concentrate on them, and Neverfell could not see what they had to do with anything.

"Perhaps a more cheerful ambience. Solphe, Merrimam, Jebeleth—the light in here is dimming. Perhaps you could go up and help the others breathe on the traps?"

Just for a moment, as she gave these instructions, Madame Appeline wore the motherly Face that Neverfell had first seen her wear in the cheese tunnels. Neverfell was not ready to see her directing that look toward anyone else, and to her surprise she felt hot needles of true jealousy in her chest. Worse still, the sight seemed to put an eagerness into the Putty Girls' step as they disappeared up a wrought-iron spiral staircase so delicate and spidery that she had not even noticed it among the false trees. After a while, the "heavens" above started to glow with a bit more vigor.

"You're going about it the wrong way, Madame Appeline," said Zouelle suddenly.

"Really?" The Facesmith's voice dripped incredulity.

"Yes." There was a long and hollow pause, during which Neverfell looked from countenance to countenance and could read neither of them. "I understand Neverfell, you see. For Neverfell, it is as if other people are part of her. When she believes they are in pain, it hurts her, like a wound in a pretend limb. So right now she is in pain for all the people she saw in the Undercity."

There was a pause. The countenances of Madame Appeline and the Putty Girls moved uncertainly from one expression to another, as though they were turning over this unfamiliar concept.

"So . . . how do we remove this pretend limb?" asked the Facesmith slowly. "How do we stop her feeling this?"

"You can't," Zouelle answered simply. "And she can't shut it out. She, well, doesn't seem to have any control over her own mind. So we have to cheer her up. We have to make her feel better about the drudges."

"I see." Madame Appeline sighed. She reached over and took hold of Neverfell's hands, and smiled sadly into her face. "Neverfell . . . I know that you were very upset by everything you saw down there, but there are some things that you need to understand. Drudges are not *like* us. They thrive on routines and hard work, whereas luxuries and comforts do not really mean much to them. They do not really feel pain or fear, any more than stone bleeds or trembles when you chip it. A few of them play at having simple personalities, but it is nothing more than an act, like monkeys dancing."

"But . . . but that's not true!" Neverfell thought of Erstwhile's mute, frustrated anger. "That's what everybody wants to think. The drudges *do* feel—they just don't have the Faces to show it. I hate it, the way they can only look calm and eager and willing to please, even when they're watching each other die. It's horrible. And I know why nobody teaches them more Faces. It's just so that everybody else can pretend drudges aren't real people. That's right, isn't it?"

"The Face training for the drudges is carefully considered," Madame Appeline answered swiftly. "What would happen if drudge children were taught unhappy Faces? They would grow up considering that they might *be* unhappy. They might look around and see unhappiness on one another's faces, and their own unhappiness would grow. If they wear a happy face for long enough, on the other hand, they are much more likely to believe in the end that they really are happy. And there's no real difference between being happy and believing you are happy, is there?"

Neverfell tried to untangle this in her head, but it writhed in her grip like a fistful of glisserblinds.

"Yes!" she blurted out. "Yes, there is! It's different! It just is!"

"I know that all this is hard to accept, but I am afraid you must. The drudges themselves accept their situation entirely, you know. And there is nothing that can be done to change it."

"You could change it," Zouelle announced, quite suddenly. "Couldn't you, Madame Appeline? You could send down Putty Girls to give free Face training."

There was a pause.

"Pardon?"

"You could, couldn't you? And then if drudges could show their feelings better, it would be harder for everybody else to treat them like moving dolls, wouldn't it?"

Neverfell could feel her face brighten. Somewhere in her mind, the great, crushing waterwheel of despair slowed and shuddered, its blades gleaming with droplets in a newly dawning light.

"Could you?" she whispered. "Could you do that?" It was small, but it was something. Zouelle was right. If everybody could be made to see the drudges as people, then perhaps everything could change. Hope began its usual puppy-bounce in her chest.

"Miss Childersin," Madame Appeline answered in tones of silky annoyance, "I know that you mean extremely well, but there are strict rules controlling the Faces that drudges can be taught—"

"Neverfell seems to like the idea," Zouelle interjected.

Madame Appeline glanced across at Neverfell, and performed a small double take. Neverfell became aware that the eyes of everybody in the grove were now fixed on her face.

"How long do we have to come up with a better solution?" Zouelle asked in a tone of utter sweetness. There was a scuffle of hands reaching for pocket watches.

"Half an hour," murmured Madame Appeline. The Facesmith gave Zouelle a glance that combined condescension, a touch of respect, and the slenderest gleaming wire of annoyance, then strode over to Neverfell, cupped her chin in one hand, and examined her face minutely. "True—the blot is not quite gone, but it is certainly a good deal better." After a long pause she closed her eyes and let out a sigh. "Very well. If that is what it takes, then I shall arrange these lessons somehow, but nothing must be said of this. Oh, Neverfell, what a strange child you are! Fancy becoming so obsessed with the drudges!"

"You'll give them sad Faces, then? And angry Faces? And rude Faces?"

"One step at a time!" Madame Appeline laughed, all kindness, and squeezed Neverfell's hands. "Let us start with discontent. If we do not keep it simple, they will get their features in a knot and end up grimacing all day. Now, Neverfell, can I speak to you privately for a moment?"

Neverfell followed the Facesmith farther into the grove and away from the others, among the glistening trees.

"Neverfell . . . I wanted to apologize." Madame Appeline's smile was sweet, rueful, and suddenly made her look a good deal younger. "I abandoned you in the exhibition room. That was very rude of me."

"No—it's all my fault. I upset you. I didn't mean—"

"There *was* a child." The words were very soft, little more than a murmur. "The memory of that child has always haunted me. She . . . died."

"Oh." Neverfell bowed as a little boat of hopes sank quietly and without any fuss. The Tragedy Range had been Madame Appeline's mourning for a lost child. A dead child. A child that was not Neverfell. "I'm . . . sorry."

"You talked about sensing a connection between the two of us," the Facesmith went on. "Perhaps that connection is shared loss. I lost that child. And you have lost . . . parents?"

"Yes." Neverfell peeped shyly at Madame Appeline through her hair. "And I don't even remember them. But when I look at the Faces from the Tragedy Range I feel like . . . like my mother is looking back at me. If . . . if she did look at me that way, she must have loved me, mustn't she?"

"Yes," said Madame Appeline, her countenance still and pure as snow. "With a fire beyond description." Their steps had led them in a circle, and they were drawing near to Zouelle and the others. "Well, perhaps it is good fortune that has brought us together, to be a comfort to each other. Would you like to visit again? We could talk sometimes, and play a game where I have found a long-lost daughter and you have discovered a secret mother . . ."

"Yes—yes! I'd love that!" Neverfell would have thrown her arms around the Facesmith if Zouelle had not commandeered her arm suddenly and with painful firmness.

"I need to take Neverfell back to the palace now," she declared. There was a curious edge in Zouelle's tone that Neverfell did not quite understand. "She has to get ready for the great jelly-tasting."

"Of course. Good-bye, Neverfell. I'm sure I will see you again soon."

Before Neverfell could say good-bye properly, she had been marched away by Zouelle, out of the grove and back into the reception room, and then the hallway beyond. The blonde girl's fingers dug deep into her arm, and Neverfell remembered the urgency of the situation.

Once outside the Facesmith's front door, Zouelle took a moment to let out a long, slow breath.

"Zouelle, you're brilliant! You persuaded her to help the drudges—I wish I could just make things happen the way you do!" Neverfell bounced forward to hug the other girl.

"Stop it!" To Neverfell's shock, Zouelle shoved her away. The shrillness in her voice was almost panic.

"What is it?" Neverfell stared at her. "What's wrong?"

"Nothing." The moment passed, and Zouelle donned a bright, gentle smile. No. 218, An Ode to Peppermint. "There's nothing wrong. Sorry, Neverfell, Facesmiths just make me tense."

"Something's happened!" Neverfell scanned her friend's face in vain for clues. "Did you find out something else? Did they catch you looking for the door? Is that it?"

"No. Nothing like that. There's nothing wrong. Can we just go? Please?"

Everything about the Face Zouelle was wearing told Neverfell that there was no problem, and that she herself was being silly in worrying.

She's one of my best friends, thought Neverfell, *and most of the time I don't know what is going on in her head at all.*

THE RENDING

DURING THE CARRIAGE RIDE BACK, NEVERFELL was so tired, hungry, and thirsty that she wanted to cry. She could feel her face crumpling with the exhaustion of it, despite all her efforts. When Zouelle spoke, her voice was a hum, a bumblebee mumble with the occasional word in it. Neverfell's mind kept flapping shut like a book.

"Neverfell!" She was jerked out of her stupor by her own name. "We're back at the palace! Look—we've made good time. Go quickly and get some food before the Grand Steward calls you."

"Is my face—"

"It's fine. It really is. It's much, much better. All mended. You don't need to worry." Zouelle gave her a blindingly confident smile.

Neverfell hugged her quickly to hide her own expression. *I know you're lying,* she thought. *I know you're lying to help me, so I won't have worry all over my face.*

Attendants led Neverfell back to the tasters' district, where Leodora ran an eye of scrutiny over her.

"Better," she muttered. "I think it's better. Let's hope it's good enough. Come and eat! Quickly! You have half an hour!"

In the dining hall Neverfell drank several jugs full of water and forced down some fennel casserole with rice. She had barely finished when her escort arrived to take her to the Grand Steward's tasting. It was larger and better armed than any that had accompanied her before. Clearly the Grand Steward did not intend to see his most prized taster stolen more than once. The horse might have bolted, but the stable door behind it was being very carefully secured.

I just have to get through the next three hours, she told herself, *and then I can sleep as much as I like.* She imagined the three hours as a space of rough gravel over which she had to hobble, and everything beyond it as rich, thick, kindly carpet.

Left-Eye watched as massive desserts were brought in on palanquins with the exotic pomp of eastern queens. His left fingers slowly tapped at the arm of his marble throne, and he gave long, slow blinks to clear the crusts from his strange, glassy lashes.

His one eye glided over the glittering confections designed for his pleasure. The first was a mighty green jelly in a cone shape, from the apex of which burst a candied flower. The sugared roots of the plant could be seen winding their way down through the translucent jelly. The second was a castle three feet high fashioned entirely from sugar and crystallized fruits, complete with a tiny spun-sugar portcullis. Third came a vast cake covered in real gold leaf, and with crunchy pearls mixed in among the nuts.

Ash, said his mind. *Ash and dull wool.* He needed his new taster. He needed to see her taste these masterpieces so they became real to him.

Here she came at last, a small figure amid her escort. As she approached from the shadows of the doorway, the light fell upon her face.

He felt a shudder of annoyance and distaste pass through the depths of his soul. The stain on her expression was reduced, but it was not gone. It was not reduced *enough*. The disappointment was bitter and maddening. How could he enjoy anything through a sour countenance like that? It would be like eating delicacies with a dirty spoon.

And then, just as he was about to make the small gesture that would doom the girl and those who had failed to mend her to a sharp and sudden demise, the girl's brow cleared and brightened a little.

His hand stilled. Perhaps the stain was not as bad as he had thought. She would do . . . for now at least.

It's Left-Eye! The one who always liked me!

That was the thought that had struck Neverfell at the critical moment, flooding her mind with relief and causing her expression to brighten. Little did she guess that her smile had just saved her from execution. The Grand Steward gave a slight nod of approval, and she took up her place on a small velvet seat a few feet from his throne, hardly believing her luck.

The first pudding was brought forward, and was introduced by its creator in such glowing and detailed terms that Neverfell had a hazy feeling that she should probably curtsy to it. She watched as a tiny silver knife was used to carve a small piece of green jelly and candied flower for the Grand Steward, and an even tinier piece for herself. Letting that little blob of jelly melt on her tongue was like suddenly running down into a glowing green valley against the wind. Somewhere a trapped flower was singing, with all the beauty and pathos of an imprisoned princess.

With difficulty Neverfell steadied herself and managed not to fall off her stool. The little bowl of moth biscuits came past, and she took a tiny fragment of one and let it settle on her tongue, dulling all flavor. She pinched her nose hard and managed to smother the inevitable sneeze.

Neverfell did not raise her gaze, because she knew that every eye would be upon her. The knowledge made her feel scraped, like a fruit rind raked by too many eager spoons.

It was only after sampling the Melodia Orchid Jelly, the Chateau Caramel, the Imperial Pineapplerie, and the rest that Left-Eye became aware of something tickling at the back of his mind. Truth be told, he was rather surprised to find that he had a back of his mind at all, since his thoughts were so soft, loose, and all-enfolding. It was blundering and bothersome, like a bat in the jaws of a lamp, and he could not see it properly.

Flap. Flap-a-flap-flap. What was it?

Something was wrong. The Kleptomancer had not yet made a bid to steal the desserts. He might of course attempt to snatch them after the tasting, but what luster was there in a meager challenge like that? The desserts would still be unparalleled, but they would be past their best. Months of calculation had gone into ensuring that they would be presented to the Grand Steward while at their very peak.

If the Kleptomancer's thefts really were designed to cause disruption, which the thief could study to understand the plans of others, what better way to create chaos than to undermine the Grand Steward? And what better way to do that than another audacious theft so close on the heels of the last? It would be a boldness akin to madness for the Kleptomancer to steal one of these desserts in such a dangerous situation, and for this very reason Left-Eye found himself growing ever more certain that the thief would be unable to resist doing so. Thus he himself had to be missing something simple and colossal.

His hand halted in its drumming. He had it. He understood. Another small gesture, and all the puddings were brought forward again so that he could examine them.

He could not be wrong. The Kleptomancer would not miss an opportunity to steal one of these puddings at their best, but the sampling itself had occurred without incident. *Which could only mean that the Kleptomancer had already stolen one of the priceless desserts and replaced it with an exact replica.*

It was so obvious now that he wondered why nobody else had worked out the truth. But then everybody else's minds did baffle him by sluggishly dragging themselves in straight lines.

Or, then again, perhaps some of them had guessed. Indeed, some of them must already know, must have noticed the change, or even helped with the theft. Which ones? And which of these puddings was an imposter?

And could it have been poisoned? He glanced across at the red-haired girl who sat nearby. She looked sleepy but noticeably alive, and any poison capable of harming him would have killed her as soon as it touched her lips. Her face at least was clear as fresh-drawn water. She was not one of the conspirators, but anybody else in the room might be.

Which pudding? It seemed to him suddenly that the melody of the candied flower in the emerald jelly had been a little mocking in its tone. Yes, doubtless, that was the false dessert. How had the theft been managed? Its creators must have been negligent at best, complicit at worst.

One small gesture of his hand, and his guards were in motion.

Neverfell missed the moment. She was rubbing her eyes during the instant that tense calm suddenly tipped over into blood and chaos. There was a horrible shortened sound, not even a cry, more like a thin slice of a cry, and some soft thuds. When she opened her eyes, she found that the men who had proudly borne in the flower-adorned jelly were buckling to the floor, dark diagonal gashes opening in their chests. Their palanquin hit the ground with a lopsided crash, and the silver platter clattered off sideways, its edge chiming against the floor, the jelly upending with a sodden murmur of melody, like a music box sinking into a well, the roots of the flower waving in the air.

She could only stare aghast and nonplussed at the red blades of the guards, hardly understanding what had happened. Next moment she realized that they were watching the Grand Steward's china-pale left hand for further instructions.

Before she could recover her senses, the hand was in motion once more.

Left-Eye knew that he had to move fast. In order to make the substitution, the Kleptomancer must have had many accomplices, among the guards, the confectioners, even the Enquiry. Why go to so much trouble just to replace a thing with its double? There could only be one answer. The Kleptomancer had intended Left-Eye to notice the switch. It was designed to throw him off balance, bewilder and madden him, throw his entire understanding of the world into disarray.

But why do so? Who would want to do anything of the sort? Left-Eye reached for a pattern that would explain it all . . . and found one.

The Kleptomancer was nothing but a cat's-paw. Left-Eye saw it all now. The thief was a tool in the hands of one who wanted to distract Left-Eye from his own plans, to keep him confused, obsessed, helpless. And who would know that the Kleptomancer's game would have such an extreme effect upon Left-Eye? Only one person.

With a series of quick signals, Left-Eye gave the order for all of Right-Eye's remaining advisors to be executed.

Right-Eye must have been plotting against him for years, nursing dark and resentful thoughts from his half of the skull. No doubt he had hidden all his schemes amid those tiresome reams of dull thoughts and schedules that he knew Left-Eye would never examine properly. Now Right-Eye was weakening him, ready to strike, so Left-Eye had no choice but to strike first.

The first advisor was neatly decapitated before anybody really realized what was happening. The second had time to offer up a scream and plaintively raise his hands before he was cut down. When the Grand Steward's left hand made the same gesture a third time, however, and pointed at Enquirer Treble, she leaped back in time to draw her sword and deflect a blade with her own.

"Hold! That's an order!" The tone of authority was enough to make the guards hesitate, confused into forgetting for a moment that Treble was not in their chain of command, and had a good deal less authority while Left-Eye was awake. She took advantage of the moment to pluck a pouch from her belt and throw it to the floor, where it burst, white powder spattering the tiles.

The guards jumped back in alarm, suspecting some attack, and a moment later everybody's eyes were streaming.

"Your Excellency!" called out Treble. "Your advisors appeal to you!"

As the stinging scent of the spilled powder reached the throne, the Grand Steward's right eye flicked open.

. . . . .

There was none of the usual easing into consciousness, sliding on his body like a glove. Instead, Right-Eye was suddenly rudely awake and aware that he was under attack. He was not alone in his own skull, and the other thing in there with him was no longer recognizable as a part of him. Rather, it seemed like a vast, maddened bat, beating at him with black wings of unreason and dragging claws across his thoughts.

His guards were attacking Treble, who was defending herself as best she could. What were they doing?

"Stop!"

They halted, looking utterly bewildered. They were staring toward his left-hand side, and he realized that his left hand must be signaling orders to them. He looked down and was infuriated by the fact that, as always, he could see only his right side, not the actions of his left. He reached across and seized his left hand to stop it from gesturing.

"Stand down! All of you! Enquirer Treble, your report . . ."

But Enquirer Treble was given no opportunity to deliver her report. Before anybody could do anything, the Grand Steward's left hand escaped from his right, and the next moment he felt a searing line slashed across his right knuckles. It took Right-Eye a second to realize that his left hand had triggered the secret mechanism in its ring and used the needle that sprang out to attack his right hand.

That needle was one of the few weapons sharp enough to pierce his skin, which centuries of carefully applied oils had left dragon-scale tough. He was immune to the poison that tipped it, and the pain was nothing, for he had long since exhausted pain's power to distract or enthrall him. What shocked him was the sudden, twisting realization that Left-Eye had gone completely mad and had to be destroyed.

"Guards! Your bows! Aim for my left side! My left eye! The left side of my throat!"

Neverfell tumbled backward off her chair, numbly staring at the Grand Steward, her skin not so much crawling as sprinting. Everything was wrong with him now. The two halves of his countenance seemed to be striving for different Faces, his mouth lopsidedly agape, his eyes struggling to look in different directions. As she watched, his left hand clawed open a secret panel in the arm of the throne, and pulled out a bodkin that seemed to be made of pale gold. A moment later both china-white hands were gripping the hilt of the bodkin as the Grand Steward wrestled with himself, writhing on the throne like a seizure victim.

The audience chamber spent a few seconds agape, and then collapsed into chaos. There had always been a crack running down the middle of the Grand Steward's personal guard and coterie of advisors. Now, without more ado, this household broke neatly in two. The guards who had attacked Enquirer Treble ceased to do so, but instantly had to defend her from another three guards who were still trying to obey Left-Eye's last orders. One of Right-Eye's favored advisors produced an illegal garotte from a bracelet and made a spirited attempt to strangle one of Left-Eye's interpreters. Suddenly an uneasy alliance had dissolved. Now was the moment to settle all grievances.

While everybody was screaming orders and counter-orders, a crossbow bolt hit the Grand Steward in the left shoulder. It did not bury itself deep, but did cause him to jerk and fall off his throne. An instant later two more hit, this time in his right leg and just below his right collarbone.

"Stop it!" screamed Treble. "Are you all mad? Stop shooting at the Grand Steward!"

"Which one?" called a guard, gripping a loaded and trembling bow.

"Either of him!" bellowed Treble. "Put your bows up! All of you! Everybody stop killing everybody!"

The Grand Steward was on the ground amid the wreckage of the jelly, rolling over and over as he fought himself. He had spent centuries developing defenses against attack, and he knew his way past all of them. He knew all his own tactics, the weak places in his armor, the creases where his toughened skin was most susceptible to a blade. When at last the bodkin fell from his hands and skittered away, he pummeled himself, each hand clawing at the opposite side of his face, pulling loose fistfuls of glassy hair.

"Stop him!" shouted Treble, her cry echoed by a number of others.

But nobody could stop him. Nobody could go near him, for none of them trusted one another with him anymore. Anybody who took a step toward him was instantly the focus of a dozen bows, and found their vista glittering with sword tips. Besides this, the Grand Steward's thrashing had triggered half a dozen traps, all designed to prevent enemies from getting too close to the throne and its occupant. A curtain of metallic gauze had fallen between him and the furor, its poisoned barbs gleaming in the pearly light. Some parts of the floor fell away, gleaming tiles tumbling into the blackness below. Steel pendulums swung from side to side with a sound like tearing silk, and venom-tipped darts thrummed from one wall to the other.

Beneath the Grand Steward a pool began to spread, but at first not everyone guessed it was blood, for it was translucent and gleamed like glass. At last he collapsed onto his back, his struggles weakening, both frost-like eyes fixed upon the ceiling. He was shuddering and appeared to be going into some kind of a fit, as if the two halves of his nature had given up on their physical fight and retreated inside his head to continue their battle.

"Physicians! Bring in the physicians!" But both halves of the Grand Steward favored different physicians, and as a furious debate broke out over which could be trusted, swords were drawn again, and the fight resumed.

So it was that only one person actually approached the Grand Steward during the confusion, for she was on the right side of the swinging traps, and of neither faction.

In the ash-filled labyrinths of the Grand Steward's mind, a war raged. One half felt that it was fighting a terrible, ice-cold, logical monster that strangled it like a boa constrictor, its monstrous scales rattling dully like chains. The other half knew only that it battled a phantom of shadow and madness that knew no shape and melted in his grasp.

And then suddenly, deep in the core of him that was both Right-Eye, Left-Eye, and neither, it came to the Grand Steward that he was dying. The body he had known for so long was cooling, numbing, passing from his control, like a demoralized army deserting in dribs and drabs under cover of night after a lost battle. *No,* sighed that greater soul as his two halves wrestled, mad with hate. *Must it be this now? Must it be this forever? An unending, slow numbing in a dying mind?*

There was still some sight in his eyes, but everything was hazy now. Staring up, he found that his view of the ceiling's delicate carvings was blocked by a blot. A blot with red hair and a pale, thin face.

Small hands were trying to stanch his wounds. They were not

doing it very well. They had made a knot out of a taster's sash and were pressing it hard against the worst wound in his flank.

Her face was upside down, but he could still make out her expression, and it filled him with a pang of curiosity. It was so long since he had seen such an expression that it took a while for him to recognize it as pity. Yes, it was true pity, without superiority or disdain. Just pain felt for pain. How strange it looked!

For a moment, he felt a sting of the same for her. Pain for pain. Pity for everything that would inevitably happen to her after his passing.

The world before his eyes fogged and extinguished, but now the maze of his mind was less dark than it had been. For the first time it seemed to him that he was not alone in there, that there was something gamboling at his side now like a monkey, something that was not the two great beasts of his consciousness, weakening under each other's claws. It prattled and had a face that changed like flame, and it led him to a room where he was to be tested.

In the great audience chamber he stood before an empty throne of marble, and stared down at the box he was challenged to open. He knew from long experience that such boxes held only horrors, but the capering companion at his side whispered that there might instead be miracles. He knelt, lifted the box, and opened the lid the tiniest crack to peer inside.

Through that narrow aperture he glimpsed not skulking, stale nightmares but blue eternities. Suddenly the song of the trapped flower was in his ears again, yet now it no longer sounded mournful and imprisoned but free and jubilant.

In an instant he saw the delusion of his five hundred years. He was not looking into a box; he was looking out of one. All these centuries his mind, his body, his world had been a box of horrors.

He took one last breath, then pushed open the lid of his prison and escaped.

SPOILS

SILENCE SPREAD ACROSS THE CHAMBER LIKE A dark pool. Every head turned to stare at the unmoving figure. It was as if they had lived all their lives at the mercy of a perilous but tireless ocean, and it had hushed and vanished in an instant, leaving stony chasms and dripping abysses full of flailing, dying sea beasts. Even the empty throne and the power it represented could not yet draw away their eyes.

Neverfell crouched shivering by the side of the Grand Steward, knowing only that her fingers could find no trace of a pulse in his chest. It seemed to her that at the last he had smiled at her very slightly, and that smile still hovered on his face.

It was during this silence that the twin doors to the audience chamber swung open to admit a stream of purple. Half a dozen Enquirers strode in, the two rearmost perfumiers with silk blindfolds. The crowd parted for them, revealing the body of the Grand Steward and the small figure crouched over him. Neverfell was suddenly very aware of the glassy blood gleaming on her hands and thimbles like varnish. The Enquirers faltered and halted, staring, then looked to Enquirer Treble.

"He's not breathing," Neverfell whispered. Her voice seemed

to have shriveled to nothing. "There's no pulse—I tried to stop the bleeding . . ."

Treble strode forward to join the new arrivals, and nobody tried to stop her. Suddenly she was not a solitary, out-of-breath woman with a sword. She was an authority figure with reinforcements.

"Somebody turn off those pendulums!" she snapped, her voice hoarse from her attempts to shout over the chaos. Several white-clad servants sprinted to hidden catches, and the razor-sharp pendulums ceased to slice the air. "Physicians! His Excellency needs attention!" The two physicians hesitated, glancing apprehensively at each other's bodyguard. "Oh, spite's bite! Go and attend to His Excellency—both of you! If either of you sees the other doing anything odd or untoward, report it to me immediately. You, guards! Train your weapons on the doctors. Be ready for my word to shoot. And let nobody enter or leave this chamber! Everybody else, stay exactly where you are. You will all be questioned in time."

Shocked out of their statue-like paralysis, both guards and physicians showed nervous signs of obeying. Neverfell shuffled backward on her knees as the doctors approached, unable to take her eyes from the fallen man, his glassy hair splayed out across the mosaic in a shimmering fan. She rubbed her fingers with her handkerchief, but they still had a sticky, pearly gloss to them. No one said anything to her, but from time to time carefully expressionless glances were thrown her way.

Is it my fault? Did I make it worse?

The doctors seemed reluctant to start their investigation, and Neverfell was just close enough to see their hands shaking.

"Your Excellency—forgive this liberty . . ." muttered one of them, apparently afraid even to touch their honored patient without permission.

"You might wish to make haste," Treble remarked icily. "After all, the Grand Steward gave orders that in the event of his death all his physicians and tasters were to be executed. Something to give you a little incentive to keep him alive." She was still recovering her breath, and took a moment to wipe her brow with her sleeve.

This reminder seemed to have the desired effect. With new eagerness leather bags were opened, pearly ointments smeared on the Grand Steward's nostrils and lips, burning censers wafted above his face, sigils drawn on his palms in a lurid yellow paste.

Neverfell was also shaken by the Enquirer's words, despite her fog of weariness and shock. The Grand Steward's tasters were to be executed after his death. Whatever Treble had said about saving him, Neverfell was sure she had watched the Grand Steward die. Now it seemed he was to drag her after him.

"Close the doors!" commanded Treble as she paced, sword still in her hand. "Nobody leaves. When the Grand Steward recovers, he will pass judgment on all who act rashly at this moment. Physicians, report! Any progress?"

The physicians gave a guilty jump. Their bags were now all but empty, and they seemed to be pouring something into the Grand Steward's ear through the point of a tapering seashell, with a shakiness that looked a good deal like panic.

"Ah . . . no, that is, yes," spluttered one. "Ah, some promising avenues . . . more time, please, more time!"

Time was given, and each second passed with the heavy tread of one who drags a body. But still there was no motion from the patient, and at last the physicians withdrew their trembling hands from the Grand Steward's glassy form.

"Enquirer . . ." One doctor spoke up, his tones muted, terrified. "We have tried everything . . . every restorative including phoenix blood . . . our instruments detect not the slightest lingering trace of life essence . . . not even an ant-stamp of a pulse . . ."

There was a deathly hush, followed by a murmur of incredulity and fear.

Enquirer Treble's step faltered. For a long moment she stood irresolute, breathing quickly, gripping her sword as if she wished to cut the physician's words out of the air. Then the tip of her blade slowly drooped.

"Peace be with him, and may his works linger long," she muttered, before rallying herself. "Everybody stay where you are! The Grand Steward has been assassinated, and every single one of you is now under Enquiry!"

"Assassinated?" The head guard's exclamation was echoed by others around the room. "But His Excellency stabbed himself to death!"

"Yes, after going completely insane without warning," retorted Treble. "There is malice at work here—poison or Perfume—and I intend to uncover it. Enquirers, to me!"

The air still bristling with tension, the Enquiry began. Statements were taken. The Enquiry's perfumiers moved slowly around the room, drawing in deep breaths through their large, sensitive noses, and sniffed at each cringing witness in turn. Pockets and pouches were turned out, clothing searched for hidden cavities, and the remaining food and drink tested on willing and unwilling volunteers.

The perfumiers were certain that the only Perfume that had been used in the chamber was the powder that had been thrown down to wake Right-Eye, and which contained nothing that would have caused anybody to go mad. Nobody who had tried the desserts showed any sign of trying to stab themselves.

"No Perfume, so it must be poison," Enquirer Treble kept

reciting under her breath. "It *must* be. Not in the desserts, then . . . but perhaps something else, something that has been consumed in its entirety, so that no trace remains to be tested—ah! I have it! The moth biscuits for damping the taste! Most of the biscuit would have been eaten in one mouthful by the Grand Steward, except for a tiny piece that would have been fed to . . . *you.*"

The last word was spoken with soft menace. Neverfell, who was leaning against the wall and letting her mind fog, opened her eyes and saw that a pair of boots had stopped in front of her. Her eyes traveled up a set of purple robes, and found Enquirer Treble looking down at her with an expression of cool loathing.

"Always *you.* Again and again, everything seems to lead back to *you.* Why is that?" The Enquirer slowly lowered herself to her haunches, so that she was on an eye level with Neverfell. In another person this might have been a friendly gesture, an attempt to seem less intimidating. In this case, however, it made Neverfell think of a cat lowering its head to peer into a mousehole. "You consumed some kind of antidote before this tasting. Didn't you?"

"Me? No! No, I didn't! I . . ." Neverfell frowned as she racked her brain to see whether there was any way she could have done so by mistake. "No, I didn't! I haven't eaten anything I shouldn't—only things from the tasters' halls, or some of what the Grand Steward was eating! Oh—except for the things that made me throw up, the ones I was given after I came back from the Undercity—"

"Ah yes, the purgatives. So the antidote must have been consumed after that. Girl—tell me everything that happened from that moment onward. Leave out nothing!"

Slowly, hazily, Neverfell set about reciting everything that had happened since her return from the Undercity, leaving out only the subjects of her conversations with Zouelle and Madame

Appeline. When Neverfell mentioned that she had slept outside the tasters' quarters, the Enquirer pounced on this fact with eagerness, and quizzed her to find out if she could have been dosed in her sleep. The Enquirer was clearly disappointed to learn that Neverfell's nap had taken place in a room bolted from the inside.

When Neverfell reached the end of her account, Treble gave a small noise of dissatisfaction, and forced her to go through the whole thing again and again, occasionally snapping questions at her. Neverfell lost her place in her story over and over, stumbled with her sentences, and felt her mind turn panicky blank every time she made the mistake of meeting the Enquirer's eye.

Please, all I want to do is sleep. The thick carpet of rest had now receded almost out of sight, and everything was gravel as far as she could see. She almost wondered whether the Enquirer would let her sleep if she pretended that she *had* taken an antidote.

"Enough!" Treble snapped at last. "This girl is to be placed under arrest." She ignored Neverfell's horrified gasp. "We can delay no longer," she muttered to the Enquirers beside her. "We must act. Rumor will already be running wild at seeing this chamber sealed off. The Grand Steward's death must be announced, and by us, and before anybody else can prepare a bid for power. Send out a call to the Court to attend in the Hall of the Gentles!"

The doors were unbarred, and messengers sprinted. Neverfell could barely keep her feet as she was led from the hall and through a waiting throng, all craning to peer at her, or into the bloodied audience chamber. Their faces were all aflutter, in desperate search for a Face they did not have. For one fleeting second, before she was borne away down the corridor, Neverfell thought she saw the pale, drawn face of Zouelle Childersin amid the crowd.

Ringed about by Enquirers, her head reeling and her wrists bound, Neverfell knew little as she was dragged into the Hall of the Gentles. She was standing in a murk starred with lanterns that seemed tiny as glowworms. She realized that they were distant, that she was at the heart of the largest cavern she had ever known. There was a reverberating hubbub of confused voices, and new lanterns could be seen scurrying in. The hall was not full, but it was filling as the Court surged in to answer the Enquiry's hasty summons.

Neverfell could dimly make out the front ranks of the gathering audience, nearly all of whom had binoculars raised to their eyes. She wondered if everybody in the hall was also minutely observing her, and suddenly felt heavy, as if their gaze had a weight.

"Gentles, Craftsmen, Elite of Caverna!" Treble's voice echoed across the vast hall, and the crowd's turbulence lulled. "I bring you only sorrow this day. His Excellency the Grand Steward, Master of Caverna, Father of Our City, has been murdered!"

The audible consternation and disbelief of the crowd rose like a wave, which broke in exclamation, then ebbed as Treble spoke again, describing the manner of the Grand Steward's sticky and sudden demise.

"The Enquiry has already determined that he was driven to suicide by poison," she finished at last, "and was betrayed by his food taster, Neverfell the outsider, whom we have placed under arrest, and intend to put to the question. His Excellency gave strict orders that, in the case of his murder, the Enquiry should temporarily take control of Caverna, in order to investigate fully and punish the perpetrators. We are thus assuming governorship of the city as of this moment."

"I am sorry, but I shall have to take issue with that."

Neverfell realized that there was a parade of tall figures marching with determination toward the dais where she stood beside Treble. They carried lanterns on sticks, so that their burgundy attire was visible to the whole Court. At their head strode a lean and familiar figure. The mouth that had spoken was one with hidden smiles in it, but for the moment they were all very, very well hidden.

"Return to your seat, Childersin." Treble drew herself up.

"Honored Enquirer, it is obvious why you wish to believe that His Excellency was murdered, since it provides you with such a fine excuse to take over the city. But I think many of us would feel happier about bowing to your 'temporary' leadership if there was the *slightest* evidence of foul play."

"And who else should govern Caverna in this emergency, if not the Enquiry?" Treble retorted sharply. "You, perhaps?"

"A council," answered Childersin smoothly. "A council representing each of the Crafts, and the interests of all the divisions of the city."

"Are you questioning the power vested in me by His Excellency?" demanded Treble. "Are you challenging the authority of the Grand Steward himself?"

Maxim Childersin let out a long breath, and suddenly it was hard to imagine that smiles had ever found a place on his face.

"Yes," he said. "I am challenging the authority of the Grand Steward. The man is dead. He went insane, threw himself into a trifle, and then stabbed himself to death. Yes, after that I *do* think it appropriate to challenge his authority."

There was a general intake of breath that seemed to leave the air thinner and slightly harder to breathe.

A long duel of stares followed. Neverfell saw neither flicker, nor could she imagine what weakness either was looking for in the other. She was having trouble keeping her mind clear, but she understood that an imaginary sword was hanging over her head, and that Maxim Childersin was putting himself in danger to stop it from falling.

"The Court shall decide the matter," called out Childersin at last. "Speak your piece, Enquirer, and I shall follow with mine. The Court shall weigh our words."

"Very well." Enquirer Treble narrowed her eyes at the vast, unseen gathering before her, and began to speak.

She gave a long, stark catalogue of all the attempts that had been made against the Grand Steward's life in the last ten years. Poison-tipped paradribbles, weakened cavern-supports, whistles whose notes made the ears bleed, Perfumes that made you yearn to swallow spiked rocks, leaping leopard-spiders, venomous thorns in counterpanes, and trained attack-bats.

"And after all this, you would have me believe that such a sudden death was not the result of malice? The Grand Steward's enemies were tireless and ingenious. And although His Excellency was not always easy to fathom, he was ever prudent, wise, and capable, and kept the city on an even keel for five hundred years. Does this sound like a man who would suddenly throw himself into a dessert and die?"

To her alarm, Neverfell could hear murmurs of assent from the unseen audience.

"Last of all, there are all the odd circumstances surrounding this girl. She is an outsider, brought in we know not how or by whom. She appeared at a banquet immediately after the death of His Excellency's favorite food taster, just in time to be chosen as a replacement. Her behavior has been bizarre and unexplained throughout. She is the key to this mystery, a key that I will turn, by hook or by crook."

Neverfell thought of hooks and crooks, and trembled. There was a long silence, and for a terrible moment she feared that Childersin had decided not to offer any answer.

"Bring the child forth," he said at last. "And bring light. Let the Court see her."

Neverfell was led forward, blinded by the dozens of lanterns that were now all but thrust into her face.

"Did you consume an antidote, Neverfell?" Childersin's voice sounded calm. "Was there a chance you might have done? Think hard."

Neverfell shook her head. "No," she sobbed. "I've thought about it, and thought about it, and . . . no."

"Look at her." Childersin had turned away, and was addressing his audience again. "Can you look at her and doubt her?

"If the Enquiry has leave to take this girl into custody, I am sure she will give a different story tomorrow. Lies can be wrung out of a witness as easily as truth. Yes, after a few hours with the Enquiry's . . . instruments, I am sure she will be willing to swear that she had swallowed an antidote, or indeed that she had flown to the moon, if that would make the pain stop. But, here and now, you can *see* she is telling the truth. There was no betrayal. There was no poison. There was no murder."

The lanterns were lowered, and Neverfell found herself blinking in the murk once more.

"My friends," continued Childersin after a long pause, "I do not deny the greatness of the Grand Steward. Caverna shaped itself around him like an armadillo's shell, and we scarcely know how we can wear it without him. He was the city's mind and soul, and seemed to be its destiny as well as its past.

"How can I say what I must without seeming to slight him?

Perhaps it is not possible. The Enquirer here has talked of the Grand Steward 'suddenly going mad.' Deep in our hearts, however, we know that there was nothing sudden about it. My friends, the Grand Steward had been going mad for months. Years. Perhaps even more than a century. And we were all too busy knocking our foreheads against the floor in fear and humility to notice each creeping, relentless step toward lunacy.

"Men are supposed to sleep. That is why they do. Have any of you ever spent time out of clock? You remember what the sleeplessness did to your mind? Think of how long the Grand Steward had gone without such repose.

"And do you pretend that you have not noticed how the two halves of his mind had been moving further apart from each other? The arrangements they had started to make to hinder and thwart each other? One of them distrusted his counterpart enough to hand out a powder so that he could be woken quickly to prevent the other from doing something foolish. Yes, when the end came, it came quickly, and perhaps we should thank our luck for that. What would have happened if Caverna had been torn by a civil war, the two opposed leaders housed in a single body?

"To us, the Grand Steward represented continuity. His persistence allowed us to play a game and pretend that everything can stay as it is now forever. It cannot. The events of this day have shown us what happens when you try to keep things from changing. Sooner or later the sleeplessness catches up with you, the paranoia about threats devours you, and your mind betrays you even if your body does not.

"Change is necessary and, deny it as we may, in the end change is always inevitable. I know it is tempting to turn now to the Enquiry, is it not? They will revere the Grand Steward's memory, they say. They will carry out his orders. They will keep things as they have always been, and through them the ghost of the Grand Steward can be kept alive, to govern, terrify, and reassure us. We can pretend that nothing has changed.

"But the world *has* changed, and we must change with it. Caverna must change to fit us, instead of us cramping ourselves to fit its confining shell. For centuries, every thought has been focused upon the will and wishes of the Grand Steward. We have disdained to cast an eye outside our city. We have told ourselves that there is nothing out there worthy of our attention, just a wilderness covered in sunburnt savages and hurricane-beleaguered shacks.

"Let me tell you, there is a rich, varied, and fascinating world out there, and *it can be ours*. Do you know how the rest of the world sees us, truly? We are the mysterious enclave where the magic of the world is fashioned. Out there, a king's ransom would be paid for a quantity of Perfume that one of our young debutantes might splash across her wrist for her first banquet. A spoonful of Paprickle would muster enough gold to pay a regiment for a year. Yes, we know that we can buy anything we choose from the outer world for tiny portions of our wares, but we are falling short, my friends—far short—of all that we could achieve.

"Why do we not send emissaries, anointed with Perfume, to every powerful nation in the world, to enslave the minds of their kings, ministers, and potentates? Why do we own no armies to conquer land for us? We could find the gold with ease. Our scouts, spice-touched, would have no equal. Our generals would have the benefit of cheese-visions to aid their strategy. Why must we look inward, and only inward, as if the world ends where the sky begins?

"Why? Because we are still prisoners of the Grand Steward's ghost. We must break free, my friends. The Enquiry has said that under his rule Caverna thrived for five centuries. The truth is it thrived for four centuries, but for the last hundred years everything has been breaking down, including our ruler himself. This girl is not to blame for the death of the Grand Steward. He had been dying for a very, very, very long time, and his span came to an end as all eras must."

The applause started slowly but gathered volume until it roused Neverfell from the stupor into which she had fallen. The votes were slowly gathered, counted, the numbers given. The Enquiry had lost. They would not be taking over Caverna. They had leave to investigate the Grand Steward's death further, and present evidence at a hearing in the Hall of the Gentles in two months' time, but they would be given no special emergency powers. A council, meanwhile, would be appointed to rule Caverna.

All of this meant very little to Neverfell. All she knew was that Maxim Childersin had given her a brief and reassuring smile. There was no longer an invisible sword hovering above her head. Childersin had marched in, risking torture and execution, and snatched her from beneath it.

HOMESICK

NEVERFELL WOKE IN A SMALL FOUR-POSTER bed with soft golden covers and strokeable curtains, in a neat, familiar little chamber that smelled of violets. Yes, it was her bedroom in the Childersin town house. Looking across the room, she could even see the outline of a dissected and partly reconstructed mechanical cockerel. The Childersins had not given her a new clock, but she could hardly blame them for that.

There were clothes laid out for her on the chair, and she felt another throb of déjà vu as she saw them. A green dress. Green satin shoes. White crochet gloves with bobbles on them. Just for a moment it seemed to her that perhaps everything that had happened since her first arrival at the Childersin household had been a dream. Perhaps she had never spilled Wine at the banquet, never served as a food taster, never been stolen by the Kleptomancer, never knelt by the dying Grand Steward . . .

There was a jug and ewer by the cockerel. She got up, discovering she ached all over, and went to wash her face, then paused before her fingers could ruffle the surface of the water, and instead peered in to see if she could make out something of her reflection.

No, it had not been a dream. All these events had happened and left their impression on her face. The reflection was indistinct and tremulous, but she could make out the expression of the eyes, and that was enough. There were other ravages as well, a series of turquoise bruises that were starting to become visible on her forearms and the sides of her hands. She puzzled over these for a short time, but in the end gave up trying to work out which of her misadventures had caused them.

She dressed, opened the door, and stepped out.

"Ah, Neverfell!" Maxim Childersin smiled. His family was in their walking garb once again, right down to the toddlers in their pudding caps. "Just in time for breakfast. Come, we are heading to the Morning Room."

The Morning Room was unchanged, and once again the blue light seemed to wipe the mist from Neverfell's mind like a hand rubbing condensation from a pane. Her head was clearer than it had been for days, and yet everything around her seemed distant and strange.

Everything was the same, and nothing was the same, because Neverfell was not the same. The Childersins had not changed; they were as tall and bright and clever as ever. Their jokes were new, but they still all knew when to laugh, and how to laugh, and how to stop laughing at exactly the same moment.

Only Zouelle seemed to be a little out of tune with the rest. The blonde girl was paler than usual, and there was something a little mechanical about her conversation. She finished her breakfast before the others and excused herself from the table early, claiming she had a private project that needed to have its runes changed.

At least I can eat what I like now, Neverfell tried to tell herself, and then found that she could not. Eating reminded her of the

Grand Steward, as did everything on the table. Smeared blobs of marmalade made her think of the ravaged jelly in front of the throne. Even the crystals of the sugar seemed to stare at her with his bleak, unreadable gaze.

"Neverfell—how are you?" asked Childersin. "You look distracted and concerned. Still a bit out of clock, are we?"

"I'm sorry. I must be. I feel like the cogs aren't biting." Realizing that she had not been clear, Neverfell hurried to explain. "Like a machine. Nothing is turning right."

"You just need time," her host told her kindly as he spread marmalade across his toast and sugared his tea. "Time with lots of sleep and no duties."

Somebody jogged the table slightly, and the water in Neverfell's glass wobbled and bobbed. Suddenly in her mind's eye she could see a prone body again, translucent blood forming a pool around it like a liquid windowpane. She had to cover her glass with a napkin before she could drive the image from her mind.

"Master Childersin," she exclaimed impulsively, "can I go out?"

"Of course! Borrow one of the carriages and go anywhere you like. But take guards with you at all times. I fear the Enquiry may still harbor designs against you."

"No! I mean, thank you, but I don't mean out into Caverna. You're going to send people into the overground world, aren't you? Can I go with them? Just to . . . I just want to see the sky . . ."

Childersin looked at her for a long moment and let his eyebrows rise in a Face that was half surprised, half amused. "What in the world made you think I was sending Cavernans up there? There is no question of letting the secrets of the Crafts out into the overground, or letting the hoi polloi romp in, bringing every disease on the planet."

"But your speech yesterday! You said . . . a rich and varied world . . . it could be ours . . ."

"Yes," Childersin answered gently and reasonably, "but we do not need to go out there to conquer it, do we? With our wealth it will be easy to hire armies . . ."

Armies. Yes, he had mentioned armies.

"You can't mean that!" But she knew he did. He did not care if he never saw the "rich and varied world" aboveground, as long as he owned it.

"We will be doing the overground a kindness," he answered, returning his attention to his teacup. "Right now it is a ghastly patchwork of petty kingdoms with short-lived monarchs, and in desperate need of a global ruler with centuries' experience behind him."

"It would give the Court a better way of ending feuds too," one of the Childersin nephews commented. "We could settle arguments through battles overground, where they can do no harm."

"No . . . harm." Neverfell could not even feel shock or anger. She could only mouth the two words to herself, wondering if they actually meant the same to everybody else as they did to her.

"And when Caverna is capital of the greater world we can expand her, start digging down . . ."

Neverfell stood unsteadily, feeling that she was going to be sick. She remembered the Kleptomancer's words.

. . . *Caverna herself is getting ready to grow or shift again, which means that everything is about to change . . .*

For a second, she could almost see Caverna as the Kleptomancer did, a murky, monstrous beauty, smiling her fine-fanged smile as she prepared to stretch and grow, shaking out her tunnel-tresses as they became longer and longer. Perhaps Caverna had already known that such an opportunity was open to her. Neverfell imagined her discarding the Grand Steward like a worn-out toy, and reaching for a new favorite, a man who could extend her empire and bring her new strength . . . Maxim Childersin.

"Neverfell!"

She did not heed their calls as she ran from the room.

"Still a little bit mad . . ." she heard as the door closed behind her.

Sprinting back along the passages to the main town house, Neverfell found that she was having trouble breathing, but not from exertion. Every moment she could remember of her life in Caverna, she had felt trapped and weighed down by the mountain above her. It had never quite crushed her mind, however, and for the first time she realized that this was because deep down she had always believed that sooner or later she would escape. *Out,* had been the beat in her heart. *Up and out.*

If Childersin's plans went ahead, there would be no true "out." In her mind's eye she saw the little scene in the painting Erstwhile had shown her, but with a stealthy shadow creeping across the land and extinguishing the sun. Of course the overground would not really be plunged into darkness, but it would become a province of Caverna. Its people would farm and be farmed like the drudges of the Undercity, robbed of their freedom and forced to serve only the interests of the subterranean city. They would feed the armies of the Court members, dying for their intrigues like pawns on a chessboard.

Her mind was too full. It would split if it could not spill. She had to find Zouelle, talk to Zouelle. Even as she thought this, she caught sight of the blonde girl ahead of her, opening a padded door and about to step through.

"Zouelle—"

"I am sorry, Neverfell." Zouelle paused on the threshold, eyes lowered, a carefully complacent smile on her face. "So many new responsibilities for the family, even I find myself with so little time. I am sure Miss Howlick will be happy to help you if there is a problem."

"Zouelle!" Neverfell felt as if a velvet-coated door had been neatly closed in her face. "I . . . I wanted to talk to *you*."

"Didn't you hear what I said?" Zouelle turned on her. The smile was still in place. Her tone was still calm, measured, and her words had nothing to do with it. "Don't you understand? Not everything is about *you* anymore. There are very important things going on. World-changing things. And those of us who have to think to stay alive, instead of just waving our face at people, are busy."

"What's wrong?" It came to Neverfell that she had been asking this question of Zouelle over and over almost since their first meeting, and the blonde girl had never answered it. "What's happened?"

"Oh, of course something has to have happened." Zouelle's calm tone was crumbling, and glints of bitterness were showing through. "It couldn't just be that you're really, really annoying, and that I'm fed up with you. I've put up with your blundering, gawking, and gushing for ages. And now you're not my job anymore."

Neverfell's first impulse was one of disbelieving recoil, and she nearly turned tail to run from the sting of Zouelle's words. After a couple of breaths, however, she managed to stand her ground.

"I don't believe you," she said, her voice shaking. "That's not it. Not all of it, anyway. You're my friend, Zouelle, and . . . and I think I'm starting to understand you a little bit. You flutter when you're upset, and right now you're trying so hard not to flutter that your Face looks glued on. I know I'm annoying. Of course I am. But I don't think you're annoyed. I think you're scared."

"Well, maybe I'm scared of you!" retorted Zouelle, the pitch of her voice rising uncontrollably. "Everywhere you go there's trouble, and now you're back in this house. Do you think any of us want you here? Why don't you just leave us alone?"

"Why won't you tell me what's wrong?" Neverfell asked in desperation. "Is it because I can't keep secrets? Then don't tell me what the problem is—just tell me what I can do to help!"

"Oh, stop it! You're always . . . opening boxes with that big-eyed look! You're never going to find one that isn't full of poison. Never!" With that Zouelle stepped through the door and slammed it.

Neverfell stared at the door, her eyes aching with tears too confused to fall. She felt as if Zouelle had reached up and snapped their friendship in two in front of her face, and she could hardly breathe for the shock of it.

But we were friends yesterday was all she could think, desperately. *Just yesterday she was helping me, looking out for me. What changed? Did I do something wrong?*

Even as she thought this, Zouelle's words came back to her and stung her hard.

You're not my job anymore.

Perhaps Zouelle had really meant it, after all. Perhaps Zouelle had been ordered by her family to look after Neverfell, and the latter had never been more than a job to her, a tiresome, difficult, embarrassing job. Now that job was over, and Zouelle had cast her off in haste and distaste, as she might a sodden glove or muddy boot.

The house was suddenly too close for Neverfell, the rooms too neat. Even the jubilant cries of the distant Childersin children as they ran from room to room, playing with the new toys Childersin had brought them, jarred upon her. This was not home.

Maxim Childersin had said she could borrow one of the Childersin carriages to ride where she chose. Nobody stopped her from walking out of the town house's front door, though four guards immediately stepped up to accompany her, and when she spoke to a driver he started readying one of the carriages.

"Where to, miss?"

Neverfell suddenly felt exhausted. For the first time she understood how Grandible might have felt when he turned his back on the Court. She had believed that nothing would make her want to go back to the cheese tunnels, but there was an ache in her, an ache to go home. She closed her eyes, and suddenly she could imagine herself back in its dim, reeking passages.

There before her mind's eye were all the rinds she had painted with vinegar. There the floors she had swept. There the places where she had doused flames or smothered butter-flies. She could almost see the thousands of days she had lost there, littering the tunnels like empty eggshells, the meat of them long gone. The old panic crept up on her with panther steps, until she could feel its breath on the back of her neck.

It isn't home anymore. Where is home?

Struck by inspiration, she opened her eyes.

"Can you take me to Madame Appeline's tunnels, please?"

Madame Appeline. Perhaps she could find a haven with the Facesmith, who had talked to her so kindly at their last parting. Neverfell's spirits immediately struggled to their feet, and even managed a small punch-drunk caper when at last Madame Appeline's distinctive front door hove into view.

Neverfell dismounted, accompanied by the guards, and gave her name at the door. Once again she was examined through the eyeholes in the painted owl.

"I am sorry," the owl told her after a long pause, in the crisp, polished tones of a Putty Girl, "but Madame Appeline finds herself extremely busy today. Perhaps if you leave your name, she can contact you for an appointment?"

Neverfell could barely frame an answer. Somehow she had expected Madame Appeline to sense how badly Neverfell needed to talk to her.

"Can I . . . can I come in and wait? Just tell her I'm here."

Another pause, and then the door was opened. Two Putty Girls with matching fashionable smiles stood flanking the door to welcome her in. The guards seemed less than happy about Neverfell leaving their company, but consented when they were given assurances that the Appeline household would take responsibility for her welfare.

"Please wait here." She was shown to a pleasant little parlor with finely carved walls. "I am afraid the mistress will probably not be free for some time—would you care for some refreshment?"

Neverfell nearly said no, then remembered that she was allowed to eat and drink what she liked now. She nodded, sat down, and was brought a silver tray of tea. About half an hour of fidgeting later, the door opened, but the figure beyond it was not that of Madame Appeline. It was Zouelle's friend Borcas, and Neverfell blushed as she realized that disappointment must be flooding her own face.

To her surprise, Borcas glided into the room, took up a cup from the tray, poured herself some tea, and sat down in a chair opposite Neverfell, her expression serene and self-important.

"I am afraid," she said, stirring in the sugar, "that Madame Appeline is busy adding brooding to a frown right now. But at least that will give me a chance to talk to you privately."

Neverfell was a little taken aback by the short girl's new confidence of manner. Borcas was looking very unlike her old self, and not only because she was no longer sustaining a painful-looking grimace. Like Madame Appeline's other Putty Girls, her hair was pulled tautly back and pinned into a bun, and her eyebrows emphasized with kohl. She had lost her nervous, puddingy slouch, and as she sipped her tea her posture was upright and a little queenly.

"Is that a new Face?" asked Neverfell, not quite knowing where she was to start the conversation. "It suits you. It makes you look less f— er . . . more thin."

"You're looking quite well too," Borcas responded smoothly, "under the circumstances." She smiled and slid elegantly through a couple more Faces, both superior, knowing, and rather expensive-looking. Evidently, becoming a full-blown Putty Girl had certain perks. "Everybody's talking about the fact you were nearly executed after the Grand Steward's death, and about the story you told in the Hall of the Gentles. And that's why I thought we should talk."

"Oh." Neverfell stared at her, a bit nonplussed. "Um, thank you."

"You see, something has been weighing on my mind." Borcas's smile, however, was not that of somebody whose mind was particularly heavy. "I found something yesterday, just after you'd left. And I thought you would rather I talked to you about it first, instead of telling anybody else." Borcas seemed to be putting a lot of pauses into her speech. Neverfell could not shake the feeling that these were *meaningful* pauses. After the longest and most meaningful pause of all, Borcas reached into her reticule and pulled out a small silvery object, which she placed in the middle of her own palm. Neverfell stared at it blankly for a second or two before recognizing it.

"Oh—it's my thimble! The one I lost last time I was here! Thank you. Was it somewhere in the guest room?"

"No," said Borcas, as if delivering the punch line to a very clever joke. "It wasn't."

Silence slowly unrolled itself, and Neverfell had the all-too-familiar feeling that she was missing something.

"Oh," she said at last. "So, where was it then?"

"That's the interesting part. It wasn't in your sleeping quarters, or in the grove, or the exhibition room, or any of the reception rooms. It was upstairs, in the gallery above the grove. The thing is, we never let guests go up there. Madame Appeline doesn't like them seeing the traps they use to create the 'sunlight' effect. She says it spoils the mystique. But there it was"—she turned the thimble so that the light sparkled on its dimpled top—"just lying on the floor. So that could only mean one thing."

Neverfell racked her brain. "That it's somebody else's thimble after all?" she hazarded.

"No, it isn't!" retorted Borcas, her smug demeanor cracking for a brief moment. "It has the insignia of the Grand Steward's household. Besides, the rooms are swept every day."

"Then . . ." Once again Neverfell suspected she had blundered into a game without any knowledge of the rules. "Then it probably is mine. So somebody must have . . . found it and . . . taken it upstairs?"

"I think you know how it got there," Borcas answered, with a smile of creamy complacency.

"Pardon?" Neverfell stared at her, baffled.

"You see the problem, don't you?" Borcas clasped her hands, and put on an earnest Face, No. 23, Gazelle Preparing to Leap Stream. "On the one hand, you're my friend. On the other hand, I have my duty to consider. Shouldn't I report this?"

"Should you?" asked Neverfell, utterly at sea.

"Well, let's talk about something more cheerful," Borcas swept on. "I've been thinking about my future a lot lately. Most Putty Girls are just Putty Girls all their lives, did you know that? Only a few get to be Facesmiths. But I was thinking, if I had private lessons from somebody with a really unusual and famous face, somebody with thousands of expressions—"

"Ooooh!" The light suddenly dawned. "I'm so stupid! You're trying to blackmail me, aren't you?"

Borcas promptly lost her serenity, her fan, and half the tea from her cup.

"What? I—that—no! I mean . . ."

"I've never been blackmailed before." For a moment it was exciting, then it left a sour crinkly feeling in Neverfell's belly. "So, you think *I* dropped the thimble up in the gallery, and you're saying that if I don't let you copy lots of my expressions you'll go and tell Madame Appeline I was sneaking around up there without her permission? Is that right? Borcas, if you wanted to copy my Faces, you could have just asked."

"I'm not talking about reporting it to Madame Appeline," snapped Borcas. "I think the Enquiry will be much more interested."

"What?" Neverfell started to develop a chill feeling in the pit of her stomach.

"There's only one time you didn't have Madame Appeline or one of us with you," Borcas went on, "and that's when you went for your 'sleep.' So, when we weren't looking, you must have slipped out without anybody seeing, sneaked up to the gallery, and then crept back into your room before anybody saw you. And that's not what you told the Enquiry, is it? You told them you just slept in the guest room for a few hours."

For the first time Neverfell was able to see the rocks under the mellow waves of Borcas's remarks. The Enquiry had been looking for the slightest hole in Neverfell's account of events. Borcas's story and the thimble in her hand might give them just the excuse they wanted to drag Neverfell off to prison and "interrogate" her.

"Oh, don't bother with the shocked and innocent looks." Borcas gave an exaggerated sigh. "They won't work on me. The only reason you're not in prison is the fact everybody is convinced that you can't lie without showing it. But this"—she held up the thimble—"is proof that you can, and have."

"But . . ."

Borcas rose from her seat, making dainty adjustments to the gleaming pins in her hair with a gesture that reminded Neverfell of Madame Appeline.

"I would love to stay, but I am supposed to be helping tweak a grimace for a Distasting later today. Mind you, tomorrow I have the whole day free. I think perhaps you will also be free. Won't that be nice? I can collect you from the Childersin household at eight, and we can spend all day together."

Neverfell only shook herself out of her daze as Borcas was leaving the room.

"Borcas! What . . . what do the stairs look like? The ones that run up to the gallery where you found the thimble? They're black, aren't they?"

"Black wrought iron" was Borcas's slightly impatient response. "Decorated with ivy patterns and grape bunches. Does that jog your memory?" With that she left the room, still holding the erect posture that made her look so much older and unlike herself.

Neverfell remained motionless, staring unseeing at the blots of slopped tea as they sank into the carpet.

She had been completely honest with the Enquiry, but there was one thing she had not mentioned to them, since it had not occurred to her to do so. She had not told them of her dream while sleeping in Madame Appeline's guest room. Now she trawled through the haunted fog of that slumber, trying to remember the details.

In the dream she had taken step after step up a stairway of black vines to a golden balcony . . . or perhaps a wrought iron stairway ornamented with leaves, leading up to a gallery ablaze with hundreds of traps. Was her dream showing her the truth through a twisted glass? Was it possible that she really *had* sneaked out of her room and up to the gallery, dropping her thimble as she did so?

Neverfell realized that there had already been a tingling sense of wrongness in her mind for some time, drowned out by all her other worries and concerns. Nothing powerful, just a niggling feeling that she had forgotten something small but important, or done something in the wrong order, or started something and not completed it. A sense that the cogs were not quite biting. A vexing tingle like a loose lash under her eyelid.

She had it. She knew suddenly when the feeling had begun, and why. Slowly she reached down, pulled off one of her little satin shoes, and stared at it.

The last time she had visited Madame Appeline's tunnels she had been exhausted. She had been shown to her little rest room, and she had collapsed into bed without even taking off her shoes. And then when she had woken she had struggled awake, slipped her shoes back on . . .

That was it. That was what had been bothering her in the back of her mind all this time. She distinctly remembered putting her shoes back on, but she should not have needed to do so. They should already have been on her feet.

What could it mean? She did not know. The Enquiry had gone over and over Neverfell's account of her actions between her return from the Undercity and the death of the Grand Steward, looking in vain for the slightest inconsistency. And all the time there *had* been an inconsistency, a minute hint of something wrong. It was a tiny crack, but through it Neverfell felt for the first time the chill draft of doubt.

THE SCREAMER
IN THE DREAM

"ZOUELLE!"

Back in the Childersin household, Neverfell banged a second time on the cushioned door of the blonde girl's laboratory. As she stood there, she felt the creeping sensation that the presence of True Wine always gave her, but more intense than usual. Something beyond the door was aware of her, and ready not to be drunk but to drink her memories dry. Time felt sour. Air tasted purple.

From within she could hear noises, an occasional shifting of a foot or clinking of glass. There was another repetitive sound, however. It was very quiet, a soft, broken, rhythmic noise that almost sounded like stifled song.

"Zouelle, I know you don't want to talk to me, but this is really important!" Neverfell followed up with another flurry of knocks.

The soft sound stopped with something like a hiccup, and it was only then that Neverfell guessed what it might have been. Steps approached the door, and it opened to show an impatient-looking Zouelle in a black apron, a runed, metallic brooch pinned to her top pocket and her hands heavy with rings.

Zouelle's eyes showed no sign of puffiness or redness. *I must have been wrong about that sound,* thought Neverfell. *She must have been chanting to the Wine or something.*

"Well?"

Neverfell swallowed hard, and leaped straight into the maw of the matter.

"I think I walked in my sleep back in Madame Appeline's tunnels. I think I did things I don't remember."

"What?" Zouelle stiffened to stare at her.

"Borcas found that thimble I lost up on the gallery above the gr—"

Neverfell got no further before Zouelle grabbed her by the collar and dragged her into the laboratory, slamming the door shut behind them.

"Have you no sense at all?" hissed the blonde girl. "Saying things like that at the top of your voice!"

Neverfell could barely register her words, so overwhelmed was she by the room in which she found herself. She had expected a cellar full of dusty casks, bottles, and the occasional set of scales. Instead, she found herself in a long, arched room rich with glyph-embroidered hangings in purple and silver. The glossy black of the obsidian flagstones was covered in chalk circles and sigils in white and pale yellow. A cloth-draped cask stood in the middle of each circle.

She had not been prepared for the musky, stealthy, predatory sense of hunger in the room. Something, or rather somethings, was hanging unseen in the air, singing their hunger so that she could feel it like a hum in her teeth. *One wrong step,* they sang, *one wrong glyph, one word out of place and you are ours.*

"Don't you see?" Zouelle was still speaking, her face taut and pale. "It's too late to start having doubts or changing your story. You gave your statement to the Enquiry, and Uncle Maxim has staked *everything* on it. He went all out to stop you from being arrested, and now his whole position—his stand against the Enquiry—his argument for setting up the Council—*all* of it relies on your statement and the notion that you can't lie. If people hear you saying that your statement might not have been true after all, you cut the ground right out from under him. You could destroy him, and all of us!"

"But what if I did sleepwalk? Shouldn't we try to work out what happened before anybody else does? Borcas said—"

"I don't know what game Borcas is playing. For all I know the Enquiry sent her to put doubts in your head."

"It's not just Borcas." Neverfell had been knocked for a loop by the other girl's forceful response, but now she was starting to recover. "When I fell into bed in the guest chamber, I was too tired to take my shoes off, but when I got up again there, they were by the side of my bed. I don't think Borcas is making things up. And I don't think *you* think she is, either. Because there's one other thing that changed while I was asleep. You. You've been acting differently ever since.

"Zouelle, I know you know something. Did you see me sleepwalking? Did you see me do something that means you can't bear to be around me anymore? What did I do? Just . . . tell me!"

"I didn't see anything. And this is all nonsense, Neverfell. You're . . . you're overwrought." Zouelle had retreated behind her big-sister manner again, but it was too late for Neverfell to be fooled by it.

"It isn't nonsense. There's more. I had this dream, and I think maybe it's like a shadow of what I was really doing—"

"Stop it!" Zouelle hissed with unexpected violence. "Stop it! I don't want to hear it!"

"But it's important! I *did* climb up to the gallery. I saw myself doing it in my dream, but I didn't know that's where it was at the time. There was a monkey with me, showing me the way, and we found a secret door, and we opened it—"

"I don't want to hear your stupid dreams!" erupted Zouelle. "I don't want to hear your stupid, crazy voice anymore! I don't want you in my house! Get out and leave me alone! Get out!"

Neverfell had not been ready for this explosion, and the first shove almost knocked her off balance, but she raised her hand in time to deflect the second. The blow struck her forearm, right on the existing bruises, and her dream suddenly flashed into her mind, shocking as a hot coal in a tub of cold water. She remembered beating at the screaming mask, remembered bruising her hands and forearms with the desperation of her own blows. But these dream blows had left real bruises, tender and bird's-egg blue.

At long last the cogs bit, locked their teeth, and began to turn. Neverfell recoiled from Zouelle, arms still raised defensively, her back to the door.

"I beat a mask to pieces in my dream," Neverfell whispered, "and it left real bruises on my hands and arms. Which means that I really was hitting something, hard enough that it should have woken me up. Bumps and grazes always woke me from sleepwalking when I was little.

"But this time it didn't. Because I wasn't asleep, was I?"

Zouelle was fluttering again, spasming between a look of mild annoyance and one of her big-sister smiles.

"I was *awake*." Neverfell could hear her own voice, sounding stark and surprised. "I sneaked out for a walk, then came back and locked the door and got into bed, and I don't remember any of it. So I must have drunk Wine that made me forget it. Somebody gave me Wine. Somebody I trusted enough to drink it. Maybe somebody who carries a vial of Wine around with them all the time, so they can get rid of mistakes.

"It was you, wasn't it? You were the dream monkey who led me to the secret room. And you were the one who gave me the Wine, so I wouldn't remember it."

Neverfell felt more wondering than accusing, but Zouelle backed away from her as if she were a storm cloud. Then the blonde girl turned tail and sped down the narrow room, in a sequence of nervous zigzag leaps, her feet finding spaces clean of chalk amid the intricate shapes and inscriptions on the floor, her plait flapping against her back and tiny talons of purple flame snatching at her heels. At the far end of the room she halted by a mahogany table, in the middle of which stood a silver goblet with tiny vials arranged in a circle round it.

"Leave me alone!" the blonde girl screamed.

"Zouelle!" Neverfell took a hasty step forward, and then halted. She could sense something changing in the room. Looking down, she realized that Zouelle's first hasty step backward had slightly scuffed the edge of one of the circles. The chalk lines were releasing lazy, luminous whorls of purple smoke, and the cask in the center was emitting a long, slow hiss. One loose tendril of smoke lapped over Neverfell's toes like a tongue, and she could feel the Wine tasting her thoughts, her most recent memories. She flinched away from the contact.

There was a crackle in the air. The disturbance had woken the other Wines in the room. One was muttering in a string of leathery pops, another yowling silently and yellowly, another watching events so hard that its silence felt like treacle. Their attention was on the young intruder, a frail, fleeting creature who had no protective amulet and no rings of lore and no idea how to command them.

The only sane option was to retreat back out into the corridor. Fortunately sanity had never really slowed Neverfell down.

"Go away!" Zouelle snatched up one of the vials, and held it aloft in one hand, ready to throw. Her long, glossy plait had lost its ribbon, and it was starting to unravel into kinked, rippling waves. "Get out of here, or I'll . . ."

"A-and behind the secret door there was a mask," Neverfell stammered doggedly. "A crumbling mask. 'What did you do to her?' it kept screaming. And about how it would never have done something if it had known—"

Zouelle gave what sounded like a sob and hurled the vial across the room at Neverfell's head. Neverfell narrowly ducked it, and heard the tinkle of broken glass, and the whisper of tiny, distant screams spreading spider legs and scampering away.

". . . and I didn't recognize its voice at first, not for ages," Neverfell continued, "not until you screamed at me just now. The mask had *your* voice, Zouelle. I don't know who you were shouting at, or when, or why, or what it was about, but I know it was you. Just as I know you were crying in here, before I knocked. Crying about something you've done. Something you'd never have done if you'd known everything. Some mistake you can't get rid of with Wine."

"You're the mistake!" shouted Zouelle. "Talking to you the first time was the worst mistake I ever made! But I *can* get rid of it. I'm a Childersin. I can wipe out mistakes and never have to think about them again. You're just grime in my head—I can wipe you away—soon I won't remember any of it! It'll all be gone!" As Neverfell watched, Zouelle reached out toward the goblet in the middle of the table.

"Stop! Don't!"

Neverfell's leaps were clumsy and inexpert. She could not remember where Zouelle's feet had touched the flagstones, so she jumped for anywhere that looked like she could land without destroying the circles. As she jumped over the sigils, pale amethyst tendrils whiplashed out and tried to catch her. One sank invisible fangs into the hem of her dress and the edge of her memory. She shrieked, kicked out, and pulled free, hearing a rip of cloth and feeling a rending in her mind as a dozen words were torn away and lost to her forever. She could sense the disappointed snap of other jaws missing her by inches.

She reached the far side of the room just as Zouelle was raising the goblet to her lips. Neverfell threw herself headlong at the vintner girl, slapping the goblet out of her hand. It flew through the air, turning over and over, spraying droplets of True Wine in all directions like dark mauve pearls. As these drops fell to splatter the floor, there was a chorus of tiny disappointed shrieks, like violin strings being scrubbed with wire wool. One plump drop fell squarely on the back of Zouelle's hand, and for a moment it looked as if she might raise it to her mouth. Then it stirred in its smoky, predatory way, and Zouelle made a choked sound in her throat, and dashed it off her skin as she would a scorpion.

For a few seconds Zouelle stared quivering at the place where the drop had been, then she collapsed to her knees and covered her face, heaving helpless, tearless sobs. Neverfell dropped to a crouch beside her, grabbed the taller girl's shoulders, and shook her hard.

"Don't! Don't *ever* do that! Do you know what it's like, having big holes in your head that you can't remember, and seams that don't match up? It drives you crazy. Crazy like me."

"I didn't want to." Suddenly Zouelle did not sound adult or big-sisterly at all. "But I can't bear the memories, the pictures in my head. I just wanted it all to go away . . ."

"But Wine doesn't make anything go away! When you bury a big memory it's always still there, like an itch right down inside your bones where you can't scratch it, or somebody walking a step behind you that you can't look at. And . . . and if we didn't remember things we wish we hadn't done, wouldn't we just run off and do them again?"

"You don't understand—"

Neverfell put her arms round the older girl and squeezed hard.

"What don't I understand? I know you've been lying to me, probably about lots of things. And I know there are probably plans inside plans inside plans, and I'm just a pawn, and that's all I ever was. Even back when we first met. And it doesn't matter, because you're my friend. You're my friend and you're in trouble. All this while you've been miserable, and I've been too stupid to notice. Now please, please, tell me! What's going on?"

"I can't! It'll just make everything even worse, for you *and* me." Zouelle raised her pale face from her hands. "Your face—"

"I don't care!" All over the laboratory Wines rippled and hissed in their casks as Neverfell's shout echoed down the room. "I don't care about my face! I'm tired of being stupid, and everybody keeping me stupid just for the sake of my face. Even if it means I have to run off and live in the wild caves with a bag over my head, I still want to know what's going on. I need to know."

Zouelle looked at her for a long time, her face pale and unreadable as a chalk cliff-face.

"It was a bit like a play," she whispered at last. "With scenes and lines. I'm . . . I'm good at acting.

"You remember how I made you curious about Madame

Appeline's hidden room? Well . . . you're right. I knocked on your door when you were sleeping in her guest chamber, and told you that I'd found it, and that I'd stolen the key. You came straight out and followed me, through the galley, and up the stairs to the grove. And . . . and to the room.

"I was standing outside as lookout while you went in. But then you went berserk, started smashing things. So I had to go in after you, and hold on to you until you calmed down. I . . . I didn't know it was going to do that to you."

"What was in there?" Curiosity gnawed Neverfell's very core.

"I don't know. By the time I came in after you, you'd crushed the trap-lantern we'd brought with us. The room was in darkness. There were masks, I think. I didn't look too hard.

"But whatever it was you saw tore you apart. When we came out into the light, I could see your face was full of flames and knives and howling and pain and . . . I couldn't look at it. Then you saw your reflection in a mirror and you panicked.

"I told you we had to wipe that bit of your memory, or Madame Appcline would take one look at you and know you'd seen the secret room, and then neither of us would get out alive. And that even if we did the Grand Steward would probably have us all executed for bringing you back with a ruined face. Then I gave you my vial of Wine, and a moth biscuit so you wouldn't have a taste of Wine in your mouth when you woke up again. I even told you where to drop the vial so I could collect it later."

"But then you didn't do anything wrong!" Reflexively, Neverfell clutched at the brightest spot in Zouelle's account. "You were just helping me look for the truth, and protecting me afterward, weren't you?" Then another detail sank in. "Oh no—I smashed things in the secret room—that means Madame Appeline must know by now that we were in there!"

Zouelle stared, then broke down into fits of convulsive, hysterical laughter.

"Oh, Neverfell!" she gasped. "You're so almost clever! If only you didn't like people so much! You still don't understand what all this is about, do you?

"Who do you think showed me the door to the secret room? Who do you think gave me the key? Who do you think kept all the Putty Girls out of the way, so we could sneak to the room and back without being seen? Of course Madame Appeline knows we were in that room. *She arranged it.*

"All the sneaking around, that whole pantomime, it wasn't to fool her. It was to fool *you.*"

"Me?"

"Yes, you. You were brought to the room so that you would see something terrible. Something that would cut you to the heart a hundred times more deeply than what you saw in the Undercity. All the horror you felt would show in your face and spoil it."

"But why?" Neverfell burst out. "Why would Madame Appeline want that?" She did not want to believe it.

"Because," Zouelle answered wearily, "she knew that when you realized your face was spoiled you'd panic, and—"

"And drink your Wine." Neverfell felt a strange, disorienting sense of buoyancy, as if the floor had dropped away beneath her and left her floating. "It was all about the Wine, wasn't it? Everything, all of this, just so I would drink the Wine, and not remember doing it."

Neverfell remembered Enquirer Treble towering over her and berating her, belligerent and unswerving.

You consumed some kind of antidote before this tasting. Didn't you?

"Oh no," she whispered. "Tell me there wasn't! Tell me there wasn't an antidote in the Wine you gave me!"

"I didn't know what would happen!" wailed Zouelle. "I just had my orders, my part to play. I only worked out the bit about the antidote after the trifle tasting. And then it was too late, and the Grand Steward was dead, and there were bodies all over the audience chamber covered in blood. It's . . . I've seen dead people before. A few. But they look different when it's my fault. They look like they know, and I keep seeing them when I close my eyes."

"But it's not your fault, if you didn't know. Listen, Zouelle, we have to tell somebody about this! If Madame Appeline really did poison the Grand Steward, and you're the only person who knows, you're in terrible danger! We could tell your uncle M—"

"Shh!" Zouelle held up a warning hand. There was a faint sound of a step outside in the corridor, and then a knock on the door.

"Zouelle?" It was the voice of Maxim Childersin. Neverfell's heart gave a lurch of relief, and she was just opening her mouth to answer when Zouelle caught at her arm and shook her head vigorously.

What's wrong? Neverfell mouthed.

Zouelle had one finger pressed against her lips in an injunction to silence, and wore a small, pleading smile. No. 144, Delicate Appeal of the Shell-less Fledgling. She gestured to Neverfell to hide behind one of the larger barrels by the wall, and Neverfell reluctantly obliged.

"Come in," Zouelle called out. The door opened, and Maxim Childersin's lean figure stepped into the room, treading with meticulous care. He too wore a black and silver apron, rings, and a rune-encrusted amulet. Glancing around him, he raised an eyebrow at the restlessness of the Wines and the fragments of broken glass scattering the floor.

"My dear girl," he said, "we all wish to throw our failed experiments at the ground from time to time, but we try not to do so. And how did you let your Wine projects get so wild? If they become any louder, they may start noticing each other. And then where would we be?"

"I am very sorry, Uncle Maxim." Within an instant, Zouelle's manner had completely changed, her hysteria and tremulousness falling away like a discarded shawl. She now had the clear and careful tones of a well-rehearsed schoolgirl about to recite poetry. "I had just finished working on that blend I was talking about and at the last moment I . . . thought better of it and threw it away from me. It smashed and woke up the other Wines, so I thought I would wait by the wall until they calmed down."

"Ah, so you have thought better of removing your memories? I am very glad to hear that." Maxim Childersin twinkled a smile at his favorite niece as he advanced carefully across the room. Now and then he stopped to chant under his breath in the direction of the Wines, rolling each "r" so that it was a soothing purr. "I agreed to your request to do so, of course, and would have let you go back to the Beaumoreau Academy to play games for a few more years, but I would have been disappointed."

Zouelle smiled blandly, discreetly retethering her runaway braid. Her eyes did not as much as flicker to Neverfell's hiding place. Again there was something eerie about her complete transformation.

"A little courage now is all it takes," Maxim added kindly. "If you can learn to stomach what has passed without running away from it, nothing else that you ever do will be as hard. Murder is like romance. It is only our first that overwhelms us. Next time it will be easier, and I promise that I will not make you work with our Facesmith friend again."

Neverfell silently gaped as one last red-hot penny finally dropped. Why had she imagined that Madame Appeline was the only mastermind of this scheme? Why had she thought that Zouelle would take orders from a Facesmith her family hated? Why had she not wondered where Madam Appeline would find a strong forgetfulness Wine with a poison antidote artfully woven into it?

She felt as if she were standing in a dim room and watching every lantern around her extinguish, one by one, leaving her to darkness and solitary stifling. Nobody was to be trusted. The plan that had ensnared her had been the brainchild of her protector, Maxim Childersin.

THE MASTER OF CRAFT

NEVERFELL'S MIND FELT STRETCHED, LIKE A frog trying to swallow a dinner plate. *But they're enemies,* she thought stupidly. *Master Childersin and Madame Appeline hate each other; everybody knows that.*

No, answered the wiser, cooler part of her head, *that's what they wanted everybody to think. What better way to hide a secret alliance?*

Maxim Childersin. When had he seen the potential in a half-mad girl with no capacity to lie? Had there been any real pity in his heart when he first visited her in the Enquiry's cell, or even then had his mind been seeing the potential, and throwing out the first tendrils of plans?

Through the bars he had laid eyes on a face like glass, somebody who could not lie without it being obvious. And he had seen a way of using that very fact to tell the greatest of lies.

Of course, thought Neverfell as the truth unfolded in her mind. *He couldn't just murder the Grand Steward in an obvious way, or the Enquiry would have taken over. He had to make the death look*

354

natural. So he needed somebody to swear blind that the Grand Steward couldn't have been poisoned, somebody that everyone else couldn't help but believe.

"I wanted to talk to you about Neverfell," Zouelle was saying, and Neverfell was jerked back into awareness by the mention of her own name.

"Indeed?"

"I wonder if perhaps she should stay somewhere else for a bit," Zouelle declared with perfect sangfroid. "Perhaps take up her apprenticeship with Cheesemaster Grandible again. The family has a lot of sensitive things to discuss now that we are on a war footing, and, while well-intentioned, Neverfell is not very good at keeping secrets. Also, she seems to be getting restless."

"Yes." Childersin had covered the broken vial with a hand-kerchief, showing the same tender reverence one might offer a dead but beloved pet. "I had noticed that. However, I do not think we can let her out of our sight, and if Grandible had her back in his care I doubt he would relinquish her again. Remember, in two months' time the Enquiry will have finished their investigation into the Grand Steward's death. There will be a hearing before the entire Court, and we will need Neverfell to testify again. We cannot afford to let her be kidnapped, assassinated, or taken beyond our reach before then."

Neverfell did pause to wonder whether he would feel very differently about her being assassinated *after* the hearing. She had a queasy suspicion that she would not like the answer.

"However," mused Childersin, "you are right that her restlessness is a problem. She needs to be distracted, diverted, made to feel that she is not in a prison. Perhaps some small outings in the carriage to see local beauty spots, or to say farewell to her fellow tasters? I will arrange something. For now, I shall leave you to finish calming your Wines."

When he had left the room and his footsteps had faded, Zouelle finally closed her eyes and leaned back against the door.

"Are you all right?" asked Neverfell.

"I . . . lied to Uncle Maxim," croaked Zouelle, and there was no mistaking the stunned terror in her tone. "I lied to him. I never dared to do so before, never thought I could without him noticing. Perhaps he did notice. Perhaps he's playing a game with me."

"Or maybe he's too busy with all his other games to suspect you," answered Neverfell, hoping she sounded reassuring. "So all this time he's been working with Madame Appeline? For how long?"

"Years, I think." Zouelle shook her head slowly. "I didn't know, not until he told me that I had to work with her to make you drink the Wine. They're . . . I think they're more than just allies. But nobody else in the family knows. I'm the only one he told, the only one he trusted enough . . .

"I don't know what I'll do if I lose his favor, Neverfell! For years I've known that he had plans for me. We all knew. That's why most of the family resents me. And now he's actually talking to me privately about becoming his successor. Which parts of the family business he expects me to take over in a year, two years, five years. What vineyards I will be governing, and which parts of the overground need to be claimed by our family. Which unguents and spices I should be taking so I live longer and think faster. Who needs to be removed, and when, so they don't get in my way. He's pleased with me. He wants to make me into another him."

"But you don't want that!" Neverfell gaped at her in horror. "You can't!"

"It's what everybody wants. I would be good at it too. Maybe I'm not ready yet, but I could learn, change, become what he wants. I know I could." Zouelle's face had returned to its habitual flutter, once more in search of the elusive Face that was nowhere in its repertoire. "No, Neverfell! I don't want it! I don't want it! I thought I did, and I ought to, but I don't. Not now. Maybe I never did."

"Then don't do it!" exclaimed Neverfell.

"But what else is there for me? Without Uncle Maxim's favor, the rest of the family will claw me apart. You saw what happened to me when they thought he was dead. And nobody else will take me as an apprentice, because they'll think I'm just a Childersin spy.

"And he's going to find out. Right now your face is one big mess of disillusionment, pain, and betrayal. It's not as bad as when you went into the secret room, but you've changed, and Uncle Maxim will be able to see it. He'll know what you know, and the first time you glance at me he'll know that I told you. That'll be the end for both of us. I should never have told you . . . I don't know what happened to me. I just . . . wanted to talk to somebody."

"And if you hadn't you'd still be going crazy with what you know, and I'd be going crazy with what I didn't know, and both of us would be alone. Right now, I'm upset but I'm . . ." Neverfell hesitated, like one stretching a limb they think might be broken. "I'm all right. I think I'm more all right than I have been for ages. Great big holes of unknown are the worst thing. Before this, I didn't know anything was wrong but I didn't *not* know, if you see what I mean. You can go mad like that. And if my face is spoiled now, once and for all, then it means I don't have to worry about it anymore."

"Neverfell," whispered Zouelle, "I . . . don't have a plan. I always have a plan, and now I don't. What are we going to do?"

It was a good question, but even as Zouelle asked it Neverfell could feel doors opening in her own head, great big simple doors that floated silently ajar with grace and ease.

"We're going to escape," she answered.

"Escape where? I couldn't bear living in Drudgery or the wild tunnels . . ."

"No. Not there. Really escape. Out. Up and out. To the overground."

"But that's insane!"

"Yes, so nobody will be expecting it." Neverfell gave her friend a wide, mad smile and squeezed her hands. "Nobody expects insane things—the Kleptomancer worked that out. How could they guess we would run away to a place full of disease where the sun cooks you till your skin falls off?"

"I don't want my skin to fall off!"

"But it isn't really like that, Zouelle! I don't remember it, and yet sometimes I think I do. It's like somebody broke my memory of it and swept up the pieces, but there are still tiny fragments, little stars of it winking at me when they catch the light. There's a brightness out there, like nothing we have here. It's blue, so blue it takes the lid off your head and blows out the cobwebs and you can see forever. And there are places where you can run and run and run. And the sky isn't just nothingness up and up and up—there are colors, beautiful colors, and you can see the birds above swimming in it. And there's smells up there, like . . . like . . . hope and your first surprise.

"Everything down here is just a painting of what's real, Zouelle. A dreg. A memory. I feel like I'm holding my breath all the time, never knowing when my lungs will just give up. The air we're supposed to breathe is up above—I can feel it."

"Neverfell, that is all very pretty, but we do not actually *have* a way out right now, do we? And even if we found one, it wouldn't do any good. If Uncle Maxim has his way, all the outside kingdoms will topple one by one and come under Caverna's control—*his* control. We could walk a thousand miles and he'd send people after us. We know too much; he wouldn't have any choice. He would never be safe until he destroyed us.

"We can't just run away from him. There aren't any half measures—that's not how it works. Unless we're playing his game, we'll never be safe unless *we* destroy *him*."

"Destroy him?" Neverfell again felt a shock like a whiplash. "You want to destroy your uncle?"

"No, I don't. He's been my best friend all my life. But I *know* him, and if we're going against him it's all or nothing. We have to destroy him, one way or another. But we can't just go to the Enquiry and tell what we know. They'd only arrest us, and then one of Uncle Maxim's spies in the Enquiry would have us murdered. We'll have to think of something else.

"But first of all, right now, we have to get you out of here before anybody else in the family sees your face and realizes how much you know. Or we're both dead."

Less than two hours later, Zouelle Childersin was standing at one of the balconies of the family's town house, watching a carriage being made ready. To look at her, nobody would have guessed that her mind was an anthill of agitation.

If Uncle Maxim finds out I had in a part in this, there'll be no forgiveness this time. Even if I escaped to Neverfell's overground, would I really be safe from him?

The overground was still an ominous mystery to her. Neverfell had tried to describe it, but Zouelle still had no clear idea that was not taken from poems or painted landscapes. The idea of the sky baffled and terrified her. Even when she tried to imagine air above air above air, something in her mind kept trying to put a roof on it. In Neverfell's face, though, she had seen something that made her also feel for a moment as if she had been holding her breath all her life without knowing it.

Her mind was abruptly dragged from such thoughts, however, as she observed a slight figure emerging from the front door below. It was dressed in a burgundy dress and veil, and it walked nervously to the carriage where as usual several Childersin servants were waiting as an escort.

Ironically, putting Neverfell in a veil had been the Childersins' idea. They had insisted upon it so that potential assassins at the palace would not guess at her identity, and a few thought that it was the only thing preventing them from seeing the rebellion on the face of their young guest. Her all-too-distinctive hair was tucked up under a burgundy-colored turban, and her skinny frame padded out with extra layers of clothing, so that she could be more easily mistaken for one of the young Childersin girls.

As Zouelle watched, the slender figure below looked up at her and raised one hand in a timid wave. Wearing her best pussycat smile, Zouelle gave a small, answering nod. It was not simply a salute. It was a signal to let Neverfell know that Zouelle's own mission had been successful, that she had tracked down Erstwhile and delivered a note from Neverfell into his hands.

. . . when the Childersins take me to the palace I will try to jump from the carriage and escape. If I do not come and find you,

then I have been caught, and Zouelle and me are done for. If that
happens, tell the Enquiry that the Grand Steward was poisoned,
and I was tricked into taking an antidote . . .

Good luck, Neverfell, Zouelle thought, feeling suddenly
powerless and exhausted.

Neverfell saw the signal with a pang of relief. At least now
Erstwhile would be aware of her plans.

Through the veil, everything around her looked wine-colored
and hazy, albeit studded with occasional stitched flowers. It was
such a fragile barrier that Neverfell was afraid every instant that
somebody would glimpse her features through it, and realize that
her heart was straining with every beat, like a prisoner yanking
at his leg chain.

She climbed into the carriage, trying not to shake. Like most
in Caverna, it was an open carriage, since closed roofs could jam
against sloping walls and stalactites. Two footmen in the very
front, to control the horses. Two guards perched on the very
back, watching behind. And Neverfell in the middle. Perhaps
it would be possible to jump out after all, if she picked her
moment, and get a few seconds' head start before any of them
noticed.

Neverfell glanced up at the balcony again, in time to see
Zouelle give her a small wave. And then the blonde girl stiffened,
fingers freezing mid-gesture.

Neverfell followed Zouelle's gaze and saw Maxim Childersin
stepping out of the front door. She watched in mute horror as he
walked over and climbed into the carriage beside her.

"The palace demands my presence, it would seem." Out of
the corner of her eye, Neverfell could see the clasping of his
long-fingered gloves with the tapering fingers. "And I thought

this might offer a good opportunity for us to have a little talk, Neverfell."

He knows — no he doesn't — he'd never have let me out of the house if he did or perhaps he does and it's a cat-and-mouse game . . .

She said nothing as the carriage lurched into motion, keeping her head ducked down, watching her veil stirring with her own breath.

"Now, I do hope that you are not going to be surly," he went on, the tiniest hint of reproof in his voice. "If I might say so, your openness and generosity of spirit have always been your best and most redeeming qualities. But I think I know what is going through your head."

Neverfell closed her eyes tight and hoped with all her heart that he did not.

"You are still upset about our conversation at breakfast, are you not?"

Neverfell breathed again, opened her eyes, and risked a small, hesitant nod.

"You really did have some fanciful notion of escaping out into the wild overground, didn't you?" Childersin's voice was sadly kind. How hard it was not to believe in that sad kindness! "Perhaps you still feel like an outsider here, and you fancy that you will find 'your own kind' out there? Perhaps a tribe of redheads with a love of licking walls? I am a little hurt by that, Neverfell. I thought we had offered you a family."

The thoroughfare was busier now. Occasionally the carriage slowed to pass another cart, the horses snuffing as their shaggy flanks brushed the arching walls, and each time Neverfell cast a glance about her, wondering if this was the opportunity she needed. But each time she was coldly aware of how quickly she would be caught if she jumped.

"Never mind," said Childersin. He patted her hand, and with a strength of mind that amazed her, Neverfell managed not to flinch. "Here is what we will do. When our family are masters of a substantial part of the overground, I will put aside a portion of it just for you. Perhaps a little island nation or something. We will have the best artists paint it for you, so that you can see what it looks like, and the inhabitants will send you gifts of tribute and letters. It will be all yours. You can choose their governor and change their laws if you like."

Neverfell listened with stunned fascination, as if she had seen a crack appear between herself and Maxim Childersin, and deepen, pushing them apart until they were divided by a colossal ravine. It amazed her that Childersin, for all his wit, wisdom, and wiles, truly did not understand why this would not make her happy. She remembered their earlier exchange, while viewing the paintings of his vineyards.

But what's the point of owning them if you never see them?

What's the point of seeing them if I don't own them?

With a quickening of the blood, Neverfell realized that the carriage was now rattling along a thoroughfare not far from Fenugreek Circle. This was a rounded cavern where various thoroughfares intersected, and was usually a higgledy-piggledy mess of carriages moving slowly around one another in their bid to reach the turning of their choice. If she could jump out anywhere and lose herself in the crush, it would be at the circle.

"Where are we going?" Maxim Childersin peered around. "Oh no, turn left here and take the long route. Avoid the circle—it gives too many opportunities for the assassin's bow."

Neverfell's heart plunged once more, and again she started to wonder whether Maxim Childersin knew all about her plans and was toying with her. Every time the carriage slowed, she desperately assessed her chances of escape. Time and again there was no turning she could run down, or the way ahead was blocked with jostlers, and while she hesitated the moment passed. She knew none of these streets, and could so easily throw away her one chance by sprinting into a dead end.

Rough cobbles stared back at her, and she was all too aware of the thinness of her flimsy shoes. For the first time she wondered whether these had been chosen deliberately to dissuade her from running.

Finally she saw the grand approach to the palace rolling out ahead, filled with gilded sedans and jostling paradribbles like gaily colored mushroom clusters. Heavy rain from the day before had found its way down crack and cranny, so that now forlorn drops were falling from the chipped ceilings. Lost rain, stained pearly pale by the ancient rock, varnishing walls and turning floors to mirrors in its doomed quest to return to the sea and sky.

Time had run out. The last chance had gone. The carriage was pulling up at the great palace gates.

Maxim dismounted, and held out a hand to help Neverfell down. The guards flanked them. Perhaps she could break from them and sprint. But she would be obvious in this serenely gliding crowd, a single frayed thread in an immaculate tapestry . . .

She was barely forming this thought, when all serene gliding was brought to an abrupt end. There was a crashing rumble that echoed from one side of the thoroughfare to the other. The air filled with clouds of stone dust, and one single screamed word.

"Rockfall!"

A second later, nobody was sane. There was scarcely a word more feared in all of Caverna. It was more terrible than darkness, more ruthless than glisserblinds. It was the awful awareness of the massive cold weight of the mountain above, the mountain that did not care about etiquette or machinations, beauty or power.

Dignity was forgotten, for what good was dignity against several thousand tons of rock? The slow of thought cringed, staring upward for cracks spreading like black veins over the rock ceiling. Those quicker of wit were already hurling themselves under anything that might withstand the brunt of a rocky cascade. Sedan owners found uninvited intruders bursting in through the doors. Others rolled under carts or flung themselves flat. Wiser souls raced to arches, counting on the masons' skill to protect them.

The only person who did not react thus was a girl in a misshapen burgundy dress and a frothy wine-colored veil, who suddenly found that her armed guards had thrown themselves prone. She twitched barely a glance to and fro, before sprinting straight into the massing cloud of pale dust.

RUNNING ROGUE

ALMOST IMMEDIATELY NEVERFELL FOUND HER-
self running blind. Rubble crunched and rolled under her feet,
bruising her soles, and she could smell newly split chalk, angry
flint. Her footing slid and she dropped to one knee, grazing it, but
was on her feet again next instant. If a wall had capsized, perhaps
there would be a new hole she could scramble through, and at
least her entourage would be loath to run into what might be a
collapsing tunnel.

Of course, I might be running straight into a collapsing tunnel.

She slithered down the other side of the unseen rubble heap,
only to see a pallid figure loom unexpectedly from the chalky
mist. It was a young woman in the all-too-familiar white garb of a
palace servant, with one hand upon an iron lever set in the wall.
Neverfell had time to squawk, but not enough to avoid barreling
into her.

"Aaaahsorry!" Neverfell staggered, and as she strove to recover
her balance the young woman took a firm grip on her collar.

"Miss?" she whispered. "Miss Neverfell?"

Neverfell could not guess what had betrayed her identity, but
decided not to stay for questions. She tried to drag herself free,

and her new captor gave a curt, curling whistle, a tiny rising note like a bird's question. A few seconds later, two more servants sprinted into view.

"Change of plan!" breathed the woman. "Breathsbait Door!"

Ignoring Neverfell's protests, the two men gripped her under the arms, lifted her bodily off her feet, and whisked her away through the settling powder cloud. The woman sped ahead, and Neverfell saw her push her finger through a hidden ring in the wall and pull. A door-shaped expanse of the mosaic-covered wall swung open.

Before Neverfell could react, the two men hurled her through this door and closed it behind her, leaving her in a narrow corridor with the woman.

"Shh!" her companion hissed. "Your friend Erstwhile told us you needed to escape. Quiet, or they'll find us."

At the mention of Erstwhile's name, Neverfell steadied herself. She was confused, but apparently among friends. Outside the door she could hear the sound of screaming, panic, rapid footfalls, shrill whinnies of horses. Occasionally there were shouted questions, the words muffled by the door. She wondered how many of them were asking after her.

"They will probably waste some time trying to find you under the rubble," whispered the servant woman. "Come!"

Neverfell found herself sidling after her soft-spoken bene-factress down cramped, narrow passages with thick carpets and velvet-lined walls. The only light entered through tiny ornamental holes in the walls, filled with colored glass. There was something dream-like about it all, not least the way that her guide glided on ahead of her without speaking.

Looking through the little spyholes, Neverfell could see familiar courtyards, fountains, and secret alcoves thick with taffeta ferns. She was inside the palace, she realized, but observing it from a perspective that few were privileged to see. These must be the servants' corridors, letting them slip through the palace unnoticed, hearing and seeing without being heard and seen.

The palace was the worst place for a fugitive. It was a den of a thousand eyes, idle, acquisitive, scandal-hungry, wary eyes. It held the headquarters of the Enquiry and the meeting halls of the new Council, and was renowned for being hard to enter or leave. It was the scene of Neverfell's celebrity, and the place where she was most likely to be recognized at a glance. It was, in short, absolutely the last place anybody would expect her to be hiding.

Of course, the hard part will be getting away from the palace again once they've started looking for me, she thought. But at the back of her mind a small, timid plan was venturing out like a fox cub.

By the time the hour was out, Enquirer Treble was making sense of the many babbled reports of the incident, and was able to strain out the rubbish and stare at the facts.

At the gates of the palace, a young girl with a covered face had leaped from the Childersin carriage and disappeared into the debris cloud of an unexpected rockfall. Ever since, the Childersin family and their allies had been frantic, scouring the streets, paying information brokers and stray-finders, and setting up unexplained checkpoints and patrols.

Enquirer Treble was in essence a hunter, with a hunter's tenacity and instincts, and relied heavily on both. This news had set her snuffing the air, like a lioness detecting the scent of an antelope sandwich.

"It's her. I know it's her," she muttered under her breath as she reached the palace gates. "Their witless witness. The outsider girl.

So their pawn has rebelled and slipped her leash, has she? We must find her. Have our men scour the city for her, particularly the route heading to Cheesemaster Grandible's tunnels."

"Is this higher priority than finding the Kleptomancer?" asked one of the junior Enquirers.

"Yes. Higher than everything else. This girl is the key to the case of the Grand Steward's death. All the other leads have led to nothing. That farce of an autopsy!" The physicians ordered to look for signs of poison had explained, as politely as they could, the difficulties of spotting "unusual symptoms" in a corpse that had blood like oozing crystal and a heart shaped like a banana.

"I had hoped to learn something from those so-called *rehearsal* deaths in Drudgery," she muttered, "but none of them bore any resemblance to His Excellency's passing. No sign of poison in the victims' bodies, or evidence that any of them went mad and killed themselves. Just a bunch of sordid, unconnected murders—some of the murderers even confessed.

"But this girl . . . the Childersins have been locking her away like a prize claret, and now they are pulling out every stop to find her. We must seize this chance to track her down before they . . . Stop! What are you doing?"

Treble had looked across just in time to see one of her men examining a mahogany sedan with a quizzical air, and tugging back the bolt that held the door closed. Her cry came too late, and the door burst open. A small, lean figure lurched into view in the gap, its narrow face all but covered by a set of multilensed goggles and a thicket of mad black hair. It waved a sextant studded with dead butterflies, and made gurgling, buzzing sounds in its throat until Treble leaped forward and shoved it hard in the chest, so that it fell back into the sedan. Treble slammed the door shut, fastened the bolt, and turned on her minion.

"Fool! Are you blind?" She pointed at the hourglass fixed to the side of the sedan. "Can you not recognize a Cartographer transport when you see one?" She turned to the foremost of the white-clad servants who were helping bear the poles of the sedan. "Why is there a Cartographer here?"

"Investigating the rockfall, my Lady Enquirer," the servant replied, bowing his head as deeply as he could without tipping the sedan. "Ascertaining whether this thoroughfare and the palace are safe." Like most of the palace servants, even when he spoke up his voice was apologetically soft, so that he sounded as if he were speaking in brackets.

"Oh, of course. And what did he—she—it say? Is the area safe?"

"Yes, my Lady Enquirer. It seems it was not a true collapse but that one of the Grand Steward's old defenses was accidentally triggered. The Grand Steward felt that if a mob were to attack his gates it would be both droll and useful to cause an appearance of a rockfall so that one or two of the rebels would be buried and the rest terrified into flight."

"I see. Very well, on you go." *Another small gift from the Grand Steward,* thought Enquirer Treble, allowing herself the rare luxury of a smile.

Inside the sedan, Neverfell held her breath, scarcely believing that the plan had worked. The black hair dye provided by the servants was not even dry yet, and occasionally she had to wipe away cold streaks of it as it ran down her cheeks and the back of her neck. The goggles fogged her vision and gave her a headache unless she kept one eye shut. On her lap lay a bundle of provisions the palace servants had given her.

Her mind was still reeling from overhearing Enquirer Treble's conversation. She had thought she might be missed, but not *this* much. The Childersins were scouring the city for her, and now so was the Enquiry. What was more, they would be waiting to ambush her on the routes to Grandible's stronghold.

For a long time the sedan bobbed gently beneath her, like a cork on the supple back of a stream. The clatter and echo of hoofs and voices gradually faded and became more intermittent.

"We are away from the crowds now, miss. It should be safe to talk," came the soft voice of the manservant carrying the front of the sedan.

"Thank you," Neverfell whispered back. "Thank you for all of this. The triggering of the rockfall defense, that was you too, wasn't it?" She recalled the female servant with her hand on the metal wall-lever.

"Yes, that was us. One of His Excellency's many mechanically triggered traps. He liked to be prepared for every emergency, so he had various devices and passages created in secret, just in case he should suddenly find himself needing to drop an assassin down a pit, or slip out of the palace, or escape from the Hall of the Gentles if he found himself overthrown and on High Trial. We were the only people he told about these precautions, so that we could make sure they were maintained and in good working order."

"It sounds like he was prepared for everything except what really happened." Neverfell felt a pang of pity. "It won't be safe to head for Master Grandible's tunnels after all, will it?"

"No, I fear not. Do you have anywhere else you can go?"

Neverfell hugged the sextant in the darkness and rocked to and fro for a few moments before answering. It seemed that she was set about on all sides by clever people who planned ahead. But brilliant people didn't predict everything, just things that made sense. They didn't expect you to sleep in your bed canopy or throw Wine across the table.

I'm not clever like the rest — I'm just a bit mad. But maybe a bit mad will do.

"I need to get down to Drudgery. Where is the best place to do that?"

"There are some descents near Musselband. We can drop you there and send word to your friend Erstwhile to meet you. But are you sure that is where you want to go? You do not have anywhere safer?"

"I think right now the safest place is where nobody expects me to be," Neverfell answered softly, hoping she was right. She held her peace for a while, but too many questions were bubbling to the top of her head. "Can I ask something? Were you the ones who kept leaving letters under my pillow?"

"Yes. I am sorry that we could not tell you."

"No. Of course not." If she had known that the palace servants were her secret protectors, she would have given it away helplessly with every glance. She winced. "It looks like all I can do is put my friends in danger."

"We are used to danger," the faceless voice assured her. "It comes with our job. Every day we are expected to carry untamed pastries and savage cheeses, advance down corridors to see whether assassins have left traps, cover for the mistakes of our betters, and risk our lives for members of the Court. We look out for our own because nobody else will. Do you know how many courtiers have been willing to risk their lives for one of us?"

"No. How many?"

"One," came the answer. "Precisely one in five hundred years."

The sedan door opened. Pulling off her goggles, Neverfell stepped out into a low-ceilinged alcove just off the silent thoroughfare, the walls etched with the whorls and rib frills of fossilized sea things. She turned toward the man who had been speaking with her, the owner of the soft-as-fur voice, and found herself looking into the face of the manservant she had saved at her first banquet.

"Good luck," he said, and with that he and his fellow servant lifted the sedan and trotted away, their feet making less sound than the stray drips falling from the ceiling to the sodden dust.

Neverfell had just started her packed lunch from the servants when Erstwhile squeaked into view on his unicycle, pink-necked with haste and spattered to the knees with mud flecks. He did not recognize her until she shouted his name and scampered over.

"You just jump into troubles like they're puddles, don't you?" was the only greeting he gave. "How did you dig yourself in a hole this deep? Mixed up in the Grand Steward's death, hunted like a rat all over Caverna—see what happens when I'm not keeping an eye on you?"

His voice was hushed, scared, and outraged, but he was there despite the danger, so Neverfell hugged him and smudged his cheek with her hair dye.

Erstwhile's part in Neverfell's escape was quickly related. He had known for some time who was smuggling Neverfell's messages out of the palace for her. "So when I got your last message I went and told them you needed to escape. Thought they might have a better plan than jumping out of a carriage."

Neverfell's tale took longer, and it took the same amount of time again for Erstwhile to run out of steam exclaiming what he thought of it.

"I never seen trouble like this! I don't know how we're going to get you out of it, Nev."

So Neverfell told him how.

"You're mad," he said after swallowing his shock. "You're *really* mad. You can't take on Maxim Childersin. He's the head of the new Council—he's Grand Steward in all but name. He probably planned this takeover for years, and you—you couldn't plan a picnic without strangling yourself with the cloth. I don't care how many of the palace table staff want to ruffle your hair and protect you, if you take on Childersin, you're a moth fighting a furnace. Give it up. Go to ground and stay there."

"I can't. And I know I'm not as clever and powerful and experienced as he is, but there's one thing that can hurt him—the truth. I need to convince everybody that he poisoned the Grand Steward.

"Let's start with those 'rehearsals.' Enquirer Treble decided they were just ordinary murders after all. Let's find out if she's right."

NEAREST AND DEAREST

GRANDIBLE HUFFED AS HE TURNED A PARTICULARLY obstreperous Whinging Bluepepper, the clamped cheese wheezing and sneezing out clouds of chalk-blue powder in complaint. Every time he used Neverfell's clamp-and-mangle turning machine, it made him more aware of the silence in his tunnels. There was no red-haired sprite to scamper along beside him now, her babble as bothersome as an itch. The prattle that had cluttered his days had been swept away in one motion, leaving them stark and empty.

He had known the first moment he laid eyes on Neverfell's face that she was an outsider. After tiring of the Court's venomous deceit, he had looked at her and seen at last somebody who could not lie to him, somebody he could trust. And so he had decided to hide her and protect her from the rest of Caverna, for he knew that her guileless face would leave her helpless among the city dwellers, like a duckling in a den of cats.

But Neverfell had not been happy in the cheese tunnels. She had grown too fast and moved too fast, and there had never been enough room for her. He had not told her she came from outside, for why torture her with thoughts of a sky she could never see?

Despite all his pains, though, the forgotten sky had called to her, and he had always known it. Would things have been different if he had told Neverfell the truth?

Wishes are thorns, he told himself sharply. *They do us no good, just stick into our skin and hurt us.*

Just as he was reflecting on the silence, however, it was broken. The entrance bell jangled, and then with increased ferocity jangled a second time.

He took down a heavily spiked morning star from a hook, and slouched through the tunnels to his front door. He pulled back the little peephatch and directed a lowering look into the passage beyond.

It quickly became clear that there were two people standing outside, both striving to place their face at the peephole. Thus he had only a view of an angry eye and a very insistent chin.

"What do you want?"

The reply was an enraged duet, all of it extremely loud and, as a consequence, only partly comprehensible.

". . . sent by Maxim Childersin of the Council . . ."

". . . Enquirer Treble sends her best respects . . ."

". . . anything you can tell us about the whereabouts of your ex-apprentice Neverfell . . ."

". . . fled from the Childersin carriage . . ."

". . . afraid for her safety and would very much like to talk . . ."

". . . to the safety of Enquiry headquarters to talk . . ."

"Lost her, have you?" interrupted Grandible. "Careless. And suppose she did run back to me, the way you seem to think. What makes you think I'd hand her over to the likes of you? Either of you?"

There was a pause, then the duet resumed, the tone far colder and more formal.

"Cheesemaster Grandible, by the power entrusted in me, I demand that you open . . ."

". . . a warrant to search your premises . . ."

Grandible's broad, yellow-stained thumb flipped a switch, and the duet gave way to coughing. He could just about see the two figures staggering away, clutching at their noses and streaming eyes. Clearly neither was a match for the scent of an overripe Plinkton Hummerbud. He slammed the peephatch shut.

Neverfell had run away. He did not need to know her reasons; it was enough to know that she had apparently fled both the Council and the Enquiry. Furthermore, he was all too aware that both messengers would now be convinced that Neverfell had indeed reached him and was tucked away inside his cheese tunnels.

Let them think that. The long-awaited siege of his tunnels was coming after all, as he had always known it would. He was ready for it. And if both the Enquiry and the Council put all their efforts into besieging his tunnels, then that might buy more time for Neverfell, wherever she was.

"Grandible did what?" Treble stared at her scorched and reeking messenger. "Then ten to one the girl is inside. How did she bypass our checkpoints? Can the girl tunnel through solid rock? Never mind. Divert men from the search and lay siege to that insolent milk-curdler. We cannot have anybody defying the Enquiry with such disdain."

"Grandible did what?" Madame Appeline sat bolt upright, and relaxed again only when her companion ran absentminded fingers through the dark waves of her hair.

"He has sealed himself in, and is firing jets of Spitting Jess acid at anybody who comes near his door. They have cut off his water and deliveries, but it is fairly plain that he has laid in supplies. It sounds as if he may have the girl hidden, but . . . I wonder. It may be that he is trying to draw attention and manpower away from her real hiding place.

"I do not intend to lay siege to Grandible's tunnels—the Enquiry will do that for us, if I know Treble. My men will be continuing the hunt for her elsewhere."

"You promised me that you could keep her under control," accused Madame Appeline. "You said there was no danger, that whatever happened—"

"And I will. I will keep your secrets safe, Vesperta. Trust me." Maxim Childersin smiled.

Quietly and for the thousandth time, Madame Appeline cursed herself. Every one of Maxim Childersin's small, dark smiles she had carefully designed for him at one time or another, to suit his face and his character. And now these smiles had more power over her than anything else in the world. It was humiliating, a Facesmith caught on a hook of her own devising.

"I think," mused Childersin, "that we should spread the word far and wide that Grandible's tunnels are under siege. That, if nothing else, may persuade the girl to come out of hiding. Her greatest weakness is her desire to protect her friends . . ."

It was a fine plan, and gave a painful twist to the cords of Madame Appeline's heart. She knew that Maxim Childersin did consider loyalty a weakness, or at least all loyalty that was not to family. She wanted to know that his first loyalty was to her, and she begrudged every hour he spent with the Childersins, every moment he spent thinking about them or for that matter anybody else. Sometimes she felt she would like to engulf him like a trap-lantern, and never share him with anyone or anything else again, not even the light. Even his obsession with ruling Caverna pained her, as if the city were a woman, and a rival.

On another day, Neverfell's Cartographer garb might have drawn more attention on the long, winding tunnel down from Musselband to Drudgery. Of late, however, the Cartographers' mood had changed from restless to downright skittish. They had been appearing in unexpected and inexplicable mobs, gabbling of shifts and changes, of twisters and tweaks, of westerleaps and southerslides. They seemed irresistibly drawn by certain places, where they gathered to stare at walls, or lay their ears against floors. Thus loose Cartographers were becoming a more familiar sight, and people avoided Neverfell but did not seem to marvel at her.

Once in Drudgery, Erstwhile led Neverfell through a baffling labyrinth of "shortcuts," most of them mere cracks and crannies that she could barely squeeze through, until Neverfell felt as if she must have been scraped even thinner than before, like a knife whetted between stones.

Deep in the bowels of the Undercity, they arrived at last at their chosen base of operations. Neverfell had realized quickly that there was only so long she could spend as a wandering Cartographer before somebody captured her and tucked her into a box. However, there was one other profession in Caverna that spent most of the time wearing masks.

The crèche matron was clearly suspicious of the grimy bandages that had been hastily used to conceal Neverfell's features, but quiet words were had and a bargain struck. Seven eggs were handed over in exchange for a set of wooden masks.

"All right," whispered the matron as she tucked the eggs in her apron pocket. "You can stay here and work as a nurse, but if there's anything fishy in this I want to know nothing about it. Understand?"

Her new young recruit nodded, gripping the wooden training masks. As she looked at them, she felt an eerie feeling in the pit of her stomach. Here were all of Erstwhile's expressions, carefully carved. They had always seemed so entirely his that it felt wrong to see them set out in smooth, impersonal pinewood.

She looked up to see Erstwhile making ready to depart.

"Holing up here is a good plan," he conceded grudgingly. "Just stay put, and keep your head down."

"You be careful too. If we're right, and those recent murders really were rehearsals, then somebody might be looking out for people asking questions about them."

"Oh, we're right," Erstwhile muttered grimly. "Don't care what old woman Treble says. I'm sure of it. Sure as I've got eyes and teeth. And don't you worry about me." With that he was on his rusty unicycle once more, and skimming away down the tunnel.

In the long, craggy crèche itself the silence was uncanny. From row upon row of tiny beds stared a hundred small faces, barely blinking, some plum-pink crumpled newborns, some with a down of wispy hair on their heads, some even old enough to sit up, but all with no more expression than a row of buttons. There were no baby cries for food, light, or company.

The only sounds were the faint murmuring of baby breath, and the clip of the nurses' tread as they walked between the beds in their wooden masks. As they drew near each bed the babies stared up at the mask, their small features struggling to imitate it. Those who succeeded were the first to receive milk from the nurses' pewter bottles; those who failed were denied milk until they did better. Occasionally the nurses even stopped to help prod infant features into the right positions, as if they were molding very delicate clay.

None of the other nurses reacted to the arrival of a new recruit among them, and only somebody with sharp eyes could have noticed that this newest nurse was younger than the others, or that the hair in her fat pigtail was freshly dyed.

Straddling his unicycle, Erstwhile skimmed and dodged through the alleys of Drudgery. The unicycle was almost a part of him, his other legs. He could halt in an instant, twist on a penny, hop sideways like a starling, and at the moment he was in a flood of other boys doing the same. The errand boys swooped like sparrows and called to each other in passing trills, whistles, or slaps on the back.

There were Enquirers loose in Drudgery. This was to be expected. What did surprise him was that there were not more. Previously, after Neverfell had been kidnapped by the Kleptomancer, the Enquiry had turned out in force, and had clearly been men with a mission. This time there were a few checkpoints, a few pointed questions, and a high reward offered, nothing more.

Good. The bloodhounds don't know she's down here. But Childersin is a different kettle of scorpions. Who knows what that sly old dog is doing? He'll have spies down here. Drudge spies. Listening out for word of Neverfell. And listening out for people asking just the sort of questions I've got to ask right now.

Skim, skim, sparrow hop, screech. A grin, a chatter with a treadmill trudger.

"Murder of Seb Blink?" The trudger shook his head slowly, his eyes gray and heavy with twelve hours of watching wooden boards rolling and rolling beneath his feet. "No, no mystery there. Brother killed him. Pushed him into the millrace just down from Greep's Dolor. Saw it myself, me and twenty others, while we were treading board. Took us all by surprise, though—they seemed so close."

Flit, weave, veer, and squeak to a halt. Drinking water at a drip pool, gossiping with the girls washing the dust out of their hair.

"Yes, it's true." A thin girl with her head on one side twisted her wet hair to wring it out. "Knock Parlet killed his wife. Thirty years together, then he does her with a mattock. They found him next to her, weeping and bleating his confession, till the Enquiry took him away."

Swerve, duck, dodge, and slow, rust specks spattering from his wheels. Helping a bent-over old woman haul a cart to the top of a sloping tunnel, while she unfolded her one big piece of news like someone shyly showing their wedding dress among its mothballs.

"Yes, I knew Job Littletoad. Never would have thought it. Always such a doting son until . . . well, I suppose he snapped. Strange, I met him just an hour before he did it, and he was as calm as pie. But he never denied what he done, they say."

And so on, through the crowds, picking up information the way a sparrow pecks up crumbs. He heard of murder after murder, and by the time he made his way back to the drudge crèche where he had left Neverfell, his mind felt blood-dipped.

He hopped off his unicycle, slung it over one shoulder, and walked in, to be met by one of the most furious whispered arguments he had ever seen. All three of the masked nurses were gesturing a lot, to show that they were shouting at the bottom of their voices. However, the argument was clearly two against one, the matron and senior nurse turning on a skinny, black-haired figure that he recognized at once as Neverfell, from the way she was twisting her hands.

"What's going on?" Erstwhile started to ask in a normal tone, but was silenced by a three-way "hush" and fingers pointed in the direction of the crèche, where most of the babies appeared to be asleep.

"You said there would be no trouble!" hissed the matron. "And yet within a day—mere hours—this girl was sneaking around the crèche trying to teach one of the children a new Face! Not a drudge Face at all."

"A horrible Face too," the senior nurse added. "Stretched, bulging eyes. I saw it before she slapped her mask back on."

"It won't happen again," Erstwhile snapped, then grabbed Neverfell's arm and pulled her away to a corner. "What goes through your head, Nev? I was only gone three hours! All you had to do was sit here with your mask on. And you took it off to frighten babies? Did they see anything except the Face you were making? Do they know who you are?"

"No. I don't think so," Neverfell answered softly. "I'm sorry . . . but I . . . I couldn't bear just teaching the babies to look obedient. I wanted to give them a new Face, to use when they're angry or upset. Only I can't do Faces, so I sort of used my fingers to pull out the corners of my mouth, and pull down the skin under my eyes . . . oh, it makes you look like a deformed frog, but it's something! And it's a Face you can teach and learn really easily, without a Facesmith or masks or anything. You just pull your face about."

"Well, aren't you the Lady Bountiful with your thousand faces," Erstwhile muttered nastily. Her words were a jagged reminder of his own limited Faces. "Try to remember that I'm risking my neck to keep you alive! Pranks like this will get us both killed. Now, hush up and listen to what I found out."

With some reluctance, he went on to repeat all that he had learned of the murders in Drudgery.

"Something smells rank in this, but I can't figure out what it is. It looks like they really were all murders of drudges by drudges. They got confessions for two of 'em and witnesses for a lot of the others. And all the murders were done different ways as well."

It was odd looking across and seeing Neverfell in a mask, almost like old times in the cheese tunnels. Somewhere behind the wood, though, he knew that her face was going through kaleidoscopic changes as she thought.

"Oh!" she exclaimed suddenly. "So that's it! Listen, Erstwhile— we've been thinking about it the wrong way, and so has Enquirer Treble. We've been looking for poison victims who went mad and killed themselves, the way the Grand Steward did.

"But it wasn't the victims who were poisoned, Erstwhile! It was the murderers. The poison made them go mad and kill the person dearest to them, suddenly and for no good reason. But the person closest to the Grand Steward *was* the Grand Steward, because there were two of him. So when somebody put the poison in his moth biscuit, both halves of him went mad and started trying to kill each other."

For a long while Erstwhile had no words. He did not care about the Grand Steward one speck. His mind was full of images of drudge wives, drudge parents, drudge children, coming home and being suddenly attacked by those they loved and trusted most.

"It's the worst" was all he could say. "It's all we have down here, each other. All treading the same wheel, shoulder to shoulder. It's one thing murdering us. But . . . using us to kill each other, that's . . ." He ran his fingernails through his hair and scrabbled it haywire. "I changed my mind. All those things you said about taking down Maxim Childersin. If there's half a pebble I can throw into the scales of that, I'm in. I don't care if he's got the world in a goblet, I want to see his head on a spike. And I bet I can find others down here who will see things the same way."

"You mean, you're going to tell people about it? Is that safe?"

"I won't tell anybody who you are, just about the poison. And no"—Erstwhile shook his head stonily—"even that isn't safe. But we need help, don't we? We got to take some chances."

A few moments later he threw Neverfell a hesitant glance.

"That frog-Face. You couldn't teach it to me, could you? Maybe I'd like to have a Face for being angry after all."

THE SECRET EXCAVATION

AT FIRST GLANCE, EVERY DRUDGE SEEMED LIKE any other. They took great pains to make sure it seemed so. Over centuries, anybody who looked like they might become a leader or spokesperson had disappeared into the cells of the Enquiry. And so they had learned how to impersonate a faceless mass.

Information, however, drifted through them all, but imperceptibly, like a drop of ink thinning into water. And so it was with word of the Grand Steward's poisoning, and about the drudges who had been forced to kill one another. An anger was building, but it was invisible to the casual eye. It burned unnoticed, like a spice that is undetectable in the first spoonful of potage but which gradually builds its fire on the tongue.

The first symptoms of it might have been spotted among the errand boys, those flitters, skulkers, and coin-snatchers. The sharp of eye might have noticed that they were a little more given to gaggles, and to suddenly pedaling away at the sound of a stranger's step. Those who succeeded in surprising them might even catch one with his fingers to his face, pulling at the skin below his eyes in a strange and grotesque way.

But the mighty of Caverna had far more to worry about than the whispers of drudge children, and so this, like many other important changes, went unnoticed. Had they known that some of said children were now carefully eavesdropping on their private conversations and reading their messages, they might have felt differently.

"So the Court are mostly stabbing each other up." The sandy-headed errand boy gave a small shrug. "Old Childersin's had four attempts against his life. Not a scratch on him, though—didn't even tear his gloves. But his enemies are all dying like flies. You heard of the Ganderblacks? All vanished, down to the tiniest tot. Folks say they was devoured body and soul by this wild black Wine they were trying to brew. All that was left behind was their clothes, hair, fingernails, and little heaps of scented blue powder."

Neverfell nodded, and mentally added the information to a growing list of details. Over the last few days a steady trickle of errand boys had turned up at the crèche to report events at Court, and in particular the doings of Maxim Childersin. They had been recruited by Erstwhile, who had told them she was a scarred relation of his, helping him investigate, and that they should leave all new information with her.

To judge by their reports, Childersin was securing his position and settling old scores. With a worried pang she thought of Zouelle living in the lions' den.

"What about Enquirer Treble? We heard rumors somebody killed her with a predatory pâté."

"Nah, though somebody had a good try. Twelfth time somebody tried to kill her since the Grand Steward died. This one left her blind for a day and turned her hair white. It was one of her own men that went for her, they say. Never found out who he was working for. But she's back on her feet, and it don't seem to have slowed her down much.

"There's one other thing. You were asking about the Facesmith Appeline? Well, I know somebody who knows somebody who knows something about her. Only he's terrified. He says that he'll talk to you person to person, only he wants twenty-five eggs and his name kept out of it."

Neverfell's heart leaped uncertainly, like a fawn in a rolling boat. On Erstwhile's advice, she had hoarded her little supply of preserved eggs to use as bribes, and subsisted on a thin gruel made from barley and moth-grubs like everybody else, though the diet left her exhausted and dull-witted with hunger. Even so, her egg supply was now severely diminished.

"I can't manage that many," she answered, trying not to sound too keen, "but I might be able to get them in a week or so."

The errand boy shook his head. "Has to be today. Tomorrow he sets off with a delving team for the wild tunnels."

Neverfell weighed the risks, but her instincts were hammering at her to take the chance. "Today I can offer an ounce of Nocteric. That's worth much more than twenty-five eggs." She had found a little pouch of the spice at the bottom of the pack the palace servants had given her, evidently intended as a valuable to trade when in extremis.

The boy drew in a breath through his teeth. "Nocteric? If it's stolen, it's traceable. I don't know if he will be happy with that." He hesitated. "Look, you better come talk to him yourself. I can't spend all day running messages between you."

Neverfell hesitated for a moment, but only a moment.

"All right."

Soon the pair of them were out on the drudge thoroughfares, amid the rush of the shift-change crowds. Neverfell wondered what her guide would think of her if he could see through her mask and realize how close to breaking she was all the time. The last time Neverfell had visited Drudgery, the sight of it had struck her mind like a fist, bruising and shattering. Now that she was living in it, she realized why none of her pursuers had expected her to flee to the Undercity.

For all its thousands of trap-lanterns, the Drudgery air was close and choking. There was the smothering odor of unwashed skin, and the reeks from the great buzzing caverns where the waste of Caverna was heaped, sorted, and washed away, or the livestock caves where herds of hay-fed goats and cows shivered in the green light and stared wild-eyed at the dripping walls.

The cramped closeness drove her near to madness. Like everybody else in the drudge crowds she had to squeeze and cram past other bodies, until she felt like part of a sprawl of maggots.

"Up here." At last the guide jerked a discreet thumb upward, and Neverfell obediently scrambled up a rope through a crack in the ceiling. It opened into a small hollow, ridged like the space inside a fist, with a rough shelf either side of the crack. A gray-faced, broad-nosed drudge man about forty years old was sitting there on one side with his knees drawn up to his chin. His hands were so covered in scars they might have been gloved in spider's webs.

Carefully, Neverfell hauled herself up to sit on the other shelf. *If this is a trick,* said the part of Neverfell that had learned from life at Court, *then you'll be caught like a rat up here.* The fact that the other man seemed just as nervous as she was did nothing to reassure her.

The negotiation was brief, and after a pause the Nocteric was accepted.

"Tomorrow I'm off with a digging team to the wild tunnels," he explained in a mutter. "Want something to leave with my family, pay their way if I don't come back."

"Tell them to keep it in its box till they're ready to sell it," Neverfell whispered back, "Now—you know something about Madame Appeline?"

The delver nodded slowly. "It happened quite a few years ago, back when I was one of a team digging out the Octopus. Do you know where that is?"

"Yes. It's near the Doldrums, isn't it?" Neverfell could not prevent her hands tightening on her knees in excitement. She remembered Zouelle telling her that the Octopus and the Samphire district were both being excavated at the time of the mysterious influenza epidemic. "Was that about seven years ago?"

"Yes—I suppose it would be about that." The delver sounded a little surprised. "Well, they were driving us to finish the Octopus fast so they could use it to link all these other districts, so we were hauling carts of rubble out of there till even the horses looked fit to buckle. All to be hauled up to the surface and scattered, the usual.

"One day when I was bringing back an empty cart past Toveknock, that used to be the turning into the Doldrums, this lady in a worn-out velvet cape and a kindly sort of Face beckoned me over. She told me that there had been a rockfall in her tunnels, but that she had it all propped up safe and didn't want to report it or she'd have Cartographers tramping all over her rooms. She said she just wanted to get rid of the rocks, and would pay to have it done on the quiet.

"I said yes." The man clasped and unclasped his fretted hands. "I think maybe I said it because of the Face she had on. Made me feel like I'd just found out I had a long-lost daughter who needed my help. So every day, after I should have gone off shift, I'd take up the cart one more time and pull into the Doldrums. The rubble would be ready and waiting in pails, and I'd load up my cart, and take her rocks away to dump with the rest. Never got caught doing it."

"And that was Madame Appeline?"

"That was her. She paid me well, so I didn't ask questions. Even though I knew the rubble never came from a rockslide."

"You're sure?"

"Sure as teeth are teeth. It wasn't cracked and crumbled the way it would be if it had just caved in; it was chiseled and broken up, like it had been torn out by a drill. There was too much of it as well. If there had been a rockfall of that size, well, we might not have heard it with all the drilling we were doing, but the Cartographers would have noticed."

"So you mean . . . you weren't the only ones digging," said Neverfell, her mouth dry and her mind whirling. Digging without official permission was one of the most serious crimes in Caverna. The wrong passage in the wrong place could collapse, flood, or asphyxiate large portions of the city. "So that's why you don't want anybody to know you were mixed up in this."

"It's not just the law that worries me." The delver glanced down through the aperture between them, as if fearful of seeing faces staring up past his boots. "The last day, when I was due to collect the final payment, I was took ill with rasp-lung, and had to send my brother-in-law with the cart instead. He never came home. They found him dead, his chest crushed. Everybody decided the cartwheel must have gone over him, and maybe it did, but I think it had help. Most people can't tell drudges apart, you see. I think that wheel was meant for me, to stop me from telling what I knew. And so I held my peace and took jobs as a delver in the wilds, hoping those that killed him never found out they got the wrong man."

Neverfell said nothing, but placed a hand on either side of her head. She felt like she needed to hold it in place until everything inside it stopped moving.

"When did all this happen?" she asked in a whisper. "It was before the Doldrums influenza, wasn't it?"

"Yes. The outbreak slowed down our work in the Octopus badly. We lost lots of Cartographers, you see. You know the way they swarm? There was something about the Doldrums that was drawing lots of them there, and when the flu broke out six of them died straight off."

"Did they ever say what was pulling them to the Doldrums?" It was all Neverfell could do to contain her excitement.

"Probably." Even with his limited repertoire of Faces, Neverfell was sure that the delver would be giving her a funny look if he could. "But I didn't ask and I certainly didn't listen. Cartographers are always happy to tell you everything they know. *Everything.* That's the problem." By this point, he was shifting nervously in his seat. "Look, I done my part. You'll give me the spice? That'll do, won't it?"

"Yes," said Neverfell distantly. "Yes. That'll do. And you're right. You shouldn't let them find out you're alive. I . . . I've got to go now. My head's full." Without further ado, she handed him the small pouch of Nocteric, and dropped down through the crack back into the passage below, where her errand-boy guide was waiting for her.

She followed him in a daze. Digging in the Doldrums, that somebody had gone to a lot of trouble to keep secret. Illegal digging, seven years ago.

Seven years. Always seven years. Everything happened seven years ago.

The bat-squeakers fretting about the Undiscovered Passage. The influenza in the Doldrums. Madame Appeline buying dresses for a child. The large anonymous reward suddenly offered for the Kleptomancer. And Neverfell's own appearance in Grandible's tunnels with no memories. All seven years ago.

What if all these things were part of the same big secret? What if something happened seven years ago that nobody was supposed to know about, something to do with me? Perhaps I knew about it—perhaps that's why somebody took away all my memories. Perhaps that's even why somebody tried to kill me in the Enquiry cell, just in case I remembered anything about it.

Now Neverfell could feel a pounding in her head, as if behind some door of the mind her forgotten memories were trying to beat their way out.

The truth was locked in her head somewhere. What secret could be so dangerous that somebody would be willing to kill her to stop her from remembering it? And who *had* been trying to murder her?

For seven years she had been safe in Grandible's tunnels. Perhaps her hidden enemies had not known where she was, or perhaps she had simply been beyond their reach. Then she had erupted from her haven and let her face be discovered, and somebody had seen her, or heard a description of a red-haired outsider girl of about twelve years, and known who she must be.

And so somebody had tried to murder her in her cage, before she could tell the Enquiry anything. And shortly after this attempt had failed . . . Maxim Childersin had suddenly come to buy her. Perhaps this was not coincidence. What if he had not been motivated by compassion, or a desire to save his niece? What if he was the one who had tried to have her murdered, and had decided to buy her only so that he would have an opportunity to silence her permanently?

But then he saw me. And he realized I could fit into his plans. And that's when he started trying to find out whether I remembered anything, or whether it was safe to keep me alive.

Neverfell recalled the questions he had asked at the time. *What have you told the Enquiry? How much do you remember before Grandible's tunnels?*

And that reprise Wine he gave me back in his study must have been a test, Neverfell realized. *He wanted to find out whether anybody else could use that kind of Wine to bring back my memories. If the reprise had helped me remember things, I wonder if I would have left that room alive . . .*

There were still things that did not make sense, however. Childersin had wanted to keep her alive so that she could play her part in the murder of the Grand Steward, and yet somebody had sent the glisserblind assassin after her while she was living in the tasters' quarters. Not Childersin, surely. Was she facing more than one unconnected enemy, then? Or a team of enemies not quite pulling together?

And what is it that they don't want me to remember? What is it that I know but don't know?

Suddenly Neverfell was jerked back into self-awareness. Following her guide through a particular arched alley, she felt the current of the crowd suddenly stop, tug forward, and then rear backward, amid cries of consternation and confusion. Suddenly she was the squished filling in a people sandwich, her masked face buried in somebody's back as they tried to recoil through her.

"Cartographers!" was the cry. "Cartographers coming! Back! Back up!" But there was no backing up into the oblivious surge of people behind. Panic leaped for Neverfell's throat like a hunting hound.

"Down!" shouted somebody else, and the crush messily collapsed to their knees, those who could covering their heads with their arms, and lay as still and low as possible. Next thing Neverfell knew there were other figures scrambling through the tunnel over the prone forms, paying no attention to whether their boots found purchase on rocks or faces. These figures gabbled, clicked, and whistled as they went, some gripping strange devices or wearing bulging eyepieces. Somebody's knee rested heavily on Neverfell's shoulder for a moment, and a boot toe scraped painfully against her ear.

Next moment the mad scrabblers were gone, farther up the passage. The crowd that could not part for the Cartographers or retreat before them had laid itself down to let them pass overhead.

Gingerly and slowly the crowd rose to its feet again, stranger helping stranger, and the flow continued. Neverfell got up groggily. Somehow being thrown down and half trampled had jolted her thoughts into a better order, and just for a single dizzy moment she wondered how she could arrange for the same thing to happen every time she was stuck for inspiration.

When she staggered bruised into the crèche, her arm was instantly grabbed by Erstwhile, who frog-marched her to a corner.

"You mad little moth! Where've you been? What were you thinking, wandering around Drudgery? And no note left for me, nothing! I am this close, *this* close, to giving up on you—"

"I'm sorry, Erstwhile, I'm really sorry!" Neverfell snatched off her mask for a moment to show him that she meant it. "I know it was dangerous, but there was something I had to chase up. And do you know what? I *caught* it." Moving to her own cot, Neverfell pulled back the straw mattress and pulled out the Cartographer disguise hidden inside.

"Caught it? What's that meant to mean?"

"It means that something important happened seven years ago, and I'm almost certain I know what it was. I think I know how I got into Caverna, why I couldn't be allowed to remember it, why the Doldrums were sealed off, and why the Childersins are never out of clock.

"If I'm right, then I know what we have to do. But I need to be sure I'm right first. Erstwhile—where are the nearest excavations? The easiest ones to reach from here?"

Erstwhile drew his breath in through his teeth, evidently disliking the direction the conversation was going. "Probably the ones out at Perilous Jut. Why?"

Neverfell held up her goggles and examined her tiny, yellow reflection in one lens. "I think," she said slowly, "I need to talk to the Cartographers."

THAT WAY LIES MADNESS

FEW CAVERNANS CHOSE TO WANDER INTO THE places where new tunnels were being mined. Why would they? Why risk the perils of chokedamp seeping from a newly opened crack, let alone the collapse of untried passages? Why endure the noise, rubble, and unsmoothed floors? And last but not least, why venture to a place where there was such a risk of running into loose Cartographers?

Erstwhile's muttered complaints on these themes were bitter and increasingly inventive, but to Neverfell's surprise he insisted on accompanying her anyway. They met only a couple of people en route, and those covered their ears or retreated at the sight of Neverfell's Cartographer garb and butterfly-covered sextant.

When it came to excavations, Cartographers were a necessary evil. Only they could tell you whether your nice new shaft would collapse unexpectedly, or weaken a set of passages above it, or unexpectedly join an underground river and drown everybody.

The character of the tunnels gradually changed, the air growing colder, the chipped surfaces of the walls lighter, less tarnished by time. The muted echoes of the thoroughfares were gradually replaced by the distinctive chip, bang, and clatter of picks on stone, and the occasional sandy rattle of shale and rocks.

Before long, Neverfell and Erstwhile passed a pit pony serenely dragging a wagon full of rocks. Its driver appeared to have twists of cloth pushed into his ears. It was not clear whether this was to protect him from the din or the words of the Cartographers. Neverfell's crazed and goggled appearance earned her only a fleeting glance, though his gaze lingered curiously on Erstwhile, who was walking a pace behind her.

"You better put cloth in your ears," whispered Neverfell when the cart had rolled by, "or they'll wonder how you're walking along with me without going mad." They cut little pieces off Neverfell's already frayed sleeves and rolled them up to make earplugs. "We're going to start meeting people soon—do you think I should start twitching and fidgeting and acting crazy?"

Erstwhile gave her a sideways glance as he chewed the cloth pieces to make them soft. "I don't think you need to change a thing" was all he said.

Many of these tunnels were propped with timber struts, their wood dusty but unblackened. Here and there, pitched wind chimes had been hung to measure the air currents, chalk marks drawn on the walls, and names of tunnels scrawled on the floor. At last they found themselves in a long horizontal shaft, where various drudges were hurrying out of side passages carrying pails of chipped rock, pouring basins of milky water down wooden flumes, or examining pale seams in the cliff-face ahead.

One of them noticed the two new arrivals, and gestured to gain Erstwhile's attention.

"Not here!" the man mouthed in an exaggerated fashion,

having evidently noticed Erstwhile's earplugs. "Take her through there. On the left."

Erstwhile nodded, grabbed Neverfell's arm, and led her through an arch to the left, then down a small, downward-sloping passage to a rather makeshift, ill-fitting door, to which an hourglass had been fixed.

"This must be where they keep their Cartographers," whispered Neverfell. "Wait here for me. It's best if one of us is outside watching to make sure the time doesn't run out."

"No, I'd better be the one to go in," Erstwhile snapped suddenly. "You're half mad already—you got less far to go if it comes to going crazy."

"Or maybe I've got less to lose." Neverfell took a deep breath, then twisted the hourglass upside down and stepped into the room before Erstwhile could object.

In the middle of the small, rounded room beyond the door, a man was sitting on a wooden chair, quite calmly. He looked about fifty years old, his thinning blond-gray hair combed neatly across his head. He wore a thick coat trimmed with graying, damp-spiked fur, and he was no drudge, to judge by his height and by the brightness and confidence of the smile he directed at Neverfell when he looked up. It was a Face that might be worn by a professor pleased to see the arrival of a new student.

His feet were bare, and his long, dirty toes kept flexing against the stone floor over and over, as if they were trying to pick something up.

"Haaah, well timed. You can help me recalculate the meridian. It has swung anticlockwise again and scattered my azimuths."

"I'm . . ." Neverfell swallowed and opted for honesty. "I'm not a real Cartographer."

"I know," said the toe-flexer. "Your butterflies are in the wrong places. But you will do. Here is your end of the string. Now walk around me in a slow circle, looking at me continually, and tell me when I look whitest."

"Sir, please!" Neverfell did not want to spend her full five minutes walking in circles. "I want to ask you something. About the Doldrums. About passages running in and out of them. About what happened there seven years ago."

"Doldrums. Dollldrrruums." The Cartographer first whispered the word, then breathed it slowly so that "dol" became a sonorous bell chime, and rolled the "r" into a drumroll. "Haven't been asked about that for a while. Such a pity it was closed off. Such a beautiful twister."

"What's a twister?" The question was out before Neverfell could stop herself.

The man beamed at her as if by asking that she had presented him with a golden chalice completely filled with chocolate ice cream. "You want to know?" he asked delightedly. "You really want to know?"

Neverfell suddenly had a strong feeling that perhaps she didn't.

"It wasn't just the twister, mind," the Cartographer went on. "Something else was happening there as well."

"Illegal digging," suggested Neverfell, slightly disoriented by how normal the conversation seemed to be so far. "Lots of Cartographers went there to find out about it. And then they died, didn't they?"

"Yes. Influenza. That's what people said." He was observing her closely, and there was something wrong with the way he blinked. Most blinkers didn't close their eyes completely, but he did, and paused an instant before opening them. Blink. Breath. Unblink. "Who *are* you?" He was still smiling, but his voice suddenly had a menacing, suspicious drawl. "Why are you dressed as one of us? Why are you here, asking about the Doldrums?"

All the sensible options seemed to involve lying or walking out and learning nothing more. Instead, on an impulse, Neverfell slowly lifted her goggles, so that her face could be seen by the light of the single trap-lantern hanging from the ceiling.

"Ahhh. You." The Cartographer sat back in his chair. Blink. Unblink. "She doesn't like you."

"What? Who doesn't?" asked Neverfell in confusion, the image of Madame Appeline's face springing unbidden to mind.

"She doesn't like you at all." The Cartographer put his head on one side and closed his eyes, apparently focusing on the sensation through his toes. "You . . . tickle."

Neverfell remembered the Kleptomancer's words about Caverna, and developed a new suspicion as to the identity of "she."

"I don't want to tickle," she murmured with feeling. "I don't want to be in the city at all. But there's nowhere else for me to go."

"If you want to go nowhere, you need the Undiscovered Passage. That goes to nowhere and nothingness. The bat-squeaks went into the nothingness, and nothing came back."

"Yes." Neverfell leaned forward to whisper. "I *do* want the Undiscovered Passage. I want to know everything about it. It appeared and disappeared seven years ago as well, didn't it? Did it happen around about the time those other Cartographers started swarming to the Doldrums? What I mean to say is, is it possible they did that because they'd realized that *that was where the Undiscovered Passage was?*"

Neverfell now had the Cartographer's undivided attention. Indeed, she rather wished something would come along to divide it, so intense was his stare. And then, just as she felt as though his gaze were boring into her forehead like a knitting needle, the Cartographer stood and walked to another door behind him, twisted the hourglass attached to it, and stepped through. The hourglass itself was murky with dust and crushed insects, and the glass appeared to have been scored by claws.

"Wait! Where are you going?" Neverfell's voice echoed uselessly in the little room. For a moment she was afraid that he had gone to report her identity. Then she began to understand what she had just seen. The door through which he had passed had its own Cartographer's hourglass. Presumably, therefore, he had gone to speak with somebody that even he could not risk talking to for more than five minutes, a Cartographer whose madness and insight were feared even by ordinary Cartographers.

Although she knew it was foolish, Neverfell could not resist running over to this second door and pressing her ear against it. All she could hear, however, was a muted conversation, which seemed to be between the man who had just left her and another who spoke in a hissing, clicking way, interrupted by the occasional short, sharp shriek. There was a pause, then a patter of steps, a metallic squeak, then the sound of yet another door being opened and shut.

There was another pause, and then Neverfell thought she could hear extremely faint hissing and shrieks, and behind even them perhaps a hint of bat-like squeaking.

The unseen door opened and closed once more, and Neverfell heard what sounded like a hissed and screamed explanation. She leaped away from the door before it too opened to readmit the short man to whom she had been speaking before.

His appearance was now even more disturbing. His hair flew up in wild antennae-like wisps, his eyes bulged, and his forehead was glossy with perspiration. Across his high brow a sooty handprint was visible, and his collar seemed to have been chewed off.

"Beautiful" was the first thing he said. "Flaws are the most beautiful thing, are they not? Like the tiny fractures in a gem that glimmer when they catch the light. And sometimes they have shapes in them, like the flecks in a perfect eye you could sink into slide down the spirals so sweet and hopeless for she never forgives but coming back to the point a twister at the kissing points of two norths with a corkscrew radiance . . ."

And if it had been nonsense, Neverfell would have been safe. But fragments of it almost did make sense, and her brain could not help but hang on to them and be pulled along, like a rider with one foot in the stirrup trailed behind a galloping horse. And it was worth it, because the longer you held on the more sense it made, only the thing dragging you was suddenly too scaly to be a horse and had far too many heads . . .

And Neverfell started to understand the beauty of flaws, those places where up and down secretly gave up their argument and shook hands, where compass points spun like a dervish, and where space itself was twisted like a wrung-out flannel. These places were the dimples for Caverna's glittering smile, her foibles, her signature. To understand them was to steal a smile, a twisted rose from her hand, a bone from between her thousand teeth.

And so it seemed that Neverfell's mind had broken out of the silly commonsense skull that had trapped it all this time, and gone lolloping off, wild as a broken bird and as formless as soup. Before her she saw the twister, a crooked pin dragging the map askew. She poured her mind into it, took its shape, started to become the twister. Ah yes, that was how it all fitted together. Now that she had folded her mind she could see that.

And then for a moment she saw a flash of something else, something tantalizing. For the tiniest instant she saw an aperture like a perfectly round cave mouth that appeared to lead to a shaft full of light. The Undiscovered Passage. It was beckoning to her, it was begging her to explore and map it . . . and it was gone. She seemed to feel the inner sigh of every Cartographer in Caverna at the memory of that passage. Where was it? Where did it lead? And why, oh why, did it vanish before they could worship it with maps?

She could find it right now. She knew she could. But it would be far easier and quicker if she gave up on her body and wandered the tunnels with her mind alone, swimming down the glittering gem-veins in the mountain's rock . . .

. . . and Neverfell came to herself to discover that she was kneeling on grazed knees, her throat was sore, and somebody was trying to twist off her ears.

She gave a squawk of pain and shook off her attacker, who proved to be Erstwhile. She was back in the corridor again. The door to the Cartographer's room was closed once more, and she could see that the sands in the hourglass had all run through into the base.

"I didn't know what else to do!" yelped Erstwhile once he had recovered his breath a little. "When the hourglass ran out, I had to drag you out, and I tried shaking you but it didn't work! You kept flailing around and shouting about the glory of loam!"

"Thanks," Neverfell croaked weakly. Her head still felt crowded. She stared down at her feet, which now appeared to be bare, and flexed her toes slowly.

"Did it work?" asked Erstwhile, peering into her face.

"Oh yes," said Neverfell. "Just for a while there I could see how it all fitted together, how things really joined and . . ." She made helpless gestures, like somebody trying to put together two halves of an invisible coconut. "I mean . . . even here it's beautiful. Just imagine that left is a kind of pink color and all you have to do is swivel it past gold and OW! Erstwhile! Ow! Let go of my ears!"

It became evident that Erstwhile had no intention of relinquishing Neverfell's ears, not until he had dragged her by them away from Perilous Jut. Even then he was clearly examining Neverfell for signs of Cartography, and the fact that she repeatedly forgot that she could not walk through walls apparently did not reassure him. At last, however, he relented and let her continue her conversation.

"So?"

"My theory was right," Neverfell began slowly. "I'm sure of it now. I asked the Cartographer about the Doldrums and he told me . . . showed me . . . oh, I can't explain! I started to understand what he was saying, and then I lost track of words, and I could almost *see* it. In the Doldrums there's a . . . a twister . . . it's a place where . . ." Numbly Neverfell groped for the concept. To her alarm it groped back, and she recoiled. "Aargh! No! Never mind what it is! It's a weird thing where geography doesn't work the way it should.

"The important bit is this: The Doldrums weren't ever properly sealed off. There's a way in. Two, in fact. The first one is out through the back of Madame Appeline's hidden room. And that's the easy part; that's the part you can work out from where things are, even with a normal brain. It's the other way in that most people wouldn't guess.

"It's through the Childersin town house. You go in through the house, out the back, down the private passage, and then, well, the twister does something so you end up in the Doldrums. The Morning Room is in the Doldrums."

"And that's it?" Erstwhile sounded deeply unimpressed. "So there's a secret tunnel between Madame Appeline's domain and Maxim Childersin's house. We already knew they were working together. That's what we just melted your mind to find out?"

"No—that's not it. That's not what they dug at all. It's all about the Morning Room—oh, I'm going to do this as a story because it's easier that way." Neverfell tugged at the ends of her hair, and was once again surprised to find them black instead of red.

"Suppose once upon a time there was a clever and powerful man who was willing to do anything for his family. Now, he agreed with everybody else that Caverna was the only place to live, but he wasn't like all the other powerful Cavernans. He always had one eye looking out across the world. And he discovered that there was something that could give his family an edge over everybody else at Court, make them smarter, stronger, and better at everything. But it only existed in the overground. You couldn't get it in Caverna—it was forbidden. So he had to look for a way of smuggling it in, and in the end he found one."

"But what was it?" asked Erstwhile. "The thing he smuggled in."

"Think." Neverfell gnawed a knuckle. "What's the hardest thing to bring into Caverna? The one thing that would never be allowed?"

Erstwhile thought for a moment, then remembered where he had left his smile. "Gunpowder!"

Neverfell shook her head. "Daylight. It's *daylight*.

"I've seen the Undiscovered Passage. Well, sort of seen it, the way the Cartographers remember it, the ones who sensed it. They say it only has one end—they think the other one goes to nothingness. The thing is, Cartographers are all in love with Caverna, and can't really understand anything outside her.

"I don't think the Undiscovered Passage goes into nothingness, Erstwhile. I think it leads out, all the way to the overground. Out of Caverna. And I think it begins in the Childersins' Morning Room. I don't think the blue light in there is done with trap-lanterns. I think it's real daylight.

"I think Master Childersin makes his family eat breakfast in the Morning Room every day so that they can sit there soaking up daylight. And I think he makes them keep to the overground clock instead of a normal twenty-five-hour clock so that it's always day when they go there, and never night.

"And the Childersins *are* different from everybody else, aren't they? They stand out, even at Court. They're never out of clock the way everybody else is. They're cleverer, their skin is shinier, they're even taller. Did you ever see the clothes and armor in the Cabinet of Curiosities, the ones made for overgrounders? They're all really big, like they're made for people six feet tall. And look at me—I come from outside, and I'm tall for my age. Well, the Childersins, particularly the younger ones, they're all tall for their age as well. So maybe the sun doesn't just fry off your skin. Maybe it makes you bigger and stronger."

"So all the illegal digging, that was the Undiscovered Passage? A tunnel leading straight up to let the sun ooze in?"

"Yes. And Madame Appeline helped by getting rid of the rubble, though I still don't really understand why, or where the Tragedy Range fits into all of this, or why I keep feeling like there's a link between her and me.

"When they finished the tunnel, I suppose they sealed it off with glass at the Morning Room end to disguise what it was, but before they did, two things happened. The first thing was that some of the bat-squeakers sensed the passage just before it was sealed, and some of them even worked out where it was and were murdered to keep them silent."

"And the other thing?"

"Something came down the shaft from the overground. Me."

UP MEETS DOWN

WITHIN HALF AN HOUR OF RETURNING TO Drudgery, Neverfell realized that something was wrong. Her first hint was Erstwhile, who kept twitching his head to look around him with increasing frequency. Only then was she aware that their progress was much faster than it had been, much easier than it should have been. The crowds were not pressing as close as they had. There seemed to be a fine, untouchable bubble around them. This would have made sense if Neverfell had still been wearing her Cartographer's clothes, but she had changed back into normal drudgewear, and covered her face with her mask again.

When Erstwhile reached out to tug at another boy's arm, the other simply continued on his way without giving Erstwhile a glance.

"What's wrong?" hissed Neverfell.

"Us," Erstwhile whispered back. "Something's wrong with us. I don't know what it is. But everybody else does." He sounded shaken at finding himself rejected by the flow of his world. "Let's just get back to the crèche. Then I'll take a walk, talk to some people, and find out what's wrong."

Neverfell felt a throb of relief when she finally saw the door to the crèche ahead. She slipped in with Erstwhile a step behind her, hurried through into the main room, and faltered to a halt.

The room was crowded to the seams. Between the cots, from which the babies peered like peas from ragged pods, clustered dozens of adult drudges, lining every wall, squatting on tables, and perching on the craggy juts of the rough-cut wall. Delvers with broken nails, treadmill trudgers, bow-backed carriers, a hundred faces so still and grayed with dust that she might have been staring down a crowd of statues.

Neverfell heard a click behind her, and turned to find that the matron had bolted the door from the inside. Stepping forward, the matron yanked the mask from Neverfell's face. Neverfell froze, but did not duck or cower. It was too late for that. They knew. All of them knew.

It was only slightly reassuring to note that most of their unblinking, unwavering stares were fixed not on her but on Erstwhile.

"Did you think nobody would find out about her?" asked one of the men squatting on the milk trolley. Neverfell's gaze flew to the source of the voice but could not work out who had spoken. None of the drudges before her held themselves like a leader, nor did the silent crowd look to anybody for orders. It was as if the crowd had chosen one person to be its spokesperson, and had done so almost at random.

"I was just . . ." Erstwhile's sentence halted, looked around itself, and realized it had nowhere to go.

"This is the outsider." It was a woman who spoke this time, wan-haired and faded. "The one everybody wants. Last time she was loose down here, the Enquiry tore half of Drudgery apart looking for her. And now you've brought her back here."

"Listen!" Erstwhile was scratching for his last threads of courage. "We have to hide her. She knows things, about the Grand Steward's death, and . . ."

His words were lost in a murmur of consternation and disapproval, a soft sound more like a fading drum echo than the sound of human voices.

"The Grand Steward's death?" Another man, with a broken nose. "Worse and worse. This girl is only a danger to us. Unless we hand her over to the Enquiry, or the Council."

"No!" Neverfell and Erstwhile exclaimed at once.

"The Council will offer a bigger ransom," came a voice from the back of the room.

"And perhaps treat us better," suggested another. "Give us more eggs for our children."

"Listen, listen!" squawked Erstwhile. "It's not just the Grand Steward! The murderers who did for him killed drudges too!"

"It's true!" Neverfell pitched in. "The last 'rehearsals,' that was them. They were using a poison that drove people mad, and made them kill their loved ones."

The murmur of disapproval died completely, and was succeeded by an absolute silence. It crossed Neverfell's mind that if stares had a sound, these were the loudest stares she had ever heard. Erstwhile had won one victory at least. Everybody was now listening.

"It was Maxim Childersin," Erstwhile continued breathlessly. "The vintner. The leader of the Council. He did it all. And he'll get away with it too, unless we stop him. And with the help of Neverfell here, we *can* stop him. We've been finding out about things he's done. Crimes that will topple him. The Enquiry hates him—this is just the chance they'll want. They'll be drooling to hear it.

"We can't prove he killed the Grand Steward, but he's done more than that. He's had a secret tunnel built, running all the way to the overground, so he can smuggle in daylight." Erstwhile had recovered now and was building momentum. "An illegal tunnel. It's right there in his breakfast room. That breaks about a hundred laws, doesn't it? Neverfell found out about it."

"Then we give the girl to the Enquiry," rasped an old man with one eye. "She can tell them about the Grand Steward and the secret tunnel."

"What? No!" shouted Erstwhile. "The Enquiry's full of torturers and murderers! We can't hand her over to them!"

"If they hate Childersin so much, they'll need her alive," came the answer. "She'll be safe enough. What reason have they to keep *us* alive if we cross them?"

"It won't work!" cried Neverfell. "If I thought it would, I would have gone straight to the Enquiry, and taken my chances at the start! Do you think I like running around endangering everybody? Yes, if I actually could get a chance to speak at the Court's grand hearing, and tell everyone what *really* happened to the Grand Steward, maybe that would make a difference. They'd all see I was telling the truth. I can't lie.

"But I never would get a chance to speak! Master Childersin and his friends have spies and agents in the Enquiry. By now he must know that I know something, or I wouldn't have run away. So if I turn up in the hands of the Enquiry he'll have me killed in seconds."

"He can do that too," put in Erstwhile. "Neverfell nearly got murdered in an Enquirer cell, just because they thought she knew too much."

"We don't have any choice" was the answering growl. The murmur of the room became louder again, the tide of feeling almost visible like smoke.

"Listen!" exploded Neverfell. "It's not just about me and Master Childersin and the Enquiry! If you hand me over, don't you see what you'd be doing? It's true, I don't want to be murdered or tortured. But you shouldn't want to hand me over either. Didn't you hear what we said about the passage?

"There's a secret shaft to the overground. Maybe the first one for hundreds of years. The only other way to the surface is the main gate where the outsiders come to trade, and that one's locked and barred and guarded to the hilt, to make sure that nobody gets into Caverna and nobody leaves. If we tell the Enquiry about the hidden shaft, they'll tear in and seal it off forever, and that'll be the end of it. Don't you see? This is a chance that none of us will ever get again if we live to be a hundred. Which we won't. This tunnel—it's not just a way of getting daylight into Caverna. It's a way out."

The murmur began again, this time with an incredulous edge to it. Again Neverfell sensed the fear of the outdoors, the dread of the burning sun. Even Erstwhile was staring at her.

"I know, I know what you all think," she protested hastily, before the sound could grow too loud for her voice to rise above it. "I know what we've all been told about the world outside Caverna. But I don't think it's true. I lived out there once, for the first five years of my life. I can't remember much, but I can remember sunlight. And I don't feel scared when I think of it. I feel . . . I feel like it's something I'm meant to feel on my face. I feel like I've gone blind, and I'm remembering what it's like to have eyes." She faltered to a halt, losing confidence before so many stony, indifferent stares.

"Keep talking," Erstwhile muttered through the corner of his mouth.

"What?"

"Trust me. Keep talking. About the overground."

Neverfell could only assume that he had sensed something in the frozen crowd that she could not, but she took a deep breath and reached for the scattered stars of memory amid the blackness of her amnesia.

It was a stumbled, piecemeal explanation, nor could it be otherwise. She started with the bluebell-wood vision she had experienced after eating the Stackfalter Sturton, and tried to describe the way the blooms had crushed under her feet, the green teeth of the ferns. She tried to find words for the way the air moved crazily and made everything shiver as if it was alive, and made your face cold. She reached for a phrase that would show them dew, and the smell of moss. She failed.

"I don't have the words!" she wailed at last. "And I know that all around this mountain there's desert and baking heat—everybody knows that. But that's not all there is. You can cross the desert, the overgrounders do all the time, and then you get to other places. Places where the grapes come from. And the spices and the timber and the hay for the animals. And the birds, they . . . they're faster, and . . . so fast you almost can't see them. Just hear them. And the sky is a thousand times bigger than Caverna, a thousand thousand times.

"Oh, I can't show you!" The frustration was an ache. "She's got us, she's got us all. Caverna. She doesn't want to let us go. Do you know what she's like? A huge trap-lantern with us inside her, digesting us really, really slowly, and not wanting to let any of us go. Maybe that's the worst kind of prison—not knowing you're in a prison. Because then you don't fight to get out.

"And we should all be fighting to get out. All of us. We should be fighting to get all of *them* out." Neverfell waved a panicky hand at the ranks of silent babies. "None of us should be down here, and maybe if we weren't we wouldn't get bowleg and stoop-back and out of clock and everything else. Even though I can only remember tiny bits about the overground, every little bit of me has been tugging and yanking at me all these years to claw my way back to it. And if I thought that I couldn't ever see it again, I think I'd go mad."

Again Neverfell tailed off, wishing for once that she had the mind and tongue of a Childersin, with their easy grace and way with words. But she was just Neverfell, a bit mad and a little Cartographied to boot.

It was a moment or two before she realized that there was no murmur of contempt or disagreement, and nobody had stepped forward to grab her by the arms and drag her to the Enquiry.

There was a pause and then the drudges turned away and began a susurration of whispers. The same phrases were audible over and over.

". . . danger every moment she is here . . ."

". . . the children . . ."

". . . crossing the desert . . ."

". . . only chance . . ."

". . . risky . . ."

"What are they talking about?" Neverfell whispered to Erstwhile. "What's happening?"

"Shh!" Erstwhile hissed back, a little shakily. "We got them thinking, that's what's happening."

At last the room-wide whispers ceased, and the drudge crowd turned back to stare at Neverfell.

"How could we escape through this tunnel, even if we wanted to?" It was the crèche matron who spoke this time. "You say it runs from Childersin's private tunnels. How could we ever reach it?"

"I don't know yet, but there has to be a way." Everything was moving too fast. Neverfell's plan had not reached this far, and yet she surprised herself with a thrill of certainty. "Yes. I'll find a way."

"You have a day," came the answer, and this time Neverfell did not look to see who spoke. "You have until the hour of naught tomorrow to come up with a plan to reach the passage. If you cannot come up with one, we must take you to the Enquiry. I am sorry. The danger of hiding you is too great."

"I understand," answered Neverfell to everybody and nobody in particular. The thrill of certainty melted away like a fistful of ice crystals. Now there was just a clock face staring down her mind's eye.

Little more than twenty-five hours, and Neverfell could not think. It did not help that Erstwhile was with her pacing in small circles, his ideas describing even smaller circles. In the end his circles got so small he nearly tripped over his own ankles.

"You bought us some time back there, Nev, or your face did, anyway. The things you were saying were just a mad old jumble of nothing, but they weren't listening to you. They were *looking* at you. That's what swung them. They could see little snippets of what you remember of the overground. Like holes with light pouring through them. They're scared, though, and they mean what they say. If we can't come up with a plan by the hour of naught, they'll hand you over.

"You don't have a plan, do you?" he added, accusingly. "After all you said, about finding a way out. You don't have any idea how to do that, do you?"

"It's just a . . ." Neverfell flailed her hands, wondering how she could make him understand the mess of tiny bubble-plans frothing around in her head, failing to make one big usable plan. "Oh, I can't think!"

"There's nowhere left to run," Erstwhile growled. "Except the wild caves. But then we'd run out of food or be eaten by cave weasels. Wherever we go, they'll find us. But we got to run. We got to. We got a day to run."

"You don't have to," Neverfell said in a small voice.

"What?"

"If I can't come up with anything," Neverfell continued unsteadily, "you should turn me in to the Enquiry yourself. At least then you'll get the reward, and the rest of Drudgery won't hold it against you anymore for bringing me here."

"Shut up!" Erstwhile took a moment to raise his hands and pull his frog-Face the way Neverfell had taught him, to show he was really, really angry. "What's wrong with you, always looking to throw yourself on the nearest spike?"

"You're right." Neverfell clutched her head again. "Yes, you're right. Sorry, Erstwhile, I just can't think straight right now."

"Right now?" muttered Erstwhile under his breath.

Those two words, uttered in a sarcastic undertone, stopped Neverfell's mind in its tracks. She lost her train of thought and gave up on it, leaving it to steam away cross-country to some dark, uncharted canyon. She even stopped breathing for a moment.

I can't think straight. But why am I trying to do that anyway? Everybody else thinks straight. That's why nobody expects me to think zigzag-hop. Which is what I do naturally.

"Erstwhile," she said, catching at the tail end of a trailing thought and letting it pull her, "I need you to wear my mask for a bit."

"Your mask?"

"Yes. And my dress."

"*What?* I'm not doing that!"

"But that makes no sense! You've been risking your life for me left, right, and center; did you think I hadn't noticed? So how can it be worse to wear my dress? It's only for a few hours, long enough that the drudges trying to keep watch on me don't notice the real me sneaking off."

"Sneaking off? Where are you going?"

"To do something I can't do if I'm being watched. I don't quite have a plan, but I think now I sort of have a plan for how to make a plan for coming up with a plan. And I can't think about it too hard right now or it won't work. Please, trust me."

Erstwhile's hands twitched, and Neverfell guessed that he was thinking of putting his new angry Face on again.

"I better not have to look after those babies," he muttered.

Neverfell drifted out of the crèche with a tattered shawl wrapped around her head, her hair straggled over her face, her arms and bare feet thickly grimed. With luck she would look like just another drudge girl coming back from a visit to the crèche to peep in on an infant brother or sister. She could only hope that any lookouts left to watch for her would be lulled by the sight of a solitary figure in her uniform and mask sitting in the main crèche and surveying the sleeping babes.

She was listening out for one particular thing, and it was not long before she heard it.

"Cartographers!" A call of panic and warning.

Neverfell was standing in one of the wider thoroughfares,

supported by clusters of floor-to-ceiling pillars where stalagmites and stalactites had met and combined. As the cry went up, the river of drudges magically parted down the middle, everybody flattening themselves against the walls. A few seconds later, three whooping, leaping figures raced through, bouncing off the chalky-white pillars.

Once again, the Cartographers were on the move. Something had happened, changed, or appeared, calling them to it as irresistibly as a plug calls water. Even now, Cartographers all over Drudgery would be twitching, raising their heads to stare, feeling the pull, and passing on the word to one another.

Before the division down the middle of the passage could close up again and fill with people, Neverfell broke from the recoiling crowds and took off after the three figures. It did not matter what was calling to the Cartographers. What mattered was that it was probably calling to all of them.

Right now she dearly wanted to speak with the most elusive man in Caverna. She did not know where the Kleptomancer had made his new lair, but she knew that he was or had been a Cartographer. She could only hope that he would be drawn to these geographical peculiarities, like all other Cartographers in Drudgery.

Following the Cartographers was no easy matter, however. They scrambled willy-nilly, caring nothing for scratches, scrapes, and bruises from misjudged drops. They waded through chest-deep pools and slithered up and down shafts until Neverfell lost all sense of where she was.

At last they reached a rather dull-looking tunnel in rough-chiseled gray-brown rock, where they all stopped dead and simply stared upward.

Soaked and cold, Neverfell settled herself down in a dark

corner and tried not to let her teeth chatter too loudly. It was eerie watching them all staring rapt at nothing, pausing only to take notes, make chalk marks on the walls, and fiddle with machinery.

At nothing? From time to time she was tempted to let her gaze creep upward toward the object of their fascination, and every time she felt an odd little thrill of panic. *That's silly,* her mind told her firmly. *You don't have to look. There's just a low and lumpy ceiling. Nothing to see.*

Within minutes another Cartographer turned up, dragging an enormous metal spirit level that struck sparks off the rocky floor. Over the next hour Neverfell saw their numbers swell to nine. Then, one at a time, they seemed to lose interest, and wandered away without a word.

At last there was only one left, and with a sense of desperation Neverfell realized that he was packing up his easel and preparing to leave like his fellows. Taking courage in her hands and throwing caution to the winds, Neverfell ran after him and clutched at his sleeve.

"Excuse me—don't go! I'm looking for somebody. Another Cartographer." She was very much aware that there was no hourglass here, and no Erstwhile to twist her ears if she started to go Cartographic.

The man turned and looked down at her. He was not old, but his eyes had a drained, stained look, like used drinking glasses.

"Maybe you're looking for me. I *am* another Cartographer." There was an odd sort of breathy rattle in his voice, like a flute made of husks. "There are lots of Cartographers I'm not."

Neverfell pushed hastily on, before his comments had time to make sense. "No—it's a particular one. He's sort of a Cartographer and sort of not. About this tall, with a drudge face, though he might be wearing a big, armored—"

"Oh, you mean the Kleptomancer," answered the stranger promptly.

Neverfell was thrown by this. "You know him?"

"We all do. But I'm sorry, he's not a Cartographer. Not really. If you want 'another Cartographer,' you'll have to look somewhere else."

Neverfell had started to turn away when his words sank in properly.

"And . . . if I'm not looking for 'another Cartographer'? If I'm looking for the Kleptomancer instead?"

"Him?" The Cartographer gave a smile that might have suited him twenty years earlier, but now looked like a glint on a greasy knife. "Oh, he's up there."

He pointed directly upward at the ceiling, and Neverfell felt an unexpected surge of panic, hostility, and rage.

"You're lying! You're trying to trick me!" Her face went hot, and without knowing why, her voice rose sharply to a shriek. "It's a ceiling! It's just a ceiling! You want me to look at it so that I'll . . . I'll . . . I have to get out of here!" She gasped for air, astonished by her own outburst.

The Cartographer did not seem upset at all but stood there shaking with silent laughter. At last he rocked forward onto the balls of his feet and peered down into Neverfell's face.

"That," he whistled, "is just what your mind wants you to think. Look. Up."

With these words, he turned and walked away. And despite a thousand thoughts trying to haul back on the reins in panic, Neverfell slowly raised her head and looked up.

Her mind had lied when it had told her there was a ceiling directly above. There was not. She had not been walking along a low-roofed passage, but along the base of a narrow ravine some thirty feet high. Some ten or so feet above her head, she could see the folded forms of sleeping bats hanging in clusters from the juts and shelves of the ravine walls. Halfway up, something peculiar happened. There were more sleeping bats farther up the walls, but they were hanging upward from their perches, not downward.

Far above her, Neverfell could see the Kleptomancer. He was dressed in his drudge clothes, his face ill-lit but just visible. He was upside down, standing as easily on the ceiling as if it had been a floor. In his arms he held a bizarre metallic bow with half a dozen levers, and he was leveling it directly at her head.

"Who are you?" he asked. There was no mistaking his still-water voice. Today, Neverfell thought the waters might have piranhas in them.

Neverfell remembered her disguise, and hastened to push back her hair to show her face. "It's me! You remember me? My hair used to be red." A moment later she remembered that the last time he had seen her she had been fleeing his lair in a stolen suit, shortly before cutting his wire and stranding him. "Don't shoot! We need to talk!"

"The outsider girl," breathed the Kleptomancer. "The one everybody talks about. The food taster. The fugitive. How do you know who I am?" His posture did not relax a jot; indeed, he seemed to be cranking one of the handles on his bow.

"You stole me from the Grand Steward after his challenge—don't you remember?"

The cranking stopped, the Kleptomancer's hand hovering on the handle irresolutely.

"You're the item I stole from the Cabinet of Curiosities?" He sounded surprised, confused, and suspicious. "But you're not a cameleopard!"

"No." Neverfell was not sure what else to say. "Er . . . no, I'm not?" Too late it occurred to her that, with his continual memory wipes, the Kleptomancer might not remember their first encounter.

"Hmm. That . . . would explain how you escaped my hideout, wired across the river, and ran away. I was rather confused by that when I read my notes. So. Why have you come after me?"

Neverfell could just make out the very point of the crossbow bolt, gleaming like a star. *If that star disappears,* she thought, *that means he has fired and I'm dead. I wonder if I'll have time to notice it's gone before I'm gone too.*

"Because I need help, and you're probably the cleverest person I've ever met," she answered, her heart flip-flopping like a landed fish. "You were the one who explained everything to me—that people who plan really well can't cope with people like you and me, the ones who do things that make no sense. They have to stamp us out or control us, or they'd always be worrying about us doing something weird, something they don't see coming.

"The Enquiry and the Council are both really scared of the way you can turn up wherever you like, only right now they're too busy fighting each other to chase you down. But if I die or get captured, then one of them gets an advantage over the other one. Which means that soon their war would be over, and the winner would be able to go after you.

"And I think that's why you haven't shot me yet. Because the longer I'm running around alive and free, the longer everybody else is distracted. In fact, I think maybe you won't shoot me at all."

The Kleptomancer hesitated, then flicked a few levers so that the bow's tension released with a hiss. He attached it to a hook on his belt, from which it hung upward. Then he took a large coil of rope from round his arm, tied one end to a spike of rock in the wall, and started trying to throw the coil toward Neverfell. The first couple of times the coil of rope descended only part of the way before falling back up to land on the ceiling at the Kleptomancer's feet. The third time it reached down to the midway point and kept falling, tumbling loose so that its end brushed the ground just in front of Neverfell.

"Tie it tight," called the thief. Neverfell knotted it securely around an outcrop, and started to climb.

Clambering up the rope was an eerie experience. When she reached the midpoint she was no longer hauling herself upward; she was abruptly tumbling headfirst. Fortunately the Kleptomancer caught her before she concussed herself, and lowered her to the stone ceiling that was now suddenly a floor. She disentangled her limbs and struggled into a sitting position, to find the Kleptomancer staring at her unnervingly.

"I stole you," he said speculatively. "Was it just the once?"

"I think so. Why?"

"Hmm. Did you used to be smaller? About so high?" He held out his hand three and a half feet above what now appeared to be the ground.

"Er . . . yes? Um . . . some years ago?" Neverfell was not sure what more to say. "That's . . . normal, isn't it? People getting bigger?"

"Yes, I suppose so." The Kleptomancer seemed to be peering through her, trying to bring something into focus, then he shook his head and gave it up. "Never mind. What matters is that until recently you were Childersin's pawn. Part of his plan to poison the Grand Steward. And now you've run from him. I suppose you are hoping I will hide you?"

"Oh no! I want you to help me topple Master Childersin, break hundreds of laws, and save as many people as will trust me." Perhaps it was just a fit of Cartography, or the effect of falling through an up-down glitch, but Neverfell found herself grinning like a lunatic. "I'm not just asking for help. I'm offering you the biggest distraction Caverna has ever seen."

"Topple Childersin? You?" It might have been Neverfell's imagination, but she thought she caught a touch of amusement amid the incredulity. "You could not topple a tower of scones before somebody stopped you. Your face betrays you at every step—"

"You know, that's a really beautiful bow," Neverfell interrupted suddenly. "Did you make it?"

"Found it, mended it, modified it" was the curt reply.

"I love machines." Neverfell's rational mind told her that she was babbling and should shut up, but it had also lied to her about there being a ceiling, so she decided to ignore it. "Everybody keeps telling me that my big talent is having a face like glass. But that's not a talent, is it? It's the opposite. It's something I can't stop doing. I leak my thoughts. Everybody can see what I'm planning.

"No, what I'm really good at is *machines*. A machine is sort of like magic. You spend ages planning it out, and put all the cogs in place, and then *bing!* You pull a lever, and away it goes. And the amazing bit is that the person who pulls the lever to start it doesn't need to understand how it works. *They don't even need to know what's going to happen.*

"I want to put together a plan just like that machine. And that's *your* sort of plan, isn't it? That's why I'm here."

There was a long and meaningful pause before the Kleptomancer spoke again.

"Do you know what the date and hour is right now?"

"Why?" Neverfell stared at him perplexed.

"You'll need to make a note of it," said the thief. "We are about to have a very important conversation, and later you will want to know exactly—*exactly*—when it started."

Here is a piece that falls between the chapters,
like a coin between paving stones.
It is a slice of silence in the middle of the melody.
It is a rough and ragged spot,
like the frill of stubs where pages have been torn out.
There is no point in looking for them.
They are gone.

TRUST YOURSELF

". . . TAKING EFFECT?"

A hand was waved in front of Neverfell's face. She blinked hard, startled by the blurred collage of light and looming faces. Reflexively she reached up to bat away a lantern that was almost touching her cheek. Stony faces regarded her without a smile or flicker, the lanternlight picking out their chipped teeth, the pockmarks on their skin, the pale ticks and squiggles of scars. Hands gripped her shoulders and arms, holding her still.

"Who are you?" she whispered. They glanced at each other, their faces shifting not a hair. *Drudges,* she thought. *They're all drudges. But who are they?*

And where am I? How did I get here? The last thing I remember is talking to the Kleptomancer . . .

"They're here already!" somebody was screaming. There was a terrible battering sound from somewhere nearby, and bellows demanding admittance.

"We have to go," snapped a man who was holding her by the collar. "Now!" Half a dozen hands abruptly released her, so that she almost lost her balance, and her strange captors sprinted as one to a small door on the opposite wall. They vanished into it, a couple of them casting glances over their shoulder at Neverfell as they departed, then slammed the door behind them. Neverfell could hear four or five bolts being thrown.

Before she could react to this, a larger door a few yards away from her suddenly burst open, and the room filled with armed men. Neverfell backed away, almost tripping over a stool, but there was nowhere to flee or hide.

"There!" The leader of the new arrivals seized her by the arm, and held up his lantern next to her face. "Yes, look! It's her. We've found her. At last. Secure the area! See if you can find the others! Break down that door over there, and see where it goes."

"What's she got in her hand?"

Neverfell stared down and noticed that she was gripping a tiny wooden cup, the inside stained dark. There was a dusky taste in Neverfell's mouth as well that seemed familiar.

The cup was snatched from her grasp, turned over, sniffed. "Damn it! She's drunk something. Let's get her to a physician quickly in case it's poison. Childersin will have our hides if he loses her to death just when he needs her."

Childersin. That word was enough to penetrate her stupor. These men worked for Childersin. She had been captured by Childersin's men. Stunned by this realization, she heard tidbits of the conversation around her.

"Looks like they cleaned out, took everything. I guess they gave up and abandoned her at the end."

"All right, everybody out! The rest don't matter. We've got what we came for."

There was a sword in every hand. There was nowhere to run. She was grabbed under the armpits and dragged out of the room down passage after passage.

Why am I here? Neverfell tried to remember but slid off a sleek blankness in her memory, like a cat failing to scale a wall of polished marble. Her hands were grimier than she had ever seen them, their nails broken, the skin covered with nicks and scars she could not recollect. Her hair was still dyed black, but now it almost reached down to her waist. There was a tangled bracelet of twine around one wrist.

"Quick! Get her out of here. The Enquiry are coming. The last thing we want is them trying to grab her from us. Go!"

The group burst out onto a Drudgery thoroughfare, and Neverfell made a belated and doomed attempt to break free. She felt sick and unsteady. When she closed her eyes to blink, she could see purple spirals rising and rising against the darkness of her eyelids.

Without ceremony, she was bundled into a closed sedan, not unlike those used to transport Cartographers. She heard locks turn and chains jingle, and the door resisted her attempts to barge it with her shoulder.

I was talking to the Kleptomancer, Neverfell thought desperately. She could recall only the first half of the conversation, after which her memories simply faded out. Even the part she could remember felt strange and flat. She could recollect everything she had said and done, but not her reasons.

I had the start of a plan—I know I did. That's why I went running off to find the Kleptomancer. And I was trying really hard not to think about it . . . and now I don't know what it was.

What was the plan? And how did it go this badly wrong?

"Hey!" She thumped the inside walls of the sedan. "Hey! Call the Enquiry! It's Neverfell! I'm in here!" Her voice sounded hoarse and rough, and she doubted anybody heard. Although she knew that if she fell into the hands of the Enquiry things would probably not go well for her, she was suddenly gripped by a wild desire to stop Maxim Childersin from winning, by any means necessary. But nobody answered.

It was a hasty ride, and she was jolted so badly that she probably would have thrown up if there had been anything in her stomach. At last the door opened, and she was pulled out into a crisp white room. The friezes looked familiar, and she guessed that she was probably somewhere in the palace.

Here she was pulled about by panicky physicians, who examined her eyes, tongue, and ears, and tutted over the flea bites on her skin, before poking her gently with needles to make sure she could feel them. They gave her emetics that made her retch hopelessly, then forced water into her mouth through a funnel, so that she ended up spluttering, with her clothing drenched.

When she finally recovered her breath, she realized that there was another figure in the room, watching discreetly from a chair by the wall. She wiped the water from her face, pushed back her hair, and defiantly tried to straighten, so that she was less of a crushed, grubby wreck. The time for trying to hide her face was over. She was tired of games.

"I'm very glad to see you, Neverfell," said Maxim Childersin. He was wearing a silvery, high-collared coat that glittered and made Neverfell think of the Grand Steward. "I never would have guessed that you would lead us such a merry chase. It has to be said that Drudgery was *not* my first guess for your hiding place."

"How did you find me?" croaked Neverfell.

"Ah." Maxim Childersin reached into his pocket, and pulled out a few letters. "That is rather easily answered." He unfolded one of them and held it up for her to see. The writing was a charcoal scrawl, but was unmistakably in Neverfell's own hand.

Neverfell's eye strayed to the top of the page, and her heart plummeted into a well that had no bottom.

Dear Zouelle, began the letter, *If you are really in that much danger, of course you must flee and hide with us. Read this letter carefully and burn it afterward. I am hiding out in the storeroom of the grub-grinding mill in the Flotsam district . . .*

Neverfell could not remember writing the letter, but it was definitely in her own handwriting.

"Loyalty," Maxim Childersin said quietly. "It always was your greatest weakness. And your strange compulsion to trust your friends, over and over again." He folded the letter and put it away. "But you must understand that Zouelle is also loyal, and at the end of the day her loyalty to her family will always win out."

He's lying, thought Neverfell desperately. *I don't believe it. Zouelle didn't trick me into telling her where I was so she could betray me to him. He stole the letters. It's a lie.*

Maxim Childersin watched her face, his impassivity colored by a hint of sympathy. *But,* thought Neverfell suddenly, *why should she think that sympathy was real? It was just another lie, something he had put on like a hat.*

"I'm sorry," he said, and sounded as if he meant it. "But as Zouelle's friend you should at least be happy that she made the right decision in terms of her own career. I have now officially named her as my heir." The little smiles came and went in his mouth, like moray eels peering out from a crack in search of prey. "It must be some consolation, though, that Master Grandible remained loyal to you till the end."

"The . . . the end?" whispered Neverfell.

"Yes. I suppose you know that he did everything in his power to make everybody think that you were hiding in his tunnels? I daresay he must have been trying to protect you by drawing attention away from you. He held out against the Enquiry's forces far longer than anybody expected, and even when they finally broke in he refused to be taken alive. We don't know which combination of cheeses he used to blow up the support pillars and collapse his own tunnels." He sighed. "The Enquiry is still digging through the rubble."

Neverfell felt her throat tighten, and her hands close into fists. *I tried so hard to protect Master Grandible, but I still brought destruction on him after all . . .*

"Ah." Master Childersin glanced at the clock. "I fear I cannot stay to talk for long. After all, we both have less than an hour to prepare for the grand hearing, do we not?"

"What?"

Neverfell could only think of one hearing Maxim Childersin could mean, and that was the hearing to decide once and for all whether the Grand Steward's death had been foul play. *But the hearing's two months away—it can't be today. Because if it is today . . . I've lost two months. Forgotten them completely.*

"I was genuinely worried, you know. I thought you might actually succeed in evading me until after the hearing was over. But it seems you were let down by your allies. Your huddle of drudge friends abandoned you at the last moment, didn't they?"

Neverfell gritted her teeth. *Erstwhile wouldn't abandon me. What happened to him? Please don't let anything have happened to him . . .*

"I wish we had more time to talk," Childersin was continuing. "There are lots of things I would love to know. *Was* it you who was trying to order several dozen pairs of smoked glasses, the tripod, the spirit level, the crossbow, and all that rope? And is it true that you were seen talking to the Kleptomancer? They . . . found his body at last. I expect you heard about that."

Neverfell felt herself blanch and start shaking.

"Ah. It would seem you had not. So you really did manage to ally with him? I must say I'm impressed. If it makes you feel any better, I am having him embalmed and placed in the Cabinet of Curiosities. A master of his talents deserves no less."

"You wouldn't dare let me testify." Neverfell felt calm, warm, and full of light. She was very, very angry, and her fears melted away like wool in a furnace. "Not now."

"Oh yes, I would. Why not? You will walk into that hall before the entire Court and you will tell them—with all the conviction of sincerity—that there is no way you could possibly have consumed an antidote while working as a taster for the Grand Steward. You will tell them you ate and drank nothing at Madame Appeline's, and that nobody could have dosed you during your sleep because you had locked the guest-room door from the inside. You will confirm everything I have been saying all this time."

"So you're going to Wine me, aren't you?" Neverfell said flatly. After all her struggles to defend her memory, the inevitability felt particularly cruel.

"Yes. I am afraid I must. You will forget everything that has happened since the day of the Grand Steward's death. We will need a story to explain such extensive amnesia, of course. Let me see . . . no doubt the kidnappers who have been holding you for the last two months must have decided to wipe your memories of your captivity, so that you could not identify them, but underestimated the strength of the Wine they forced on you. When you were rescued, you were in a state of shock, so that you only came to your senses just before the hearing . . . Does that not sound plausible?"

It did. Neverfell swallowed drily.

"To tell the truth," continued Childersin, "I am reluctant to do this. Over a relatively short period you seem to have developed into rather an interesting and formidable young person. The Wine is being brought over now, and after you drink it you will go back to being sweet, trusting, helpless . . . Well, you remember how you were. The person you are now will cease to exist. So I wanted to drop by one last time, just to say good-bye." He smiled sadly and turned to leave.

"I see." Neverfell's chest felt tight. "Master Childersin?"

Childersin paused mid-stride on his way to the door, gloves draped over his hand.

"What is it, Neverfell?"

"You won't win, Master Childersin. I won't let you."

"You don't have a plan," Childersin said very gently. "You don't have any allies. You don't have your freedom. And very soon you won't even remember why you might want to cause trouble for me anyway."

"I am going to stop you, though." Neverfell felt heat rising from her chest to her face, and with it a wash of strange strength. "I will, somehow. Look at me, Master Childersin. Look in my face and tell me I'm bluffing."

Childersin looked at her for a long moment. He did not tell her she was bluffing. He did not tell her anything. In the end he shook his head slightly, and left without a single word.

After Childersin and the physicians had departed, a group of female servants in Childersin livery entered, bearing a ceramic bath, buckets of soft water, and crumbly cakes of soap wrapped in pink leaves. Neverfell watched them peel off her clothes with an odd sense of distance. It was so much like her first arrival at the Childersin household, and so different. Back then she had felt as if she were being rescued. Now she saw exactly what was happening. The Childersin family were cleaning and polishing a tool. Soon they would wash her memory as well, and there she would be, innocent, doe-eyed, and grateful to all of them.

The Childersin maids were not meeting her eye, she noticed. Whenever their gaze touched her face by chance, they physically flinched and looked away. She could only assume that her face was currently too painful to look at, just as it had been when she was first thrown into an Enquiry cell.

So busy was she with such hollow thoughts that she almost did not notice the twist of paper. It was woven into a thin plait that was half-hidden by the dank rats' tails of her hair. When a comb was hastily dragged through her tresses, the twist pulled free and fell to the floor. Glancing down at it, Neverfell made out grayish streaks and shapes on it that looked slightly like letters.

Nobody else had seen it. She covered it quickly with her heel, and then when she was sure that no one was looking, discreetly nudged it behind one foot of the bath.

"Come on, my dear." Neverfell was guided into the bath, where she was scrubbed and soaped, and dye washed from her hair until the water ran purple. All the while her mind kept straying to the twist of paper, and expecting somebody to notice it, exclaim in surprise, stoop to pick it up. She could only be grateful that the servants were so squeamish about looking at her face. One good glance would have shown them that she was hiding something.

When they helped her out and toweled her, she pretended to stoop and scratch her toe, scooped up the twist, and hid it in her hand.

Only when she had been dried, dressed, and combed was she allowed a fleeting moment alone. With shaking hands she untwisted the graying fragment, and held it close to a lantern to make out the few faint words scrawled on it.

Everything will be fine. Trust yourself.

The handwriting was her own.

It soon became clear that Neverfell would have no more moments alone. Dressed in a green dress and green satin shoes once again, she was walked firmly back to the sedan and locked inside it once more. As it bounced along, she sat twisting and untwisting the little message.

Everything will be fine. Trust yourself.

What did it mean? How could everything be fine? Trust herself to do what?

Neverfell ran through scenario after scenario in her head. The Childersins were going to give her Wine. Perhaps she could knock it out of somebody's hand, or spit it out, or make herself throw up before it could eat her memories.

The sedan stopped. "Ah, there you are, miss. She's inside."

Neverfell heard the locks unfastened, and as the door opened a crack she threw herself against it, hoping to burst it open and make a bid for freedom. The guards outside, however, seemed to be ready for such a move and seized her, wrestling her to a standstill, her kicks made useless by the satin shoes. Her wild glares alighted immediately upon the girl standing a few yards away from her.

Looking into the face of Zouelle Childersin, Neverfell felt her faith crumble. There was no pity there, no pallor, no sign of conflict at all, only the small, confidential smile that always suited the blonde girl so well. There was a small corked vial in her hand.

"You'll need to hold her mouth open," said Zouelle. "And keep her steady. We don't want drops of Wine on the green silk."

Neverfell was pinned to the side of the sedan, and her nose pinched shut to force her to open her mouth. Zouelle stepped over, carefully and daintily. Her dress was made of the same silvery fabric that her uncle had worn.

"I'm sorry," said Zouelle. She did not sound sorry. The words were just cold, melodic noises, like the notes from a glockenspiel. "But you'll forgive me, you know. In just a few minutes you won't blame me at all."

Neverfell tried to struggle as the Wine was poured onto the back of her tongue, but her mouth was held shut until she had no choice but to swallow.

Back in the sedan Neverfell doubled up, spluttering, knowing it was too late to spit out the Wine. Its taste was opening and spreading on her tongue like a hundred water lilies. She could feel it blowing like sparks across her memories, and feared every moment to feel them burning away.

"Name!" A barked demand from outside.

"The food taster Neverfell, due to testify . . ."

"Ah, the taster! She's due in there now; the proceedings have been halted to wait for her arrival. Quick, through there!"

Don't forget, Neverfell willed herself as the sedan lurched into a jog. *Don't forget. Maxim Childersin killed the Grand Steward. Remember it. Remember it.*

The door was flung open, and a couple of attendants in palace white leaned forward and plucked her out of the sedan, hurrying her along a grand hallway so that her feet barely touched the ground.

Just hold on a little longer, Neverfell begged herself. *Just long enough to tell everybody the truth.*

Mahogany doors ahead were swept open by eager hands, and she was half led, half carried into the vast Hall of the Gentles. It was brighter than on her previous visit, and she could see it more clearly. It was shaped like an amphitheater, with stepped seating sloping up on all sides. She was at the lowest and most focal point, standing on a small, brightly lit stone dais, with a wooden rail all around her that made her feel caged.

It seemed to her dazzled mind that the entire Court had turned up to watch her. A sea of Faces surrounded her, half-hidden by raised binoculars or opera glasses. There was a faint scent that she recognized as the smell of singed Paprickle. Evidently those toward the back of the vast hall were using the ear-enhancing spice to avoid missing a word.

Her hands shook as she leaned against the rail, and her vision misted. There was a burning sensation in her head. She clenched her eyes shut, but there was nothing she could do to hold out against it. The Wine took effect, and something in her mind was peeled away.

When she opened her eyes again, everything looked different to her. Suddenly there were no purple spirals, no conflicts, no doubts. She slowly relaxed her death grip on the rail and looked around her. To the left, on a black iron platform adorned with briars, stood Enquirer Treble, her face still bulldoggish but her hair now startlingly white. A matching platform on Neverfell's right supported Maxim Childersin in his silver coat. Looking out across the lavishly dressed assembly, Neverfell could make out a patch of burgundy, doubtless the Childersin family attending en masse.

"Neverfell the outsider," intoned the Enquirer. "Are you ready to testify?"

"Yes," said Neverfell. "I'm ready now."

"Very well." The Enquirer raised herself up and leaned forward, everything in her bearing designed to let the witness know that her story was about to undergo trial by fire and bombardment. "Two months ago, you gave a statement to the Enquiry. You told them that while working as a taster for the Grand Steward you could not possibly have been fed a poison antidote. Correct?"

"Yes."

"Now, my first question is—"

"Yes," Neverfell interrupted, "I did say that. But I was wrong."

The murmur of confusion rose to a roar within seconds. At the back of the amphitheater, Neverfell could see the various courtiers who had taken Paprickle clutching their ears in pain as the noise levels increased to unexpected levels.

"What?" exclaimed Treble, in astonished tones.

"I was tricked. By Maxim Childersin and Madame Appeline. I found out afterward what they had done, which is why I ran away, because I knew I couldn't hide from them how much I knew."

Maxim Childersin's Face of kindly encouragement had frozen there and been forgotten. He turned his head to peer off toward his seated family, and Neverfell guessed that he was scanning their ranks for Zouelle. Neverfell, however, was quite sure that he would look in vain for the distinctive blonde plait and silver dress. Zouelle would have made herself scarce within minutes of delivering the all-important Wine.

Neverfell's heart was beating so hard she could hear its velvety thump, and yet she had never felt so strong, so serene. Her memories were sparking red and gold where the Wine's influence had touched them, but they were not burning away; they were flaring back into life. She was not forgetting. She was remembering.

· · · · ·

A recollection opened before her like a flower. It was a memory of a conversation with Zouelle, held a few weeks before in a closed sedan.

"*So you really want to go ahead with this?*" *Zouelle fretting at her own gloves, white-faced.* "*Letting Uncle Maxim catch you?*"

"*It's the only way. If I want to speak to everybody in the Court all at once, it has to be at the hearing. And if I want to reach the hearing alive, it has to be because your uncle thinks I'm there to testify for him. And since we can't let him get wind of our plan that means I can't afford to know about it myself, or he'll read my face. I have to blank out two months of my memories, at least for a while.*"

Zouelle sighed. "*All right. I'll do my part. Uncle Maxim thinks I'm working on a Wine to make you forget you ever suspected him, so that he can give it to you when he catches you. I should be able to switch it for a reprise Wine at the last moment, something to bring back the memories you need to testify. Timing will be important, though. We only want you remembering the plan just before you testify. So you can't afford to get captured until the very last moment.*"

"*Thank you, Zouelle.*" *Pause.* "*I'm sorry . . . I'm sorry if I say anything cruel to you while my memories are missing. I'll probably think you betrayed me to your uncle.*"

"*Neverfell?*" *Zouelle asked in a small voice.* "*How do you know I won't?*"

Shrug. "*I just do.*"

I still don't have all my memories, thought Neverfell. *But I'm sure there's a reason for that. I trust myself.*

And I know exactly what I have to say next.

CATS AND PIGEONS

HARDENED VETERAN THOUGH SHE WAS, IT TOOK Enquirer Treble three whole seconds to struggle through her sense of shock. Ever since the death of the Grand Steward she had been facing setback after setback. A "set-forward" of this magnitude left her reeling.

She could never be sure what Maxim Childersin's plan was. However, she was about a thousand percent certain that this latest development was not part of it.

"Halt these proceedings!" he was shouting. "This child clearly believes what she is saying, but her mind has suffered—her recent ordeal in the hands of drudge kidnappers . . ." Treble saw one of his hands creep up to adjust one of his buttons, and her presence of mind returned to her in a rush. Perhaps it was a harmless gesture, but more likely a signal to some assassin to end the child's life before she could say more. His tool had turned against him and would cut him if it was not cast away.

Treble tapped twice at the balustrade, giving a signal of her own. She had arranged certain precautions to protect the witnesses. Now she would probably find out whether they had been enough.

"Let the witness speak!"

". . . but I didn't really guess until Borcas, one of Madame Appeline's Putty Girls, came to find me and told me that she had found my thimble somewhere else in the tunnels. And then the shoes thing just confirmed it. And then when I ran away and started investigating . . ."

Neverfell was speaking fast, trying to ignore the way that Childersin and Treble from time to time made small, seemingly meaningless motions of their hands. She guessed all too well the nature of their silent battle.

She flinched as a vicious-looking feral wasp appeared before her face, sting curved to attack. A second later a large bat swooped before her with the grace of a pendulum's swing. After its passing, the wasp had gone.

Treble gestured again, and somewhere in the heart of the audience there was a wooden thunk, followed by a thin and plaintive scream.

"Continue," snapped Treble.

"Well, I've actually found out quite a lot over the last couple of months," Neverfell went on, as memory after memory opened in her mind like books. "The hardest part was tracking down samples of the poison. It was tried out on some drudges, who ran off and killed their loved ones, but of course they died or were executed and nobody kept the bodies. But, as it turned out, the poisoners threw away some of their leftover samples down the nearest waste chute, so we just had to find a place among the waste heaps where all the rats were killing each other. We've saved you some of the killer rats, Enquirer, though they're a bit dead. But you might still find some of the poison in them.

"There's more, though." Neverfell took a deep breath and

launched into her last assault, even as a poison dart whistled past her ear. "I know the Childersin secret. The reason his family are growing up taller, stronger, cleverer, and never out of clock. Master Childersin has been giving them something magical and special, something he had to smuggle down from the overground. And he didn't tell anybody, so his family would have an advantage over everybody else. He even killed people to keep his secret.

"The Childersins have been dosing on it for seven years, getting bigger and better and brighter, while everybody else gets paler and duller and further out of clock. It's the Childersins' secret golden medicine, and they want it all to themselves."

The confusion in the audience was escalating into uproar. News of the Grand Steward's assassination had shocked them, and set them desperately rethinking their alliances. But this revelation was a different matter, arousing their personal wrath, envy, and outrage. There was a treasure that had been hidden from them, something that could have been theirs. The burgundy patch that was the Childersins had now formed a neat spearhead, driving its way toward the nearest exit, while beleaguered on all sides.

"This court is in disorder! I demand a recess!" shouted Childersin, and before anybody could react, he marched out, slamming the door behind him.

"Guards!" Treble bellowed. "After him! Detain him!" She turned back to Neverfell. "Tell me of this smuggled medicine. Where is it?"

"I'm afraid I can't tell you that," Neverfell declared meekly. "And that's not what you should be worrying about right now anyway, Enquirer. You see, there's about to be a lot of chaos . . ."

Another recollection unfolded before Neverfell.

She was sitting next to the Kleptomancer on a narrow ledge

over a dark abyss, while bats whirled around them like tea leaves
in a stirred cup.

"You know a lot about the Court, don't you?" she asked.
"Secrets you found out through stealing things and watching the
ants scurry. People's schemes and plans."

"What is it you need to know?" responded the Kleptomancer.

"Lots of things. And it doesn't matter what they are, as long as
nobody is supposed to know them. We need a big distraction, don't
we? Lots of chaos. We want the Court too busy squabbling to stop
us. So I guess I want to take lots of cats and throw them in among
as many pigeons as possible."

The Kleptomancer was unreadable, but Neverfell thought that
somewhere inside he might be smiling. "Cats," he murmured.
"Yes, I think I can manage cats."

". . . because right now the Lossbegoss family are planning to
murder the Quelts by sneaking poison into their soap," Neverfell
explained enthusiastically, "and the Quelts are too busy to notice
because they're preparing to invade the Brittlecrag district,
which isn't really full of diamond seams the way people say,
because that's just a lie put about by the Tarquin Alliance. Oh,
and there's probably going to be a huge battle between all the
unguent makers as soon as they find out where old man Tobias
really hid his huge stores of Millennia Oils just before he died.
Um, they're inside the great clock at the Chiselpick Crosspath,
by the way . . ."

Uproar had escalated into anarchy. All truce had dissolved.

"Order!" shouted Treble. "You, girl—this evidence is not relevant
to the case! The medicine! Tell me about this illegal medicine!"

"I'm sorry, Enquirer, but I can't. And I'm pretty sure I've said
everything I came here to say."

"You are hardly in a position to hold out on us, girl!"

"Enquirer," Neverfell said slowly, "do you really think I would have walked into this court if I didn't have a way of getting out again?"

"What? What way?"

"I don't know." Neverfell gave Enquirer Treble an enormous smile, as bright and mad as a sun soufflé. "Do you like surprises, Enquirer? I do. Just as well, really."

It is fair to say that what happened after that was a surprise to everybody in the courtroom, including Neverfell.

Somewhere high above in the shadowy, stalactite-fanged ceiling, a trapdoor flipped open, revealing a darkened hatch. From this darkness a coil of wire whispered down, unraveling and unraveling as it fell, until the bottom end brushed the dais on which Neverfell stood. Then with a singing, metallic whine, a stocky figure in a gleaming metal suit and goggled mask dropped out of the trap and slid down the wire, to land with a jolt beside Neverfell.

"Seize . . ." began Treble.

A metal-scaled arm was thrown around Neverfell's middle. An armored hand flicked two belt levers.

". . . that . . ."

With a lurch, Neverfell was dragged aloft as the armored figure whizzed back up the wire, carrying her with it, the whine of the mechanism rising to a screech. The dais dropped away, and she was staring down at a receding sea of frozen, upturned faces.

". . . girl!" finished the Enquirer in a deafening yell as both soaring figures disappeared upward through the hatch. The court vanished from Neverfell's view as the trapdoor flapped shut.

Neverfell found herself in a cramped, musty passage, filled

with dusty, criss-cross timbers. Her sudden rescuer released his crushing grip around her middle, and unfastened his belt clip from the wire.

"It's you!" Neverfell squeaked as she recovered her breath. "Is it you?"

"What answer are you expecting?" The voice that echoed from inside the goggled mask was muffled and reverberating, but unmistakably that of the Kleptomancer.

"You're alive!"

"You say a lot of pointless things."

"Where are we?"

"A passage built by the Grand Steward." A soft voice by Neverfell's ear made her jump and look around. There were three palace servants close by, one of whom was bolting the trapdoor. "As we told you before, he set up many precautions—including a secret escape route from the Hall of the Gentles should he ever be overthrown and find himself on trial for his life."

"I can't stay." The Kleptomancer stepped forward, and shook Neverfell by the hand. "Everything is happening according to schedule. If I am to take full advantage of the distraction you have given me, I need to leave now and attend to *my* plan. Good luck with the rebellion!"

"Er . . . thank . . . thank you," whispered Neverfell. Then as the Kleptomancer vaulted over the nearest beam and sprinted away into the darkness his words penetrated. "Wait—rebellion? What rebellion?"

"Explanations take time," murmured the nearest servant. "You had better drink this."

Neverfell was passed a tiny corked bottle of smoky, churning Wine. There was a label in her handwriting.

"Don't worry. Drink me."

She downed it, and for a moment the world convulsed. Then new memories came out like the stars.

"O-o-o-o-oh. *That* rebellion."

Enquirer Treble stormed back toward her headquarters in the palace, flanked by two purple-clad bodyguards. As far as she could tell, she was the only person trying to work out what was happening and make it stop.

After the startling disappearance of Neverfell, the Hall of the Gentles had emptied in no time flat. All the different factions and families had surged out, some to escape the anger of their peers, some to pursue those fleeing, some no doubt to seize what advantage they could during the confusion, some to follow private vendettas, and some to hide until the whole thing was over.

Neverfell's string of revelations had caused more chaos than if she had hurled a dozen bombs into the listening assembly. Such words coming from anybody else could not have had the same power, of course, but everybody looking at the girl's face had known that she was telling the truth . . .

"She did it on purpose," hissed Treble. "I know she did. But why? Why expose Childersin, and then cause so much chaos that we cannot pursue him properly? I know him. Even now he will be looking to turn all this to his advantage. Men—be alert. He will probably try to have me assassinated any moment n—"

Enquirer Treble had a good set of instincts. Two faint, metallic scraping sounds caught her ear, one to her left and one to her right, and before her mind had even registered them as the sound of drawing swords she had already flung herself to the ground. Looking up, she saw that her two bodyguards had managed to impale each other while stabbing at the place she had been a moment before. They crumpled to the ground, one even managing a surprised Face before he expired.

"Not *again,*" snarled Treble as she clambered to her feet. "Core of the earth! Is there anybody working for me who is actually working for me?"

She strode on alone, dabbing a touch of Perfume behind her ears and on her wrists as she went. This was not one of the soft, serpentine scents that many in the Court used. This was a Perfume meant to terrify, to subdue.

Out of my way. I am Death in purple. I look through you, and see the lies squirming in your heart like worms in an apple.

"Enquirer Treble!" Another Enquirer sprinted to meet her, and showed signs of panic as he came within range of her Perfume.

"What is it, Mellows?"

"It's the drudges!" faltered the new arrival.

"The drudges? What about them?"

"They're rising. Hundreds of them, surging up out of the Undercity. They've overrun Pale Point, Gammet's Groove, Whichways, and the Squirms. Last seen, they were making for Spoons . . ."

"They're heading for the palace," muttered Treble. "So that's it—that's why that girl set us all at one another's throats! She wanted us distracted, to give that stinking rabble a chance to rise up against us. Secure the palace! And all the stores! They must not capture any True Delicacies, or they will be the very devil to subdue." Pursuing Childersin would have to wait.

She reached the palace, only to receive abundant confirmation of the news. The long-docile, patient, phlegmatic drudges were rising, boiling out of cracks and chutes like so much dirty water. Treble tore around the palace, terrifying all the courtiers and guards she could find into common sense and unity, forcing them to ready themselves for siege.

However, there was worse news. The water pipes that usually nourished the whole of Caverna were now empty. Messengers sent from the purification departments near the surface soon brought an explanation. The rotating belts that usually hauled water up from the Undercity's deep-running rivers had ceased to move. Drudgery had cut off the Court's water supply.

Before long, the encroaching drudge tide could be glimpsed from the palace gate. Hundreds, not thousands, just a fraction of the population of Drudgery, but still an army of dangerous size, and all wearing cloth nose-guards so that Perfume could not affect them.

Never in her life had Enquirer Treble so wished that gunpowder was permitted in Caverna. She understood why it was banned, of course, and had worked hard to confiscate and destroy all samples of it that had ever been smuggled in. However, just for a second or two she did imagine what it would be like to be able to repel an army with weapons that smoked and roared and sent dozens of metal missiles into enemy flesh at once.

On the other hand, she was considerably better prepared than the enemy, most of whom appeared to be armed with little more than rocks and laboring tools. They showed no fear, however, and as the Enquirer peered through a spyglass she realized that every drudge confronting the gate was doing something odd to their face. They were using their fingers to pull down the skin below their eyes and tug out the corners of their mouths.

Each on its own looked grotesque and a bit comical, but there was something alarming about seeing a hundred faces distorted in that way, and Enquirer Treble's excellent instincts told her that she was looking into the Face of revolution.

Then we shall show them the Face of authority, with a frown they will never forget.

"We cannot hold out against a long siege without water," she said aloud, "so we must break their will fast. Rout them by any means necessary, then pursue and set up barricades so that they cannot flee back to Drudgery to gather strength or supplies. Trap them in unfamiliar tunnels without food or water, and they will make terms in no time. Look! Here they come!"

With a roar, the drudges began a surge toward the gate, hurling rocks and shards as they went. Their charge was brought up short, however, amid a rain of crossbow bolts, ballister shot, and a splattering of hot oil. It seemed that the attack had barely started before it was abandoned, the drudge horde routed.

"They are fleeing into the Painted Parades! Perfect! Block up the passages behind them! We will trap them in the Samphire district and the Octopus!"

Forth charged her guards, hastened with spice, and tunnel after tunnel was hastily blocked with wooden barricades.

"They'll negotiate when they see that they're stranded without supplies," muttered Treble, allowing herself a second to wipe her brow, "and Drudgery will come to heel when they find we have several hundred trapped hostages." Her plan had succeeded. It had been easy. She fought against a nagging worry that it had been too easy. "You there—go and ask the servants whether the palace has sustained any damage."

And this, as it turned out, was *not* easy. The palace servants were not to be questioned, or for that matter found. During the chaos of the attack and rout, every single one of them had disappeared.

. . . . .

The Childersin family arrived out of breath, having ridden their carriage ponies into a lather. Not one of them had suggested waiting for Maxim Childersin. If anybody could survive alone and on his wits, it would be their patriarch.

"Seal the doors behind us!" shouted the uncles to the servants as they stormed in. "There is a howling mob not five minutes behind us! We must prepare to hold siege."

"Yes, sirs!" called Mistress Howlett. "Miss Zouelle told us what had happened. We have been making preparations."

"Zouelle came back here?"

"Why, yes, she arrived half an hour ago."

Glances were exchanged. It had not crossed the mind of any of the family that Zouelle would come back to the town house. It was plain to all of them that Neverfell must have been given the wrong Wine, and that the fault must lie with Zouelle. While a few suspected her of deliberate treachery, the rest assumed that she had used another concoction by mistake, then realized her error and fled before the rest of her family could find out. None of them harbored any kindly feelings toward her, however.

"Where is she now?"

"I believe she went down the passage toward the laboratories and the Morning Room, sir. She said she had some work to do and should not be disturbed."

"Did she now?"

A moment later, the massed Childersin uncles were stamping their way down the passage. No conference had been needed. It had occurred to them that if they were to rid themselves of Maxim Childersin's tiresome little favorite, there could be no better time. Maxim himself was absent, and the girl had blotted her copybook badly enough that they could surely be excused for taking action against her. Zouelle's golden days were over.

"If she had any sense," one of them murmured, "she would have fled to one of our rivals, instead of heading into a dead-end set of tunnels and leaving herself with nowhere . . . to . . . go." His voice trailed away.

They had just turned a corner, and were now gazing down the stretch of tunnel that included the doors to the laboratories. Every single one of these doors was now open. Half a dozen barrels stood in the corridor, and the floor was a cat's cradle of criss-crossing and interlocking lines, sigils, and circles, hastily drawn in chalk.

The Childersins stared as their vintner minds struggled to grasp what they were seeing. All their pet projects, minor, major, and misbegotten, had been rolled out into the corridor. All the Wines were awake and feral, the scruffy sigils barely holding them in check, and already they were sensing one another and bristling. The air was thick and rasped against the Childersins' cheeks like paper. A careless step into this danger zone might be enough to set all the Wines lashing out blindly, and if half a dozen True Wines started to fight, they would tear holes in reality like cats in a paper bag.

Beyond the barrels and the curtain of quivering light, they could just make out the kneeling figure of Zouelle, adding some finishing touches in chalk.

"Zouelle!"

She looked up, scrambled to her feet, and fled, just in time to evade a crossbow bolt that chipped the wall behind her and ricocheted down the tunnel.

"ZOUELLE!"

Zouelle did not stop running until she reached the Morning Room. There she fastened the door behind her, and took a moment to recover her breath.

She had made good use of her half an hour but had been hoping it would take the rest of the family longer to get home. However, her efforts in the corridor would hold them back for now. Her only worry was that Uncle Maxim would manage to evade the Enquiry and return to the town house. He would have a much better chance of undoing the damage she had done, and taming the Wines.

Hurry, Neverfell, she thought. *Hurry.*

Meanwhile, Neverfell herself was making all haste through the Grand Steward's secret escape route, while her escorts helped fill the gaps in her memories.

"So Master Grandible is alive?" Neverfell could barely speak for relief.

"Yes," confirmed one of her companions. "He used a hidden exit to escape—I believe it was one that you discovered."

"The rabbit hole," whispered Neverfell. "That wonderful rabbit!"

The twisting route led at last past a dusty brocade throne, next to a great bottle of water and a chest of provisions worth a king's ransom. Evidently these were laid down in the event the Grand Steward found himself hiding for some time.

Beside them had been placed a rough cloak with a hood and a pair of good boots in Neverfell's size. These were handed to her, and she donned them quickly.

"Take this as well." The nearest servant opened the chest and pulled out a small teardrop-shaped vial. "Perfume, just in case you need to win somebody over in a hurry. It will irresistibly draw people to you."

"Though they might wonder why I'm holding my nose," whispered Neverfell, but pocketed it anyway.

The passage ended in a hatch, and once she and her three

guides had dropped down through it they found themselves in a little-used thoroughfare, the horse dung on its rough road stale and dry.

"Do you remember what we're doing now, miss?" one of the servant women asked gently.

"Yes . . ." Neverfell scraped at her memory to see if she knew the woman's name, and found to her joy that she did. "It's Clarelle, isn't it? Yes, I do. We're going to the Doldrums. We're going to make sure the route there is clear for the drudges."

Thankfully, they encountered next to nobody as they strode hastily along the byways. However, all the while the twisting tunnels brought Neverfell echoes of the sounds of conflict—cries, metallic clashes, rumblings that sounded worryingly like rockfalls. *I caused that. Did I cause that?* She could not decide how to feel about it. Instead, she thought of Zouelle waiting in the Morning Room and trying to hold off the rest of her family, and all the people counting upon her to scout out the Doldrums.

They weaved through the Samphire district, and edged along the Octopus, until a broad thoroughfare came to a sudden stop. It had been blocked off by a solid wall of heavy stone blocks, thickly mortared round the edges so that no air could squeak past.

"That must be it," Neverfell said aloud. "The old entrance to the Doldrums." She bit her lip as she examined it. Battering down the wall would make a lot of noise, but she had chosen this option rather than asking her allies to battle their way into the Doldrums through Madame Appeline's abode. That would inevitably have involved bloodshed, and she had already caused enough of that.

"Somebody's coming," murmured Clarelle. Neverfell pulled up her hood just in time as half a dozen girls sprinted round the corner and continued running. They wore simple white dresses, their hair tied neatly back, and Neverfell recognized them as Putty Girls belonging to Madame Appeline. A few seconds later, a handful of men in cream-colored livery came racing round the corner.

"Ah, let them go. It's Appeline we were told to find. And it looks like she must have escaped." The men turned and walked back the way they had come.

"That's the livery of the de Meina sisters," whispered one of Neverfell's guides. "The Facesmiths. After you denounced Madame Appeline in the Hall of the Gentles, I suppose they thought they had a good excuse to attack her." Neverfell could well believe it, as she recalled how bitterly the sisters had spoken about Madame Appeline.

Neverfell directed a quick glance at her companions, then set off after the men, at a discreet distance. Just as she suspected, their path took them to the front door of Madame Appeline's abode.

The aforementioned door, however, was now off its hinges, having suffered some splintering impact. A long timber lying before it had evidently been used as a battering ram. There was a substantial crowd outside, not all of them wearing the livery of the de Meina household. This mob, however, seemed to have expended most of its energy, and was in the process of drifting away. A few of its members were having to be helped hence, sporting what looked like crossbow wounds, testimony to Madame Appeline's security measures.

"Any sign of the Facesmith?" one of them shouted.

"No," came the call from within. "We've searched everywhere. She's not here."

"Get the Putty Girls to tell you where she is!"

"Too late. They've all run away."

As Neverfell watched from round the corner, the last of the

triumphant force finally departed, some of it carrying away familiar-looking furniture. In the end there were no further sounds of life issuing from beyond the broken door.

"Miss Neverfell?" Clarelle brought Neverfell out of her own thoughts. "I should go back to the forces at the gate and tell them the way is clear."

"Yes," answered Neverfell absently, and then realized what she was staring at. "Yes! Clearer than we expected. We don't have to bash down the wall into the Doldrums after all. We can go in this way, through the secret door."

After a quick conversation, it was decided that Neverfell would remain by the broken entrance, to keep an eye on it and make sure the route through Madame Appeline's tunnels remained clear. The other two servants would retrace their steps through the thoroughfares, so that they could stand as lookout at different junctions in the Octopus, and bring warning if a large and hostile armed force approached from the direction of the palace. Neverfell took up her position just outside the shattered door, while the two servants disappeared back the way they had come.

Standing so near to the door was an eerie experience. Neverfell was not close enough to see much through the splintered gap, but she could make out the gradual darkening as the trap-lanterns within let themselves fade, one by one. It was like watching a creature die, and gradually lose the sparks of life. It filled her with pity and fear, and made her wish that the last faint glimmer of light at the far end of the corridor would die out and be done.

Despite herself, Neverfell drew closer to the door, even fingered the ravaged wood. Looking down the corridor, she could see the shattered remains of the door to the reception room, and through it into Madame Appeline's grove. The far end of the corridor and the reception room were swathed in darkness, but as she stared and blinked it seemed to Neverfell that the distant murk of the grove was less inkily black than it should have been.

Slowly she realized what this meant. Somewhere in the depths of these devastated tunnels, a trap-lantern was still softly glowing and glowing. This could mean only one thing: Someone down there was breathing.

FACE OFF

*OF COURSE THE RAIDERS DIDN'T FIND MADAME
Appeline. How stupid of me. They didn't know she had a secret
passage. She could have slipped through the hidden door, waited
until they'd finished shouting and looting, then come back.*

It was strange, but, staring down the corridor to the tiny,
almost imperceptible glimmer of light, Neverfell felt afraid in a
way that she had not while facing down Maxim Childersin, or
testifying before the Hall of the Gentles. She still felt a sense of
connection to Madame Appeline, of linked destiny. Before, it had
seemed like a bright rope she could cling to, or perhaps even
climb to reach somewhere she belonged. Now that she knew of
the Facesmith's betrayal, the sense of connection was haunted,
twisted, a black chain leading away from her down the shadowy
corridor ahead.

It almost seemed to be pulling at her, reeling her in. She was
just telling herself that there was no reason to venture in alone,
that she could wait there on lookout until reinforcements came,
when another thought hit her like a brick.

Zouelle.

If Madame Appeline was down there in the darkness, the Facesmith would not wish to dare the streets where she might meet prowling mobs sent by her rivals. Instead, sooner or later, she would flee to her close and secret ally, Maxim Childersin. She would make haste down the secret passageway to the Morning Room, and there she would find a girl she despised. A girl she could blame for her own denunciation before the Hall of the Gentles. Zouelle Childersin, alone, undefended and unsuspecting.

Perhaps she had already had that idea. She could be heading for the secret room and the passage beyond at this very moment . . .

Neverfell wiped her perspiring palms on her clothes, and stepped forward into the corridor. Running off to find the departed servants would waste valuable time and leave the area unguarded. The black chain of inevitability hauled her in, step after step.

As she advanced, the few surviving traps glimmered into life and showed her scenes of devastation. The table in the reception room was overturned, the floor crunchy with broken crockery. Neverfell stooped for a trap-lantern and took it with her.

The sight of the once-beautiful grove clutched at her heart. Nearly all the millennia-old crystal-trees had been shattered, leaving nothing but kaleidoscopic stumps like broken tusks, and glistening shards scattering the moss carpet. She stooped and picked up one long shard. It was cloudy cream and rose in coloration, streaked like an expensive sweet. It was narrow, sharp, and cold in her hand. Neverfell did not know if it made her feel more safe or less.

At one point, she passed yet another broken door, and glimpsed into one of Madame Appeline's treasured galleries, half the alabaster masks still hovering sublime in their lines, the others lying on the ground like so many skittles.

She passed on, and did not notice the farthest of the pale faces let out the breath it had been holding, and slip silently from the line.

It was difficult to find the stairway, so spidery-fine was its outline, but at last her lanternlight gleamed upon the ivy-like whorls. Heart in her mouth, Neverfell climbed the spiral stairs, the metal ringing slightly under her feet. Only then did it occur to Neverfell that she was re-enacting her motions from her dream-that-had-not-been a dream, on the day of the betrayal.

She did not hear another set of feet walking carefully through the shattered grove behind her, making sure that they did not crunch on the fragments of crystal.

As she reached the top, all around her a faint glow started to bloom. She stepped forward onto the gallery, which proved to be a long, metal balcony fixed to the wall, just six feet or so below the roof of the cavern. Clustering on the gallery, the ceiling, and the upper parts of the wall were the largest trap-lanterns that Neverfell had ever seen. One of them was about nine feet across, its crusty skin glowing just enough for her to make out the pale rings and honey-colored blotches. No wonder the false sky of the grove had blazed so brightly, and no wonder it had taken the Putty Girls so much puff to keep them shining.

In her dream, a monkey had led her to the hidden door. Now it was the frail will-o'-the-wisp of reawakening memory that drew her on. Very carefully she edged round the greatest of the traps. It stirred slightly, its great jaws opening like a beast hunting in its dreams, then closing again. She drew her fingertips down the smooth tiles of the wall until they found and tugged at the hidden catch. A door swung open away from her.

The last time I entered this room I went mad. Zouelle had to hold me down.

She tightened her grip on the lantern and stepped into the room.

It was a small room, and there were hundreds of faces in it. Some were molded in clay or cast in plaster, but most were drawings, rapid but detailed sketches in colored pastels or charcoal. They were all images of the same woman, Neverfell could see that at a glance, and with a shock of familiarity she recognized again and again expressions from the Tragedy Range.

The woman was not Madame Appeline. Her skin was dappled and her hair long and red. Her eyes were large and gray-green. Her features were gaunt, agonized, and infinitely expressive. The pictures seemed to be arranged in some kind of sequence. In the pictures to the left of the door the woman was merely thin, but as Neverfell's gaze darted frantically through the images around the room, she could see her growing frailer and more haggard. The woman was dying before her eyes. Finally, on the right-hand side of the door was what looked like a death mask, the cheeks fallen in, the mouth expressionless at last.

There was another small door set in the opposite wall, but Neverfell scarcely noticed it, because her gaze was drawn to the mural immediately above it. It was a sketch in pastel and tempera, drawn directly onto the plaster of the wall itself. It showed a full-length image of the woman, so that the manacles round her legs were visible. A red-haired child was being wrested from her arms. The faces of both woman and child were full of utter anguish, and had been sketched in the most meticulous detail.

On the floor at Neverfell's feet were the remains of a clay mask that had been smashed to pieces. To judge by the fragments, it had shown the face of a child, her expression contorted by grief and rage so terrible that one expected to hear it screaming. When she looked at it, Neverfell's hands and arms throbbed with remembered bruises.

The room seemed to be shuddering, and Neverfell realized that her lantern-hand was shaking. There was a feather-faint noise behind her, and she spun round.

There was one Madame Appeline face in the room after all. It was between her and the door to the gallery, and it was not a mask.

Neverfell flung herself backward as Madame Appeline's arm slashed down, and the bodkin aimed at her face missed by inches.

"You're not my mother." Neverfell could hardly find the breath for words. "*She* was." She gestured wildly with her shard at the dozens of images of the red-haired woman. "And you killed her."

"She was ill when she came here." Madame Appeline's heart-shaped face wore one of the tender Faces from the Tragedy Range, but now that Neverfell had seen the original she knew it for the cruel mockery it was. "All I did was let her die."

"Why?" erupted Neverfell. "Just so you could draw her expressions, and use them as Faces?"

"Just? Did you say *just?* Ebbing away before my sketchbook was the most useful thing she ever did. Before my Tragedy Range, Faces were varnish. I made them into true art."

Something inside Neverfell seemed to crack with these words. She gave a croak of pure anguish and rage, and lunged at Madame Appeline with her shard of crystal tree. But at the last moment the muscles of her arm seemed to weaken. Although the flesh and bone before her belonged to a cruel and calculating enemy, the expression it wore came from the red-haired woman in the pictures, from Neverfell's own mother. It was a stolen Face, but Neverfell could not strike at it, and Madame Appeline knew it.

"You," hissed the Facesmith. Her tone was poison. "I never asked for *you.*

"I had the perfect bargaining position. Maxim Childersin

wanted to build a secret shaft to the surface, one that he could reach through the twister behind his town house. So he needed the help of somebody in the Doldrums. My tunnels were ideally placed, so he approached me.

"I told him my price. I wanted an outsider with a particularly expressive face, one I could study in extreme situations of my choosing. Preferably with green eyes, so that her Faces would suit me well. *One* outsider.

"And his agents in the overground found me the perfect specimen. They told her of the oils in Caverna that could cure her illness, and she paid them all she had to smuggle her into the city. But she would not leave her child behind. And when she was lowered down the shaft, there *you* were, in her arms."

"You hate me." Neverfell could not understand the icy vitriol in the Facesmith's voice.

"I have always hated you. The first moment I saw you, there was something in your face . . . I found uses for you, of course. Your mother managed her finest Faces when you were pulled from her arms, but your face—no child should have looked so angry, so implacable. You made my blood run cold."

Half-forgotten fragments of memory were whirling into place. The scene from Neverfell's Wine vision came back to her, now with new clarity.

The same thing, every day. The half an hour in her mother's arms so warm, so short. Then the dry click of the clock striking naught, and the strong hands dragging her away. Screaming and screaming, losing her grip on the beloved hand one more time, and being thrown into the cupboard room . . .

"Your blood has always been cold," said Neverfell, her voice shaking.

"I have sensibilities!" snapped Madame Appeline. "You bruised them, shattered them. After your mother died, your face became a thorn in me. So Childersin gave me Wine to make you forget everything. I gave you the finest luxuries so as to sketch your reactions, and I bought you a dozen dresses, the better to set off your expressions, but all the time I sensed that your vengeful self was just buried. Waiting for its chance. And then one day you vanished from my tunnels. Disappeared completely. That infernal Kleptomancer!"

Another two pieces of the puzzle. It was the Kleptomancer, then, who had stolen Neverfell at the age of five, and left her, on some long-forgotten whim, in Grandible's tunnels. And it was Madame Appeline who had offered the reward for the master thief's capture, desperate to reclaim the child who knew too much.

"I never forgot you," continued the Facesmith. "That a child's face could hold so much rage, so much defiance . . . it did not seem possible. I have created a thousand Faces, and always I feared seeing that one expression of yours pushing through the others. It would be like seeing a ghost.

"Perhaps you blame me for taking your memories? I left you clean. Purged of all your ghosts. *I* am the one who has been haunted all my life. Haunted by *you*."

The Facesmith made another unexpected lunge, and Neverfell dodged aside, one hand raised to protect her face. The bodkin point traced a painful line across the back of her hand. The dance of stab and dodge had moved the pair of them around each other, so that it was now Neverfell who stood with her back to the door.

"And then one day I *did* see you," hissed Madame Appeline. "Large as life, and in my tunnels. I knew you at once. Maxim promised that you would not live to threaten me, but his assassin failed to drown you. And then when he went to the Enquiry to buy you, he changed his mind and decided to keep you alive. But I knew—*knew*—that I would be safe only if you were dead. If only the Zookeeper had been worth the fee I paid him!"

"You stole my mother's Faces," whispered Neverfell. "You stole them, and you sold them, and you walked around wearing them and using them to make people do what you wanted. You used my mother's Faces on *me*. And all the time you were her murderess or close enough. All that time you were trying to murder me."

"Do not look at me! Not with that face!" Madame Appeline was shaking from head to foot, the feathers in her hair quivering like insect antennae. "Just as you looked when you were an imp of five. I should have snuffed you out then!"

Madame Appeline made another pounce and slash, and Neverfell again leaped back, the motion carrying her out through the door and onto the gallery. All around, the traps eased into light once more, sensing the frenzied movements and the rush of rapid breaths. Some were blindly gaping, their fangs so fine and pale they looked like fringes of fur.

Madame Appeline struck out with her bodkin again and again like a giant stinging insect. Neverfell dodged, dodged, dodged. All the while the shard was in her hand, and her mother's tender gaze was before her, pasted onto a murderess's face.

You're not my mother.

You're not my mother.

You're not my mother.

"You're not my mother!" Neverfell lashed out wildly, scarcely knowing whether she meant to wound or to parry. "Take off her Face!" The shard drew a long oblique line upward, and almost entirely missed. Almost, except for the very, very tip, which just nicked the chin of Madame Appeline's precious alabaster face, causing a tiny pearl of blood to swell. The Facesmith gave a wail of utter horror, clapped a hand to her chin, and leaped backward.

It was a leap too far, and in the wrong direction. Directly behind Madame Appeline lay the largest of the traps, monstrous mouth agape. Neverfell had just enough time to see the Facesmith fall sprawling into its maw before its upper jaw descended, the fine teeth meshing like two combs locking together.

An eerie silence fell. Despite everything, Neverfell's conscience smote her, and she tried to prise the jaws apart, but in vain. After years fed on grubs, the trap had found prey worth its maw, and it sat there intractable, wearing a grin wider than any the Facesmith had ever designed. There were no signs of life from within.

Neverfell ventured slowly back into the hidden room once more, and stared around her at the hundreds of sketches. They were pictures of pain, but also strength, tenderness, endurance, love.

She was looking at me. The love in all these Faces . . . it was meant for me.

Neverfell took down one of the pictures of her mother, and placed it carefully in her pocket.

The frontrunners of the drudge army met up with Neverfell just as she was returning to her post by Madame Appeline's broken front door. To her delight, Erstwhile was among them. He was gruff as ever when she nearly squeezed him in two with a hug.

"It worked," he summarized curtly.

It had been, Neverfell now remembered, the part of the plan that had caused the most heated debate. There was simply no way to bring hundreds of drudges to the Doldrums without somebody noticing, even if the Court was in chaos. The plan that was finally concocted was audacious in the extreme. Instead of trying to sneak up from Drudgery, the drudge masses would rise and pretend to attack the palace. Then the drudge army would let itself be "put to rout" and "flee" . . . toward the Doldrums, in just the direction they had wished to go in the first place.

"They fell for it," Erstwhile pronounced with pride. "Half the Court—the half that isn't tearing itself apart right now—is holed up in the palace, hiding. And when we ran away, they thought they'd won. Nobody tried to stop us. They even put up barricades behind us! So now if anybody wants to chase us they got to come through those first."

"Did . . ." Neverfell scarcely wanted to ask the question. "Did anyone get hurt?"

Erstwhile looked stony again, then gave her shoulder a short, slightly painful punch. "It's a war, Nev. Everyone knew the odds. And we only lost a couple out of four hundred. Just take us to your precious sky so it's all worth it."

Four hundred drudges and their children, all trusting in my plan. Neverfell did not know whether to be staggered that there were so many, or saddened that there were not more. This was not even one-tenth of the population of Drudgery. The others had agreed to rebel but had not been willing to leave Caverna for the hazards of the unknown overground. *I suppose not everybody can bear to give up everything they have ever known, however bad their life is.*

The passage beyond the hidden room took a number of twists before coming to a dead halt with a trapdoor set in the roof. When Neverfell pushed this up, she came out under the breakfast table in the Morning Room.

"Zouelle!" Neverfell ran to fling her arms around her friend. "You're here! You did it!"

"Neverfell!" Zouelle returned the hug. "You took so long I thought you'd been caught! My family still hasn't found a way through the hazards I set up in the corridor, but it's only a matter of time. Let's hope it's long enough."

Drudges of all sizes and ages were pouring out from beneath the table now, and peering around the room. The white tablecloth, the pristine silver, and the crystal dishes earned only a brief glance, however. All eyes were fixed on the ceiling immediately above the table.

Zouelle had unscrewed the large, blue glass hemisphere that had fitted into the ceiling, and left it on the table. In its place could be seen a round hole, some three feet wide, from which a mousy-gray radiance was emitting.

Neverfell clambered unsteadily on the table and peered up into the hole. The shaft soared up and up, a faint glimmer telling her that the walls were mirrored. It ended at the farthest point in a tiny dull coin of light.

Sky. I can see the sky.

Her spirits took off like a flock of doves, and she almost expected to see them spiral upward toward that dim luminescence in a flurry of white wings. The sense of relief was so intense that she almost collapsed. Only then did she realize she had been secretly fearing that she had been wrong about everything, and that she might find herself looking up into a nest of trap-lanterns like those above Madame Appeline's grove.

She looked around at her waiting allies, who all seemed to be holding their breath.

"It's the way," she said huskily. "It's open. I don't think the sun's up yet, but . . . I can just about see the sky. Look! See for yourself!"

Instantly there was a crush of people around Neverfell wanting to crane and peer up the shaft.

"What's that smell?" whispered one of them.

"Overground." Neverfell could feel a smile trying to split her face. "Freedom."

"Nev—we got to hurry!" Erstwhile gestured to a machine that three drudges were maneuvering out of the floor hatch. It looked like a cross between a tripod, a crossbow, and a multipronged grappling hook. "You sure this contraption is going to work?"

"I don't know." Neverfell stared at it. "What is it?"

"Don't you remember? The last reprise must still be taking effect." Zouelle passed her another vial of Wine. "Drink this—that should sort it out."

Neverfell downed the Wine, and then stared at the device with dawning realization and glee. "Oooh! I built this! Hee hee hee hee!"

"You're really not reassuring me, Nev," growled Erstwhile.

"No, no, it'll be fine." Neverfell grabbed the contraption and started erecting it on its tripod on the table, directly under the hole. "Ah . . . probably. Shaft's a bit wider than I thought, but, um, the prongs are *probably* long enough. As long as I get everything symmetrical." She checked the built-in spirit level, propped one tripod leg with a piece of rag, and squinted up the shaft again. "Got the rope? Good. Tie it to the thingy. Here we go!"

She pulled a trigger, and six steel strings loosed and thrummed at once. The central bolt was fired upward, unfolding its four prongs as it went and dragging the rope up with it. Neverfell could hear the shrieks of the prong-tips scraping against the mirrored walls. After the shrieking stopped there was a pause, then a clattering clang. She gave the rope several good yanks, and the grappling device failed to tumble down on her head.

"I think it's worked. I think it's hooked onto the top!"

Erstwhile scrambled on to the table and grabbed the rope. "If I fall down, it wasn't," he muttered, and started to climb. After what seemed an age, Neverfell felt a signal of three short tugs on the rope. A rope ladder was tied to the end of the rope, and after a second the unseen Erstwhile started to haul it up.

Three more tugs on the ladder. Erstwhile had made it secure.

"Everybody—line up and start climbing!" called out Zouelle. "We don't know how long we have."

Maxim Childersin was having the most frustrating day he could ever remember in his unnaturally long life.

It had started badly, with the Enquiry's insistence that the hearing be held considerably before his family's usual hour of rising, throwing his entire schedule into disorder. He rather suspected that Treble had arranged this on purpose. She seemed to do everything in her power to annoy him, not least by her repeated refusal to be assassinated.

His irritability at missing breakfast and his usual dose of morning light, however, had been eclipsed by everything that had happened since. Try as he might, he still could not quite understand how the hearing had ended in such utter disaster. He felt like a chess master who, two moves from achieving checkmate, suddenly sees a live kitten dropped onto the middle of the board, scattering pieces.

There must be some way to pull everything back, he told himself as he cleaned his sword and returned it to its scabbard. *There must be a way to recover from this. I know there is. Nine times out of ten, defeat is in the mind.*

Defeat had certainly been in the minds of a host of his allies that he had encountered fleeing from the Hall of the Gentles. It had required all his charisma and some discreet use of Perfume to rally them. Now at least they seemed to have regained their composure, and it was with a substantial honor guard that he now walked the increasingly dangerous thoroughfares. The coterie of Enquirers who had just tried to arrest him had fared badly.

A change of plan is needed, that is all. A bloodier one, perhaps, but that cannot be helped. We are in too deep to falter. I must rally the rest of my allies, so they do not go to ground, or make cowardly deals to escape punishment.

The first people he had to bring into line, of course, were his family. If not, they would doubtless cut one another's throats in a fit of ambition.

He was pleasantly surprised to see that the mob besieging his town house was considerably smaller than he was expecting, with no sign of the formidable Enquiry forces, who he could only assume were busy dealing with the overall chaos. The besiegers were considerably more surprised to be attacked from behind by a superior force, led by the man they had expected to be skulking inside the town house.

By the time the battle was over, the little street no longer looked like an idyll. Plaster was cracked, swing-seats shattered, and bloodstains marred the sugar-sparkle of the housefronts. Childersin stepped over the prone figures that strewed his porch, and gave a coded rap on the door.

His family was overwhelmed to see him and had a hundred things to report. The news that Zouelle was in the house, however, set him striding down the passage toward the laboratories and the Morning Room.

Upon seeing Zouelle's handiwork in the corridor, he was filled at once with acute pride and intense disappointment. As he had always hoped, his young heir was showing every sign of being a cunning contriver and a remarkable and audacious vintner. However, she had ultimately failed to display what he prized above all things—family loyalty.

It was easier to enrage Wines than to calm them. It was easier to create mayhem than to impose order. But Maxim Childersin had been alive for many centuries, and had taught Zouelle everything she knew.

Gently he began to advance a little at a time, performing the calming incantations, leaving his family to chain and roll away the subdued barrels one by one, so that they could follow. He had pressing matters to discuss with his favorite niece.

In a steady stream, the drudges poured out of the floor hatch, and up the rope ladder into the shaft. Time was of the essence, so they could not wait for one to reach the top before the next started climbing. Neverfell's heart lurched every time the ladder creaked. It was the strongest rope ladder they had been able to find, and even now she wondered if it could cope with so many drudges all climbing it at once.

Not all the climbers were drudges either. Still wearing their neat, serviceable Faces, the palace servants had quietly turned up en masse, taken their place in the queue, and disappeared up the ladder. To Neverfell's colossal relief, Cheesemaster Grandible had also appeared, wincing at the bright light and toting a sack of his tenderest cheeses as gently as if they were infants.

Was she still angry with him? No, somewhere along the line her anger had fallen away, like a forgotten coin tumbling from her pocket. As his grim gaze came to rest on her face, however, she felt her cheeks burn.

"Yes, I know," she said in answer to the unasked, for there was no time for explanations. "Yes. My face is spoiled."

Grandible's jowl wobbled and creased. Then, for the first time that Neverfell could remember, he changed to a Face she had never seen before, a frown more ferocious and alarming than any she had seen.

"Who the shambles told you that?" he barked. "Spoiled? I'll spoil them." He took hold of her chin and examined her. "A bit sadder, maybe. A bit wiser. But nothing rotten. You're just growing yourself a rind at last. Still a good cheese."

Neverfell's eyes misted over, so that she barely saw Cheesemaster Grandible as he vanished up the ladder.

"Oh no!" Zouelle had her ear pressed to the door that led back toward the Childersin household. "I can hear my Uncle Maxim! I thought the Enquiry was supposed to arrest him! Why is he here? That block I set up might hold off the others, but it won't slow him down for long. Everybody climb faster!"

"They can't climb any faster!" protested Neverfell. Many were carrying babies or infants in satchels or papooses, while others bore crippled or elderly relations piggyback as they climbed.

Her words were barely out when there came a sound of confusion from the tunnel below the floor hatch. Instead of clambering out at a careful pace, drudges were suddenly scrambling up into the room with every sign of haste and panic.

"What is it?" Neverfell caught at the arm of one of the errand boys. "What's wrong?"

"Map-freaks," he gasped. "There's map-freaks creeping in behind us, don't know where they came from. Dozens of them. Weaving and singing and waving things. We're piling up furniture behind us to block their way, but they just keep coming . . ."

"Oh." Neverfell clapped her hands to her mouth. "Oh no! Why didn't I think of that?" Her eyes strayed to the blue glass hemisphere that had once covered the base of the shaft. "The Undiscovered Passage! We've just removed the seal that stopped the bat-squeakers from being able to sense it! Which means now they know where it is, and that means they've told all the others . . . Oh, we're going to have every Cartographer in Caverna here!"

"Do we have anything to slow them down?" called Zouelle, her ear still pressed against the door.

"Perhaps I can talk to them and persuade them to go away!" exclaimed Neverfell. "The palace servants gave me some Perfume. They said it would . . . oh. Draw people to me."

"That is very nice, Neverfell," Zouelle answered levelly, "but right now *precisely* the opposite of what we need."

Drudges boiled into the room, and before long it was full.

"I'm the last!" shouted a frail drudge woman finally, as she pulled herself out. "Close the hatch! They're coming!"

The hatch was closed and bolted, and dozens of willing hands turned over the breakfast table, laying it upside down on top of the hatch to hold it shut. The dresser was dragged against the door to the Childersin tunnels.

"Climb! Climb!"

Twenty people waiting to climb. Fifteen. Ten. Two.

The trapdoor under the upturned table started to rattle, and the table jumped a little. Barely a second later, the door that led to the Childersin household shuddered in its frame, as if somebody had barged their shoulder against it.

"Go!" Zouelle shoved Neverfell toward the ladder. "Climb, Neverfell!" There was no time for argument. Neverfell grabbed the ladder and started to clamber up into the shaft.

Thus it was only Zouelle who was still in the Morning Room when the door burst inward with a crash of falling furniture.

Crystal goblets shattered, silver platters rolled across the room, and the doorway filled with Childersins, Maxim at their head.

The Face that Uncle Maxim was wearing as he pushed his way through the wreckage of the makeshift barricade was one that Zouelle had never seen before. Instinctively she knew it was reserved for enemies of the family. It froze her to the spot, like a guilty five-year-old. But she was not five years old, nor would any concession be made for her youth.

She had taken on one of the great chess masters and failed. Of course she had. Now she and her accomplices would be hauled down off the ladder, and his men sent to kill those who had reached the desert. Once too often, Zouelle had tried to play a game too big for her.

And then, just as she was thinking this, the table and several floorboards shattered, flinging up fragments, and through the jagged hole leaped Cartographers, with eyes like fire and sawdust in their hair.

The Childersins were armed with swords and daggers. The Cartographers were armed with nothing but surprise, but really quite a lot of surprise. Thus the Childersins were, for a crucial moment, thrown onto the back foot as the mapmakers lurched toward them, buzzing and mewling, the dim light gleaming on their astrolathes.

"Cut them down!" shouted Maxim Childersin sharply. "Do not let them talk to you!" As he slashed at the encroaching Cartographers with his sword, Zouelle remembered how to move, snatched at the ladder, and started to climb.

Hand after hand she climbed, expecting every moment to feel a sword through her leg or a halting hand around her ankle. Only when she felt the ladder lurch in her grip did she look down. Fifteen feet below her, she could see another figure starting to climb the ladder. It was Uncle Maxim, her dear mentor and protector. She could go no faster, because of the queue of climbers above her. The rope of the ladder was too thick for her to cut with her pocket dagger.

"Neverfell! The Perfume! Drop it to me!"

Looking up she could see Neverfell stare down at her in bemusement for a second, then fumble in her pockets. The vial dropped fast from the red-haired girl's hand, gleaming like a raindrop, and Zouelle nearly lost her balance snatching it from the air.

"Zouelle." Childersin's voice was soft and reproving. "Do you really think my will is so weak that you can talk me around, even with Perfume?

"No." Zouelle pulled out the stopper with shaky hands, and upended the vial so that its contents rained downward past her. "But I think it will work on the Cartographers."

The Perfume spattered over Maxim Childersin's head and shoulders. There was the tiniest pause, and then a scuffle of motion. Other figures appeared at the bottom of the shaft, squeaking and gabbling, goggle-clad and groping. They scrambled up after Maxim Childersin, seizing his ankles and coattails, pulling him down off the ladder.

Zouelle felt her heart beat harshly as she watched her mentor disappear beneath a heap of Cartographers, his hands flailing at the mirrored sides of the shaft and failing to find a grip. As she started to climb again, her hands slippery with perspiration, she wondered how many Cartographers her Uncle Maxim had killed to hide this shaft, and whether those below had any notion of it.

She was not sure that they would care in any case, even after having just seen him cut down some of their number.

Cartographers had no room in their mind for malice or revenge. They would not hate him, or try to hurt him.

They only wanted to talk to him.

Caverna was falling apart.

Enquirer Treble knew it, in every nerve and fiber of her body. She heard it in every fleeting chaotic echo that the twisting tunnels brought to her. She felt it in the tremors of the ground as distant battles let loose with their heaviest weapons, or dissolved into stampede. She found it in every report that floated to her, like scraps of a tattered banner. And still she stormed and shouted and fought the chaos, delaying the moment of utter collapse, forcing her underlings for just a little longer to be more afraid of her than of the descending anarchy.

"How could you lose an entire rebel army?"

Nobody had an answer. They could only report the facts. The drudge horde had been successfully chased from the palace gates. They had been successfully contained within a set of middle-city passages as planned. Their routes back to Drudgery had been successfully cut off. And then, within an hour, all four hundred of them had disappeared.

"Well—send scouts! Send a group of . . ."

Treble trailed off mid-sentence. She had, of course, been about to suggest sending a set of drudge runners out into the tunnels to report on proceedings. A fine plan in any situation where the drudges themselves were not the problem.

With every passing moment, she became more and more aware of the thousand ways in which the running of Caverna had relied upon the silent toil of the drudges. Over and over she tried to do or arrange some simple thing, to order a message sent, or debris cleared away, or rubble brought up from the mines to create a barricade, or provisions fetched, only to remember that drudges were not at her disposal. She felt like an amputee, reaching out reflexively with an arm she no longer had.

The drudges, the invisible machinery of Caverna, had ground to a halt. Nobody was clearing away the wreckage of battle or hauling up water. Nobody was bringing up grubs for the lanterns, some of which even now were starting to dim and flicker. And when the stifling darkness came, the Court factions would still be tearing one another apart like fighting ferrets.

"Go there yourself, and take two men with you. Drudges do not melt away like chocolate. I want a report within half an hour!"

Her men departed, and she guessed that even now they were considering changing their allegiance as soon as they left the palace, if indeed they were not already in the pay of somebody else. She felt a sudden need to be alone, to clear her head for a moment in the one room where fear did not choke the air like smoke. When she reached the Grand Steward's audience chamber, she found it unguarded and pushed open the door.

All around the walls, the lanterns glimmered into faint life, and the white walls and pillars gleamed like those of a tomb. A tomb for the Grand Steward, and perhaps a tomb for Caverna too.

How did he manage it? How did he keep track of a hundred threads, plots, patterns, conspiracies for so many centuries? Perhaps I am a fool, thinking I can hold together his city after his death.

Motion caught her eye, and she realized that the sharpened pendulums that had been installed to defend the throne were swinging to and fro across the room with silken swishes, just as they had on the day of the Grand Steward's death. At the far end of the room, she heard the sound of somebody slowly exhaling a carefully held breath. A distant lantern flared into life and showed her that there was a figure sitting on the throne. He was clad from head to foot in scaled armor, his face hidden by a goggled mask. It was the Kleptomancer, and he held a strange bow leveled directly at her chest.

"I knew you would come here sooner or later." The intruder's voice was perfectly level, like a glass of still water. "Like an old hunting dog to bay on your master's grave."

After dodging so many murderous blades, Treble cursed herself for letting herself be caught off guard and without a weapon in her hand. *No groveling,* she resolved. *I have stormed my way through life; I can storm my way out of it.*

"I have no time to talk to thieves or assassins," she said. "Either kill me or surrender."

"I had a third option in mind," said the Kleptomancer. "I would like to help you save Caverna. You can hear her dying screams. So can I."

"And what can you do?" The hopelessness of the situation descended upon Treble, folding its dark wings around her. "A madman with a bow, who cannot even remember his own name."

"You are the only person trying to keep order," answered the thief, "but you have everything upside down. You face rebellion from the drudges, and you try to crush and terrify them back into submission. You face disorder from the Court, and you try to reason with the courtiers, to bring them back into line.

"Those drudges who still remain in Caverna have tasted rebellion and have nothing to lose but lives filled with misery. Fear will no longer work. You must bargain with them. The courtiers are crazed with their own greed and rivalry. Reason will no longer work. You must terrify them."

"How?" The Enquirer could hardly bear to see a thief defiling her master's throne, but there was something so calm in his words she could not quite cast them aside as the babblings of a maniac. "How should I bargain with these drudges?"

"Talking to them would be a good start. You will hear their demands soon enough."

"And how should I terrify the Court?" Pride prevented Treble from admitting how sadly the Enquiry was diminished in numbers.

"By threatening them with something more terrible than the drudge rising, more dangerous than their rivals, more heartless than Childersin and all the other would-be tyrants. Me.

"Enquirer, right now I have two dozen ways of destroying everybody in the city. I have spent ten years putting them in place a scrap at a time, in between meaningless thefts and shallow shows. At this moment the water-lifting belts do not turn because I have sabotaged them, nor shall they unless I choose to repair them. The palace servants have confided to me all the secret measures put in place by the late Grand Steward, including those that would lay waste to all within. Furthermore, I may not have gunpowder, but I scarcely need it when I have True Cheese. Right now I have wedges of Stackfalter Sturton placed deep in rocky walls where, if they explode, they shall flood whole districts with poison gases and water from the underground rivers."

"You would not do these things!" Enquirer Treble was driven by outrage to take several steps toward the throned figure, despite the leveled bow, despite the swinging pendulums. "If you destroy Caverna, you destroy yourself, and Drudgery from which you came!"

"Enquirer Treble, I am what you have called me. A madman. That fact is well known. The Court will believe such threats from me as they would from few others. Drudgery, as I have said, has nothing to lose and everything to gain. And now I will tell you what is happening out in the city that you cannot see. I will tell you who is fighting whom, and how they can be stopped. I will even carry your messages to them. And faced with our ultimatum, they will crumble."

"Our . . . ultimatum?" Enquirer Treble had halted just before the swing of the pendulums, and against her face she could feel the breeze of their passing. A gulf of madness was opening at her feet, but there was no other path available to her.

"Yes, ours. The last Grand Steward could be murdered because he could be found. I do not intend to be found. This is the only time I shall sit in this throne, the only time I shall give orders in person. Which means that I shall need somebody to run my city for me, and carry out my commands. You will be my face, my voice, and my hands."

"Why me?"

"Because you are halfway honest, Enquirer, and it has not killed you yet. Because when you came into this room, it was not to try out the throne. Because you will fight a fight long after it becomes hopeless. And because I can predict you. And that is how I know that you will leave me now, go to your room, and read the packet of orders I have prepared for you."

Treble would have liked to defy his expectations, but in truth she was overwhelmed by a surge of relief. She had, she now realized, entered that room in the hopeless hope of receiving orders that would give shape to her life once more. Now she had them.

After Treble had departed, the Kleptomancer sat for a while longer on the throne of white, considering the situation carefully.

"Yes," he said to himself at last. "Yes, I believe I can see how things will go. Everything is secure. My new hunting dog is good enough that she will bring all the hares to ground."

It was done, then. He had completed his most recent objective, and was now permitted to open yet another of the letters he had left for himself. Pulling it out of his pocket, he broke the seal, opened it, and read.

If you are reading this, you have successfully stolen Caverna. Your Great Plan has reached fruition. Enjoy the rewards of your success. Incidentally, your sanity is probably a ruin, and you should avoid drinking any more True Wine for the rest of your life.

He examined the letter for secret postscripts, held it to the light, shook it, and peered at the seal, but it yielded no further information. For a long, long time he sat there staring at it.

So that was my Great Plan?

Here he was, unexpectedly at the end of all his machinations. He stared unseeing at the paper in his hand, realization slowly unfolding in his breast like a rose.

Of course. This was why he had become a master thief, to achieve this theft of thefts, this masterpiece of larceny. All the time, fascinating and terrible Caverna had been his goal. While other Cartographers had sighed in vain after the beauty of her treacherous geography, he had decided to win her with cunning and threats.

All along Caverna had been his opponent and his prize, and she had never suspected it for a moment. He had fooled her, fought her, and defeated her. She would be furious, no doubt, would hate him, rail against him, and look for ways to destroy him, but he had outmaneuvered her, and now she had no choice but to play things his way. Unlike her earlier favorites, he was her lord, not a plaything to be tossed aside when she was bored.

And yet, for the first time in ten years, he found himself at something of a loss.

I have succeeded. I have won. I rule the city.

I wonder what I was planning to do with it?

The pearly light grew brighter and brighter as Neverfell climbed. She did not let herself look up yet, but she could now see the creases in her grimed knuckles, with a starkness that had never been possible by traplight. The air was cold and fresh, and sang in her ears.

Out, beat her heart. *Out, out, out.*

"No traps . . ." Somebody above her was panicking. "There's no traps . . ." And of course there were no traps in the glassy shaft.

"We don't need them!" she shouted upward, hearing her voice echo tinnily. "We'll never need them again! Haven't you noticed? You're breathing! *Breathing!*" She was filling her own lungs again and again, feeling a rush of air so fresh that it prickled in her chest and across the skin of her face.

A strange noise echoed from above, a liquid, metallic string of notes, ending in a long and eerie whistle.

"What's that sound?" went up the whisper, and there were a few terrified gasps. Something warm was running down Neverfell's cheek, and she realized that it was a tear.

"A bird," she whispered. "It's a bird. A wild bird, singing."

Somewhere above a giant was sighing, yawning, and then roaring. The drudges in the shaft dissolved into a clamor of dismay.

"It's the wind!" Neverfell was blind, mad, hungry for the overground, and it was all she could do not to tear her way past the others on the ladder. "Come on! I'll show it to you! I'll show it to you all!"

And then the dull gray light was growing brighter, and the ladder ran out, and she was climbing out of the mouth of a rocky spout onto a plain of rubble. Above her was no roof, and no roof, and no roof, up and up and up until she wanted to scream for joy, and above that the great lead and silver sky-billows went rolling slow as smoke and vast as a hundred mountains. In among it a little piece of bright silver was washed and tumbled like a fingernail clipping, and she knew it was the moon. All around misshapen rocks lurched and leaned, as if they were craning for a better look at the fugitives. Some rose in unsteady posts and lintels, showing that they were the last crumbling remains of walls long since tumbled and worn away. To one side loomed the huge black mass of the mountain, carving a great expanse out of the sky.

"Look! It's . . . it's . . . look!"

She spread her arms as if she were a plant soaking up the sky. Then she became aware that everybody else around her was hunkering down to the ground, staring about them like hutch-bred rabbits. None of them looked at the sky. None of them dared look more than ten feet away from them. All kept their eyes fixed on the ground.

"Neverfell . . ." Zouelle was crouched beside her, clutching at her sleeve, her eyes also fixed upon the ground. "Is this . . . is this your overground?"

Neverfell choked back the exultant laugh that had been forming in her lungs. With a wrench, she suddenly saw this dark, looming landscape as her friends did, her friends who were flinching from the incomprehensible wind and the chill gaze of the moon.

"No—just a bit of it. Just the start. It gets better." She raised her voice. "You have to follow me. Downhill, this way. And we have to go fast. Whatever happens in Caverna—whoever takes over—somebody will come after us. Somebody will want to stop us from escaping."

Progress was slow. Drudges clung to one another, staring about, and Neverfell was aware that a few had turned back, preferring to climb back down into the depths of the underground city. She could not stop them. They were thrown into panic by the rough cries of crows, the booming of buzzards, every mysterious grating and whistle that echoed among the crags.

The light all around was getting brighter, and something inside her chest started to swell until she felt it might float her aloft like a balloon. Colors were showing in the rocks that cracked and crumbled underfoot. There was an amber glow in the sky ahead now, a gleaming crust on the underbellies of the clouds.

"Everybody! Put on your smoked glasses!"

There was much fumbling in packs, and suddenly hundreds of drudges and palace servants wore spectacles with round, dark lenses. It was part of the preparations made for every fugitive, for who knew how tender, cave-dwelling eyes would deal with true daylight?

And then the first spear of sunlight showed over the rippled horizon, and everybody forgot to flee or cower. The eastern sky lazily paled to peach, with frills of white cloud lost in it, and the wind ceased its restless roaring, freshened, and found purpose. The dark and ominous rocks slowly flushed with purples, dark reds, dull golds, blue-grays. Birds were black bullets, too fast to be seen, and air was wide and wild and had somewhere to be in a hurry. There were scents of baked dust and dry dew and the hot-cold smells of a world awakening.

The slope laid itself out before them, jagged as a toothline, descending toward the foothills and then the blue and gold dunes, and somewhere beyond them the world where the trees waved and the brooks ran and the seas champed at the bits of the shores.

And Neverfell led the way down the slope at a run. She slithered and stumbled and fell and recovered and galloped and leaped, and there was no wall to stop her and no roof to bang her head. Above her the pale sky was turning fiercely blue like a mermaid's eye. The wind ran with her, its roaring as loud as the breath in her ears.

EPILOGUE

BY THE OASIS WEST OF MOUNT CUSP, YOUNG
Pelrun the goatherd met with a strange pilgrimage. He knew at
once that they belonged to the little people who lived beneath
the mountain, for they were small, pale, and had faces like dolls.
All wore discs of dark glass on their eyes, and held cloth shields
on sticks over their heads to keep off the sun. They spoke only
their own strange tongue, but he cut the fruit from some prickly
pears and gave it to them to show he meant no harm. The little
people tasted the soft pink fruit, and though their countenances
were as stone, several of them wept, he knew not why.

He brought them to his village, and one among the fairies, a
golden-haired maiden who was taller than the rest, used signs
and mime to trade a vial of rare Wine for camels, water, cloaks,
and guides across the desert. Pelrun himself traveled with the
strangers as far as the grassy plains.

At the time he did not know whom he was escorting. Later,
many would speak of Zouelle the Vintner and Grandible the
Cheesemaster, the first Craftsmen to leave their home among
the little people and bring their magical Crafts to the overground
for others to learn. Pelrun saw only that these fairies were

uncommonly fascinated by common things, that they could spend hours raptly gazing at a butterfly, or cupping handfuls of stream water as if the sparkles were jewels.

One thing struck him as strange above all else. Among these fairy folk there traveled a young human girl with flame-red hair who gabbled happily with the little people but seemed to know no human tongue. He guessed that she must have been stolen by the fairies very young, and raised by them as one of their own.

When they reached the parting of the ways at the edge of the desert, it seemed to him that she thanked him, though he could not understand her words. She was not pretty, but her face showed her heart so clearly one could not help but understand her. As she clenched the grass between her bare toes, her smile was like the sun swimming through blue eternities.

ACKNOWLEDGMENTS

I would like to thank Martin for accompanying me on cheese-making courses and into cave networks, and listening patiently to my incoherent burblings about monkeys and glowing carnivorous plants; Rhiannon, Deirdre, Ralph, and Reuben for their invaluable feedback; my editor, Ruth, and the rest of Macmillan for letting me write a book that sounded crazy even to me; my agent, Nancy; Kathleen McGrath for copious information on sleep and insomnia, and for coming up with the idea behind the Morning Room; Professor Chris Idizkowski for his expert insights into sleep, blue light, and the biological clock; Dan for letting me quiz him about brain lobes; Liz Wootten for inspiriting an entire character by mispronouncing the word *kleptomania*; Felix; the Yarner Trust cheesemaking course; the caves and cheesemaking demonstration at Cheddar Gorge; the subterranean alleys of the Real Mary King's Close; the Chislehurst Caves; the grottoes of Quinta de la Regaleira; the Hellfire Caves; Grutas de Lanquín; The Củ Chi tunnels in Vietnam; the underground dwellings of Matmata; the Seattle Underground Tour; and the Legendary Black Water Rafting Company, with whom we floated down Waitomo's underground rivers, stared at glowworms, and jumped off waterfalls to our hearts' content.